TOUCHDOWN

Kickoff

USA TODAY BESTSELLING AUTHOR

EMMANUELLE SNOW

MEDORA BEACH UNIVERSE

Wrecked series
Cast Away
Ride for a Fall

Touchdown series
Kickoff
Game Plan

All titles available at
emmanuellesnow.com

OTHER BOOKS BY THE AUTHOR

ALL TITLES AVAILABLE AT EMMANUELLESNOW.COM

CARTER HILLS BAND UNIVERSE

Carter Hills Band series
False Promises
Blindsided
Forevermore

Whiskey Melody series
Sweet Agony
Cruel Destiny
Beautiful Salvation
Wild Encounter
Brittle Scars

Upon A Star series
Last Hope
Midnight Sparks

Love Song For Two series
Fallen Legend

Rising Star
Snowbound

Standalone novels
Wicked Love

All titles available at
emmanuellesnow.com

TRIGGER WARNINGS

Disclaimer

My books are realistic and emotional love stories.

I'm an advocate for mental health, and some topics could be sensitive for certain readers since they are portrayed as close to real life as possible.

I've listed the potential trigger warnings for each title on my website.

Be advised that those trigger warnings could potentially be spoiler alerts for the storylines.

Those sensitive topics have been written with the utmost care and respect. Please reach out if you have questions or comments.

The Medora Beach universe contains sexuality, mature

content, and language not intended for people under 16 years of age.
For other readers' sake, please avoid spoilers in your reviews.

Thank you and have a wonderful day!

Emmanuelle

emmanuellesnow.com

*Don't suffer in silence.
There's always someone to offer you a hand
and pull you out of the darkness.*

(And don't fall for Nathan Fucking Bellevue.)

BECOME A VIP

TO NEVER MISS A THING

Snow's VIP

Join **Emmanuelle Snow's VIP newsletter**

Be the first to know about new releases, giveaways, sales, and special events. And step into a space where big emotions are celebrated, love is messy and beautiful, and stories linger long after the last page.

emmanuellesnow.com

Snow's Soulmates

Join Emmanuelle Snow's Facebook VIP group, **Snow's Soulmates**, to chat with her and other readers, get updates, and more bonus content.

facebook.com/groups/snowvip

TOUCHDOWN SERIES

Mason and Craig Pierce are football gods in their little town of Elk River, Michigan. Seniors in high school, their lives are already outlined: Graduating and playing ball in college before joining the pros. They believe nothing can stand in the way of their dreams until long-buried secrets are exposed, threatening to unravel their carefully planned futures and put in jeopardy their relationships with the girls they love.

Mason Pierce is everyone's favorite quarterback. Girls wish they could steal his heart, and guys wish they could be him. But Mason's heart isn't available, already set on Melinda Shepard, the one girl who won't fall for his charm or his football glory. Truth be told, she's been resisting their easy chemistry since the day she moved next door to him. When their lives entangle one night, and Mason saves her from a fateful event, their non-existent relationship is quickly upgraded to friendship. One that comes with a high dose of attraction neither of them seems to be able to escape. But behind her star swimmer and straight A student persona, Melinda hides secrets of her own that could put her future and her blossoming relationship with Mason at risk.

As pain, lies, and unsaid words mix, do Melinda and Mason have a chance at love, or is their relationship doomed from the start?

THE MEET-UP

FIVE YEARS AGO

PROLOGUE

I THINK YOU ARE PRETTY.
FOR A GIRL.

Wiping the sweat along my hairline with my sleeve, I watched the moving truck as it parked in front of the house next door. A man about Dad's age climbed out, followed by an older boy, probably in high school, who looked just like him. No doubt father and son. Both stood with their fists on their hips, observing the house after the boy removed the *Just Sold* sign from the front lawn.

I wondered if they were the new owners.

Mom had told me there would be a kid about my age moving next door, and I'd been shooting hoops all day, trying to catch sight of him. I couldn't wait to have a new best friend since most kids in our street were either babies or teenagers.

Craig, my older brother, said earlier I looked like a creep, but I didn't care.

Since Lee, my old best friend, moved away last month, I had been wondering what his replacement would look like.

The father-son duo rounded the box truck, opened the rear roll-up door, and entered the cargo area only to come out with their arms full of boxes seconds later.

The man spotted me and offered a warm smile. "Hi there."

I returned his greeting with a wave.

Maybe I really did look like a creep after all. Not wanting them to think I was being weird, I focused on the ball in my hand.

From the time I was old enough to throw, I'd been obsessed with balls. Footballs. Basketballs. Baseballs. Anything I could toss, dribble, or hit. Passing a ball was my special power as Mom called it.

According to Dad, I had what he called *one heck of an arm*. I could throw with precision and barely ever tired out. Last summer, my parents had enrolled me in baseball and football camps. Since then, the latter had become my sport of choice. I loved everything about throwing a pigskin across a field in a perfect arc and watching the receiver catch it mid-air. Each time, it filled me with pride. It helped that my brother's sport of choice was also football. While my special power was throwing, his was catching.

And we worked great together. *Like a well-oiled machine*, Dad often said. Yep, Craig always anticipated my moves as I did his.

Right now, I was alone and couldn't play catch, so basketball was my only option to blow off some steam and busy myself.

Handling the ball with ease, I shot from the sidewalk

into the basket. "He shoots and scores." Pivoting on my feet, I dribbled some more, pretending I had some fierce opponents hot on my heels. "Mason Pierce is the player to watch this season, ladies and gentlemen. No wonder he's going pro next year." Craig always made fun of me when I faked being a commentator, describing my own plays, but I didn't care. I had to get used to it because playing for the big league was my future—and my dream.

I feinted a spin to the right, only to go left and shoot a three-point hoop from an imaginary top of the key. The ball slid smoothly through the rim fixed above the garage door. Pride coursed through my blood, and I pumped my fist.

"Wow, you're good."

I jumped around at the sound of a small voice behind me. A girl with long, wavy brown hair and turquoise eyes that glimmered with curiosity under a hitched brow stood a few feet from me. For a second, I lost myself in the pool of her eyes because they looked like the ocean on a sunny day.

"Who are you?" I asked with a sigh, scanning the length of her, wondering if my wishes had gotten mixed up because I seemed to have landed a girl-neighbor instead of a boy-neighbor.

"Melinda Shepard. I guess I live next door now. We're moving in today."

"Oh." My shoulders dropped. She was not a boy-neighbor. I wanted to say something else, but my words were stuck in my throat, and I had no idea how to get them out. This kinda sucked. Big time.

The forgotten ball rolled between my feet down the pavement, and I bent forward to retrieve it before it reached the street.

"Are you a student at Elk River Middle School?" she asked.

"Yes, I'll be in seventh grade. Going to be twelve soon."

"I'll be in seventh grade too. I turned twelve at the beginning of the summer."

"We're the same age? Wow, you're tall. Like tenth-grade tall."

She shrugged. "Mom too said that the other day when we went shopping. Will you be on the school basketball team? You're pretty good. You should try out."

"No. I play football. I'll be on *that* team. I only play basketball when I'm alone and have nothing fun to do. Mom doesn't want Craig and me to play video games so—"

"My mom doesn't even want me to watch TV other than on Saturdays when we have a family movie night." She shrugged. "How old is your brother?"

"You ask a lot of questions. How old is *your* brother?"

"He's my half-brother, and he's seventeen. We're not super close. He's into music and hates everyone. His mom died when he was little, and he's still angry about it. Dad says he'll learn to live with it eventually. Not sure therapy helps him, though. He wants to move out and be an adult and record an album."

"Oh. My brother's name is Craig. He's my best friend…most of the time. He plays football with me. He'll be in seventh grade too. You'll meet him."

Her eyes rounded. "You guys are twins? Cool."

I shook my head. "Nah. We were born ten months apart. People always assume we're twins. I skipped fourth grade, so we're in the same grade now." I sighed. "My parents treat me like a baby even though we have the same birth year. Mom sometimes says we were twins who chose not to share the womb at the same time. Anyway, it's not *that* interesting."

"I think it is. It's like you're twins but not *twins* twins. It's weird, but it's still cool."

An idea popped up in my head. "Wanna play?" Maybe I could teach her the game, and she'd become decent enough to fill in when Craig was busy. It wasn't too far-fetched an idea. Anyway, I was out of options and tired of playing by myself. It became boring after a while. I could use a friend.

"Sure. You better bring your A-game, though, or you'll lose," she said, assurance clear in her tone. She tipped her chin up and adjusted her white T-shirt and pink shorts before getting into position before me. "I'm not joking about basketball."

I watched her every move, impressed she knew all about the game. None of the girls at school loved playing ball. They always complained in gym class when we teamed up for basketball or soccer.

"You know the rules?" I asked, just to make sure. My heart was beating faster, excited at the idea I had someone to play with. For real.

"My dad and my brother. They taught me the game. I'm pretty good at it. Our love for basketball is one of the things my brother and I connect over."

I blinked as she stared at me with her game face on. "Wow." I gawked at her, not sure what to say. She wasn't a boy, but she was my age, and she liked to play ball. My new neighbor wasn't exactly the friend I had wished for, but I could work with that.

Melinda crossed her arms over her chest, tilting her chin in defiance. "So? Are we playing, or are you gonna stare at me all afternoon? I can't wait to beat you."

She had attitude and confidence, and they reminded me of myself. Maybe we would get along fine, she and I.

My lips curled into a large smile, and I snapped out of my Melinda-trance state. "Yes. Let's play. I'm Mason, by the way. Mason Pierce. Ready?"

She unfolded her arms, bent at the knees, and leaned forward, seriousness painting her face. "Ready." She nodded. Once. I believed I fell in love right then.

We played for the rest of the afternoon. Melinda was good—not as good as me—but a decent enough opponent. She knew how to dribble, and I couldn't look away when she controlled the ball, my gaze following each movement of her tanned legs.

Her hair swept her shoulders. Each time she got too close, the smell of her orange blossom shampoo filled my nose, and butterflies took off in my stomach when her bare skin rubbed against mine.

Foreign sensations invaded me, and I sorta enjoyed the excitement they brought. I had never noticed that Lee or any of my friends smelled good, so maybe it was a girl thing. I didn't hate it, though.

Perhaps having a girl-neighbor wouldn't be so bad after all.

We lost ourselves in the game, pausing only to drink water from the garden hose attached to the side of the garage or retie our shoelaces.

Melinda's cheeks were red from exertion, and it was a good look on her.

I could tell she too liked basketball from the stars shining in her eyes and the upward curve of her lips when she scored. I smiled whenever she did because she looked happy—and proud of herself.

"I have an idea," Melinda said after a while. "Let's play H.O.R.S.E. The winner gets to decide their prize."

I frowned. "Like what?"

She twisted her lips, thinking. "Whatever. Winner's choice."

"Anything off limits?" I was already thinking about what I'd ask for if I won.

She shrugged. "Nah. Unless it's weird."

"Okay, then. Get ready to lose."

The challenge seemed to spark a newfound confidence in her because her eyes turned to slits and her game face returned. "We'll see about that."

Oh, I loved how cocky she got. Was my new neighbor as competitive as I was? Right now, I wished that was the case because it would make things more interesting. I was so ready to kick her ass and show off my skills. I was Mason Pierce. I never lost. And now, I even had an endgame.

"Fine, you win," Melinda conceded a while later, tossing the basketball back at me, bending forward, her palms on her knees, catching her breath.

"Can I decide my prize now?" I asked, breathless, but unable to stop the grin taking over my face. Winning had been harder than I thought it'd be. Melinda Shepard didn't go down without a fight. She'd put her whole heart into our game until the last second. "You were not kidding. You are good at this."

"Told you." Her breathing slowed, and she sat on the lawn, stretching her legs before her. "We had a deal. Tell me what you want. Candies? Popsicles? Iced tea? I can even bake you banana bread."

I dropped next to her, twisting blades of grass around my finger. "Do you have plans tonight?"

She seemed to hesitate for a second. "Huh…no. Mom said nothing about our having plans. She's too busy unpacking."

"Then we'll have dinner and watch a movie in my backyard together."

"Backyard?"

"Yes. Dad has an old projector we use sometimes to screen movies in the garden on a white sheet. It's Saturday night, so you're allowed to watch a movie, no? Isn't that what you said earlier?"

"I guess. Mom said our family nights would start again next week because unpacking is the top priority before school starts."

"Perfect. Do you like pizza?"

Her face flushed. "Duh, yes. Do you know anyone who doesn't like pizza because I don't."

"No. That would be silly." I chuckled. "Mom makes the best homemade pizza."

"Huh…Mason… Are you sure it's okay with your parents if I come over later?"

I nodded. "Yep. Mom says my friends are always welcome at our house."

"I'll ask my parents first, okay? They are super protective of me. Like a lot. My best friend Jolie, back in New Jersey, said it was a bit too much sometimes."

"Wow, you moved from New Jersey? It's like *far* far away"

She bobbed her head. "Super far. Three-day drive to be exact." She moved to her feet. "Nice game, by the way."

I stood and dusted myself off. "Can I walk you home?"

"You wanna walk me home? I live right next door."

"I'm a gentleman. And we can ask your mom together."

We walked side by side without a word. It felt weird to go to a girl's house. I never really had a girl as a friend before.

Mr. Shepard opened the door when we climbed up the front porch steps. "Hi again," he said when he noticed me. "Mel, I'm glad you made a friend on your first day."

I stood next to her and held out a hand as I'd seen my father do many times. "Sir, my name is Mason Pierce. I live next door. Can Melinda come over and have dinner at my place tonight? We'll have a picnic in my backyard and swim and watch a movie."

Mr. Shepard studied me with a serious expression. "Will my daughter be home before nine, Mr. Pierce?"

"Yes, sir. I have an eight-thirty curfew."

Mr. Shepard nodded. "I see. Will you keep her safe?"

"Always. I'll watch over her. So, can she come?"

Mr. Shepard brought his attention to his daughter. "Mel, do you wanna go?"

She nodded fast. "I would love to, Daddy."

"Okay." He looked at me. "It's settled then." He turned around, picked up a notepad from one of the boxes stacked in the foyer and a pen from his pocket, and scribbled something before handing me the piece of paper. "Please ask your parents to call me to confirm, okay? This is our number."

I took the note he offered. "Sure. Cool." I tried to act unaffected, but inside my chest, my heart was pounding very fast. "Like five o'clock?"

Melinda nodded with a smile, and I hurried away, not sure what to do now that I had asked a girl over. I had never been on a date before. Was that what it was tonight? A date? My heart rate accelerated at the idea. Craig would be jealous because he had never invited a girl home before either.

I jumped down the stairs and watched her over my shoulder one last time. "I'll see you around five."

———

"Wow, you did this?" Melinda asked when she walked into my backyard later, her dad by her side, as she looked all around her.

I shrugged like it was no big deal when, in fact, I'd spent over an hour setting it all up with Dad. I had laid a blanket and some pillows in one corner of the yard for our picnic. Mom had made a pitcher of lemonade for us, and I'd helped her bake cookies. I hoped Melinda loved cookies as much as I did. I had added extra chocolate chips just in case. Dad had installed the projector and put two chairs on the other side of the pool, with a white sheet pinned to the wooden fence in front of them.

We'd put a large float we could drift on while watching the movie in the pool, and my inflatable basketball pool game was ready, in case Melinda wanted a rematch in the water.

"Did you bring your swimsuit?" I asked, gesturing to the red shark-patterned swim trunk and sleeveless white shirt I was wearing.

"Yes." She tugged at the sleeve of her purple dress to reveal the strap of her bathing suit. "I also made cupcakes. Here." She handed me a plastic container.

"Cool."

Mom joined us and started a conversation with our new neighbor while Melinda and I stood next to them in silence.

Feeling awkward, I rocked on my heels, wondering what to do or say next. "Huh...do you want lemonade? Mom made it for us."

"Sure." Melinda followed me to the small table. She looked around as if searching for something. "Is your brother home?"

"No. It's just us."

She nodded. Seconds later, her father said goodbye.

"Dinner will be ready in half an hour. Come get me if you need anything, or if you wanna go for a swim, I'll send your dad to watch over you, okay?"

We both nodded as she returned inside.

Melinda offered me a small smile. "Your Mom looks nice."

"Yeah. She's the best."

She fidgeted with her fingers while I scratched the back of my head as silence stretched between us.

After a few long minutes that seemed endless, I pointed to the front yard. "Do you think we should play a game?"

"Yes. I think I can beat you this time," Melinda said, puffing her chest out.

"You think?"

"Yes." She dropped her bag on the ground and bent down to retie her shoes. "Come on, Mason."

We played for the next thirty minutes, both of us sweating, too invested in the game. The score was tied. Fifteen to fifteen.

"If you score, you win," Melinda said. She stood before me, her hands on her knees as I dribbled the ball, her gaze following all my movements.

I stepped to the left, pivoted on myself, passed the ball through my legs, and aimed for the hoop. Melinda's eyes lit up. She raised her arms, blocking me. I shifted my weight to my right, positioned my arms, and tossed the ball. It spun around the rim, again and again. We both watched, jaws hanging, eyes big.

Until it slid through the net.

I shot my arms up in victory. "I win," I screamed before I noticed the defeated expression on Melinda's face. "Huh…it was close. I thought it wouldn't go in."

"You did good."

For a moment, I wondered if I was supposed to have let her win. Maybe it was the gentlemanly thing to do on a date. But would Melinda enjoy the victory if she knew I had cheated? Nah. I know I wouldn't love winning because my opponent tricked the game. My belly growled. "Are you hungry? We could eat now. Dinner should be ready."

"Sure."

After we inhaled the pizza and desserts, I flipped on a switch, and dozens of garden lights illuminated the backyard.

"Wow, Mason, it's beautiful," Melinda said, her hands cupping her heart. "Like it's a fairy garden."

I high-fived myself in my head. She was pleased with the setup, and it filled me with joy. I had missed her smile when she'd lost the basketball match earlier, and I was happy I had done something that brought it back.

I peeled my shirt off, and Melinda removed her dress, both of us standing in nothing but our swimsuits.

Dad joined us. "Ready?"

"Yes," we said at the same time.

While he put the movie on, Melinda and I climbed on the float, sitting next to each other. Dad sat on one of the loungers with a newspaper, far enough to give us some privacy and not eavesdrop on our conversation, but close enough to keep an eye on us just in case we decided to get into the pool. For the next hour, we glided on the water, engrossed in the action on the screen, paddling with our hands to keep the float facing forward. Every few minutes, I glanced at Melinda, mesmerized by her smile and the way her hair swept her shoulders every time she laughed. Having a *girl*friend wasn't too bad so far. Sure, she didn't crack jokes like Chase always did, and I didn't wrestle with her like I would do with Craig, but I still loved her company. It was different from hanging out with the boys, but a good different.

The movie was almost over when I took a deep breath and enveloped her hand in mine. My heart drummed in my chest so fast I believed it would escape.

Melinda turned slowly. "Mason? What are you doing?"

I shrugged, trying to look unaffected. So far, she hadn't pulled her hand away from mine, so maybe she liked it as much as I did. "We're on a date..."

She watched me with a funny expression like she had drunk sour milk.

"What?" I asked. "I won the game earlier, and you said I could choose anything if I won. So, I invited you on a date."

She studied me with her turquoise eyes. "A date? You never said anything about a date before."

"Huh, well... I thought it was obvious."

She stared at me, not saying anything.

It felt like thousands of ants were marching through my stomach. I thought girls liked to go on dates. Was I wrong all this time? Before I chickened out, I spoke the words lingering on the tip of my tongue. I spoke fast because I had never said something like that to a girl up until now. "I think we should date for real. You love playing ball, and we're friends now... It makes sense. Don't you agree?"

She blinked a few times. "But we are too young to date. I'm only twelve."

"My friend Lee, who used to live in your house, had a girlfriend last year. They dated for eleven days, and they were almost twelve. We are older. And...I think you are pretty. For a girl."

She said nothing for the longest time. "You want us to date?"

I bobbed my head fast. "Yeah."

"Okay. I will only date you on one condition."

My heart started to bang again in my chest. I was ready to agree to anything she asked of me. *Almost.* "What?"

"Let's race to the other end of the pool. If you win, I will be your girlfriend. If I win, we're never dating."

My mouth popped open. "Never? Like never *ever* ever?"

She nodded and held out her hand. "Yes."

"Huh…can we still be friends?" I had no idea what dating would change between us, but it sounded more serious. More grownup. After all, in a few days, we'd be in seventh grade. "If I lose, I mean." I wasn't scared to lose. I was good at holding my breath under water and always won when I made bets with Craig.

"Maybe. But I prefer to have girls as friends than boys. Boys always get into trouble. I have a big brother, remember? He plays hockey, and he dates girls. *Lots* of girls. Mom always says there's no rush and he should take his time to find a nice girl instead of looking desperate. Anyway, he's cocky and doesn't like to follow rules. Dad has *a lot of talks* with him in private about his behavior. I overheard them talking many times."

I shook her hand. "I won't get into trouble. I swear."

She studied my face for a moment like she was trying to decide if I was speaking the truth, then nodded without saying anything.

We positioned ourselves on the float on one side of the pool.

"Ready?" Melinda asked. I nodded, and before I could take a full breath in, she dove forward and swam to the other end as if propelled by an engine. It took me a long second to get into motion, hypnotized by the way her body speared through the water.

I touched the wall seconds after her. "Whoa. How did you do that? You were fast. Like super extra lightning fast."

Her smile brightened her entire face. "I'm gonna be on the school swim team this year. I practiced a lot over the summer."

I blinked, still surprised she had beaten me. "You are really good."

"Thanks. It's like you and football. It's no big deal."

My happiness slipped away. "So, does this mean we're not dating? Like ever?"

She shrugged. "Sorry." She grabbed the edge of the pool and lifted herself out of the water, gathered her stuff, and neared me as I dried myself. "Thank you for inviting me tonight, Mason. I had fun."

She inched closer and dropped a kiss on my cheek before grabbing her bag and running away. She turned once to watch me over her shoulder. "For what it's worth, I think you are pretty too. For a boy." She didn't wait for my reply as she reached the driveway and disappeared behind the line of trees separating our properties, the sound of her wet footsteps on the pavement echoing behind her.

For a long moment, I stayed there, watching the same spot, wondering what I had done wrong.

When I couldn't decide, I grabbed my stuff and followed my dad inside.

Once in my bedroom, I neared the window when I spotted movement next door. Melinda's parents were sitting in their backyard, sipping wine. I watched her as she joined them. Sensations I'd never felt before tingled low in my body. Even though I tried to shift my gaze away, I couldn't. I had no clue what was going on with me since she had come over to play basketball earlier, but I didn't want to share her with the guys once school started next week. I wanted Melinda to be *my* special friend. Chase would be all over her on Monday. He loved girls, and she was new in town, so he would want to make her his special friend too. He had dated Samantha Johnson for a whole month last spring, so he had experience, while I didn't. He had even kissed her on the lips. He said it was gross, but he was ready to do it again.

I had to find a way to let the guys know I'd played with Melinda first and called dibs on her. That she was *my* friend. After all, we already had a date together. It had to count for something.

Tonight, we had a great time until I opened my big mouth and messed it all up. Why did I have to tell her we were dating? I had seen Chase's older brother flirt with girls many times. He always told us the trick was to look confident. I was pretty sure I'd nailed that part. He also said to invite them to eat, which I had, and to set the mood. I had done that too. Melinda had even commented on it. I had followed all the steps. I had no idea why she didn't agree. We had fun together, and she could play ball. Mom even said to Dad earlier that Melinda and I had chemistry, whatever it meant. Yet, after she won the race, she'd run away from me as if I had cooties.

She looked up my way, and I lifted a hand to wave at her, but she turned around before I could.

Seconds later, she entered her house, and I sighed.

Was this what being rejected felt like? Because I didn't like it. It knotted my stomach.

Lying on my bed, I dreamed about the girl with the sparkling eyes who made my heart race.

ELK RIVER HIGH

SENIOR YEAR

CHAPTER 1
YOU'RE THE LION TO OUR KITTENS

Three months ago

Chase, my best friend, honked twice after he parked in my driveway. I grabbed my overnight and sleeping bags and beelined for his pickup truck, dropping my stuff in the cargo box. I entered the garage after punching in the code to open the door, to grab the cooler I had filled earlier and the five-person tent my parents kept in there.

"Need a hand, man?" my friend asked through the rolled-down window.

"Nah. All good. I hope Rusty brought his tent because I swear this thing can only sleep five people if they are either women or little kids. No way can we all fit in."

"If he hasn't, he's sleeping in his car, and we keep the tent for ourselves."

We bumped fists.

"Deal."

"Is Craig riding with us?"

I shook my head. "Nah. My big bro is at Paige's. Sheldon is picking him up. It's just the two of us."

I locked the front door, then hauled myself onto the passenger seat once I made sure I had my wallet and my keys.

"Mase, I don't know whose idea it was to go camping to celebrate the end of our junior year but remind me to thank him."

"That would be me. Thank you very much. I appreciate the fact that you can admit it is the best idea. I checked the map yesterday, and we can go cliff jumping within a twenty-minute hike from where we are setting camp. There's also an indoor karting track in the next town over if it rains and the ground gets too muddy to go to the campsite or if we're bored and need a plan B."

"See? This, right there, is why you're the captain. You always plan ahead, unlike me, who just follows the parade."

I clapped his shoulder with a snicker. "It's okay. That's why we're friends—"

"Best friends."

"Whatever. Best friends. Because we complete each other."

He tapped the steering wheel with his palm. "True. You're the yin to my yang."

"Chase, don't say things like that. It's…huh…cheesy. And weird."

"Nah, it's poetic. Would you prefer the up to my down or the puppy to my kitten?"

"Kitten, really?"

"What? You like me. And I know for a fact you like pussies. Pussies are cats, and kittens are pussies too. It all makes sense."

I lowered my sunglasses over my eyes, flipped my cap forward, and slouched in my seat. "Gosh, this weekend trip is going to be *sooo* long."

"Nah. It will be perfect, kitty." He grinned at me. "Absolutely fantastic."

Two hours later, Chase pulled onto a gravel road and followed a sinuous path between the trees leading to a clearing by the riverbank.

"We're here," my friend announced.

We had just climbed out of his truck when two cars pulled up behind us, both filled with some of our teammates.

"Paige didn't hold you hostage?" I asked my brother when he came to stand beside me.

"Ha. Ha. Very funny. She's spending the day with Mel before she leaves for the summer."

"Wait, what?" I reeled in my surprise, trying to sound nonchalant instead. "Melinda is leaving for the entire summer?"

"Yeah. Going to her grandparents' in Jersey or something like that."

"Oh. Cool." *Nah. Not cool.*

"Anyway, Paige was more than happy to kick me out because they had plans."

Rusty joined us. "Hey, Cap. I was thinking of setting up the tents there." He gestured to the clearing with a finger. "That way, we'll have enough space for a bonfire in the middle. What do you think?"

I pointed my thumb at my chest. "What do *I* think?"

"Yeah. You're the man in charge."

"Nah, man. I'm in charge on the field. Not when the season is over. Find someone else to lead your sorry asses. I'm on vacation."

"Too bad because all the guys voted and you're the lion to our kittens."

"Please tell me you didn't ask Chase for his opinion." Only my best friend could come up with such a ridiculous metaphor, and he had a weird obsession with kittens today.

"Too late. Anyway, what do you think?"

"Whatever, man." I sighed, annoyance building inside me. I really didn't want to manage our camping trip. "Do what pleases you."

———

"Who's ready for some cliff jumping?" Sheldon asked as soon as we were all up the next morning.

We hadn't slept for more than just a few hours last night, too engrossed in the retelling of stories of the previous school year, sipping beer, and roasting sausages over the bonfire.

"Not me. I can't swim," Seth said. "I need my feet to touch the ground at all times."

"You're going to play ball in college next year and you can't swim?" Sheldon asked. "Are you joking?"

"Nah. I'm not a fan of water. I'll thrive next year. I'm more worried about you guys. How will this team survive if I'm not there to protect you on the field? You'll see, you'll miss me."

"Miss who?" Craig asked, scratching his temple. With his disheveled brown hair—the same shade as mine—and stained T-shirt, he looked nothing like the usually well-put-together guy he was.

"Nothing." Sheldon stripped off his sweatpants before sliding board shorts up his legs.

Jackson covered his eyes with a hand. "Jesus, Sheld, hide your junk. It's too early in the morning to be exposed to your balls."

"You're just jealous, Pettyfer. You wish you had balls of steel like me instead of a pussy."

"Says the man who lacks self-confidence. I'm not gonna respond to this."

Sheldon tied the drawstrings of his shorts. "Whatever. As I was saying, I'm going cliff jumping. Who's in?"

"It could be fun," Craig said. "I need caffeine first, though. I have no clue how to reboot my brain this morning. Mase, that camping mat you brought is the worst. I would have slept better on a bed of nails."

I sighed. "Stop being a brat. Next time, bring your own camping gear if you're not happy." I turned to Sheldon. "Count me in. As long as I'm fed first."

Chase buttered a few slices of bread and placed them on the mesh grate along with last night's potato leftovers over the dying campfire. "Breakfast will be served in a minute, guys."

"That's breakfast?" Rusty asked.

"Yep. Since none of you fuckers moved a finger to do anything, that's what we'll have. We'll keep the eggs and bacon for tomorrow morning. I'm too hungover to prep anything right now. There's orange juice in the red cooler, and my mom sent a portable coffeemaker that is somewhere in my truck, so help yourselves. If you can figure out how to make it work."

An hour later, we were all overlooking the lake from the cliff. Half a dozen people were sunbathing on the other shore, girls floating on tubes and guys throwing a ball around. The sun was shining bright, a perfect beginning to our summer vacation. Starting Monday, we would have different schedules, all of us having secured summer jobs, so this weekend was our one chance to hang out together before school and practice resumed.

"You sure it's safe?" Seth asked. "It's kind of high."

Sheldon neared the edge. "I've jumped from much higher than this last summer." He peeled his shirt over his head and kicked off his shoes. "I'm going first. Watch and learn, pussies."

Before we had time to register his next movement, he walked back to the tree line to gain momentum and ran, screaming "Yahoo" at the top of his lungs when he propelled himself airborne. Seconds later, a loud splash echoed from below, and someone on the opposite shore wolf whistled.

Jackson walked closer to the edge and looked down. "He made it."

Sheldon hollered something, but we couldn't hear him from up here.

Jackson turned to face us. "You guys all gonna jump?"

"Yep," I replied at the same time the guys said, "Yes."

"Are you sure it's deep enough? There are boulders. I can see them."

"You gotta jump straight ahead, and you'll be fine. People have been cliff jumping here for decades. My old man used to camp here when he was our age. Don't ruin the fun, Pettyfer. Anyway, watch me execute a perfect front dive pike." Rusty extended his arms over his head in some sort of stretching exercise. "I should have been recruited by the Olympics diving team. I'm that good."

"Only when you're wasted," Craig said.

"You wish." Rusty folded his body in two, grazing his toes with his fingers. "The trick is to warm up properly. And also, flexibility. That's what makes me popular with girls." He rotated his upper body to the left and then to the right. "See? Flexibility."

"Like that?" Seth asked, imitating him, but also walking on his tiptoes like a ballerina. "Sure, you look gracious enough, Rust. It's not the Olympics team that will recruit you, but a ballet company." He continued to do one ballet position after the other.

"Man, are you sure football is your sport?" Craig asked. "You're too good at this to just be a coincidence."

"Shut up. My mom owns a dance school." Seth twirled. "She's been teaching me since I was a kid. Said it would help with football. Just sayin'." He moved into another position. "You guys should try it. As Rusty said, it's all about flexibility."

"Stop making fun of me," Rusty growled, pushing Seth in the chest. "You're stealing *my* show."

Everything happened in slow motion. Seth's ankle rolled on a rock, and he lost his balance. He flapped his arms at his sides, worry creeping into his gaze. His lips rounded in an *O*. Before any of us could react, he fell backward.

Rusty shook his head. "Good riddance."

"Didn't he say earlier he couldn't swim?" Craig asked.

We heard water splashing down below.

"Oh." Rusty neared the edge of the cliff. "He's not coming up for air."

"What are you all still doing up here? I thought some of you would have jumped by now." Sheldon, who had hiked back, was now standing next to us and staring down at the water. "What are we looking at?"

I didn't think. I just reacted. No way would my friend drown. Not on my watch.

"*Massse.*" My brother's worried voice was all I heard as

I plunged forward, headfirst, with no safety net to hold me back.

The sound of bones and rocks colliding reverberated through me. This was bad. I resurfaced and spotted Seth holding on to a rock feet away, his face white as a ghost. Thank God, he was alive. I tried to move my shoulder to swim in his direction, but winced as pain radiated across the right side of my body. No, this couldn't be happening. Not now. Not months before the last year of my high school football career. Not when scouts were coming to our games to watch me play, and I was at my pinnacle.

Tears prickled the back of my eyes. I clenched my teeth, doing my best to keep the pain away. In vain.

What did I just do? Did I mess up my entire future?

CHAPTER 2

LAST NIGHT WAS A MISTAKE

Present

Planting my feet on the hardwood floor of my bedroom, I buried my face in my hands, debating what my next move should be. I glanced over my shoulder at Lydia, the girl in my bed, tangled in steel-blue sheets, her blonde hair spread across the pillow. I would have to wash them later today. No way could I go back to bed tonight with her scent lingering on my sheets. We were done and over. Hooking up with Lydia was just one amongst a lot of bad decisions I had taken over the summer.

I inhaled, never enjoying the next part. "Hey, wake up. You gotta go."

A low snore exited her mouth, and she stirred in her sleep, eyes still closed.

I pushed her bare shoulder with my fingers. "Hurry. You need to leave. If my parents catch you here, this won't end well for either of us. You know the drill."

It did the trick because her eyelids fluttered open and she stared at me, her brain clearly not registering my desperate tone. "Your parents? I've never even crossed paths with your parents the four times I was here in the past."

From the pile of clothes we'd discarded on the floor last night, I found my neon-colored boxer briefs and pulled them up my legs. Now on my feet, I spun to face her. "Huh…yeah…my parents. The people who own this place and sleep down the hall."

Stretching her arms while she sat, Lydia eyed me as if I was speaking another language.

"You, here at my parents' house. You, so need not to be here. I'm not interested in getting caught, and I have other plans today." I swooped her clothes from the floor and placed them on the bed. "Here. Get dressed."

She shaped her lips into a pout and batted her eyelashes. "Mase, I thought we'd get breakfast and spend the day together. Isn't that what it should come down to between us? We've done this dance often enough. When are we gonna take the next step?"

I shook my head, erasing the images forming in my brain, and sighed. "Huh…us? Like you and me?" Yes, I was acting like a jackass on purpose. Blame it on the lack of sleep or the early morning hour that cast last night's actions into a new perspective, but I couldn't wait to be alone. Since I couldn't leave my own house, Lydia had to go. "You serious?"

She bobbed her head, watching me.

I frowned, pretending not to get what she meant.

"We'd be good together, Mase."

Lydia stared at me with eagerness, but wariness entered her gaze now that I locked eyes with her in what I was sure looked like a *don't go down this path* expression. "There is no *us*, and there will never be. It was clear from the start. You said that's what you wanted too. A few unattached nights of fun that came with no promises. You agreed to it. I never promised more than that. I can't… I just can't. Anyway, you're using me."

"No. I am not. I want us to be together. Officially."

I snorted. "Come on. Be honest here. You're always after me when you break things off with Copperman."

"Dave and I, we're done."

"No. I've heard this many times before. You two are always on and off. He'll say he's sorry for whatever he has done this time, and you'll go back to him. You always do. It's like you're only with me when you wanna piss him off. Like you have some sick QB fetichism. The Cowley High Cobras are our number-one enemies, and it won't change. Fraternizing with the girlfriend of—"

"*Ex*-girlfriend."

"Whatever. Sleeping around with the girlfriend of their quarterback is like asking to get beaten up by the entire team. No, thanks, I'll pass."

I should have never let her sleep here last night. It had been a rookie mistake.

Yesterday, after an afternoon of excruciating pre-season football training during which we ran drills for hours, I went out with the boys to grab some food. We were about to leave when I saw the only girl I'd ever loved climbing into Nathan Fucking Bellevue's pickup truck, and I panicked. Lydia was there, ready to patch the hole in my heart for a night, and I took advantage. Now she was spinning this *there's an us* crap on me at this hour, too early for me to be able to react nicely about it. My heart would never be able to beat for anyone else other than the one it had set its sights on, no matter how much I tried to. It was stupid. I knew it, but I was doomed, and I had accepted my fate a long time ago and rolled with it. If only I were brave enough to make a move, put myself out there, and be honest about my feelings, all this clusterfuck, and Lydia being here, could have been avoided.

I stepped to the left to open the dark curtains framing my bedroom window, revealing the off-white walls and charcoal trims. A queen-size bed with a striped black-and-charcoal comforter that Lydia was currently wrapped in—*ughhh*—was positioned against the wall next to the door, facing a desk with a dresser and a small A-frame dumbbell rack. A few posters of my idols were pinned on the wall above them. My room was quite simple, nothing too fancy. From here, I could spy on the house next door, but I averted my eyes before I was tempted to do so. "Now it's daytime which means you gotta go. You really don't wanna face my dad in the morning."

A weird feeling stirred in the pit of my stomach as the words left my mouth.

I hated being that guy. Elk River High's adored quarterback, whom the girls only saw as a trophy they could seduce. Yet, I pretended the role suited me and that I didn't care about anyone else but me when, in fact, I wasn't interested in any relationship unless it was with *the* girl. The one my heart beat for. And so far, she couldn't care to give me the time of day, so I acted out and ended up hooking up with Lydia to forget. What a joke.

Lydia moved to her knees on the mattress, not taking the time to cover her bare tits. "Mase, you can't be serious. Can we please rethink this relationship?" she asked, motioning a finger between us. "What we have is precious. We get along great. There's more to it than sex. This thing between us has nothing to do with Dave. I swear."

"Nope." I popped the *P* to emphasis my answer. "No relationship here. No breakfast cuddles. No kissing in the school hallways. We don't have anything precious because we don't have a thing, to begin with. Last night was a mistake. You and I, we're done. I don't wanna be that guy anymore. Anyway, I was clear on the specifics when you decided to tag along yesterday. You knew what you were getting into. It's better to part ways now than to get mixed up in something neither of us is ready for."

"But—"

"No but. It's for the best. I'm going to take a shower, and the door will be locked. Don't try to get in there with me." Grabbing my phone from the bedside table, I checked the time. *Eight-o-nine.* "My folks will be downstairs in twenty minutes. You better be out before they get up." In any other circumstances, I would have kissed her good-bye, but right now I felt sick to my stomach and was desperate to get as far as possible from the girl hinting at an *us.* Just the thought sent cold chills through my being. No, I wouldn't mess things up more than they already were.

Under the stream of scorching water, I hung my head low, pressing my forehead against the tiled wall. If only the hot jets could erase last night's mistake. And so many nights similar to this one. I was being an idiot. I knew what I was doing, but I couldn't stop. Because I had no clue how to pretend I wasn't broken.

CHAPTER 3

MY BEHAVIOR WAS A DEFENSE MECHANISM

Wearing a pair of washed-out jeans and a navy-blue cotton T-shirt that molded to my broad chest with the number twenty-two—my jersey and lucky number—printed in white on the front, I ran downstairs. I was ready to jumpstart my day and see if Lydia had left. There were no traces of her in my bedroom when I got dressed, and it erased some of the discomfort swirling inside me.

In the kitchen, Craig was sitting at the island with his girlfriend, Paige, two steaming mugs set before them on the counter. Just like the rest of the main floor, the room reminded me of a cozy ski chalet with its oak cabinets, cream walls, and black countertops and appliances. It had vault ceilings and a breakfast nook with a built-in corner oak bench and a square table framed by two large windows covered by dark teal-blue heavy linen curtains. It opened on the dining room on one side, and the wooden staircase on the other.

"Hey, you guys," I said, stealing Paige's coffee and bringing the mug to my lips while taking the stool across from her. "How is it going, babe?" I leaned forward to plant a chaste kiss on her cheek. "When did you get here?"

Paige never spent the night. My parents had strict rules about girls staying over—rules I broke at least once a month. Not Craig, though.

Her clear laughter warmed my insides. She and I had that kind of relationship. "Good. Got here fifteen minutes ago. Met your *friend* in the driveway." She made air quotes around the word *friend* with her fingers. "Mase, I won't repeat what she said. But, geez, some words were not meant for tender ears."

I flicked my free hand in a dismissive gesture. "Babe, don't believe everything you hear."

My brother removed the mug from my grip and put it back in front of her. "Don't *babe* my girlfriend, man. We've been over this many times already. Get your own coffee and your own girl and call my girl Paige. Stop flirting with her."

I winked. "Don't mind him, *babe*. He's grumpy in the morning." I took another sip of her coffee, and she let me. Yes, we were friends, and I shamelessly flirted with her in a non-sexual kind of way every chance I got. Paige was family. She was a great audience, always laughing at my lame jokes and cheering me on even when I acted like an idiot. Yeah, my brother had hit the jackpot with his girlfriend.

Paige mirrored my smile, her fingers intertwining with

my brother's, using her other hand to tame his tousled hair in an affectionate manner. "He's not."

I lifted one brow, and she chuckled.

"Okay, maybe a bit. Caffeine should kick in and chase his moodiness away. Eventually."

I smirked, and her grin widened.

"Stop teaming up against me," my brother complained, unable to keep his face straight as he said it, a smile breaking free when he shook his head. "What happened with Lydia? I had to put a pillow over my head last night to muffle her moans. She kept screaming *Harder…Mase,* and I almost puked in my own mouth. You're lucky Mom and Dad's bedroom isn't next to ours; otherwise, you would have gotten caught this time around."

We both knew Lydia wasn't much of a screamer, but Craig loved to mess with me for the sake of it, so I indulged in his game and displayed my cockiest smile. "What can I say? I have talents, man. Don't be jealous. If you ever want pointers, I'm always available to teach you how it's done in case you lack technique." He rolled his eyes, and my humor died down. "Anyway, that was the last time. She won't be coming back."

"Trouble in paradise?" Paige asked with a knowing smile.

"Well, I may or may not have deserved her anger this morning. I dropped her ass...for good this time. She was getting clingy."

"Man, you gotta stop doing that." Craig ran a hand through his hair. "For some reason, girls like you even though they know you don't date them, and you take nothing seriously. Don't bring girls home if you are going to kick them to the curb the next morning. If you invite them over and let them spend the night, they'll expect more from you. Think about it."

Between us, my older brother was the more responsible one. The rule follower. Perhaps it was the fact he was older, or he had inherited more genes from our mother that made him super serious and shit—the opposite of what people expected from me. Cracking jokes—even when I'd rather cry—taking nothing seriously, and acting like I was over everyone and everything had become my way of coping. All. The. Freaking. Time. Over the years, I'd gotten good at hiding my feelings from the rest of the world, plastering a fake smile on my face.

"And, Mase, messing around with Lydia Santos is asking for trouble. The last thing the team needs is to have David Copperman and Jayden Clarke on their backs off the field. The rivalry is fun during football season, but those two will go crazy if they learn you've been hooking up all summer with their QB's girl. Everyone knows Copperman has a soft spot for this girl. Even if they're toxic together. And the fact that she's Clarke's cousin makes things even more complicated. He's super protective of her. I heard his dad tried to get her transferred to Cowley High, but the school board refused. Take your player-ways elsewhere. Far from the team. It's our last year, and we should make the most of it instead of messing it all up for a girl who, by the way, is using you to make her boyfriend jealous. This shit will come to bite you in the ass eventually. Take my word for it."

"It won't happen. As I said, we're done."

"This isn't like you. Acting like a dumbass. I don't know why you keep up with the charade. Aren't you tired of people thinking you're all looks and no brain? You're worth much more than who you pretend to be. Since what happened three months ago, you're even more reckless than usual."

I made a cutthroat gesture. We had agreed we wouldn't talk about what had happened at the beginning of the summer. It was between my brother, my teammates who were present, and me. Nobody else had to know. No need to alert anyone and make the coaching staff or scouts worry about my ability to throw a ball.

Paige's attention drifted between us. "What happened three months ago?"

"Relax, bro. It's no big deal. It's just a character I'm playing. People enjoy this version of me. And it makes me popular with the ladies." *I could be convincing when I needed to be.* I addressed Paige. "By the way, nothing happened. It's just Craig messing with me. Sibling rivalry and shit."

She sighed. "Sounds dumb."

"It is, babe."

Craig shook his head. "Whatever. I think it's stupid. One day, you'll realize you were an idiot for giving high school kids so much power over you. Hiding behind that identity isn't smart. I love you too much to let it ruin the person you truly are."

Or maybe I wasn't as convincing as I thought I was.

His words stung. Craig had no idea about the thoughts invading my brain. He had no clue I was scared shitless that my reckless jump had impacted my dreams. He also wasn't aware that I was trying my best to protect my heart from getting hurt. My outgoing persona was a shield. Because I feared rejection. As long as I didn't put my heart on the line and didn't give a damn, it was safe from getting broken, right?

Sometimes, I still thought about the night my neighbor told me boys were trouble. I was just an innocent kid with big ambitions and a soft heart back then, but her words had stayed with me all this time. Some days, I still wondered if she could tell at the time how I'd turn out. If she knew I'd become trouble for real.

These days, despite the fact I joked around a lot, a big part of me was still that child, scared his dreams wouldn't come true. Rejected for the first time. See? My behavior was a defense mechanism. I didn't need a shrink to explain it to me. I was well-aware. Didn't mean I knew how to break the cycle, though. And the persona my friends had thrust on me. I pushed the thought away, not wanting to dwell on the past and not ready to obsess over things I couldn't control.

"I'm sixteen. Nobody should take anything I do or say too seriously." My argument was pathetic. Even I could recognize that much.

"You're about to turn seventeen. In a year, you'll be an adult. And Paige and I, we were already together at sixteen. Your age shouldn't be an excuse for using your dick more than your brain. It's pretty lame."

Paige nodded. "True."

"Don't be on his side, babe. I need you on my team here."

"Sorry, Mase, but you brought this upon yourself." She huffed a breath. "You make questionable choices some-times. And they come with consequences." *Like I didn't know.*

I sighed. I didn't plan on being on the hot seat this early on a Saturday morning. I addressed my brother. "Maybe you inherited all the mature genes, and I got the player ones because there were none of the good ones left for me." My attempt at a joke fell flat, but I would say anything to get out of this lecture.

"Mase, one day, you'll find a girl made just for you, and you'll stop pretending you don't care about anyone else but you." Paige squeezed my forearm. I really liked her. She always possessed the right words to ease the storm unleashing inside me. "You are one of the good ones. I just wish you would start giving yourself the credit you deserve. The real you is more than enough. You are genuinely a nice guy. Never doubt it, okay? And stop pretending otherwise."

I nodded. Yeah, Paige was a sweetheart, and nobody could argue that fact.

She and Craig had been dating for almost two years now. A lifetime in teen years. The three of us were about to be seniors at Elk River High, Michigan. Through the years, Paige had become a sister to me, and my favorite pastime was to rile my brother about her. They were disgustingly in love and spent all their time together. Too often, I ended up being the third wheel in their relationship. A position I despised despite the fact I liked their company too much to walk away.

Craig and I were both star football players for the Elk River High Bears. He was the wide receiver, and I was the quarterback. On the field, we were a force to be reckoned with. I had no idea if it was our shared DNA or just good chemistry, but we were unstoppable when we played together. In addition to our close relationship on and off the field, my brother and I hung out with the same crowd. Most of my friends were his friends too.

The sweet aroma of freshly baked cupcakes hit my nostrils. I pointed to the oven with my thumb. "Babe, did you make those?" I asked, trying to steer the conversation far away from my life and my screwups.

Paige was an excellent baker. I had no idea why she didn't wanna pursue it as a career after high school, but she'd said it was a hobby for her, nothing more.

"Yeah. Thought you guys might like some to jumpstart

your day. You've been training like crazy for the last couple of weeks. You deserve a treat."

"Red velvet?" I asked.

"What else?" Paige retorted, aware they were my favorites.

I lifted my hand to high-five her. "That's my girl."

My brother groaned. "Mase…"

I ignored his grimace. "What's on the agenda today?"

He shook his head, deciding not to join in on my humor. "Sheldon's dad has secured a bunch of tickets for the races this afternoon." He fished his wallet out of his back pocket and slid four tickets toward me.

"Who's going?"

My brother shrugged. "We're all going."

"Who's all?"

"Huh, everybody. Someone you're trying to avoid? Another girl you pissed off lately?"

I dragged a hand over my face. "Nah. All good. Just curious."

Only one question pinballed through the walls of my skull: *Would she be there?*

Melinda Shepard had been gone all summer and had returned yesterday.

Last night, in the few seconds I saw her, she disappeared with Elk River High's resident bad boy. Dressed in a teal number that made her eyes pop, with her brown hair loose over her shoulders and her smile disarming, I couldn't look away the entire time she glided from the restaurant to his pickup truck. I watched her like a freak, hiding in the shadow of the building next door, my heart bouncing inside my chest. I had no idea what went down during the time she was away, but she appeared taller, more confident of herself, and definitely hotter than I recalled. Perhaps it was my mind playing tricks on me since I'd been on a Melindawithdrawal phase for months, but the sight of her had cast me under a new kind of spell, and now that she was back, I was aware I was screwed more than ever before. That girl had gotten under my skin years ago and had no idea about it. Yes, I'd been madly in love with her for as long as I could remember—or since the day she had moved into the house next door with her parents and half-brother, five years ago, and had rejected me for the very first time.

We were strangers for what felt like forever after that fateful day. I might have killed our budding friendship and pushed her away for good on the first day of seventh grade when I'd put her on the spot and embarrassed her in front of everyone. With age came insight, and I'd realized over time that it wasn't the smartest thing to do. But I was a kid back then and thought I was being smooth about it. From that moment, Melinda had acted as if I didn't exist. Until Paige and Craig started dating and our groups of friends merged, and she couldn't avoid me anymore. Except for the last three months when she'd been away, and like a stupid lovesick puppy, I'd missed her.

Anytime she was around, I had a hard time keeping my cool. I became a nervous wreck and cracked more jokes than usual or flirted with all the wrong girls.

Yep, my defense mechanisms were warped when it came down to her. Something broke inside me every time we breathed the same air. Yeah, I grew into a defective version of myself. In so many ways. I was always saying stuff I didn't think through, talking too loud, and pushing myself out of my comfort zone. For what? A chance to draw her attention.

So far, all my attempts had been in vain. She hated me. I was pretty sure the attraction was one-sided. This year, if I wanted a chance with her, I would need a brand new game plan. Something incredible that she wouldn't be able to resist because, so far, Melinda Shepard had never indulged me or made me believe we could ever be friends —or more.

High school started in two days, and I was already angsty at the idea of seeing her every day after months spent living in two different states. My summer had felt like a never-ending saga without a single glimpse of her. The only news I'd received was through Paige, and only when I extracted them from her, trying to be as subtle as I could get. Yep, that was me. King on the field, lame on the love scene. Melinda had blown my attempt once, and I was in no rush to be rejected again. Thus came my rule to steer clear of the dating scene. Unless it was with her. Why I was still obsessed with my neighbor after all this time was a mystery to me. But hey, Mom had told me once that you can't choose who you love, so maybe that was the case here. Whatever.

"Are you coming?"

My brother's voice pulled me out of my spiraling thoughts. I felt my cheeks warming up as I zeroed in on him and prayed he wouldn't be able to guess what—or rather who—had invaded my mind.

"Where?" I blinked, not sure what we were talking about just now.

"Did you listen to anything I just said?"

"Huh…"

"Huh?" My brother snickered. "That's your answer? Seriously, I thought Mom and Dad taught you how to speak when you were two."

"*Bla-gadda-ta-ma.* Better?"

"So much more articulate, baby bro. I knew you were fluent in English. Anyway, back to business. Are you in?"

I still couldn't recall what we were talking about before I'd zoned out.

"C'mon, Mase, pay attention. The races. Later today. Are you coming?"

My mind switched back to the girl next door.

Would Melinda be attending? Geez, my Melinda Shepard problem was getting out of hand. No matter what I did, my brain always reeled back to her.

My pulse kicked up at the thought the fourth ticket was hers. I would think she would be eager to spend time with her friends after being away for so long, no?

"Fine. Count me in." *New game plan.* The idea I could switch things around between Melinda and me this year filled me with renewed hope. I had to make the most of all the opportunities that presented themselves. "What time are we leaving?"

"Two. We're all going out to dinner afterward."

I nodded. "Okay. I don't know if I have plans yet. I'll confirm later." If I sounded too interested, Craig and Paige would know something was up with me. The best thing I could do was to act nonchalant. Interested enough, but not too much. Inside me though, there was a fireworks show going on. Jitters danced in my belly. I couldn't stay still. Two o'clock was hours away. Time was moving too slowly. I had to get out of here. Do something. Clear my head. Exert my body.

I jumped to my feet to bolt when my brother grabbed my wrist.

"Mase, wait."

"What? I'm going for a run. I need to breathe some fresh air, and running will help chase away last night's mistakes."

He fixed me with a stern gaze and bunched eyebrows. I knew this look. Craig was about to use his big brother card on me. The one that only came out whenever he thought I was being an idiot. "Mase, tell me you are done with Lydia Santos."

I offered him a tiny smile. "Yeah. Not going there again. I won't screw with the team. You have my word."

"Whatever it is you're trying to prove or fix by sleeping around won't do it."

"Yeah, yeah."

He lowered his voice. "How's your shoulder? Coach was hard on you all week."

"Okay. Don't worry about me. It's all good." I gave my shoulder a roll back as if that proved my affirmation.

"Are you still in pain?"

Sometimes. "I'm not… I don't… I'm fine. Gotta go." I jerked away from his touch, fearing he could tell all my secrets if he looked at me too closely.

The state of my right shoulder was nobody's business. No way would I ever let it slow me down or restrict my movements this season. It was senior year, and I planned to lead my team to victory for the second year in a row. My mind drifted to my neighbor—again.

Melinda and Paige were best friends. The last thing I wished for was to complicate the relationship between the four of us and for them to think I wasn't being serious toward their friend.

I had to prove myself first. I knew that. I'd be halfway there if only I could figure out how not to turn into someone else when Melinda was around.

Fixating on something other than my physical pain was the distraction I needed right now. And Melinda Shepard was the chosen one.

Rushing to my room, I changed into a pair of dark mesh shorts, a worn Heather gray T-shirt with cut-off sleeves, and runners.

I came face to face with my dad on the landing, dressed in a deep-blue terry cloth bathrobe, his dark hair spiking in all directions, and his eyes red and still swollen from sleep. "Morning, son." He rubbed a palm over his two-day-old stubble.

I chuckled. "Wow, Dad, the night has been rough." I motioned to his hair, and he used a hand to try to tame the beast. "Keep trying. It's stuck like that." I shrugged. "I hope it's not forever, or you'll have to shave it."

"Oh, well." He sighed and dropped his arm to his side. "Not sure your mom would find me handsome if I go bald. Anyway, too little sleep and too much on my mind."

"Well, there's always coffee downstairs if you need a pick-me-up. Going now. Bye."

I jogged downstairs, and when I entered the kitchen, Paige and Craig had disappeared. Only the smell of freshly baked cupcakes hinted at their earlier presence. I swallowed a protein bar in three bites and downed a glass of water before making my way outside to stretch.

The storm swirling inside me resembled a mixture of excitement and anticipation at the idea I could prove to Melinda I was done being the stupid version of myself. I had no clue how to interpret it. It felt different from the jitters I felt before a game or the doubt and anxiety that crippled me when I tried something new. This agitation in my stomach was foreign, and I couldn't wait for it to settle down.

CHAPTER 4

MY BROTHER IS WEIRD, GIRL

From my position on the front deck, I had a partial view of the Shepards' house. I cracked my neck and stretched my glutes, positioning myself in the only spot where I had an unrestrained view of their porch. Just in case Melinda magically appeared. A line of mature trees between our houses made it almost impossible for me to see anything from here. From my bedroom window or the back deck, I had a much better chance to catch movements next door because their angle made it perfect to spot any activity going on in their backyard. Over the years, I had gazed multiple times at Melinda doing her late-night laps in the pool during the summer. She was on the school swim team and was pretty amazing at it. I knew college scouts had been watching her because I'd heard her father tell mine one day. Crestwood University, a college a little over an hour's drive from here, renowned for its academics and athletics programs, had shown interest, amongst others. They had shown interest in Craig and me too. Even offered us a full ride if we played football there next year.

My brother and Paige had their sights on Thompson University in Philadelphia, though. Paige couldn't wait to move away from our little town and live in a big city. My brother was so head over heels in love with her that he would follow her anywhere. Even if her college of choice ended up being in Antarctica. It helped that Thompson U had one of the top football programs in the country, so both would thrive there. Craig wasn't compromising his future by following his girlfriend.

If Melinda got into Crestwood U, then I would attend too. Maybe I was pussy-whipped just like my brother. The only problem, in my scenario, was that the girl had no idea I would follow her to the opposite side of the globe if she asked me to.

I stretched my quads and then my arms over my head one last time, ready to go. With a sigh, I glanced at the house next door again, annoyed that I hadn't spotted any signs of life there in the last ten minutes.

The front door behind me opened, and I almost expected it to be my brother when Paige joined me, a container full of freshly iced cupcakes in hand.

"Hey, Mase. You still here?"

I craned my neck to meet her eyes. Paige was tall enough—about five-eight, the same height as her best friend—but I towered over her by at least six inches. "Yeah. I just finished stretching. I was about to leave." I gestured to the street with my chin.

With long dark blonde hair and gray irises, Paige was pretty. Level-headed and smart, I understood why my brother was so enamored with her. She and Melinda had been best friends since the first day of seventh grade. The day I'd made an ass of myself at school—and humiliated her in the process—and my neighbor turned her back on me and killed whatever friendship we might have had.

Paige shoved her other hand into the pocket of her shorts and twisted her lips.

"What's wrong? I know you well enough to tell when something is bothering you. Spill it."

She remained silent.

"Is it Craig? What did the sucker do this time?" I lifted a brow, waiting for her to confirm. "Did he do something to piss you off?"

We both knew my brother was way too serious for his own good sometimes and would never do anything to anger his girlfriend. Even though they were still in high school, Craig and Paige were *that* couple. The one you looked up to. The one that made sense from day one. The one you envied sometimes when you were alone in bed at night. Yeah, they were disgustingly adorable together. And meant to last. The forever kind of love.

The upturn of Paige's lips hinted that she thought I was being funny, but the frown marring her forehead indicated there was still something bothering her.

"What's wrong, babe? You know you can talk to me. Always." I pulled her down to sit on a step next to me. She placed the container behind her on the deck.

Unlike my brother who hated my calling his girlfriend *babe*, Paige had never complained about it or asked me to drop it. She and I shared our own special bond.

"Did Craig confide in you about something?" she asked, staring straight into my eyes.

I would never be able to spin shit to her because she would call me out on it. "No. Why?"

She shrugged. "He's been acting weird lately."

I bumped her shoulder with mine. "My brother *is* weird, girl." The sound of her chuckle warmed me up. "Nothing new there. It was about time you caught up with the fact."

"He is not. He's focused. Smart and talented. And he knows what he wants. I admire him."

"Maybe. He's still weird, though. He's seventeen and acts like he's thirty most of the time. He should go out more, party more, enjoy his youth more. Just sayin'. He gotta live before he's all grown up and has a bunch of responsibilities. I can't be fun for the two of us forever. He has to step in and do his part. There must exist a way for him to loosen up a bit. Do you think they offer classes in college for that? Maybe he should join a fraternity next year. Those guys sure know how to enjoy all the perks college has to offer, no? Have you thought about joining a sorority instead of staying in the dorms? You and Craig would make a cute Kappa Gamma Whatever couple."

"*Kappa Gamma Whatever couple*? It sounds terrible." She exploded in a fit of laugher. "Anyway, for your information, not all of us want to get shitfaced or sleep around all the time, Mase…or join Greek life. And for your own good, please never move into a frat house. That would be a nightmare waiting to happen. Steer clear of drunk college kids and you'll be all right. By the way, in case you weren't aware, one day, you'll have to grow up too."

I lifted my hands between us as if to protect myself and put my most scared face on. "Me too? Are you serious?"

Paige bobbed her head, laughing.

"Oh geez, I should have been warned. Why is it that nobody ever told me? *Moooooom*?"

Paige planted a hand over my mouth, shutting me up.

My teasing died down, and she dropped her hand.

I rubbed my jaw. "Let's see. I know he's been stressed about college. Since junior year, we've had all these scouts calling us and promising things. Craig has been waiting for Thompson U to make an offer. Hopefully, when they come to see him play later this fall, they'll get their heads out of their asses, and it'll be a done deal. They already showed interest in me last year. He should be next. He has those late-night meetings with Dad in his office once a week. Neither of them will tell me what it's about."

"They do? He didn't tell me about them either. Has he told you he's been re-thinking our college choice? Is it because of the tuition fees?" Alarm swirled in her eyes.

"Nah. Even if he doesn't get that full-ride scholarship, our tuition fees are covered, no matter what. Mom and Dad have made sure we'd both be good on that front before we even turned one. It's flattering to know your number one school also wants you, that's all. I'm sure it's nothing. You two are fine?"

"Yes." She rubbed her palms on her thighs, looking nervous. "I-I think so. He's being quiet about all this… He usually confides in me. This time, it's like he's keeping something from me, and it's annoying me. Every time I broach the topic, he says I'm worrying for nothing."

I draped an arm over her shoulders and drew her closer. "Hey, Paige. My brother is madly in love with you. Never question his feelings, okay? No matter what's going on in his head or in his life, I'm sure if it's important, he'll tell you. Otherwise, he doesn't wanna worry you with stuff he has no control over. Don't overthink it. I'll keep an eye on him for you. Just in case."

She sighed, and her shoulders sagged forward. "I know. You're right. It's probably nothing." Her voice was soft, barely audible. I hated seeing the defeated expression shadowing her face. "Thanks…for keeping an eye out. I appreciate it."

Knowing my brother, he would never hurt her on purpose or hide things from her unless he thought it was in her best interest. I meant everything I said. I would never lead Paige on either. I respected her too much to feed her bullshit.

And I wasn't privy to Craig and Dad's secret conversations either. I too felt left out sometimes.

"Mase…I'm worried about you too," she said after a long stretch of silence. "You've been acting out more than usual in the last couple of weeks. I can tell when something is bothering you. You look agitated these days. Anything you wanna talk about?"

Okay, I was clearly more obvious than I thought.

"Summer training has been a bitch. Coach wants me to lead the team to State again this year. It's a big commitment. Most guys are seniors, and this is their last year playing. Many have no interest in playing in college or won't be recruited. It's their final shot at this. I don't wanna let them down. With Seth now in college, our starting cornerback has big shoes to fill. The pressure is real."

Never would I tell her about my infatuation with Melinda. That secret was not meant to be shared. Even with her best friend.

"You would tell me if it was something else?"

I nodded. "Probably."

"Good. And for what it's worth, I intend to enjoy my senior year and make the most of it."

"That's right, babe. Senior year is all about having fun and making memories."

"Well, that's the plan. I won't do crazy shit, but I'll try to get out of my shell a bit more…go to parties and stuff." She stood, ready to leave.

"Where are you going? I thought you just got here."

She pointed next door. "Mel is back from her vacation. We have a *loooot* of catching up to do. I arrived early because I wanted to spend some time with your brother first. He's going to the gym with Sheldon, so we'll meet you guys later. Are you riding with us to the races?"

"Who's us?" *Please say Mel. Please say Mel.*

"Huh, Craig, Mel, and me. Who else?"

"Oh, okay." My pulse accelerated, and I fought the urge to pump my fist. "Yeah, okay then… I'll ride with you guys. Sounds good." Did I nail the nonchalant, unaffected tone? A beat passed and Paige didn't call me out on it, so I guessed I'd fooled her. "I'm going now, and I'll see you later."

We faced each other when I rose to my feet, and she hugged me. Standing two steps below hers, we were almost face to face.

"Thanks for reassuring me, Mase. And if you wanna talk, I'll always make time for you."

I clutched the back of my neck and glanced at my feet before meeting her eyes. "Thanks, babe."

"Oh, and I left you cupcakes inside. I put your name on the lid. Your mom said she'll make sure you get them when you come back."

"You're the best. Craig is a lucky bastard."

Her smile lit up her face, her cheeks turning an adorable shade of pink. Gone were her worries. For now. "See you later."

She picked up the container and hurried next door. At a lazy pace, I jogged after her, hoping to see Melinda when she answered the door, but instead, it was Mr. Shepard who greeted her.

"Hey, Mr. Shepard." I waved at the man, fixing earbuds in my ear.

He returned the gesture. "Good morning, Mason. Enjoy your run."

"I will."

The only thing filling the silence other than the music in my ears and the pounding of my shoes on the pavement as I accelerated the pace was the drumming of my heart. Not from exertion, but from anticipation.

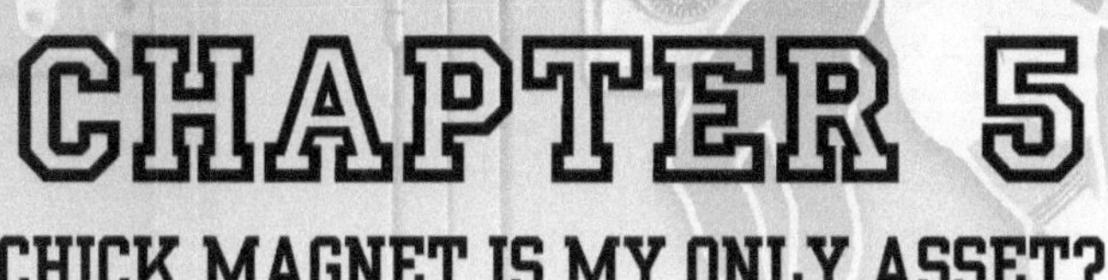

CHAPTER 5
CHICK MAGNET IS MY ONLY ASSET?

Craig pulled his Jeep into Melinda's driveway. The girls were sitting on her front porch steps, deep in conversation. Just then I realized my brother and I were dressed almost identically: board shorts, white T-shirts, and baseball caps. "Did you do it on purpose?" I asked, gesturing between us with a finger. "You copied my go-to outfit. I don't care if we're born in the same year, we are not twins. And even if we were, I would never do the twins-dressed-alike thing with you. Find your own style."

"I can't help it, Mase, if you feel like always copying me because I'm the most handsome between us and you idolize me too much. It's okay. It should pass when you grow up. I can't believe mom thinks you are her fashionista son." He snorted. "Yeah, right. Everyone knows I set the trends and that you're just a follower."

"Do you hear yourself? Identity theft is a real thing. By the way, I recognize the shorts you're wearing as being mine, so please don't pretend you bought those."

"Well, I found them in the stack of fresh laundry on my bed this morning. I assumed they were now mine. Honest mistake, man. Or what we used to say? Finders keepers?"

"You wish. What are you? Five? We both know you always steal my shit because you think I'm the better-looking sibling. It's time you admit it."

"Mase, Mase, Mase... Stop complaining."

I sighed. "Sometimes, it feels like I've landed an annoying sister instead of a brother."

"Shut up. You know you can't live without me. You'll realize it next year when we attend different colleges."

I said nothing because I possessed no argument to deny it.

Craig honked, and Paige's cheeks flushed when my brother killed the engine and waved at her.

I turned to him. "Really? You saw her like five hours ago."

He shrugged. "What can I say? I love her so much, man. You'll understand when you find the one."

As he spoke, I locked eyes with Melinda. Where Paige was willowy, Melinda was athletic. Her shoulders were defined, and her curves more generous. One hundred percent my type. Something flashed in her gaze. Defiance, anger, indignation? We hadn't seen each other in months, so unless my morning fight with Lydia was common knowledge already and it affected her somehow, Melinda had no reason to be upset at me. I didn't care about her attitude, though, because the sight of her, looking pretty in denim cut-offs and a red top, stole every molecule of my breath away. With her sun-kissed complexion and the caramel highlights she'd gained by spending the last three months at the beach, she looked alluring. I was so weak when she was involved. In my twisted mind, even when she pouted or rolled her eyes at my lame jokes, I found her irresistible. Yep, there probably existed no cure for this kind of sickness.

She flipped her ponytail over her shoulder, and the scene imprinted on my mind in slow motion. My heart raced in my chest. Paige told her something, and Melinda's lips dipped into a crestfallen expression. Something was bothering her, I could tell, and I wished I could bring happiness back to her features. If only she'd let me in. In my wildest dreams maybe, not in this life, though. After a moment, Paige moved to stand, and Melinda broke eye contact with me. I rubbed the column of my throat and looked away, trying to appear unaffected when inside I was all but calm. I had missed our staring contests while she was away. Whenever we engaged in one, it was like neither of us could break it, and yet it had never evolved into a conversation or more.

Slipping my cocky suit on, I climbed out of the car when the girls neared us. "Hey," I greeted them with the biggest smile I could muster. I winked at Melinda before I spun around to face Paige. "Babe, why don't you sit at the front?"

"You sure?"

I shrugged. "Yeah. Lover boy is lovesick when you're not around. I'll ride in the back." I discarded my cap and ran my fingers through the mass of light brown waves also known as my hair, messing them up probably more than they already were. Girls usually loved my just-woken-up look, and it kind of became one of my trademarks over the years. A stupid part of me wondered if Melinda loved my tousled hair too…or if she liked anything about me at all.

"Mase, there's more room for your stupidly long legs at the front," Paige argued.

"I'll be fine. It's only a twenty-minute ride." I held the door open for her while she slid onto the passenger seat. "And I'll be in great company."

Melinda's eyes transformed into weapons—aimed at me. I winked again. Even though I wanted her attention on me, when she did give it to me, I wasn't sure how to act. When we all rode together, I usually sat at the front with my brother, because yeah, my legs were squashed at the back, but a guy had to suffer sometimes for the greater good. Doing my best to pretend to be interested in the scenery, I felt Melinda's gaze on the side of my head. Glad to know I wasn't the only curious one. Perhaps she wasn't so indifferent to me either after all. The hammering of my heart quickened. The thought of her date last night ending like mine sent a weird feeling through my body. It felt as if someone had blocked the airflow to my lungs. I knew I was being a hypocrite about not wanting her to date other guys, but I couldn't care less. I hated the idea of Nathan Bellevue's hands all over her body or kissing those pink lips. I clenched my jaw, my molars about to fuse together under the pressure. *Relax, Mase,* I told myself. *She could have been with that sucker right now, but she's not.*

"Did you hear about Rusty's latest feat?" Craig asked, putting a stop to my inner turmoil.

I directed my attention to him. "No. What did he do this time?"

"He was high as a kite last night and jumped into Johnny Wilson's pool from the roof, pretending he was flying. The rumor is that his dad is trying to do some damage control with Coach so he doesn't get kicked off the team. You know how it is. Mr. Street usually brings his checkbook along when Rusty messes up. Maybe we'll get those new jerseys after all."

I dragged a hand over my face. "Geez, sometimes it feels like I'm the captain of a bunch of first-graders."

Russell's family owned three of the four car dealerships in town. His father was known to buy his way out of any situation.

"Remember when the golf balls prank went horribly wrong last year during rivalry week?" Paige asked.

"Yeah, well. It's football, babe. Coach has forbidden us to partake this year. I'm sure some of the guys will still try to get into trouble, though. I can't believe Mr. Street would pay the fine this year again if things turn to shit."

"Uh, it's your job, Captain," my brother teased, "to keep your guys in line."

I shrugged. "A bunch of stupid and horny teenage boys thinking they're indestructible. Easier said than done."

"And you're not one of them?" Melinda asked from beside me, her tone clipped.

"I'm not what? Irresistible? Hot as hell?" I meant it as a joke, but it sounded pretentious as hell. I wouldn't win any brownie points with stupid replies.

"No, Mr. *My Ego Is Too Big For My Own Head.* I meant a stupid and horny teenage boy doing idiocies." She tipped her chin up, challenge swirling in her eyes.

"Maybe I am, but my dream to go pro doesn't involve acting like a shithead and getting caught and spending the night in jail. It's still fun, though. The thrill of the forbidden. It's tradition, and we usually have a blast during rivalry week. As fun as it is, I just don't wanna get involved this year because my college career is more important than pranking our rivals. But these guys are my teammates, and I won't let them down."

"I second that," Craig chimed in. "Mase, no wiser words have ever left your mouth. Hopefully, the guys will follow your lead."

Melinda folded her arms over her chest, looking unimpressed.

I scanned the length of her, relishing the swell of her breasts peeking from the neckline of her top. I looked away before she could call me out on it.

She snorted. "Wow, you guys are a bunch of followers."

"It's called being part of a team." I offered her my widest smirk. "We don't snitch on each other, and we work as a unit on and off the field."

"That's stupid. I'm glad I'm on the swim team and not the football team."

I winked at her. "Me too. I agree with that statement one hundred percent."

She scrunched up her nose, studying me for a second before retreating to her side of the seat with a groan. She mumbled "Perv" under her breath. It wasn't the reaction I'd hoped for, but it was still better than no reaction at all.

My thoughts tangled in my brain as I watched her profile. Why did I always have to say shit when she was involved? Why couldn't I just keep my big mouth shut like any smart guy would do?

To satisfy my need to touch her without being obvious about it, I stretched my legs, bumping my knee into hers. I held my breath, waiting to see what she would do.

No reaction.

After a moment, she huffed a breath and moved her legs, breaking the sole point of contact between us. Pretending to adjust my board shorts, I opened my legs wider, my knee resting against the side of her thigh. A zing ran through me. Like tiny electric tingles spreading under my skin and messing with the thumping of my overzealous heart.

From the front seat, Paige glanced at Melinda over her shoulder, then at me.

What's wrong with her? I mouthed.

Girls' stuff, Paige replied.

"Mel, we can skip the races and do something else if you want," Paige offered, minutes later.

Melinda sighed and twisted in her seat, severing the physical connection between us again. "Nah. It'll be fun. Gimme a minute to find my groove back."

Paige nodded and swiveled to stare out of the windshield, satisfied with her friend's answer.

For the umpteenth time, I checked the time on my phone. Only three minutes had passed. How could twenty minutes feel like forever?

I huffed a breath, ran my fingers through my hair—now a messy disaster for sure—and extended my left leg again, hoping for the slightest contact. Anything to ground me and kill the angst swirling inside me. In vain. In my imagination, Melinda would realize I was desperate for her attention and spin around, look at me, and indulge me by striking up a conversation like we were best friends or something. Or lodge herself in the crook of my arm, admitting she'd been in love with me all this time and we should go on a date. If only real life was as simple and love was as straightforward as the game, right?

All day, I'd been waiting for two o'clock to ring, and now that it was here, my new game-plan project was lacking. It was in dire need of some brainstorming and a real course of action. I shook my head, disappointed in myself.

From the shortest conversation known to humankind between the girls, I could tell I was right earlier, and something was bothering my seat neighbor. A part of me was desperate to put a smile on her face. To make her laugh because the sound was truly amazing. Also, it would be fun to have a ceasefire for a few hours so we could test once and for all if we still shared some chemistry.

Shutting my eyes, I tried to come up with a joke that would ease the weirdness in the air—or at least decrease the tension tying my stomach. Nothing. It was like my brain cells had been fried. I couldn't come up with anything funny. My mind was blank, and my brain refused to reboot. The restlessness inside me multiplied. I wiped my palms over my shorts.

Slouching in the seat and widening my legs a little more, I attempted once again to rub my knee against Melinda's. Since when had I no better move than this with girls?

Melinda leaned forward to grab a lip gloss from her purse she had set on the floor, and I moved my leg out of her way. She offered me what resembled a tight-lipped smile, and my stupid heart galloped in my chest like she had just made a love declaration. After coating her lips in glittery pink, she returned her gaze to the scenery passing by, and my hopes for some interaction died. Why couldn't I come up with something smart to say? Anything. I wasn't usually shy. And I always had a comeback ready on the tip of my tongue.

Now, though? Nothing. My thoughts were frozen inside my head.

I watched Elk River, our small Michigan town about fifty miles northeast of Traverse City, through her window. Bordering the Grand Traverse Bay, it had the small-town charm while being close enough to the big city, so we had all the amenities within an hour's drive. Other than the chilly winters, I loved everything about my hometown. Right now, all we could see were trees and more trees, a few businesses lining the road, and a strip mall. Nothing exciting enough to suck in Melinda's interest.

A notification on my phone jolted me out of my thoughts. I fished the device out of my pocket and unlocked it, thanking, in my head, whoever saved me from my own stupidity.

JAX

Throwing an end-of-summer bash tonight. You in?

Jackson Pettyfer was a left guard for the Elk River High Bears and one of the coolest people I knew. Always in a good mood and ready to party, he had gotten the nickname *The Organizer* a few years back when he always found an excuse to throw a rager. Even when we were in middle school, he would come up with all kinds of ideas to have a group of friends over. Now that he was in high school, his parties had switched from *video game and soda* nights to *booze and midnight swim* themes.

My phone chimed three times with incoming text messages.

JAX

Ten.

My uncle's cabin by the lake.

Spread the word, everybody will come if you're there.

My lips curled into a smile, and I typed a reply.

ME

You're only using me for my popularity with girls and my social skills. Is that it?

JAX

Yeah. Pretty much. Can't stand your ugly mug otherwise.

ME

Chick magnet is my only asset?

JAX

That and throwing a ball.

Bring beer. And a crowd.

ME

Fine. Let me see what I can do.

"You guys have something planned for later?" I asked Craig and the girls, relieved to have something to talk about and break that awkward silence once and for all.

My brother watched me through the rearview mirror. "Told you we were having dinner with the guys later."

"Yeah, but I mean after dinner."

Paige turned around in her seat to look at me. "What do you have in mind?"

"Jax is throwing an end-of-summer bash at the cabin by the lake. You're all invited. You coming?"

She shrugged. "Could be fun." Her attention drifted to her friend who had been oddly silent so far. "Are you in?"

"I suppose."

Paige's eyes shone with glints. "Okay, people, we're going. We need to let loose before school resumes in two days. Senior year means attending parties and opening ourselves to new experiences."

I nodded my agreement. "Nothing like a night at the cabin to end our summer break on a high note. Let me text Jax. We gotta bring beer."

"We can do a pitstop after dinner," my brother said. "I

know a place where they don't check IDs as long as we pay cash."

"You do? Never thought of sharing that piece of useful information with your baby brother before?"

He shook his head, a smirk forming on his lips. "Yeah, well, I'm surprised I'm the guy providing the information right now. Between us, you're usually the one in the loop, man."

"Life would be boring if I was perfect all the time. I love it when you're the one teaching me stuff. After all, that's the reason you were born first."

My brother's grin took over his face.

"I'm glad we're doing this," Paige said.

"Me too." The tension straining Melinda's shoulders seemed to vanish, and a tiny smile shaped her lips. "I need this. To let loose."

I pumped my fist. "Good. We have a plan, people."

The weird silence that had enveloped us until now dissipated. The energy in the car had transformed, the heaviness a thing of the past, and now we were back to being ourselves. I relaxed in my seat, the need to entertain the crowd gone.

Paige and Melinda were chatting about some movie I'd never heard of, and Craig kept stealing glances at his girlfriend every few minutes. His hand stayed attached to hers as if he feared she could disappear any second. Something was different, though, in their interactions, and for the first time, I noticed what Paige had hinted at this morning and wondered what was troubling my brother.

Craig eased onto the highway and pushed the gas, and the Jeep swerved. "Oh, yeah," my brother hollered, his lips tilting into a wide grin, as he winked at his girlfriend. Since we'd removed the Jeep's soft top before we left, the wind blew our hair, and right now, it felt like summer would last forever. I clutched the cross bar above our heads, enjoying this moment of freedom where everything seemed possible.

Paige waved her arms in the air and Melinda laughed, whatever bothering her minutes ago seemingly forgotten. Her smile was back—contagious and blinding.

"Okay, listen," she began. "One night when I was in Jersey, I was getting ice cream with some people I worked with when this couple walked in. The guy had planned to ask his girlfriend to marry him. With the help of the employee working behind the counter, he had hidden the ring in her cone. She took a big bite and almost swallowed it. You should have seen his face when she choked on it. The poor guy. It was like the entire place froze, waiting to see how it would play out."

"And?" Paige asked.

"She didn't swallow it. She pulled the ring out of her mouth and started crying. The guy got down on one knee, told her what she meant to him, and they walked out of there engaged."

"Wow. So romantic." Paige cupped her heart and swiveled in her seat, her gaze traveling back and forth between Craig and me. "Take notes, guys. Girls love big gestures. A lot."

My brother brought their joined hands to his lips. "You do?"

She smiled back. "We all do, right, Mel?"

"Yes." She shrugged. "Can you blame us? Movies and books have been teaching us about romance all our lives and to expect fairytales. Girls have standards. Anyway, this was the most action I saw in New Jersey this summer. It was fun, but hanging out with my grandparents got old after a few weeks. I'm glad to be back."

I absorbed each word escaping her lips and burned to

memory every one of her features, familiar but also different from how they were three months ago. Sharper angles and softer curves.

"I can't believe Nathan Bellevue vacationed at the same place you did. How small is this world?" Paige asked. "I hope he treats you well, or he better run fast when I come after him."

My brother's glanced at her. "God, you're hot when you get all protective and shit."

She glowed at the compliment, a pink shade tinting her cheeks. "Thanks."

"Ah, I understand now." My brother watched Melinda through the rearview mirror. "That's why you two know each other."

"His granddad lives down my grandparents' house. He was in New Jersey for a week, and we spent some time together. He wasn't the same Nate he is at school. Anyway, we just had dinner last night. Nothing to feed the rumor mill."

I thanked my brother and Paige in my head for bringing up the topic and putting to rest the questions swirling in my head.

"Hey, Mase," Paige said, stealing my attention. Was she about to deliver more insider information about her best friend? "You won't believe what…" The first notes of a pop song playing on the radio captured her attention, and she toyed with the knob, increasing the volume. Turning backward in her seat, she lifted a finger in my direction. "I'll tell you later. We cannot ruin a good song."

The chorus started, and both girls belted the lyrics at the top of their lungs using their fists as microphones, not a care in the world about their singing abilities. Flushed cheeks and bright eyes, with the breeze lifting their hair, happiness radiated from them.

A slice of my heart swelled at the sight. I wished every day could be like this moment. Carefree and filled with joy—and love. And that the girl would be mine and not hate my guts. The four of us together against the world.

Craig cocked his head toward me and grinned. I mirrored it because it was impossible to deny the girls' contagious enthusiasm was rubbing off on us too.

The song ended and another catchy one began, and their singing resumed.

Resting my back against the door, I pretended to stretch my legs, my only goal to watch the girl beside me. Her eyes were full of life, her ponytail sweeping across her shoulders with each bob of her head. Her rosy lips, thanks to the lip gloss she'd applied earlier, looked good enough to devour. Melinda Shepard was a sight for sore eyes. And no matter how many times I told myself to look away, the truth was I couldn't. My entire being couldn't resist her magnetism. Despite myself, I homed in on her mouth as she sang every word.

I would give up a lot to be able to kiss those pouty lips once. Feel them on mine and decide if they tasted as good as they looked.

All I needed was one chance to make a move and prove to her I wasn't the cocksure guy everyone believed I was. When she had been away this summer, I'd made a promise to myself. I wouldn't make a move on Melinda Shepard until I was sure she knew she wasn't a joke to me and that I was serious about my intentions toward her. If I had only one chance to make her fall in love with me, I wouldn't risk it.

CHAPTER 6

NATHAN FUCKING BELLEVUE

Ten minutes later, Craig parked in the gravel lot behind the tracks. The car races at the old speedway should be entertaining—they usually were. The scent of gasoline and hotdogs from the concession stands saturated the air, and the sound of engines being pushed to their breaking point vibrated through the small stadium. An enthusiastic crowd cheered and clapped as we took our seats. The races hadn't begun yet, and the drivers were just testing the tracks and their vehicles, but still, excitement was palpable in the air.

The drivers got into position. A horn resonated somewhere, but it sounded miles away.

Somehow, I didn't wish to be here anymore. Awareness took over my entire body. My senses were acute. Even my breathing hastened, and I wasn't even moving. The problem with today's races rested on the girl sitting right in front of me, capturing all my attention, no matter how hard I tried to ignore her. She hadn't talked to me since we arrived, mostly acting as if I didn't fucking exist.

I had to forget about her. And fast.

Every smile she sent Paige, who sat next to her, each flick of her ponytail over her shoulders, or even the clap of her hands when she got excited watching the cars circling the dusty track, I missed nothing. Not a single one of her movements. As if all of them were playing in slow motion. A waft of her fruity shampoo hit my nose. Her laughter spread through me like a caress. Right now, I couldn't care less about the action down on the speedway.

Every inch of my body was tensed, and I swallowed, trying to ease the discomfort invading me.

Since when did someone—a girl—bother me so much? And yet, her presence acted like a dagger straight through my heart because she couldn't care less about my existence.

My clothes felt too tight on me. At one point, she cocked her head to ask Craig something, pointing at the tracks, her smile bright. The sparkle in her eyes could probably be seen from space. Melinda Shepard loved the competition. That was what made her so good at her sport on meet days. I almost combusted when her eyes landed on me for a fraction of a second. I was back to being that eleven-year-old boy with a crush on the girl next door.

She turned around, engrossed in the action before us. "Go. Yes. Like that." She jumped to her feet, cheering and stamping, as dust rose up around the cars, hiding them from us, and only the high-pitched whine of the gearboxes could be heard. "Faster. Yes. Pass him on the right."

She pumped her fist when the cars crossed the finish line. People screamed and clapped as the guy who finished first held his helmet over his head, grinning like an idiot. I had no idea who he was or if he was any good since I'd been too distracted the entire time he had circled the track.

Melinda spun around to talk to my brother but lost her balance, and her palm splayed on my thigh when she fell forward. My heart rate picked up, and my entire body sang as her hand lingered there for longer than needed.

I took a deep breath in, trying to relax. In vain. Melinda Shepard was touching me. Her hand was on me. I swallowed, not sure how to react without scaring her away. Time idled as I steadied my breathing, trying to look unaffected. For a long second, we fixated on each other. The imprint of her palm burned my flesh through the fabric of my board shorts. This time, the glint shining in her eyes looked nothing like the swords she usually threw at me. I feared if I blinked, they would disappear. As if an invisible string tied us together, we both leaned into each other. The moment she realized her hand was still connected to my leg and we were about to collide, she removed it. A puff of air left my lungs at the same time.

"Sorry," she murmured, shaking her head like she was trying to escape whatever spell had taken us hostage.

I tried to speak, to say something, but I nodded like a fool instead. *Smooth, Mase. Real smooth.*

Chase, my best friend, sitting on my right, elbowed me in the ribs, breaking the weird trance I had fallen into. "Man, it's Novak's turn." He pointed to the tracks. "He's doing it. How sick is that?"

My attention returned to the starting line. Something loosened in my chest, and I breathed easier.

Indeed, Novak, a guy four years older than us who had survived leukemia back in high school, climbed behind the wheel of an old white sports car with the number thirty-nine painted in red on the side—his old football jersey number. My friends and I all jumped up from our seats, and we applauded and wolf whistled. The guy was a legend in Elk River. Years ago, the town had organized charitable events to aid him and his family through their ordeal. From paying hospital bills and helping him with his doctor's appointments to offering to drive him back and forth to his treatments in Traverse City and giving him moral support.

The energy buzzed in the outdated stadium.

The thirteen of us in our little section were a mad crowd as the engines roared to life and the cars spun around the track, leaving clouds of dust behind.

Third on his last lap, Novak maneuvered a last-second passing and crossed the finish line in second place. His girl-friend jumped into his waiting arms the moment he exited the vehicle, locking her legs around his waist and kissing him senseless.

Something pinched my heart as I watched them. I wanted that. A girl who loved me for me and would jump into my arms after a win on the field but also just because she felt like kissing the shit out of me for no reason other than we loved each other.

I cocked my head and turned to crack a joke, trying to ease the knot forming in my chest. "Hey, babe. I—" I scanned the bleachers, searching for the girls, but they had vanished. "Where's Paige?" I asked Craig, trying to sound chill about it.

"Restroom break and then to grab snacks with Mel. Want something?"

"Hotdog. All-dressed."

He lifted an eyebrow.

"The season hasn't started yet. I'm allowed a cheat day." I usually avoided junk food and empty carbs during football season as much as possible.

"Not complaining. They're getting me cheese fries. I'll call them."

"Get me some too."

We high-fived, and I directed my attention back to my friends.

———

Most of us arrived at the cabin Jackson's uncle owned a little after ten. I'd ridden with Chase and my brother and stopped to buy beer while Paige and Melinda were driving his car.

Set on a five-acre lot surrounded by thick woods, the two-story property offered enough privacy for our parties, the neighbors too far away to be bothered by the noise and loud music. A crowd filled the front lawn, and other people were on the dock, cheering the ones using the rope swing to dive into the lake. Guys flaunted their six-packs while girls paraded in tiny bikinis, scraps of fabric leaving nothing to the imagination.

Mindy, a girl from school, neared me as soon as I hopped out of the car. "How are you doing, Mase?"

"Good." I continued toward the front door, avoiding her wandering hands, flanked by my brother and Chase on either side of me. "Seen Paige?" I asked Craig.

"Nah. She messaged she was inside with Mel minutes ago."

I nodded and weaved through the crowd, the deafening beat of the music pounding in my head the closer I got to the front porch.

I scrunched up my nose when the pungent scent of weed wafted in my direction, its smoke suffusing my nostrils.

Someone bumped into me as I climbed the steps,

booze splashing the front of my shorts. *Great, now I looked like I pissed myself.* "Watch where you're going," I barked through gritted teeth. "Idiot." I slid to the right to avoid a girl juggling too many shot glasses, steering clear of another unwelcome spill.

Music blasted from inside, the sound earsplitting even from the other side of the wall.

Chase pushed a couple about to jump each other's bones on the front porch while I reached for the doorknob, desperate to escape this circus.

The house was crowded, every one of my cells throbbing with the intoxicating beat of the bass.

"This is a zoo," Chase said with a shake of his head. "None of Jax's party has ever been this crowded before."

Sweat pearled on my nape. Too many bodies cramped in such a small place wasn't my definition of fun. I loved crowds, but only the ones sitting in the bleachers and cheering us on.

"Let's drop this in the kitchen and make our way outside," I said, barely able to drag fresh puffs of oxygen to my lungs, pointing with my chin at the booze we were all carrying.

Chase nodded.

"Going to find my girl," my brother said, forcing his way through the crowd, with us hot on his heels.

We entered the kitchen, and I halted, the scene playing in front of us making the blood boil in my veins, my mood turning sour by the second.

Melinda was cuddling with Nathan Fucking Bellevue, both sipping from the same beer bottle and smiling at each other. He leaned forward, whispering sweet nothings in her ear as she giggled.

My jaw tensed.

Heat crept up my back.

With keen eyes, I assessed the situation, trying to keep calm and banking the hot fury awakening inside of me.

My hands curled into fists once I dropped the two twelve-packs onto the counter. Before I could do or say something I'd regret, I darted away, shouldering the screen door open with a bang, not caring if anyone stood on the other side and got swept by it.

"Asshole," I cursed as I kicked the door shut behind me.

Mindy cornered me the moment I stepped onto the porch, trying to wind her arms around my waist. Clingy much? Geez. With a gentle push, I sidestepped and lifted a hand. "Not in the mood."

A pout formed on her lips. "But you never are anymore. What have I ever done to you that you won't even try to kiss me?" Her whiny tone grated on my nerves.

Jesus, I was so done with all this bullshit. "Nothing." I faked a smile and walked away. "It's an *it's not you, it's me* kinda situation," I said over my shoulder. I heard her complain from behind me, desperate and demanding, but I blocked out her words as I plodded toward the lake, following the narrow path between the trees. The musky aroma of the damp soil and spruces enveloped my senses. Sitting on a rock in the shadow of a tree, I watched the crowd swinging from the rope into the clear water under the moonlight. One of my teammates was running around, a girl scooped over his shoulder, holding on to her backside, a beer clutched in his other hand. They both giggled as he pretended to throw her into the lake, only to catch her at the last second.

The chatter of happy people was the background noise to my running thoughts. Closing my eyes, my fingertips found my temples, massaging the tension away. I forced a deep breath in, and another one for good measure.

Some of the annoyance tightening my upper back melted away. Yet, I wasn't ready to join my friends and fake that I was fine when I was clearly not.

Nathan Fucking Bellevue. What a waste. I was sure his name followed the definition of douchebag in the dictionary. Yeah, I bet the term had been invented with him in mind. He was nothing more than a jerk with a handsome face. He talked a good game, and girls fawned over him, but that was the extent of his talent. I couldn't understand how Melinda Shepard could fall for his charades. She was smart. Smarter than most people I knew. How could she not see how much of a loser the guy was?

My breath hitched.

The aura of danger that followed him around always caused friction amongst our friends. Last year, he got punched in the face after he tried to coerce a girl to give him head in the janitor closet during gym class. She wasn't a willing participant in his little game and had kicked him in the junk. Hard. Nathan had dismissed the fact she had a boyfriend—and two older brothers. He then missed two full weeks of school after the three of them rearranged his face that night. Rumor had two of his teeth were fake now and that he'd gotten a nose job to correct the damage his face had sustained.

I dragged one palm over my face, unable to quiet my troubled mind. Nathan Bellevue was bad news. A crippling feeling knotted my insides. I could tell this would end badly, but I had no clue how to warn Melinda without sounding like a lunatic. She and I weren't even friends. I knew the girl well enough to know she would tell me to mind my own business if I got involved. If anything, my meddling in her life would push her further into the devil's arms. Unless I got to Paige first. Perhaps she would listen to me and warn her friend. And yet, would it make me look like a jealous asshole instead of someone who cared? Crap. I had no idea how to proceed.

A drink would taste amazing right now, and it would probably help settle my buzzing anger. But it would also mean I might get drunk and do or say things I would regret. Like, start a fight with Nathan Bellevue just because I was indeed a jealous bastard and I thought he was a piece of shit. Or take Mindy up on her offer because a distraction would help me cool my temper. My stomach curdled at the thought of her mouth on me.

Two things I didn't need—or crave.

Instead of enjoying a night out with my friends, here I was, sulking on my own, not knowing how to react to Melinda's actions and how to prevent her from getting hurt. I knew I was being a hypocrite because I often attended parties with a girl locked under my arm even when I was aware of Melinda's eyes on me. More often than not, I played the part of the player like the role had been created for me—damn the consequences—putting more distance between us instead of trying to shatter the wall of ice that stood between us and fixing our relationship. And here I was, tonight, upset—and hurt—that she was flirting with another guy in my face when I had no right to be. I was being served a taste of my own medicine, and I hated every second of it. Yeah, jealousy didn't suit me.

I sighed and hung my head low.

When did I turn into such a loser?

CHAPTER 7
IT LOOKS BETTER ON YOU ANYWAY

"I'm out of here," I told my friends as I joined them in the kitchen a while later.

I scanned my surroundings. Craig was busy talking to Jackson about a pro football player who had just broken a record, and Chase was cheering on a game of beer-pong. Paige was sitting on the kitchen island, chatting with a bunch of girls, laughing and drinking from a red plastic cup.

Sheldon's face snapped in my direction. "Already? It-It's not…it's not even midnight yet." He crooked his arm and rested it on my shoulder. I could smell the tequila on his breath. "What's up, Captain? You can talk to me, *youuu* know." He lifted a finger. "I'm *suuuper* good at keeping secrets. Like a *suuuper* secret-keeper."

"I'm just not in the mood, man."

"Is it because Shepard left *withhh* Bellevue?"

"When?" Gosh, I hated sounding so desperate. I cleared my throat. "What do you mean by *they left together?*"

"Just that he…*huuuh*…he invited her…he invited her to go on a 'walk.'" He used his fingers to draw air quotes around the word *walk*.

"And why would I care?" *I cared a whole lot.*

"*Cappp*, I might not be the smartest guy on the team, *buuut* I have eyes, you *knooow*. I've seen how *youuu* always look at her like she's *reallly* special. Like she's *youuur* girl."

Here was the proof I wasn't as subtle as I thought. "Yeah, well… Do you know where he took her?" Angst awoke inside me. I hated the feeling of my heart banging too hard in my chest and my blood turning to ice. It usually happened when I was playing a game that mattered. When we were losing and the pressure became unbearable because I had to find a way to pull us out of the hole.

"*Nopppe*, but I can assure *youuu* he didn't take her upstairs."

"Good." Some of the knots in my stomach loosened at that piece of information. Still, Nate had been drinking earlier. I had a hard time believing Melinda would ride home with his sorry drunken ass. Unless he possessed some kind of charm girls found impossible to resist—even her. Dammit.

Sheldon nudged me. "Hey, *Cappp*. Are you *stilll* leaving?"

I nodded. "I'll see you on Monday at school. Don't do anything stupid."

"Follow *youuur* own advice." He dropped his arm, and I sidestepped him. "Take care." He lowered his voice. "If

I… If I see your *girrrl*, I'll make sure she's safe, *okkkay?* Like *suuuper* extra-safe."

"Thanks, man."

"Always, *Cappp*."

Outside, the night air filled my lungs, bringing me a sense of calm. Keeping my head down, I snuck away, escaping the mass of people trying to strike up a conversation with me.

I trudged toward the cars parked at a weird angle across the patch of grass lining the driveway, with the intention of walking home. The forty minutes trek should be enough time to flush away all the remaining flecks of anger coiling me tight.

I stopped by my brother's Jeep to grab the hoodie I had left there earlier and slipped it on. I resumed my walk when the sound of a heated conversation a bit further on my right stopped me in my tracks.

The breeze carried the voices of a guy and a girl arguing.

"I'm not doing this with you. I already said no. Twice."

Every cell in my body froze. That voice. I would recognize it amongst a thousand others.

Bracing myself for a fight, I clenched my fists at my sides. If Fucking Bellevue had done anything to hurt Melinda, I would kick his ass to Neptune. In just a few strides, I zigzagged through the parked vehicles until I spotted Nathan's pine-green pickup truck with the "Fuck The World" sticker on the slider.

"Stop flirting with me if you won't open your legs for me."

The distinctive sound of a hand slapping a cheek resonated in the night. "That's my girl," I whispered to myself, pride filling me at the idea Melinda had put this jerk in his place.

"You bitch." Nathan's tone had gone from annoyed to pissed. "You wanna touch me? Is that it? Then I'll show you—"

I saw red. Enough that fury blurred my vision.

From a distance, I saw that Nathan had Melinda pressed against the back door of his truck, one knee between her legs and the full length of his body caging her while he held her hands above her head like she was at his mercy. She had no way out of this. The jerk had at least forty pounds and a few inches over her.

Silent tears rolled down her cheeks. "Let…let me go. Please, I-I don't want this. I wanna…I wanna go home. Don't do this."

"Shhh, relax. It'll be fun."

She shook her head. "You're wrong about me. I thought we were friends. I'm not who you want."

His grin turned devilish as he leaned back. "Friends? Nah. See? I don't agree with you. A sweet little pussy like yours is exactly what I crave. Let me take care of you. I didn't waste all this time on you over the summer to get nothing in exchange. I'll make this worth it, trust me."

"Please. No. *No, no, no.* Nate, don't do something you will regret."

"Touch her and die." They both went rigid at the sound of my voice.

Nathan didn't have time to finish his sentence before I tackled him and tossed him aside.

Melinda watched me with big, teary eyes, her back molded to that jackass's truck frame, her arms folded around herself like a shield.

The sight of her, shaken and scared, fractured a piece of my heart.

My pulse went haywire as I took in her ripped shirt and unbuttoned cut-offs. Nearing her, I pulled her into my arms, careful not to squeeze her too tight in case Fucking Bellevue had hurt her. Her sobs doubled in intensity as she buried her face in my chest, her frame feeling much smaller in my embrace. How many times had I dreamed of having her in my arms just like this? And the first time it happened, it was because she had almost been assaulted by a fucker. With her body taut against mine, I held her until her muscles relaxed and she calmed down, then wiped her wet cheeks with my thumb. "Are you okay? Did he hurt you?"

With careful fingers, I pushed her hair back, studying her face, searching for clues—or his marks on her porcelain skin.

She watched me for a long moment before she whispered a quivering "*Nnnn*-o."

"Gimme a sec, okay?"

Her voice sounded broken when she said, "O-okay."

A cocktail of emotions swirled inside me. I had to cool off, or I'd do something bad like re-rearranging the fucker's face. He kinda deserved another facial makeover and a brand-new nose.

I let go of Melinda, and seconds later, charged in the direction of Nathan trying to lift himself off the ground.

"What's wrong, Pierce? You want her as a sidepiece too? Pretty sure she's untouched yet. No doubt she'd be the best lay in all Elk River High. Come on, have you seen that ass of hers? I've been dreaming of riding it for a while now."

My wrath spiraled to a new high I'd never experienced before when he flashed a crooked smile my way. "Asshole, shut your mouth, or the only thing you'll ride is my fist."

"I'm not greedy, man. We can share. She can blow you while I fuck her hard and fast from behind."

With one hand, I fisted the collar of his T-shirt and

lifted him two inches above the ground. "You son of a bitch. She told you *No.* She fucking said *No.* N.O. No. That's the first word you learn as a baby, you dickhead. You're a sick psycho. Is something wrong with your hearing, or are you as much of a creep as everyone says? You're speaking about her like she can't hear you. Are you dumb? She's not a toy you can play with. Didn't Mommy Bellevue teach you to respect women growing up?"

His face turned a dark-beet color. "Fuck off, Mr. Football Star. Don't disrespect my mother."

"Whoa, you're even more deranged than I thought. You won't let people talk shit about your precious mommy, yet you assault girls in parking lots. It makes total sense."

"It's okay for you to get a buffet of pussies but not for me? Take a long hard look in the mirror before accusing me of any wrongdoing."

"Wow. Here I thought you had some brain matter left. Guess you're not that lucky after all. The difference between us is that I never force myself on a girl, you sociopath. Ever heard of consent or are you too dumb to understand the meaning? I'll give you one warning. No second chances for freaks like you. If I ever catch you giving my girlfriend—or any other girl—trouble, you'll deal with my fist." I reared my arm back, ready to make the motherfucker understand my threat wasn't just for show when a small hand curled around my biceps and the voice that had haunted my dreams for so many nights filtered through my murdering thoughts. My whole being relaxed under her touch, and the anger raging in the depths of me decreased a notch.

"Mase... He's not worth it. Don't injure your good hand for him. Release him. Please. Do it for me."

Closing my eyes, I debated my options in my head. The idea of aggravating my condition because of this idiot and risking the football season and messing further with our chances to play at State—and my future—didn't appeal to me right now, so I dropped my arm. Yeah, I didn't need another injury.

"Thank you," Melinda murmured from behind me.

With a big shove, I pushed Nathan back. "You're lucky she's defending you. Now get lost before I change my mind."

In his drunken state, he twirled and stumbled, landing on his front, no doubt eating a mouthful of dust as his face kissed the ground.

My hand gripped Melinda's. Our palms fused together, and her fingers held on to mine like a lifeline. Nothing had ever felt so right before. "Are you sure he didn't touch you?" I asked. The thought of Nathan putting his hands on her made me choke on my breath.

"He wasn't able to..." Her voice sounded a bit shaky. "You stopped him just in time before he... Oh God, I don't even wanna think about it. I really thought we were getting along..."

"Hey, it's okay. As long as you're unharmed, it's all that matters."

She nodded, staring down.

"Don't blame yourself. Some psychos are good at hiding their agenda." Just then, I noticed the bruises forming on her wrist.

"Fuck." I stepped back, ready for my fist to explain stuff to Nathan, who was still on the ground, when Melinda stopped me once more.

"It's nothing. I'm okay. Mase, please don't fight."

"I'm gonna kill him. I swear, one day, I'll kill this jerk."

She cradled my cheeks with her hands, and the expression on her face captured my eyes. "No, you won't. Listen to me. You are better than him. Never let your rage take control of you. Don't stoop down to his level. He's not worth it. Besides, he didn't do much. It's nothing."

"It didn't sound like nothing to me."

She swallowed, emotions flashing across her features for a split second. "It could have been much worse."

"Want me to grab you the sweater Paige keeps in Craig's Jeep?"

Melinda glanced down at her ruined shirt. "Nah, I think I can manage. Thanks, though." She tied the bottom in a knot, hiding the damage, before fixing her shorts. She exhaled a long breath and forced a smile, unable to hide the tremor in her voice. "Huh…all good."

"You sure?"

She swallowed and smiled, trying to project fake confidence. "Yep."

I hung my head and nodded. "Okay, then. You should go back to the party. Don't stay out here all by yourself." I didn't give her time to reply and walked in the direction opposite to the cabin. Feeling eyes on me, I glanced at her over my shoulder.

Melinda eyed me with a frown. "Where are you going?"

"Home."

"Home? Are you going to walk there?"

"Yep." I turned my head, waving at her over my shoulder. "See you later, neighbor."

Before I could put too much distance between us, she caught up with me. "Mason. Wait." She appeared in front of me, blocking my escape. "Why did you tell Nathan I was your…huh…girlfriend?"

A groan formed in my throat. "I meant *girl* friend. Not girlfriend." I swallowed. "Obviously."

She searched my face as if she was trying to decipher the words I hadn't spoken out loud. If she looked too closely, could she tell I'd just lied to her and the truth was that the word *girlfriend* had tumbled out of my mouth and it didn't even bother me because it felt right when I said it? Afraid she could read my thoughts, I skirted her and continued my retreat.

Melinda jogged after me and grabbed my arm from behind, slowing me down. "Stop."

"Nah, I'm out of here. Already told you."

"What happened?"

"Nothing except Asshat over there." I pointed behind me where we'd left Nathan.

"You're riled up because of what went down with Nate minutes ago?"

I muttered something under my breath, not in the mood to explain the extent of my feelings for her and why I was in such a piss-poor state. "I'm done. You should really go back to the party instead of staying here all by yourself since—" I cocked my head and looked at her, losing my train of thought.

We stared at each other for an infinite second. Awareness spread through my body at her proximity.

She let go of her grip on me as if our connection had set her fingers on fire and rubbed her palm over her shirt. "Can I…huh…can I join you? Walk home with you, I mean… I don't feel like being here anymore either."

"Fine." I shrugged. "Whatever pleases you." I fished my phone out of my back pocket and shot my brother a text. "Told Craig we were leaving."

"Oh…okay. Thanks."

For the next ten minutes, we walked side by side in silence. The energy between us wasn't as uncomfortable as I thought it would be. More like charged with something hard to define instead. It felt as if our silence translated the secrets none of our words could, an unspoken conversation nobody else was privy to.

"I thought you hated me," I said after a while.

"You just saved me from being assaulted. The last thing I feel for you is hate."

I nodded once.

The night was dark now, thanks to a thick cover of clouds. Not even a sliver of the moon or a tapestry of stars lit up the sky anymore.

The treetops danced, and we heard an owl somewhere in the distance and crickets chirping around us. Our footfalls blended with the night sounds.

The breeze picked up, and Melinda shivered, hugging herself to keep warm.

"You cold?" I asked.

She turned her head to look at me. "A little. It's fine, though. I'll survive."

Before she could react, I slipped off my hoodie and handed it to her.

Melinda pushed it back with a hand. "Keep it. You'll be cold too."

"Nah, I run hot. Don't worry about me." I placed it in her arms. "Take it. I insist."

"Thanks." She put it on, and on her, it landed mid thigh. Something close to possessiveness flooded my heart.

We continued our stroll, new silence falling upon us.

Our neighborhood looked different in the dark. Other than the one car that passed us, the streets were deserted.

"Are you ready to resume training and all?" Melinda asked when we crossed the park and took the path circling the soccer field.

I shoved my hands into my pockets. "Yah. The guys are ready. Pre-season training has been good. Coach believes we have another chance at State this year."

"Nice."

"How's yours? Are you ready to go back out there?"

She swallowed and twisted her hands in front of her. "I think so. There's a lot at stake this year. I can't screw this up. My future and my college application depend on my being not only great, but also exceptional. I won't accept a second place. Being the winner of the losers isn't good enough anymore. First place is my goal."

"Love the ambition. I can relate." I paused. "It's okay to have great and not-so-great-days too, you know. It's sports. It's part of the game. Losing is not always a bad thing."

She halted, watching me with a scrunched-up face like I'd said something terrible.

"When you lose, it teaches you something valuable..." I shrugged. "Like how to improve your technique…how to perfect your mindset... Then you appreciate each victory much more and you're humbler about your performances and your wins."

"When you say it like that, it makes sense." We resumed our walk. "The thing is… There's this girl… Emery Mellencamp. She swims for McKinley High. She always climbs to the top of the podium. Always beating me by milliseconds. She's good, like really good, you know. The truth is that…I wanna beat her so bad. First place and all. Not just for the medley relays, but solo too. I know I have what it takes. I just need to be consistent and push a little more. I gotta see that my efforts and dedication are paying off… That I can be the best. More than once. Sure, I win against her often, but overall, she's still number one."

"I respect that. I like being at the top of my game too. I thrive on being the best." We turned into our street. "Just make sure you do it for the right reasons. Being the best, I mean."

Melinda blinked, looking confused.

I glanced at her to make sure she understood what I was saying. "Do it for you. Not for anyone else. It has to be *your* victory."

"I won't… I-I'm not. It's me I'm challenging."

"All right." Silence stretched between us. "Sometimes I feel like I'm the product of everyone else's expectations of me." I couldn't believe I was confiding in her about my own insecurities.

"What do you mean?" She stopped to look at me, but I kept my gaze locked on the ground instead.

"Like I've become whoever other people wished I'd turn into instead of myself. Not just on the field…but elsewhere too. In my life in general."

"Can't you just refuse to partake in whatever they expect from you?"

I shrugged. "It's not that easy... The game is all mine. Nobody is forcing me to play or to be great at it. It's the other things… I'm not my true self around a lot of people." I avoided her eyes, feeling naked as I disclosed the piece of information I usually kept quiet about. "Anyway, forget I said anything. I'm just in a foul mood tonight. Don't worry about me. I'll be okay. *I'm* okay." *Because you're here with me and not with that jackass.*

"You sure? It's fine if you're not. Nobody will hate you because of it."

I added nothing.

Minutes later, we stopped on the sidewalk in front of Melinda's house. "Thanks. For walking me home."

"Anytime." I turned to leave but spoke before she could let herself in. "And Mel? Keep the hoodie. I've almost outgrown it, and it looks better on you anyway."

She looked flustered under her porch light. "Huh…you sure?"

"Yep."

"Okay. Thanks?"

I bobbed my head once and strolled toward my house.

For a while, I stood in the entryway, immobile, not sure how to define my night.

Did Melinda and I finally share a moment?

Because it oddly felt like we did.

I had no better way to describe the time we'd spent together tonight and the camaraderie we'd experienced for once. A warm flicker inside my chest confirmed my theory wasn't too far-fetched.

Moments later, I climbed the staircase and locked myself in my room. Lying on my bed, I tried to make sense of the last hour. Before I could come up with an explanation, my eyes closed, and I lost the battle as sleep claimed me.

CHAPTER 8

CALL ME NURSE PIERCE

Chase jogged after me as we left the athletic building. Our early training session had been exhausting, and right now, I was looking forward to my morning classes.

"Why are you in a hurry?" my best friend asked, sliding the strap of his bag over his head. "School resumed only a week ago, and nothing is urgent enough that you gotta rush to class."

"I have to go to the office to switch my Calculus and Biology classes. They're supposed to gimme my new schedule. Anyway, you know how much I hate being late."

"I'll come with you then."

I looked at him with a raised eyebrow.

Chase lifted his hands in surrender. "The new girl working the front desk. She's hot. Just saying."

"Like forty-hot?"

"Nah. More like thirty-ish-hot. Not certain so I gotta go there…you know…with you to make sure."

I poked his shoulder. "Man, can't you find girls your own age? You almost got Ms. Richardson fired last year because you were shamelessly flirting with her."

"I'm a love machine. What can I say? No lady can resist my undeniable charm."

"Keep believing that, Romeo."

"And I love older women. They're not clingy, and they have experience." He waggled his eyebrows. "If you know what I mean."

"Seriously, I'm starting to think you have mommy issues."

"Nah. Just too much love to give."

I was in and out of the main office within five minutes. My friend left when he realized the girl at the front desk wasn't working today.

I bumped into my brother before I made it to my homeroom. "Watch where you're going, bro. Get down from your love cloud. Us, mere mortals, live down here."

He smiled at my teasing. "I'm late. I walked Paige to her homeroom. I can't believe we have no classes together this semester. It's like they did it on purpose."

I unfolded the sheet of paper in my hand to analyze my new schedule. "I think I'm with your girl in social studies." I folded it back and stuffed it in my jeans pocket. "Gotta go. My homeroom is on the other end of the east wing."

"You're not in my homeroom anymore?"

"Nah. They reworked my schedule because it didn't fit with training hours on Fridays." The late bell rang. Ugh, I really hated being late. I clapped my brother's shoulder. "I'll see you later."

The rest of the day passed in a blur.

It turned out I had two classes with Paige, one with Chase, and none with Melinda or Craig.

The bell rang at the end of the last period, and I shoved my books into my bag as students got up in a shuffle of chairs and loud chatter, then rushed outside the classroom.

Tanya, the captain of the cheerleading team and a girl I'd hooked up with once a long time ago, waited for me outside my English lit class.

"*Heyyy* Mase," she purred, the sound grating on my last nerve.

"Sorry, Tan, but I don't have time for whatever this is." I had to get to practice.

She wound her fingers around my arm in an iron grip, and she followed me as I weaved through the mass of students ready to go home, the buzz of their voices surrounding me.

I offered her my fakest smile, not in the mood for anything related to her. "There's somewhere I have to be. You know how Coach hates it when we're late. I don't feel like running extra drills to make up for my tardiness." I yanked my arm away from her hold, but she grabbed it back as soon. Jesus. We used to be friendly, she and I. For the sake of the school spirit. Not anymore. I hated everything she represented, and I was done with that life. People pleasers and panty droppers weren't in my job description anymore.

"We haven't hung out together in ages. I miss you. The last time I saw you was before summer break, and you were with a bunch of people and didn't acknowledge me.

Do you miss me?" She batted her fake eyelashes as if it could make me jump back in bed with her.

That night had been a mistake, with a giant capital *M*. The next morning, Tanya had planned our whole future, only to sleep with one of my teammates two days later, thinking I would react. Even after I had admitted to her that we would never have a do-over. Yeah, well, her revenge plan failed because I didn't give a damn about whose dick she sucked. If only she could get the memo, it would save us both a lot of trouble and awkward encounters.

"I told you once. It was a mistake. We're not compatible. I have no interest in pursuing with you whatever it is you have in mind."

"Can we at least spend time together?" Was she really this clingy, or was it all an act to dig her poisonous claws into me?

"Nope. My schedule is full. I'm busy. And not in the mood."

I yanked my arm free with more force than necessary, and she struggled to keep her balance.

"Can…we…huh…at least be friends?"

God, was she deaf or just stupid? *Just stupid, I guess.*

"I don't think so. We have nothing in common, and I already have plenty of friends."

She moved in front of me, stopping my escape, and crossed her arms over her chest. "Is it about Lydia Santos? I heard you two were an item over the summer. Is this some sort of devious plan to get back at Cowley High? Because you know she'll go back to Copperman in the end, right? Sorry to be the one delivering the news. I hope you're not in love with her because it would be heartbreaking to waste time on a girl who will never love you back." She winced and pretended to gag. "C'mon, Mase.

You and I both know you can do better than her. If the goal was to mess with the Cowley High team's mind, then you're a god. Screw them."

I was so going to be late. "Seriously, Tan? Being a bitch is so last year. Grow up. And if I hear another word against whoever I spend time with, you and I will have a problem."

She batted her eyelashes again. "Oh, I like Mason's game face. I can be your problem anytime. Is role play something you might like? We could bring the whole *quarterback-captain of the cheerleading squad* thing to the bedroom. I think it could be fun. Is that what you had in mind?"

I blinked. "What? I don't even know what you're talking about. Tan, stop being delusional about us. Not happening. Please, move. I have places to be, and you're in the way."

She yelped as if I had just slapped her. "You don't have to be cruel, Mason. Unless it's foreplay, I'm not sure it turns me on."

She was impossible. Seriously, was this a prank and someone was filming this exchange? "No foreplay. No nothing. We're not together and never will be. Now, go annoy someone else, and let me be."

Her lips swelled into a pout, and she twisted a strand of her hair around her finger. "You are no fun, Mason Pierce. You used to be the life of the party and this school."

"We'll continue this entertaining conversation some other time."

I walked around her to leave when she splayed a hand over my chest to stop me, moving to the tips of her toes to kiss my cheek. "Oh, so we *will* get together, right? I can't wait." She winked.

Jesus. This was getting more ridiculous by the second. "Whatever."

I stormed forward only to halt when I noticed Melinda,

who was squatting down and picking up her scattered stuff from the floor, her face curtained by her brown hair. Wearing a purple striped shirt with jeans and black ballet flats, she looked beautiful. We hadn't really crossed paths since the night I'd walked her home a week ago. I wouldn't call us friends, but at least we had proven we could be civilized around each other, and she hadn't ripped my face off since. I kneeled beside her and lifted her books in my hands. She looked at me. Her face was paler than usual and her eyes, glassy. She motioned to stand, but I stopped her with a hand. "Hey, are you okay?"

She swallowed, avoiding my gaze. "Yeah. All good."

We stood at the same time, and she snatched her books from my arms to stuff them into her bag.

"You don't look so fine to me."

She stepped back, putting distance between us, eyeing me with an expression I couldn't decode.

"Mel?"

Her eyes rounded, and her hand flew to cover her mouth. Without an explanation, she spun on her heel and emptied the contents of her stomach into the nearest trash can.

"Fuck. You're not all right." I went to the restroom to fetch paper towels and handed them to her so she could dab her mouth. "Come, sit."

"No. I'm great."

"Stop lying. You are not okay. Are you being stubborn on purpose, or is it a me-thing?" I kept my hand on her arm in case she got dizzy and lost her footing.

"Mase, I said I was fine. Let go of me."

I did as she asked. "Whoa. Are you always this charming when you're sick?"

Her eyes threw daggers at me, but some of the tension in her back vanished. "Sorry. It's just that… Never mind."

"What is it?"

"Nothing. You should be at practice. You'll have to run extra laps if you're late."

"How do you know?"

"I heard Sheldon complaining about it last year."

"Who cares? You're sick, and you look like you're about to faint. I couldn't care less about being late."

She squinted. "Why?"

"Want me to spell it out for you? Because I care about you."

She snorted. "Yeah, right. Mind your own business and leave me alone. I can deal with my shit all by myself."

"What has gotten into you? Are you asking for a fight? Is that it? Want me to scream at you? Tell you to go fuck yourself instead of making sure you're all right?"

She folded her arms over her chest. "Maybe." She looked away, avoiding my gaze.

"What the hell. Are you mad at me? I thought we were way past that. It's been years, so get over it."

Her eyes widened and filled with something resembling hurt, and I regretted saying those words out loud. Melinda and I had never discussed what went down between us all those years ago. Still, now wasn't the time to bring it up. Raking my brain, I couldn't find a reason why she would be pissed off at me right now.

Melinda turned her face away, ignoring me.

I cocked her head using a finger. "Talk to me. What is it? I thought we were good after the other night. A cease-fire of sorts or something like that."

The pads of my fingers tingled where we touched. Over the last minute or so, my skin had made more contact with hers than it had in the past five years combined.

She closed her eyes. "Nothing for you to worry about."

"It's not *nothing*. Can you please not shut me out when we're having a conversation?"

She opened her eyes one at a time. "Happy?"

I couldn't leash in the smile that broke free on my lips. "Better."

"FYI, we're not having a conversation. You are the only one talking."

"Why are you answering me then?"

Some of the fight left her, but she kept her stance rigid. "I owe you nothing."

"Mel… Help a guy out. I can't fix whatever is wrong between us if I don't know what is actually wrong between us."

"I've never asked you or expected you to fix anything." She bit her lower lip. "I… You…" She raised a finger between us. "Hold that thought." She ran away, her hand cupping her mouth. Seconds later, she threw up in the same trash can as before.

"Okay. I don't care if you hate me right now. I'm driving you home."

"No."

I bought a bottle of water from a vending machine behind us and twisted the cap off before placing it in her hand. "Drink."

She wiped her mouth, then raised her hand toward the bottle. "Don't boss me around." She took a small sip, nonetheless. "Your team is waiting for you on the field."

I handed her the bottle cap, and she screwed it back on. "They'll survive. It will give Summerfield a chance to show what he's made of."

"Summerfield?"

"He's QB2, and the guy has no chance of being the starting quarterback this year as long as I'm playing, so I'm sure he'll enjoy taking my spot at practice. Follow me."

She dug her heels in and refused to move. Under the recessed lights, her skin appeared greener than it should be.

"What about Tanya?" she asked.

I crossed my arms over my chest. "What about her?"

"You two looked like you had plans for later. Don't change them because of me. I can take care of myself."

"No plans with Tanya. Nope. Not happening."

She watched me with a curious gaze.

"Mel, I swear. She's the last person on my mind."

I didn't let her argue or question the statement, just lifted both our book bags and hauled them over my shoulder. Holding her hand in mine as if it were a common occurrence between us, I led Melinda outside to my car. She didn't try to remove her hand from mine, which gave me hope we could really put the past behind us once and for all if we tried. After I helped her sit on the passenger seat and closed her door, I rounded the car and fired the engine. I hadn't even pulled away from the parking lot when she started shivering. I cranked on the heat, and warm air blasted through the vents. I kept my window an inch down so I wouldn't be the one barfing due to the suffocating heat enveloping us as I drove her home.

We stopped at a red light, and I pressed my palm to her forehead. "Whoa, you're burning up. How long have you been feeling sick?"

She shrugged. "I've been having this pounding headache for the last two days. It's not going away. And then I had the chills during third period. I couldn't eat anything at lunch because my stomach hurt, so I'm thinking food poisoning or indigestion. Anyway, I'm sure it's nothing. A virus maybe."

"Well, I'm sure it's not nothing."

She heaved beside me, and I passed her the plastic bag I kept in the pocket behind my seat. "Just in case."

"Thanks."

We made it home five minutes later.

"Are you okay on your own?" I asked as I helped her out of the car, then kept a hand on her lower back in the event she required some support.

"Yeah. Don't worry."

I noticed the empty driveway. "Where are your parents?" They were usually home early, and their cars were always parked by the garage door by four o'clock.

Melinda closed her eyes and inhaled. I bet the cold air helped with the nausea. "Out of town. My dad had a work thing, and they're spending the night in Traverse City."

"In that case, I'm spending the night here."

She stared at me and blinked twice. "No. You are not. That would be awkward. It's just a stomach bug. Nothing sleep and a hot shower won't cure. I'm not your responsibility, Mason."

I shrugged. "Too bad. It's not up for discussion." We entered the house after I stole the key from her and unlocked the door.

"Mase."

"Mel."

"I'm safe and sound. Go back to practice or whatever you do in your free time."

"Don't be silly." I pointed to the couch. "This is my bed for the night."

"No. You're too big for the couch." A snicker exited her mouth, and the sound soothed a part of my soul. "Go home, Mase. I'm sure your bed is much comfier and has more room for your stupidly long legs, as Paige would say. I'll call you if something's wrong."

"We've never even shared contact info."

"Oh…"

I opened my palm. "Gimme your phone. I'll rectify that." I added my number and handed it back to her.

"I have your contact info now, so you can go."

"No nonsense. Sorry, but I'm not leaving. You shower, change, and go to bed, and I'll play nurse for the night. Your face is a scary shade of pale right now. It's not a good look on you. You really shouldn't be alone."

Melinda looked at her device and giggled, the sound a melody to my ears. A tinge of pink colored her otherwise grayish complexion. "Nurse Pierce?"

I grinned. "Yep. Now, if you are a nice enough patient, I'll reward your behavior."

Her eyes lit up. "And what's the prize?"

I pushed my hands into my pockets. "Not sure yet. It depends on how good a girl you are and how much you listen to Nurse Pierce's orders."

"And what if I don't?"

"Then that's for you to find out."

CHAPTER 9

JUST FOR THE RECORD,
I ALWAYS WRAP IT UP

We moved to the kitchen, and I rummaged through the cabinets to find glasses. Unlike the kitchen at my house which was all wood and dark tones, the Shepards' was bright. The white cabinets and floor contrasted with the slate-gray hue of the countertops and the stainless-steel appliances. A panoramic window stretched the entire length of the countertop between the refrigerator and the oven, offering an unobstructed view of the backyard. After they moved in, the Shepards had done some home-improvements, and the house that once belonged to my childhood best friend was similar but different from the one I remembered.

"I love what you guys have done to this place." I poured us both some water and put hers on the kitchen island. "Drink this. I'm sure you wanna get rid of that horrible taste."

Melinda stood still, her eyes fixed on me, but her mind seemingly miles away.

"Mel? Did you hear a word I said?"

She blinked. "Huh… Sure."

"You really sure?"

"Yeah. All good. It-it's weird having you here in my kitchen." In a slow perusal, her eyes trailed over the length of me before locking onto my face. Whatever she saw seemed to have pleased her because a ghost of a smile tipped up her lips.

I felt self-conscious under her attention. "Happy to know you have a nurse fixation."

She shook her head but stopped, pressing both sides of her skull with her hands. "New rule. No joke. It… Gosh, it hurts." She took a sip of water and glanced at the staircase. "I think I'll lie down before I take a shower. I'm spent." Before she could reach the stairs, she doubled over, clutching her abdomen. "Ouch. It hurts… It hurts so bad. Like someone is stabbing me with a super sharp, burning knife."

I neared her in three strides. "Do you wanna sit?"

She motioned no with her head, covering her stomach with both hands and taking deep breaths in.

"Want me to drive you to the clinic?"

Again, she shook her head. "It'll be…" She sucked in a sharp breath and spoke through clenched teeth. "It'll be over soon."

I surveyed every detail of her face, trying to find clues to an illness that could explain her pain, but came out empty. "How long has this been going on?"

"Not so long." She pressed her lips together, jaw taut, and closed her eyes. "It's fading now." She straightened after a few seconds, forcing a timid curl to her lips.

"You okay?"

"Yeah. I will be. My stomach is all over the place right now. Don't worry."

"Go to bed. Please take some medicine for the fever. It will be useful for that headache too. If you don't, I'll stick a thermometer into—"

Her eyes rounded, worry playing across her features.

"Your mouth."

"Oh." She relaxed her shoulders and nodded slowly.

"Glad to know you have a dirty mind in addition to a nurse fixation."

She pinched her lips together and averted her eyes before changing the subject. "Mase. Thanks. For taking care of me. You don't have to, but still, I appreciate it."

"I'm sure you would do the same for me. Go to bed. Now. Nurse Pierce says so, and you gotta listen."

With small, slow steps, she disappeared upstairs, and I used the time to go home to shower and change after I sent Coach a message about missing practice and texting my brother so he wouldn't look for me.

"Mmm, it smells delicious," Melinda said when she joined me in the kitchen and sat on a stool two hours later.

I watched her from the corner of my eye. Her damp hair was loose over her shoulders, the tips soaking parts of her violet oversized T-shirt. Even dressed down and sick, she still looked like the most beautiful girl I'd ever seen, a vision my body had a hard time resisting.

"Good, you're up." I turned to fully face her, a ladle in one hand and her mother's raspberry-pink *Kitchen Queen* apron tied around my waist. Earlier, I had changed into a pair of washed-out jeans riding low on my hips and a simple white T-shirt.

"Oh, wow. While I was out of it, you've turned into a stay-at-home nurse slash chef. Tell me I'm asleep and this isn't real." She did her best to keep a straight face but failed because her mouth turned up at the corner as she stared at me.

"Not a dream. I'm right here. I thought of going shirtless, but since you're sick, I thought my awesomeness would be too much to handle and could blind you, but I can fix it if it helps you get well faster. After all, I caught you ogling me earlier."

She poked her tongue out, and I winked, loving the light blush coloring her cheeks.

"By the way, I came to check on you half an hour ago, and you were snoring."

She propped her elbows up on the counter and buried her face in her hands before watching me through her fingers. "Mase, you are incorrigible. You can keep the shirt on. And just to set the record straight, I don't snore. And I didn't ogle you earlier."

"If you say so. Anyway, when you're done lying to yourself, I wanna inform you that I made soup if you're hungry. Chicken and noodles. My specialty."

"You did? You cooked for me? It's not from a can?"

"Don't underestimate your nurse, Shepard. I'm the real deal. Anyway, it's not a big deal. My mom gave me a few pointers when I went home to shower quickly and grab my overnight bag with a change of clothes. She had some leftover chicken and said we could have it. All I did was chop veggies and make a broth."

"You made a broth?"

"Yeah. I'm a man of multiple talents. It's about time you catch up with the fact."

"I never doubted it, but I'm still impressed. Your mom

was okay with your spending the night here? Something we still need to agree on, by the way."

"She said she'd raised trustworthy men who took care of those important to them and she was proud I was skipping practice and sleeping over if it meant making sure you were okay. She also told me to use condoms if you and I were sexually active."

The blush on her cheeks turned into an adorable shade of crimson. "Mase. Huh… It's not like that. What did you tell her?"

"That you and I were friends and that I was here as Nurse Pierce and nothing else."

She blew out a breath. "I won't be able to look your mother in the eye ever again. This is embarrassing."

I moved closer and held her hands in mine. "No reason to feel embarrassed. Nothing to lose sleep over, okay? Just for the record, I'm putting it here. I always wrap it up, so my mom has nothing to worry about."

"Thanks for this very personal piece of information I've never requested."

I curtsied. "You're welcome. Back to business. How are you feeling? Did that nap help with the headache?"

"Yeah. I'm still lightheaded, but I'm actually starving." Her stomach grumbled as if on cue. "The medicine did wonders for the fever, though."

"Awesome. Do you feel like eating? Soup is usually my go-to food when I'm sick. I also filled the refrigerator with a collection of sports drinks and ginger ale, just in case."

"Wow. You thought of everything."

"I've tried." My face felt warmer as she watched me with something close to admiration.

"Sports drink. Until I'm confident I can tolerate real food."

"Purple or pink?"

"Wow, I have a choice?"

"Yep. I chose my favorite flavors because I had no idea what you like."

"Huh…pink?"

"You relax. There are blankets and pillows on the couch. Now go. Nurse's orders." I waved her away with a hand. "I'll bring you that drink and then finish up here."

"Thanks." She padded to the living room, leaving me alone with my own thoughts.

Melinda was curled up into a ball on the couch when I joined her. Sweat beaded on her forehead, and her eyes were glassy, her teeth digging into her bottom lip like she was in extreme pain.

"Hey, talk to me. Where does it hurt?"

"It feels as if someone is stabbing my right side again." She pointed to her abdomen, and tears filled her eyes. "It hurts like hell." She took a few deep breaths. "It…it comes and goes. Hard to explain. It's not much of a burning knife now but more…but more like somebody is sawing my body in two and then taking a break before getting back at it with a vengeance."

Her forehead wasn't hot, so at least the fever hadn't come back. "You're not feverish, but let me grab you more medicine. It's not normal to be in so much pain. You sure you don't wanna go to the clinic?"

"Nah. The pain meds helped earlier. I'll be good. I just need to take it easy for a little while."

Once the pain decreased and she relaxed a bit, I spread a blanket over her and positioned the pillows behind her back so she could take a sip.

She ate half a bowl of soup after she made sure she could keep the sports drink in. "Whoa, you were not kidding. This is delicious. My compliments to the chef when you see him."

"I will. Mom always says you should sprinkle love in your food when you prep it. That always makes it better. Shhh…it's our family's secret ingredient. Don't tell anyone."

She mimicked zipping her lips. "Your secret is safe with me. If you decide to become a chef someday, I'll eat at your restaurant."

"I'll reserve a table just for you by the window."

Melinda nodded once. "We have a deal." She handed me her bowl, and I discarded it on the coffee table. "If you were not destined to play football, what would you do?"

"Career-wise?"

She hugged her folded legs, resting her chin on her knees. "Yeah."

"That's a good question. I don't wanna disappoint you, but I wouldn't work as a chef."

"Bummer."

"I know." I thought for a second. "I love fixing cars, so that could be an option, but I don't feel like it would fulfill me. I need action in my life, something that keeps my blood pumping or requires my full attention. I would also love to start something. A business, a foundation, a… huh…whatever. Have my own venture to nurture and do something I'm proud of. I never really thought about it before."

"I like that. I can see you as a CEO or in a position of importance. You possess natural leadership. It would suit you. I just don't see you dressed in a suit working behind a desk and carrying a briefcase around and wearing Oxford leather shoes."

"God, me neither." I scratched the column of my throat. "I would be terrible at it. Just thinking about wearing a tie every day and I feel claustrophobic."

She snickered. "Yeah. Forget about the suit and tie five days a week. You look better in jeans anyway."

"I do?"

She cast a glance down. "It's my feverish brain talking. Don't listen to everything I say."

"Stop making excuses. You don't have a fever right now. Anyway, while we're at it, anything else I should add to the growing list of things you like about me?"

She pinched her lips together and shook her head.

"Fine. I'll let it slide…for now. What about you? What do you wanna study in college?"

She smiled. "Public relations. I love the idea of helping someone or an organization improve their image. Even if they mess up, everyone deserves a second chance in life."

"Everyone?"

"Nah." She grimaced. "Not really, but most people do. I would have to work for someone with a conscience, though. I would never be able to help…let's say…a business that exploits others or someone who abuses other people…or who harms children." She yawned. "Anyway, sorry I'm boring you."

"No. You could never bore me. I like that you wanna do good, not just defend others because they pay you to do it."

Her eyelids fluttered close. "Mase, do you mind if I nap?" She massaged her abdomen in slow circles. "I'm sore and tired as if I've trained for hours. My belly feels like a war zone."

"Need my help to lie down?"

"I think I can manage. Thanks for staying here with me." She removed pillows from behind her back and flipped to her left side next to me on the couch.

I adjusted the blanket over her. "You sleep. I'll watch over you."

All evening, Melinda dozed on and off. At some point, she shifted position when a surge of pain woke her up, and now her head was resting on my thigh, and my arm lingered on her shoulder. I tried to watch a movie—I really did—but all I could focus on was her body pressed against mine and the soft rise and fall of her chest with each breath she took.

She stirred in her sleep, and her head rubbed against my groin. As if I had been tased, my body reacted to her every movement. Careful not to wake her up, I scooted to the side just a tiny bit and tipped my head back. I stared at the ceiling, breathing in and out slowly before closing my eyes and counting from fifty to one in my head. That did the trick because the tension in my lower body decreased. I blew out a puff of air and forced my attention back to the TV screen, still unable to focus on the action playing in front of me.

Nothing about tonight felt real. I was hanging out with Melinda Shepard at her house, taking care of her like it was just another day for us, and she was almost asleep in my arms.

Around eleven, I carried her to her bedroom. We had school in the morning, and I believed she would have a more restful night if she slept in her own bed. She twitched in my arms once but never woke up as I tucked her in.

CHAPTER 10
HIS TRUNK IS TOO BIG FOR HIS BODY

The sound of a muffled thump woke me up with a start. I looked at the time on my phone. One fifty-seven in the morning. It took me a moment to recall where I was.

I rubbed the sleep away from my eyes with my fists, on high alert, as I sat in the darkness. Perhaps Melinda had woken up to pee or grab another dose of painkillers because the fever had returned. Or she had fallen off her bed.

I was about to check on her when I heard it. Whimpering sounds coming from upstairs.

Jumping over the couch's backrest, I climbed the stairs two at a time, and when I flicked the switch, the hallway light cast the house in a golden glow.

Curled up on her side on the wooden floor, I believed for a second Melinda had fainted. She looked so small and fragile right now.

"Mason—" My name sounded like a plea on her lips.

"Mel? You awake?"

Tears rolled down her cheeks. Sobs shook her. She hugged herself, rocking from side to side.

I rushed to her, squatting next to her, my hand flying to her forehead. "You're burning up. Did you fall? Are you hurt? Talk to me."

"It… It hurts. Inside. It… I can't breathe, and I feel like I'm going to throw up." She pushed a hand over her mouth. "Ohmygod…ouch. Make it stop. Mase, please. I'm dying. They're drilling…they're drilling a hole inside me. I-I can't move. I tried to stand." Her lips quivered. "And I fell. Help me. Mase, do something. Ouch. I think I'm gonna pass out. What is… What is wrong with me? Ouch. Mase, please. Don't let me die."

I pulled her into my arms, cradling her shivering body. "I'm driving you to the hospital. Unless you want me to call an ambulance."

She shook her head. "No. You. Drive. Me." She screamed when waves of agony radiated through her, piercing my very soul. Her fingernails dug into my forearms. "Mase, I can't bear it. It…it hurts everywhere." A loud cry left her lips and made my blood curdle. "Tell me the truth. Am I going…am I going to die?" She lifted her head to look at me.

"Don't move. Stay still. I'll carry you. Mel, I'm here, okay? I won't let anything bad happen to you. You have my word. Trust me."

"Okay. Don't…don't leave me."

As I made my way downstairs, Melinda's body grew limp in my arms. Her skin was warm and sweaty from the fever. As gently as possible, I placed her on the backseat of my car, pushing the strands of hair sticking to her face away with my fingers before rushing back inside to grab a blanket to cover her. The entire drive, I talked to her, but only guttural sounds passed her lips. At least she was still with me. Alive and breathing. I strangled the steering wheel with a death grip. I had no idea what was going on with her, but it appeared serious. At a red light, I pivoted in my seat to watch her. Once again, she was lying on her side, hugging herself.

"Mel, hang in there." I stretched my hand to caress her shoulder. "We'll be there in like five minutes, okay?"

No answer. Only growls of pain.

The light switched green, and I let go of her. "I'm doing my best to drive you there quickly, and in one piece. Don't quit on me, okay? Be brave for just a little longer."

After I parked at the emergency drop-off, I lifted a non-responsive Melinda in my arms. "We're here. I'm with you. I'm not going anywhere." Her eyelids flickered but remained closed as we entered the hospital and fluorescent lights shone above us. I pressed my lips to her forehead in a fervent prayer. "You are safe now."

———

I was holding her hand when Melinda woke up almost three hours later. The adrenaline had worn off, and exhaustion had settled over me. I pushed it back at the sight of her regaining consciousness. "Welcome back to the land of the living, Shepard."

"Mase? What—" She coughed, and I brought a cup of water with a straw to her lips.

"Drink this."

She did, but her voice sounded hoarse when she asked,

"Where am I?" Moisture filled her eyes, and they appeared bluer than their usual turquoise shade.

I traced the side of her face with my knuckles. "You had appendicitis. I drove you to the hospital, and you underwent emergency surgery. That's why you may feel drowsy right now. They said you should come back to your senses soon. Your parents are on their way."

Her gaze traveled around the room. "Appendicitis? Surgery?"

"Yes. You're out of the woods now."

She blinked, and I wondered if all the drugs in her system were affecting her understanding of the situation. "The woods? Were we outside?"

"Nah." A hint of a smile tugged at my lips. "Just an expression."

"Oh. How did you manage to be in this room by my side? I'm pretty sure it's family only."

"I told them I was your twin brother. No way would I have let you wake up alone after surgery. I thought you might like to see a familiar face."

"I do. Gosh, I can't believe you did that." She laughed but stopped, wincing in pain. "It still hurts."

"Take it slow so you don't rip out your stitches."

"Stitches? Mase, did you say I had surgery? Was I in an accident?"

Definitely the drugs. "No accident. Appendicitis."

"Oh." She yawned. "I'm tired."

"Sleep. I'll be here when you wake up."

"Where are we?"

"Hospital. You had surgery."

"I don't like this dream."

I squeezed her hand resting in mine. "Don't worry. It's gonna be okay."

"I-I…" Her eyes closed, and her breathing evened

before she could finish her thought. For the next hour, I watched her sleep, praying everything would really be okay after all.

An hour later, Melinda's eyes opened, and she eyed me with a frown. "Am I still dreaming, or is this real?"

"All real."

"So, we really were in the woods, and I had an accident."

Our earlier conversation replayed in my mind. She was adorable and had no idea.

"No dreams and no woods. And no accident. You had an appendectomy... Huh, they took out your appendix earlier. You are safe and sound now."

"A-appendectomy? No, it's impossible." New tears filled her eyes. "I can't be sick. Not now. I have a meet next weekend. I need to qualify. This is senior year. I refuse to be on the sidelines."

"Easy, tiger. You need the rest. Don't stress over a meet. Now isn't the time." My fingers landed on hers in a gesture I hoped was comforting.

"You brought me here? I don't recall a lot. All I can remember is the pain and that I was feverish and confused. But the pain...it was bad."

"You were barely coherent on the way here. The doctor said another hour and your appendix would have burst. It was a close call, but I'm Nurse Pierce, and I told you I'd keep you safe. That's my job."

"Mase, you saved me... Again." She flipped her hand around to intertwine our fingers. The tears pooling in her eyes looked different now, more like gratitude tears.

"I didn't *save you* save you, but let's just say I am glad I insisted on playing nurse tonight. Who knows what would have happened if I hadn't been sleeping on your couch?"

"Thanks. For being there." Her lips trembled. "I can't believe I'll miss the next meet. My team needs me."

Melinda's brain on painkillers was a fascinating thing. We were having two different conversations at once.

"Yeah, well, I know the feeling. When that concussion glued me to the bench last year, I became a lion in a cage after only two games. You'll get through this. You're stronger than appendicitis. If it brings you some sort of peace, I'll check with your coach. To make sure it doesn't affect your college offers, the rest of your season, or anything else."

"You would do that for me?"

"Yes. As long as you take the required time to heal and don't rush back."

"Oh…okay. I can't believe I had surgery. I really thought I had food poisoning or a virus. Thank you for bringing me here."

I nodded, watching her. My lips parted. I had so much to tell her but changed my mind. Now wasn't the moment to spill the contents of my heart. "I'm relieved you're out of danger."

"Me too."

"I have something for you. It's not much, but I hope it will bring you some comfort."

She frowned, and I fetched the stuffed animal I'd bought from the hospital gift shop while she was undergoing surgery.

Her face lit up. "Wow, it is adorable." I had chosen a pastel-blue and lilac stuffed baby elephant. She twisted the animal in her hand and looked at me with a quizzical gaze. "Mase, are the drugs playing tricks on my mind, or is *Mason* written on its foot?"

I gave her a half-shrug. "I promised you earlier I would get you a prize if you were a good girl and listened to

Nurse Pierce's orders. There were none with the name *Melinda*. What can I say? Now, you'll think of me each time you cuddle with it."

"It's not the medication messing with my brain. You still are terrible, but somehow it suits you." Her eyes sparkled with emotion. "Thank you. I love it. Very much." She kissed the elephant's head and brought it to her heart like it really comforted her. "I almost died tonight. And I didn't, because of you. I will make Mason the elephant a superhero cape."

"I'm sure he'd like that."

"Do you want one too?"

"Nah. Thanks, I'll pass. You could get me a trophy, though."

"I'll think about it." We exchanged small smiles. "Do you think I'll be able to swim again?"

"Yeah. You just need to take a little break."

"Okay." We stayed silent for a full minute. "I'm so tired. It's like I've been buried alive after being stomped over by a mammoth. Everything is heavy and hurts. Not like before, but still, every inch of me is sore."

"You should sleep it off." I glanced at the clock mounted on the wall. "They'll come to inject you with another dose of painkillers soon. I'll talk to Paige and visit you after school if you're still here."

"That is nice of you. I like this version of you."

Yeah, well, me too.

I moved closer and kissed her forehead. "Rest." My entire body woke up at the contact. I'd just kissed Melinda Shepard. Well, her forehead, but still, my lips were on her skin. This night was nothing like I expected, but I wished to be nowhere else. "I'll watch over you. I'm not leaving your side unless I have to."

She extended her arm to clutch my hand, and seconds later, her steady breaths informed me she was asleep.

A knock resonated on the door sometime later, and I presumed it to be the medical team, but instead, Mr. and Mrs. Shepard walked in, followed by Dr. Shinde, the surgeon who had operated on Melinda.

"Melinda, honey," her mother said nearing the bed while her dad stayed by the door to talk to the surgeon. Tears shone in her eyes as she took her daughter's other hand between hers.

Melinda's eyelids fluttered open, and she squinted, looking confused. "Mom?"

"I'm here, honey. How are you doing?"

"Huh...I'm okay…I think." She closed one eyelid as if keeping both open took too much energy from her. "I-I had surgery… That's what the real Mason said." She winced. "My brain is made of jelly... I…huh…I can't remember how I got here, and I won't be able to swim next weekend. Mason is a hero, and I'll make him a superhero cape. But not the real Mason…the other Mason. The one with the big purple trunk."

Mrs. Shepard gasped, her attention ping-ponging between her daughter and me, her gaze filled with questions. From where she stood, she couldn't see my namesake because he was hidden under the covers.

"It's true. He's like an elephant, and his trunk is too big for his body. I love him because he's my gift. For being a good girl. Mason said so."

"Mason said so?"

"Yes. He tucked me in bed earlier. And I fell asleep on his lap. Why is my stomach so sore?"

I buried my face in my free hand. Mr. Shepard would have kicked me out of his daughter's room without a second thought if he had caught even a fragment of what she had just told his wife.

Mrs. Shepard blinked a few times, looking like she swallowed a sour pill. "Melinda, honey. Let's forget about elephants and big trunks for now, okay? I'm so relieved you're all right and out of danger, and this is what matters. The rest, we'll deal with it later."

I leaned toward the bed. "Jesus, Mel. You can't say stuff like that. Not in front of your mom." I turned to face her mother. "All that she said was only about Mason *the elephant*. Not the *me*-Mason. He's a stuffed animal I gave her after the surgery. We just happen to have the same name."

Mrs. Shepard nodded and dropped her shoulders. "Thanks for clarifying, Mason. I appreciate it."

"It's hard to keep up with her pain-med brain. She's quite entertaining. Anyway, I should go." I stood up and neared the bed, her hand still nestled in mine. "Mel, I'll see you later, okay?"

Sadness took over her features. "No, Mase. You can't go. You didn't get your trophy."

"We have all the time in the world to figure it out once you're back on your feet. There's no rush."

"Oh…okay. You sure?"

"Yeah. Rest for now." I kissed her forehead and walked away, releasing her fingers. A void opened inside my chest, and I missed the connection of our joined hands.

Dr. Shinde took my spot next to Melinda's bed.

"Did you make a hole in my body?" she asked him.

"Yes, I did." He offered her a small, comforting smile. "Let me run you through the procedure, and then I'll answer all your questions…"

I blocked out the surgeon's voice and turned to leave when Mr. Shepard stopped my escape. "Thank you, son.

For everything." He held out his hand to shake mine. "You should go home and get some sleep. You did good last night."

"I did what anyone else would have done in the same situation."

"No. You saved our daughter's life."

"Thanks." I bowed my head, feeling vulnerable as he watched me with a gleam in his eyes before pulling me into a hug.

"I'm proud of you, son. You should be proud of yourself too."

He released me, and I coughed to chase the ball of emotions lodged in my throat. "I'll talk to all of you later and will come back to visit her after practice." I spun on my heel to watch Melinda one last time.

Her eyes met mine and stayed locked there for a long moment, sending my heart into overdrive.

"Night, Mason not-the-elephant," she said after a while. It wasn't the middle of the night anymore, rather early morning, but I didn't correct her.

"Good night, Mel." I broke eye contact and made my exit. The door clicked behind me, and I released a shaky breath. "I love you," I murmured, looking at the door.

When we'd arrived at the hospital earlier, my stomach had knotted and my heart had capsized in my chest, because I thought I might lose her. It made me realize, for the first time, that what I felt for her was unlike anything I'd ever experienced before. It was love, a feeling foreign but all-consuming at the same time. A feeling I hoped she would reciprocate one day.

CHAPTER 11
I'M NOT BEING COCKY, JUST STATING FACTS

"**Y**ou're aware of how she is. She can be intense sometimes. I was about to go nuts. We argued for an hour last night before she even considered it. I know she means well, but she's just suffocating me," I heard Melinda tell Paige as they were getting their textbooks from their lockers.

"I'm glad you're back." Paige looped her arm through hers. "You tell me if you don't feel well, okay?"

Before she could say anything, I stole Melinda's bag from her grip and moved to stand behind her, speaking close to her ear. "Tsk-tsk, Mel. What do you think you're doing?"

She sucked in a breath, and shivers lined her spine and

lit up my entire body as my front brushed her back. I was glad our proximity affected her as much as it affected me.

"Hello to you too." She spun around and folded her arms over her chest, a frown creasing her forehead. It was cute when she pretended to be angry. "What do *you* think you're doing?"

I mimicked her stance. "I asked you first."

She extended one arm to grab her bag, but I held it above my head, which made it impossible for her to reach. She sighed and dropped her arm down with a grimace. "Huh…coming back to school. Isn't it evident?"

I rolled my eyes as if she was exasperating me, not hiding the smile forming on my lips. "I mean, why are you doing the heavy lifting? I was there when your dad said you're not allowed to train or lift anything over ten pounds for at least two weeks."

She stretched her arm in my direction again. "It's a book bag, not some heavy weight. Give it back."

"No."

"No?"

"That's what I said. I'm not in the mood nor do I have time to weigh this thing of yours, which means I'm confiscating it. Until further notice. Not risking it."

Paige snickered from beside her, and Melinda blinked in surprise. "You what? Stop with the nonsense." The first bell rang. "Mase, I gotta go to class. Are you going to follow me around like a shadow and deliver my books to my classes all day?"

I smirked. "Yep. That's the plan."

"No. I refuse. I'm not a baby. And I certainly don't need a sitter."

"Well, I'm your caregiver so."

Paige blinked. "Since when?"

"Since I've turned into Nurse Pierce." I flashed them a bright smile.

"Nurse Pierce?" Paige asked, her eyes drifting back and forth between Melinda and me. "You guys are weird. It sounds like a porn reference. What am I missing?"

Melinda shook her head and sighed. "Nothing. Mase, can we not do this here?"

"If you have a complaint to lodge, you'll have to talk to my superiors after hours."

She sighed, looking part amused and part exasperated. "Fine. You wanna play delivery boy all day? Suit yourself." She pivoted and removed Paige's bag from her grip and pushed it into my chest. "Since you're insisting, I'm sure Paige would love your services too, Delivery Boy."

My smile turned into a full-blown grin. "My pleasure, ladies." I waved them forward. "After you."

Melinda held my gaze for a long moment, her annoyance vanishing.

As we walked toward their homeroom, my brother joined us, draping an arm around Paige's shoulders and pulling her in for a kiss. "Where are you guys going?"

"Class," Paige said.

"And what's with all this?" He gestured to the bags hanging from my shoulder.

"Book delivery," Melinda said.

"Using Mase's services," Paige added.

"Why?" My brother's eyes traveled between the three of us.

Paige elbowed my side. "Because Mase is feeling chivalrous this morning. I think he's scared his arms required some more weight training before Friday night's game."

"Whatever, I'm stealing you," he told his girlfriend. "Just for a minute." They disappeared around the corner, and just like Craig had done minutes ago, I rested my free arm around Melinda's shoulders, doing my best to look confident and praying she wouldn't push me away.

"Why didn't you tell me you were coming back today?" Wanting to test a theory, I spoke close to her ear like I had minutes ago, and once again, she shivered. Yeah, she really was affected by my proximity. I filed that piece of information away for later. Along with her nurse fixation and how good I looked wearing jeans. "I would have driven you to school myself."

"I only learned about an hour ago that my prison sentence had been lifted."

"That bad, huh?" I asked when we got in step

"They worry. All the time. But I'm doing much better. I had to get out of the house for my sanity. By the way, were you also listening to my conversation?"

"Never. I walked in when you were complaining about your mom."

"I have a visit scheduled with the surgeon in three days to remove the stitches on my abdomen. Mom didn't want me to come back to school before then. What she doesn't understand is that the sooner I return to my life, the happier I'll be. She's like this helicopter parent who won't let me breathe on my own. I had enough. I miss the pool and I miss swimming. While I was at home, I missed being here too."

"How long until you can resume training?"

"Two to three weeks. It's way too long in my opinion. I feel fine. All I did while being on bedrest was watch TV and read books I wasn't invested in. Mom kept checking up on me every thirty minutes. She fed me comfort food, as she called it, and I'm pretty sure I've gained twenty pounds. I have eaten enough in the last week for years to come. I'll have to up my training game now if I want to perform and go back to where I was or else I'll spend my season eating other swimmers' dust. No, thank you."

"I may be able to help you with that," I offered. "Some jogging, a bit of yoga, weight training. I'm sure we can get you back in shape in no time."

"You think?"

"I believe it. Call me Trainer Pierce."

"Jesus, you won't let it go, will you?" She snickered, the sound addictive. "And tell me, since when are you a yoga guru?"

"When I hurt my shoulder sophomore year, it actually helped with my flexibility, and I regained the momentum I had lost. I like to include a session or two weekly in my workout routine." *And even more so since I injured it again last summer.*

"Mason Pierce in a pair of yoga pants. Never would I have thought I'd witness this one day."

"You'll see. People say my ass looks awesome in those. And the color of the spandex makes my eyes pop. It's a win-win outfit. I should wear it more often."

"Stop throwing yourself flowers. They're almost the same as football pants."

"And how does my ass look in football pants, *Mel*?"

The slight blush on her cheeks confirmed my suspicion.

My grin must have reached both ears. "Yep. No need to tell me. I can read it on your face. See? I'm aware my ass is extraordinary. I'm not shy to admit it."

Melinda backhanded my chest. "That ego, Mase. Better watch it before it swallows you whole."

"All under control. I'm not being cocky, just stating facts. Anyway, let me know when the doctor clears you to train again and if there are restrictions, and we'll start from there. With the training, I mean."

Her eyes sparkled, and she squeezed my forearm.

"Thank you, Mase." Neither of us moved for what felt like an infinite minute. Her fingers glided to wrap around my wrist, her thumb caressing my pulse point. Could she feel the pounding of my heart? Melinda stepped closer, narrowing the space between our bodies. A loose strand of hair fell over her right eye, but before I could tuck it away, she did, and the spell that had descended upon us dissipated.

I swallowed hard as I said, "Anytime."

We stopped by her homeroom. "Let me know if you're sick or anything. I can hide you at my place if you don't feel good enough to be here and you don't wanna go home either."

"Paige already called shotgun on that role." She offered me a hint of a smile. "Thanks, though. For offering. I didn't know jailbreaker host was also one of your many titles."

"Just so you know, Paige isn't a certified nurse. She won't know what to do with a jailbreaker. She may report you. Just sayin'. It would be much safer to run things by me instead."

She raised one brow. "And you are?"

"I'm the most qualified person to take care of you. No doubt about that. I think I proved it to you the other night. You can't deny it."

"How poetic."

"Hey, Mrs. Belleville," I greeted the teacher when Melinda and I walked into the classroom.

"Mr. Pierce? Have you transferred to my class and I'm not aware?"

"You wish. I know you miss me this semester, Mrs. B, but no. I'm here to deliver book bags."

Paige joined us, her lips red and swollen and her face flushed. "Sorry," she whispered to Melinda.

"Book bags?" The teacher's eyes ping-ponged between the three of us like my brother's had earlier. "Whatever. Nothing surprises me anymore when it concerns you, Mr. Pierce."

"Thank you," I said with a huge grin, deciding to take it as a compliment.

Mrs. Belleville stared at me over her glasses. "Who said it was a good thing?" The curl of her lips betrayed her humor. "Make it quick." After a moment, she waved us off and turned around to answer a student's question.

"See you after class, ladies." I faced Melinda and took her hand in mine. "Wait for me. I'm serious."

"Fine." She sighed like I was asking her the impossible, but then she grinned, and I knew she would do as I said.

Feeling light on my feet, I sauntered away, humming.

When I entered my homeroom, I bumped into Lydia Santos. I'd done my best to avoid her since school had resumed. "Ugh, Mase. Watch where you're going. Or better, stay away from me."

Before I could prevent myself, and feeling my classmates' stares on me, my cocky persona took over. "That's not what you used to say." I winked at her.

Lydia gave me a slow once-over, her red-painted lips parting. "I'm with Dave now, so you better not try anything."

"Come on, Lyd. We're history. Not interested in rekindling anything with you. I always knew you'd go back to him. Told you, you were using me. No hard feelings, though. It's like I'd already predicted the future when it concerned you."

If looks could kill, Lydia's would have annihilated me right on the spot. I weaved through the desks to reach the last row and slouched in my seat, dropping my bag on the floor.

"Hey, Mase," Tanya, the cheer captain, purred, leaning toward me and pushing her black hair over her shoulders in a gesture I bet she thought was seductive. "If you have some free time later, I'd need your help in physics." She pouted as if it would help her case. "Wanna come over tonight? We could also practice biology if you're up to it. I kinda need to refresh my memory on human anatomy. I have a quiz coming up soon."

"Sorry, Tan. This ship has sailed. Find someone else."

"But I gotta find a tutor or I'll flunk, and you know if I don't keep a high enough average, they'll kick me off the squad. Help a girl out."

I pinched my lips together to avoid saying something I might regret. "Sorry, I can't. I'm working after practice. Tonight and every other night. My schedule is fully busy these days."

"You working? I thought your daddy was all about you and Craig focusing on school and football until you graduate."

"What can I say? I'm a nurse now, and it's taking a lot of my free time."

She snorted. "You, Mason Pierce, a nurse? Feed me better bullshit."

I fixed the most shocked expression onto my face. "I take my job very seriously. Don't mock me. Anyway, it's none of your business."

Mr. Stenberg, our teacher walked in, calling for silence. I faced forward, tapping a rhythm on my jean-clad thigh with a pencil, ignoring Tanya's heavy gaze that I could still feel on me.

For the entire class, I watched every minute ticking on the clock hung over the board in front of me, waiting for the bell to ring, so I could return to my book bag delivery duty.

"Who are you taking to Homecoming next week?" Chase asked a few days later as we sat at our usual table at the back of the lunchroom, the Bears' unofficial reserved section. Other than the team, only girlfriends were welcome to sit with us. Most times, I thought this rule was stupid, but hey, it was our chance to get together during and after football season. Craig was my brother by birth. Along the way, my teammates had become my brothers on and off the field.

The idea of inviting any girl other than Melinda to our school fall dance knotted my stomach. I had wanted to ask her to Homecoming last year, but she had picked up a shift at the movie theatre where she worked a few hours a week and made it pretty clear to everyone she wasn't going, so I had missed my chance.

I ended up accepting Hilary Jones's invitation and had run back home pretending I had the flu when she tried to kiss me. Not my finest moment—and a big contradiction to my usual ways.

Homecoming was the biggest weekend of the year, and the stakes were high. Not only was I expected to give a speech at the pep rally and lead our team to victory, but if the rumor mill were right, I'd be crowned Homecoming King again this year.

"I haven't decided," I lied, pushing my chicken salad away, not so hungry anymore at the thought Melinda would reject me if I asked her to accompany me. I sighed. Our friendship might not have been solid enough to risk it. We'd just reconnected. My life seemed to be an eternal catch-22 situation when it came to her.

"Gigi cornered me after chemistry this morning, and I accepted to be her date. Jude is going with Laura, and

Landon asked Mel. I'm sure anyone in your fan club would jump at the chance to be your date." He laughed, draining his bottle of water in two gulps. "Sometimes, I'd love to be you for a day, man. Sounds easy enough."

I scratched my temple. "Yeah, well, it's not that simple."

He snorted. "Yeah, right. You're Mr. Popular and Superstar all wrapped up in one. There are guys with way less going on for them. Just sayin', man."

"Like you can complain. You've been dating girls since before you even hit puberty."

He pointed to himself. "I'm a good catch. What can I say?"

His previous words hit me. "Landon asked Mel?" I took a sip of water to flush the sour taste from my mouth, trying to act as if I didn't care. "What did she say?" My heart squeezed in my chest at the idea they would go together and perhaps end up dating. "I didn't know he had a thing for her." I spoke the words through clenched teeth, unable to relax my jaw as images I would prefer to never imagine invaded my mind.

"Don't know. Why would you care?"

I shrugged and stretched my legs out on the chair across from me. Lunch hour was almost over, and most people had left to pick up books from their lockers before classes resumed. "I don't. It's just…unexpected. That's all."

"The girl is hot," Chase said. "Why would he not?"

"Yeah…well… You might be right."

"Like hell I am. I'm always right." He jumped to his feet. "I'm out of here. I gotta make a pit stop at the admin office before the next period. I lost my student ID."

"Again? We're only one month into the first semester and you've lost it twice so far."

"Told you already. The new girl working at the reception is a nice piece of ass. What can I say? My eyes can't get enough. That rack she's trying to hide under those blouses?" He brought his joined thumb and forefinger to his mouth in a chef's kiss gesture. "Divine."

"Fucker."

He chuckled. "See you later." We fist-bumped, and he sauntered away with a pep in his step that only his infatuation over a girl could explain.

I scanned the almost-empty cafeteria, my gaze snagged by one of the girls sitting at the far-end table gathering her stuff. Melinda pushed her brown hair behind her shoulders and smiled at something Paige said. When her gaze drifted in my direction, a new tightness grew in my chest. We eyed each other from a distance, neither of us breaking the contact.

Like an idiot, I waved at her. What else could I do when I was too late to ask her to Homecoming? Unless Landon got abducted by aliens or changed schools, I had no chance of accompanying her. How stupider could I get? Seriously, I had never shied away from asking a girl out before. I was losing my touch around Melinda Shepard. Big time.

I studied her, wondering why she hadn't told me she was going with him. Sure, we'd been talking more since her appendectomy, but I was right in thinking our friendship needed a stronger foundation to blossom. Still, the idea of watching her and Landon together all night strangled my insides. I was pretty sure I would lose it if his lips ever connected with hers.

Melinda waved back, rescuing me from my drowning thoughts about her kissing some other guy, before walking away with Paige and their friends. I watched her retreat, admiring her strong set of swimmer shoulders and that tight ass in those jeans. I missed the time when I was her official book bag carrier for the week it had lasted. Back then, I had an excuse to talk to her. Unlike now.

I wouldn't attend the dance. I preferred missing it to being miserable all night if I had to invite anyone else. My stomach churned just thinking about Melinda dancing with Landon, knowing she would pamper herself for hours just for him.

Not a chance.

Fucking bastard.

The gears of my brain overheated as I chastised myself. Why had I waited so long to ask her to the dance? Why had I been so chickenshit, to begin with?

If I could kick my own ass, I would do it without any hesitation.

I emptied my tray into the nearest trash can, grabbed my stuff, and made my way out of the nearly deserted cafeteria.

Not in a hurry to meet my friends, I dragged my feet toward my locker. Three girls stopped me to inquire if I had a date for Homecoming—very subtle—and a guy from the school paper asked questions about our next game.

Realization hit me. I was Mason Pierce, captain of the football team and their beloved quarterback. Everyone expected me to show up at the homecoming dance and be a role model for the rest of the student body. For a moment, I wished I was all but famous in these hallways and was a regular Joe that nobody cared about. Except one person. I passed a row of lockers and punched the first door, regretting it when pain shot down my arm.

I couldn't injure myself. Not now. Not when we were playing Cowley High, our biggest rival, a little over a week from now. I had to be at the top of my game. They were a bunch of sick bastards, always eager to fight and cheat to claim victory. I had told my teammates that being the better guys would make the victory sweeter in our eyes. Hurting myself was not how we would win that game.

And if the word had gotten out to Copperman that I had hooked up with his girl last summer, they'd be out for blood—my blood.

"Fuck my life," I said as I grabbed books from my locker, pushed the thought of Melinda and Homecoming far away, and sauntered toward my next class, pumping myself up for tomorrow's game instead of thinking about next week's.

CHAPTER 12

I WOULDN'T KISS YOU, EVEN UNDER TORTURE

The crowd erupted in applause as we won the game. Twenty-eight to eighteen.

School had resumed a month ago, and so far, we were having a perfect season. I congratulated the boys, hugging them. Paige ran on the field, and my brother caught her. Geez, these two. It was hard to imagine that two years ago, Paige was this shy girl, never standing out, and always ignoring the football team whenever we would walk by her.

"One hell of a game," I told Sheldon, inching closer and bumping his fist.

"I swear, man, that last hit stole all the oxygen from me. For a second, I thought the guy's elbow had punctured my lungs."

"They put up more of a fight than I expected. Much better team than last year." I wiped the sweat grazing my hairline with my sleeve. "We underestimated their defensive line."

"Yeah. I'm glad we still kicked their asses and showed them who the real champs are."

"Keep your cockiness for when we win State, man. Being humble is a great quality. You should try it."

"I'm Sheldon *Cocky* Rice, man. Humble isn't my middle name." He laughed with his head tilted back, turning his attention to Rusty. "Hey, man. Wait for me." He jogged away, leaving me all by myself.

From the corner of my eye, I noticed Paige and Craig still busy whispering love promises to each other, lost in their own world, with her looking so small against his giant, uniformed self right now.

"Awesome. We could—" my brother said before I interrupted him, jumping between them and forcing them apart.

Paige landed on her feet and poked her tongue out at me.

"How is it going, lovers?" I said, making kissing sounds with my mouth and draping my arms around their shoulders, ignoring her grimace.

"Get lost, man," Craig said, pushing me back with a hand on the side of my chest.

A loud laugh broke free. "Sorry. You're my ride to the party tonight. And making out in the middle of the field on school property is super gross." I made an exaggerated puking sound. "I thought you two knew better."

"Wow, look who's talking. Mr. *Making Out At All The Wrong Places*. Anyway, you should take a night off. Cool down. Learn to be by yourself from time to time."

"Thanks for your concern, though." I clapped his

shoulder. "Big brother, don't worry about me. After tonight's win, the girls expect me to be there. They will all beg to kiss me and make it better." I pointed to the scratch covering my right arm from elbow to mid-forearm that I got after being tackled minutes into the game. I hated every word leaving my mouth, yet I spoke them like I meant them, as if I thought I was being funny.

"That ego," Paige said, chuckling. "Mase, you're a lot, you know that, right?"

I puffed my chest out. "I'm Elk River High's best quarterback in their history. I'm just playing the part, *babe*." I winked and rubbed her cheek with a finger. "Girls love a confident man."

My brother sighed. "Don't *babe* my girlfriend, loser."

"Don't be jealous I'm the better-looking sibling, bro— we've already agreed on that—and the most successful one with the ladies. Anyway, I have my eye on a girl."

"Just one?" Craig asked with a frown.

"Who is she?" Interest brightened Paige's eyes. "Do we know her? Is she a student at Elk River High?"

"Paige, are you ready?" Melinda asked, dangling her car keys as she neared us, interrupting the interrogation.

I thanked her mentally for her sick sense of timing.

At the sight of her, dressed in a maxi denim skirt with a slit at the front and a white long-sleeved top, my heart froze in my chest. Melinda Shepard had no idea how beautiful she was, which made her even more alluring.

These days, our interactions were friendlier than they'd been in years, but I still felt unsettled around her.

"Hello, my favorite patient," I greeted her, beckoning her with a finger. "Come here." She moved closer, and I pulled her into something almost resembling a hug. She fit perfectly at my side. I filled my nostrils with the sweet scent of her orange blossom shampoo. Letting go of her, I kept her close, an arm locked around her waist. "Let's leave these two to their tongue play." With my chin, I motioned to my brother who was back with Paige in his arms, his tongue down her throat. "Ugh, we don't need to see their tonsils. It's disturbing." I steered us in the opposite direction. "Tell me something, Mel. Why aren't you begging to kiss me after tonight's win?" I waggled my eyebrows, with a smirk pasted on my lips. "I played amazingly, don't you agree? Go ahead, shower me with praise. I'm used to being idolized by the ladies."

She nudged my ribcage. "Oh Mase, you wish. I have to admit you did great tonight, though."

"It's okay if you're not ready to kiss me yet. I won't hold it against you this time around. As long as you can admit how wonderful I am, though. We're almost family, you and I, and honesty is a value families share."

"We're almost family? Care to explain it to me?"

"Paige and you are joined at the hip, and she's dating my brother...or should I say she's almost married to my brother by the looks of it... So, you and I, extended family. See? Super simple."

"It's really not a stretch. You are almost right." She chuckled, and I joined her.

"About that kiss?"

She rolled her eyes in the most dramatic fashion. "Huh, sorry, but no. I wouldn't kiss you, even under torture."

I laughed, trying to cover the sting of her words. "I know you know I'm the one for you. I'm just waiting for you to be honest with yourself and catch up with that fact. For five years, I've been biding my time, waiting for you to admit how you really feel about me. Put the guy out of his misery already. It's bound to happen anyway. Why not make it official now and stop wasting precious time?"

"Not happening. Anyway, I'm sure there're dozens of girls waiting for you at that party. You won't miss me."

I pinched my jersey as if looking too good for school and winked. "What can I say? Everyone wants a piece of *The Mase.*" *Shut up, man.* Why did stupid words always leave my mouth every time she was around? Like my filters were defective. Why did I portray myself as a player? Dammit. What was wrong with me? Melinda would never see me as anything else if I didn't get my act together. The goal was to get out of the friend zone, and here I was, digging my own grave and burying my heart at the same time. Since I'd just been promoted to said friend zone, I couldn't jeopardize it too soon.

"Ugh, you're a pig when you want to be." She slapped my chest and pushed me aside in a teasing way. But it was the expression on her face that said she wasn't amused. She was trying to hide her disgust with a half-smile, the sight breaking me.

"Can I be *your* pig, though?" *Seriously, Mase, shut the fuck up.*

"Oh geez. Let's end this conversation right now before you say something else that scares me away."

"Your loss, Mel. Guess you'll never know how incredible a kisser I am."

"Hard pass," she scoffed, a hint of a smile grazing her lips, humor returning to her features. "I'm sure you won't have any trouble finding someone desperate enough so you can sink your victorious tongue down her throat."

"If I follow your logic, then you admit I'm the best?"

"Did you hit your head tonight? It's unhealthy to be this cocky."

I cupped my heart with a hand. "See? I knew you couldn't resist me. You and I, it's true love, baby, don't you see it?"

We stared at each other for a long minute. A glint shone in her eyes, and she blinked it away. How I wished I could translate her expressions and read her mind.

The air became charged between us, thick with awareness.

She swallowed, and I got entranced by the movement of her throat. I zoned in on her eyes, which was much safer, but soon got lost in the turquoise pools of her irises. My heart hammered in my chest. My hands became moist. Melinda parted her lips like she was about to say something but swept her bottom lip with her tongue instead. I was burning up. How could she do this without knowing how wild it made me? I stepped forward, my feet not asking for my permission as they moved of their own volition, erasing every bit of distance between us. My fingers grazed hers. Little particles of electricity tickled their tips. I became super aware of every one of her gestures and the pattern of her breathing. Melinda stared at me, her eyes big and full of an emotion I couldn't name, but that my body liked a lot.

The silence between us grew heavier.

Could she feel the pull like I did?

She parted her lips on an exhale, and her gaze descended on mine.

The pulse point in her throat throbbed.

This was it, the moment I'd been waiting forever for.

I leaned in and she blinked, killing the moment.

"Whatever, Mase. Go annoy someone else." There was no fight or teasing in her tone. It sounded more like a resolve.

"You won't get rid of me so easily." My voice sounded huskier than usual. Almost breathless.

She cleared her throat. "Knowing you, I've never expected anything less."

Right now, I couldn't tell if our banter was disguised flirting or friendly teasing only. No matter what, something was brewing between us. I sensed it in every fiber of my being.

I pushed her chin up with a finger so I could look into her eyes. "Seriously, though. How are you doing?"

"I'm fine."

"You swear?"

"Yes. Don't worry about me, okay?"

I pinched the sleeve of her sweater, the small gesture meant to keep her close to me. "I…huh…listen, I gotta go. Coach will want to talk to the team…" *Will you wait for me?* I picked up my helmet and fiddled with the strap. "I'll see you around…" *Please say something. I would rather spend my night hanging out with you than going to another stupid party I couldn't care less about.* I raised a hand and waved at her. *Don't let me go. Promise you'll be here when I return.* I hated myself for not being brave enough to reveal the feelings I'd been carefully tucking away for all these years.

"Bye, Mase." Melinda's voice had an edge to it. "You played well tonight. You should be proud of yourself." She waved back at me before nearing Paige and my brother. I hated being dismissed by the only person I had ever wanted to be seen by.

Turning to leave, I called over my shoulder to Craig and the girls, "I'll catch up with you later, guys." I pointed to the athletic building with a hand over my head. "Come on, bro."

"I'll be right there," he said before murmuring something to his girl and kissing her.

Hurrying toward the rest of my teammates heading for the locker room, my helmet hanging from my fingers, I kicked myself mentally for acting like a fool whenever Melinda was around. No matter how many times I told myself to say and do the right things when it concerned her, I always ended up acting like a pretentious and over-confident jerk who I barely recognized. I was trying to show her this other side of me, but sometimes, I failed because I got so nervous and forgot she wasn't someone I needed to impress.

Jogging forward, I facepalmed myself. I needed to up my game. Find a way to make Melinda see me as the boy I was and not just the stupid little brother of her best friend's boyfriend. The guy living next door—or the arrogant jackass I could be around everyone else…and now, around her too. Damn.

First order of things, get rid of my reputation as the guy who only slept around.

Melinda would never be just a one-night story, and if I wanted her to believe me, I had to clean up my act and stop screwing around for the sake of it. Mason Pierce Improved-Version would soon be underway.

CHAPTER 13

SOMEONE DIAL 9-1-1

The next Thursday, after football practice, I met a dozen of my teammates, including Craig, at Space Burger. We were playing Cowley High the next day. It'd been a long time coming, and we needed some team bonding before the big night. When I sat down, they were all laughing at Sheldon's antics as he tried to convince the waitress to accompany him to the homecoming dance two days from now. The woman, Juliet, according to her name tag, was hot, but she was at least a decade older than him. That was Sheldon, though. Always aiming for the impossible—and doing things out of the ordinary.

"I'll buy a basket of chicken wings and tip big every Saturday night for the next six months if you agree. Come on, who wouldn't want to accompany a guy as handsome as me? If you refuse, it will be your loss, beautiful."

Juliet blushed, shaking her head, clearly affected by our friend. "I wish you were at least five years older," she said. "I would have gone with you. I'm too old for you now."

"Old?" He slapped his chest in fake hurt. "Never call yourself old, beautiful. Perhaps today is a no, but give me nine months and I'll be eighteen, and then our age difference won't matter anymore," Sheldon said with a wink. "I'll come every Saturday night, as promised, and court you until you say yes."

"Oh Jesus, you're a stubborn one, aren't you?" The grin on her face made her eyes sparkle.

"Woman, you've seen nothing."

She sighed. "I'll punch your order in, then be right back with your drinks, guys."

When she left, Chase started the retelling of his latest date when more of the team walked in.

The conversation switched to the following night's game. I cringed internally when it drifted to the dance and everyone's date. My teammates' priority should be football, not getting laid.

"Okay, people. We have an important matter to discuss. I kid you not, guys, but Pierce Junior has no date," Chase announced to the table. The guys on the team often used Junior and Senior to differentiate Craig and me when they called us by our last name. Something Coach had started during freshman year.

I killed my best friend with the laser beams my eyes had turned into, and he winked in response.

Fucker.

All eyes around the table were fixed on me.

"You don't?"

"Are you sick?"

"What's happening to you?"

"Pierce Junior out of his game? Unbelievable."

"Someone dial 9-1-1."

My friends' reactions were immediate.

"Screw you, Chase," I told my best friend, who laughed his heart out. His grin widened. With a shake of my head, I turned toward the rest of the table, lifting my hands in surrender. "Stop getting worked up about it. I've been thinking… Will you guys forgive me if I ditch Saturday night?"

Silence fell upon us as everyone stared at me.

A series of *Ooohs* and *Aaahs* followed. Confusion took over most of my friends' faces.

"Hey, come on, it's just a dance. You guys chill out. We'll win the game like the amazing champs we are and give the crowd the best football they've ever seen, and then you guys wear some tux to impress the ladies and make me proud. I'll just sit this one out."

Chase's face fell. "Geez, you're serious." He blew out a breath. "Man, it's not just a dance. It's tradition. Homecoming. The biggest weekend of the year. Football, music, chicks. It's like the trifecta of high school. That plus blow jobs and booze."

"C'mon, I still have time to make traditions. I don't feel like going." I shrugged, trying to look convincing. "It's no big deal. And it gives one of you suckers a chance to be crowned Homecoming King. You should all be thankful that I'm removing myself from the competition." I plastered my best devilish grin on.

"One point for Mase," Sheldon said. He extended his arm over the table, and we high-fived. "Challenge accepted. I'll be your king, guys, but I would prefer if you called me *Master*."

"Ugh. Never. Sheld, please don't encourage him. Mase

is rarely wrong, but right now he is. Big time." Chase pointed at me. "Mase, you're the captain. Homecoming and football go hand in hand, man. You, Mason Pierce, are our king, and the troops need their king to show them the way. If you don't go, then we should all abstain." He nodded once as if it gave weight to his argument. "I'm sure girls are already lining up to give you head in an empty classroom to celebrate our future victory. Would you deprive them all?"

"Geez, you sound like a knockoff Shakespeare, but a perverted version of him. Stop with the drama. It's just a dance. I don't need a bunch of followers or a blow job from some random girl. You guys go and make the most of it. It's not an all-or-nothing kinda situation. It's just a school dance. What are you? A bunch of middle schoolers? Get over it already."

A hand clapped my shoulder. Someone poured me a glass of soda. If I had announced I was going to die, not sure my teammates would have reacted any worse.

"Something is wrong with you," Rusty said, with a sigh.

"Definitely," Jackson replied.

"Guys, stop it. I'm fine. Can we please talk about something else? We have a game tomorrow, and we should all focus on that instead. We gotta crush Cowley High. Losing to them isn't an option."

Craig's eyes locked on mine across the table, and he shook his head. Even though he asked me at least once a week, I still hadn't told him the identity of the girl I had a crush on. I was surprised he hadn't figured it out by now. He was usually good at reading me without my telling him about my thoughts. Or perhaps he knew and was just waiting for me to spell it out. Whatever.

I wouldn't open up about it unless Melinda and I made

it official. And from the look of things, that status wouldn't be easily obtained—not by a long shot.

"Paige is part of the homecoming committee. You could at least make an appearance," my brother said. "I'm sure she'd appreciate it. My girl has spent weeks working on the decor. You're part of this team and this family, and the least you can do is show up where you're expected."

As if she had been summoned, Paige and a group of girls—minus Melinda—joined us and pushed a table against ours to create more seating and sat down. I straightened my posture, readying myself in case Melinda and Landon walked in together for whatever reason. I was being ridiculous, yet I couldn't prevent myself from reacting. I relaxed my shoulders when I noticed she wasn't coming, even though a part of me wished she was here too. My head, my heart, and my entire being were conflicted when it came down to the one girl who had the power to make me lose my mind all the time.

"Your girl what?" Paige asked, leaning into him when Craig tugged her closer. He kissed her forehead, and she smiled back at him.

Chase jumped in. *Traitor.* "Your man was telling Mase he should get his head out of his ass and come to the dance on Saturday night. We're going to win that game tomorrow and be badass superheroes in white tights, and everyone will expect him to show up. Craig said that Mase can't miss it because you worked so hard on the decor, and he wants him to support you because you're family or some shit."

A look of love shone in her eyes when they landed on my brother. "You're so sweet." She grabbed his hand in hers and kissed his palm. God, they were nauseatingly in love sometimes. Her attention switched to me seconds later. "Mase? Is it true you're not coming?" She flicked her wrist.

"Mel already ditched it last year. How can you both miss traditions?"

"Ah, that's exactly what I said," Chase chimed in. "Traditions, man. They're important."

"Shut up, Chase," I grumbled through gritted teeth. "We've been over this already."

Paige watched me with a laser focus as if she could guess whatever thoughts were swimming in my head. "Mason Pierce, you better have a good excuse."

I shrugged. I had none.

She studied me for a little longer. "What are you not telling me? You're hiding something. It's obvious."

"Don't try to be a mind reader, babe. It's a waste of your time." I paused, trying to come up with a not-too-far-fetched excuse she would buy. "Too many school dances. It gets old. I'll attend prom. That's where I draw the line."

"No Winter Formal?"

"Nope." I popped the *P*, putting fake assurance into my reply. "I'm starting new traditions."

She threw her arms up in the air. "Fine. Whatever. Do what you want. I'm not gonna force you to come, but prom is non-negotiable. If you bail on us, you'll hear from me for years to come." She pointed a finger at me. "I was thinking…we should go camping after prom. All of us. It could be fun."

Silence fell around the table. Some of us recalled how last year's camping trip had ended.

"Mase, remove that sour expression from your face. You love camping too much to miss the opportunity. This way I'm making sure you hold up your end of the bargain. And this time around, it won't be just a boys' trip. We're all going."

I killed the past memory as new images formed in my mind.

Me, Melinda Shepard, and a tent.

The idea brought a fresh wave of hope. A deadline. An endgame.

Could I make the girl fall in love with me by the end of the school year? I wasn't a guy usually fearing dares. Except this one was in my head and not for anybody else's sake but mine.

Yeah, I could be the guy she needed me to be by then.

"Okay, we have a deal, babe," I told Paige.

She stretched her arm over the table, and we shook on it.

When her smile split her face in two, I knew that no matter what happened, she would never let me get away with it down the road.

The challenge was on.

———

"Hey you," I greeted Melinda once she exited her car. I had just made it home and spotted her headlights from down the street and decided to wait for her.

I adjusted the strap of the bag slipping from my shoulder and neared her.

Her car keys jingled as they hung from her fingers. "What are you doing here?"

"I had dinner at Space Burger with the team. Some of your friends were there too."

"I had a meeting with Coach. To go over my training program." Her lips tilted up. "I've been cleared to train and compete again." Her turquoise eyes sparkled with glee.

"You have?" Before I could register my own movements, I pulled her into my arms. The smell of her orange blossom shampoo assaulted my nostrils.

After a few seconds, Melinda relaxed against me. She

rested her small hands on the dips of my hipbones, and time stopped. My heart thrashed in my chest. As if someone had electrocuted us, we both jumped back, keeping a safe distance between our bodies. The air was charged with something galvanic.

She adjusted the navy-blue varsity school sweatshirt she was wearing over a pair of jeans and white running shoes. The semi-athletic style—very similar to the one I was sporting right now—looked good on her.

"I wanted to come and see you after dinner," she said, breaking the awkward face-off.

"You did? Missed me too much already?"

"Not yet. I was wondering if you were still up for helping me train. I gotta get back in shape and shed a few pounds."

I snorted. "You? Lose weight?"

"Yeah, well, I have to get in the best shape of my life. Maybe not shed pounds but increase my lean muscle mass. These next few meets are important, and I can't afford to slack off right now or be slow."

"We could go for a run in the morning."

"Don't you have a big game tomorrow night?"

"Yes, but I would go for a run anyway. We'll go slow and see how you feel. Six thirty?"

"Huh…yes?"

I cocked one brow. "Yes? Or yes. Are you scared I'll beat your ass, Shepard?"

"Ha ha, real funny. We both know I can't beat you at running, *Pierce*. But yeah, six thirty is fine with me."

"Awesome. I'll meet you right here when you're ready."

"Deal. Night."

We both turned to leave when I stopped and whirled around. "And, Mel? If it's hard at first, don't let it discourage you. I'll be right there to help you, okay?"

She nodded, a somber expression painting her face. "Thanks."

I was in bed by eleven, trying to catch some rest since tomorrow was going to be a big day. Unable to quiet my racing thoughts, after tossing and turning for a couple of hours, I dressed in a pair of old sweatpants and a hoodie and made my way downstairs. I faced my mother when I entered the kitchen. A quick glance at the oven digital clock told me it was almost one in the morning.

"Mase, I thought you went to bed hours ago?" she asked, a worried expression clouding her face. Her light brown hair was piled at the top of her head, her blue eyes boring into mine. My mom and I looked very much alike and shared most of our facial features, but hers remained soft through the years while mine became more angular the older I got. Even though Craig and I were very similar, he inherited most of our dad's genetic traits.

"I did…huh…I tried. I couldn't sleep." The game tonight, the homecoming dance on Saturday night I was ditching, Melinda and Landon going together, and our upcoming jogging date. The game was the only thing I should be anxious about, yet the idea that Melinda and I would spend many hours together multiple times a week made me restless. I couldn't screw this up. Helping her out with something that meant a lot to her was my chance to prove that I wasn't some immature idiot but rather someone trustworthy. And that we could be more than friends and our chemistry was still there even after all these years.

"Want me to make you some tea? I was having trouble sleeping too. Your dad is snoring. He's been working longer hours these days, and I think it's finally catching up with him."

I eyed the front door. "I think I'll go for a walk."

"In the middle of the night? You would tell me if your insomnia was serious, right?"

"Yep. It's just the pressure of the game. Nothing else. Playing against Cowley High always does that to me. There's a lot at stake."

"I don't want you to fall into old patterns. Do you remember? During sophomore year, the recurrent bouts of insomnia before games had been a huge problem. Even your grades suffered."

"Fully aware. I swear it's not like that this time around."

"Are you still doing those breathing techniques when you feel overwhelmed?"

"Yeah. And I'm trying to do more visualization. I'm getting much better at it. Coach says it shows, and my game has improved too. I'm still not good at meditation, though. I find it hard to sit there and not do anything for fifteen minutes. My mind never shuts up when I have no distraction."

"You, my son, are so much like me. Craig and your father can sleep through an earthquake. We're the emotional ones, even though we try to act like everything is fine all the time. It's okay to be vulnerable sometimes, Mase. Growing up, I had no options and had to deal with it, but you have choices nowadays. Society is much more forgiving about anxiety and other mental struggles. It's okay if your mind wanders when you do mediation. Give it some time. As long as you keep trying. That's all I'm asking." She cradled my cheek with a palm. "I want you healthy, physically and mentally. Always."

"I'm all right, Mom. I swear."

She watched me for a long moment. "Do you recall my friend Susan?"

"Yeah, why?"

"Remember I told you her nephew got recruited to play professional baseball next year?"

"Yeah, so?"

"He was in a car accident two weeks ago. Drunk driver. Broke his hips and two ribs. His baseball career is over."

"Shit."

"Language."

"Sorry. Why are you telling me this?"

"Because... I know playing professional football is your dream, but you never know what life has in store for you."

I raised one brow. "And what's that supposed to mean?"

"When you go to college next year, choose a major that interests you. Don't just go to college so you can play ball. In the long run, if things don't work out as you're hoping then you have a plan B."

"Geez, Mom. Depressing much? What has gotten into you?"

"It's true, Mase. You might not see it now because you are young and healthy and thriving, but sometimes things happen, and the choices you make will impact your future."

"Playing football *is* my future. It's all I'm good at and all I'm interested in. There's nothing else for me."

"Are you sure?"

"Yep. I won't let anyone or anything get in the way of my playing pro dream."

"Don't you think that poor boy must have said the same thing about his baseball career?"

"Probably. It sucks that his gift has been stolen from him, but how is it related to my situation?"

"It's not. I want you to remember something. Most things in life happen for a reason. Even if it's hard to see the endgame sometimes. Maybe Susan's nephew is destined to find a cure for cancer or to be the best college baseball coach in history. Or maybe he's supposed to be a spokesperson against drunk driving and inspire people around the country with his story. I have no idea. I just don't want you or your brother to rely only on football and forget there's a life outside the sport. I don't like it when you put so much pressure on yourself. And I hate the fact you have insomnia because of a sport ruling your existence when it shouldn't. Perhaps you're destined to play in the big leagues and be the best quarterback of your generation, but maybe you're supposed to do something else too. Something that doesn't take a toll on your mental and physical health."

"Impossible."

"If you say so. Anyway, pick a degree you like. If, eventually, you gotta do something else with your life, then you won't be miserable. It would make me very sad if you were."

"Seriously, Mom. Where is all this coming from? Are you okay? I have no intention of retiring from football anytime soon. And neither does Craig."

"I know, Mase. It's just…that poor boy's story got me thinking. As a mother, I can't help but imagine what would happen if it were you or your brother navigating such a situation."

"Well, it's not. We're here, healthy and thriving. If you always imagine the worst, you'll only worry about us."

"I already always worry about you two. It's my job as your mother. Also, I know football players are prone to injuries. Concussions are no joke, Mase. Your brain is precious. It's not worth gambling with it. You experienced it firsthand last year. I don't want you to live with long-term consequences. You're still growing."

"Mom, stop. My brain is fine." I hugged her petite

frame before releasing her. "Craig's brain is fine too. Don't lose sleep over this, okay? And I've already decided I'll study business next year. See? I'm thinking long shot. It will open doors for me if needed. Melinda asked me a question the other day, and it got me thinking too."

"You two have been spending more time together lately."

I shrugged. "It's no big deal. We're friends."

She raised a brow as if to say *Yeah, right*. "Anything else I should be aware of?"

"No. I will be helping her train so she can get back in shape."

"She's a nice one, Mase. Don't hurt her."

"Never. I would never hurt her on purpose, Mom."

"Good."

"And, Mom? It's gonna be all right. You've always known football was in our DNA. We didn't choose the sport, it chose us."

"True. I remember when you were just a little kid and you stepped on that field for the first time. It was magical. It was like you'd done it a thousand times before. Still, I won't ever not worry about you two for as long as you both play."

"I bet I would do the same thing if I were in your shoes."

"How's your shoulder? I noticed you've been icing it more than usual in the last few months."

I rotated my joint as if to prove to myself it was moving like it should. "It's good, Mom. All good. I'm being careful, and I'm not icing it because it's bothering me, but more as a preventive measure. It's me being smart about my health and my future." *And maybe also because it feels a bit stiff these days, and my worst nightmare would be to be benched as a result of not being able to throw a pigskin the way I used to.*

She nodded. "Okay, then. I trust you, Mason. You would tell me if you were in pain?"

"Yes." Not this time.

"I love you."

"I love you too, Mom."

"I'm glad we had this talk. Are you still going on a walk?"

"Yep. Just need to clear my head. I won't be long."

"Want some company?"

"Nah. Go to bed. I'll be back in an hour at the most. Night." I kissed her cheek. Darkness enveloped me as soon as I stepped on the front porch. There was something oddly calming about the fact that I was alone, wandering around the neighborhood when everyone else was asleep. A light breeze swept across my face, and the earthy smell of petrichor in the air the rain had brought in an hour ago delighted my nostrils. It reminded me of summer, and somehow, I found it soothing.

"You can't sleep either?" a small voice asked when I passed the Shepards' house.

"Mel?" I spotted her sitting on the wooden bench by the front door, hugging her knees, covered in a thick blanket. I neared her before I could realize where my feet were taking me. "What are you doing alone in the dark at this hour?"

"Thinking."

I cocked one brow. "About?"

"Stuff."

"Yeah, I was thinking about stuff too." I hesitated for a split second. "Want company?"

"Sure." She scooted on the bench and freed a spot for me next to her. "Blanket?"

"Thanks. I'm fine. Wanna tell me what's on your mind?"

She exhaled. "Not really. What about you?"

"Cowley High."

"Oh. Is the rivalry thing still going strong?"

I nodded. "Sometimes I freak out because of all the pressure I put on myself. Like losing isn't an option. Not against them. The team would despise me if I couldn't bring in a victory tomorrow…well…tonight now, I guess. Anyway, the stress is real, and usually I'm fine, but there are times when it keeps me awake at night. I don't wanna disappoint people who are counting on me."

"Whether you win or lose, it's not your fault, Mase. It's a team thing, not a one-man show."

"True, but the pressure is my own doing. I hate letting down the people I care about. I feel like it's my duty to take my guys to victory. To prove we're unbeatable. It's stupid. I'll shut up now."

Her fingers grazed mine, and I shivered under the feather-like touch. "It's not. What you feel is not stupid, because if you feel it, it means it's important to you."

I shrugged.

"When things get crazy in there," she pointed to her head, "I like to make a list. Of things I can control and things I can't. I do that before every meet. What I wear, what I eat, what playlist I'm listening to in order to get in the zone, or the number of hours of training I put in a week are things I have control over. My opponent's swimming abilities, their training schedules, or how many hours my teammates put into their own training are things I don't have control over. I focus on my own stuff. If I decide to eat a chocolate cake instead of a protein shake before a competition, I'm harming myself and also my teammates if I can't perform like I should. If I put in the work, eat healthy, and train like I should, then it's harder to blame myself if I don't obtain the results I expect."

"What happened to the girl wanting to win, no matter what, a few weeks ago?"

"Still here. I swear. Now she's trying to only zero in on the things she has control over. I'm trying to let go of the winning obsession and give my full attention to other things leading me there instead."

"Is it working?"

"I'll tell you when I climb on the highest step of the podium next time."

"You should be my motivational coach when I doubt myself." I elbowed her in a teasing manner.

"I'm not as much in control as I'd like to be. Not sure I would be a great role model. It's pretty messed up in my head sometimes."

We remained sitting there in silence for the longest time.

"Before I left, my mom told me a story about a guy who lost his chance to play pro because he got into a car accident. Now she's freaking out and said I need a plan B other than football. I don't want her to worry, but I also don't want to have to think about another career choice because if I do, it feels like it could become true, you know? Like if I don't open that door, it can't exist. I'm rambling."

"Nah. Your mom is right. When you realize you could have died, it changes your perspective about things. She loves you and wants what's best for you. But she also doesn't want you injured."

A comfortable silence stretched between us as we both got lost in our thoughts.

"Yeah. We should go to bed," I said after a beat. "I have no idea what time it is, but I'm sure six thirty will come soon enough. I wouldn't want my student to ditch her first training. Unless she needs the rest."

"Nah. She'll be there. Early and ready."

We both moved to our feet, and I opened my arms, hating myself for looking like I was out of my game and insecure about myself. Melinda hugged me quickly and then stepped back.

"Night, Mase. Only focus on what you can control. The rest is not your job. Trust that the universe—and your teammates—have your back, no matter what."

"Will you be there to cheer us on tomorrow?"

"I wouldn't miss it for the world."

I watched her as she retreated inside, replaying every word my mother and Melinda had spoken tonight. *Focus on what I can control.* I could do that.

CHAPTER 14

IT WOULDN'T BE GOOD FOR
MY HARD-ASS COACH REP

I stretched while I waited for Melinda to join me. In my defense, it was only six fifteen. After our talk last night, I did what she said and made lists in my head until I couldn't keep my mind active and fell into a deep slumber.

"And I thought I would be the first one here," a voice said from behind me.

I pivoted to come face to face with Melinda wearing black running tights molded to her strong legs, a matching fleece, her brown hair tied in a high ponytail, and a pink headband covering her ears. We were dressed almost identically minus the headband that I had replaced with a knitted hat. My body reacted at the sight of her, tightening everywhere. Even dressed like this, I found her sexy as hell.

The crisp morning breeze did nothing to cool down the hot-as-lava blood circulating through my veins. I jumped on the spot, stretching my neck and rolling my shoulders back, trying to show my body I was the one in command.

"You're up early, Mase."

"Always ready, Shepard." I winked before morphing into coach mode. "From now on, until the end of the five-mile loop, you can call me Coach Pierce. I'll get your blood pumping, your pits sweating, and your glutes aching." I lowered my tone and dropped the act. "Unless you tell me five miles is too much and you'd prefer walking instead of running."

Her smile was a permanent fixture on her face now. "Nah. All good. I tested myself on the treadmill yesterday, and I can keep up. I'm ready to go when you are, Coach."

I nodded. "That's the spirit. Let's stretch a bit, and then we'll walk for half a mile so you can warm up. The last thing you need is to hurt yourself by diving back into your training too soon."

"Okay."

For the next five minutes, we stretched, silence heavy between us. I caught Melinda ogling me a few times, and I returned the favor.

I jogged in place. "Shepard, you good to go?"

"When you are."

After a short walk, I switched the pace to a light jog. Melinda kept up with me. The huffs of her breaths, the sound of our footsteps, and the thumps of my overexcited heart were all I could hear. We ran down the street, crossed the park at the end, circled the pond, and took the walkway bordering the river, before slowing back to a jog as we neared our street.

Melinda bent forward, her palms resting on her knees, gasping for air.

"You did great, Shepard. It was your first training in weeks." I held out my hand, and we high-fived. "Wanna ride together to school?"

"Nah. You have that game tonight, and it's easier if I take my own car. Thanks for the offer, though."

I shrugged as if it were no big deal. "We could stick to jogging all weekend and start some weight training next week during lunch hour and alternate with yoga. What do you say?"

"Should work for me."

"Awesome." We strolled back home, stretching as we did. We stopped in front of her house. "I'm proud of you, Shepard."

"Thanks, Coach."

I removed my beanie and raked my fingers through my hair. "Listen, I thought about what you said last night...about things I can control and things I have no control over."

She stayed immobile, waiting for me to continue.

"I think I can focus on that." I closed my eyes and breathed in before bringing my attention back to her. "Can I tell you something I've never told anybody else?"

"Always. Your secret is safe with me."

I motioned for her to sit on the lawn, and I plopped down next to her. "It's my right shoulder. It's been bothering me for a while. I lied to my mom last night and said it wasn't, but it's stiff." I rolled it back as if to make the statement true. "Stiffer than usual. I haven't told Coach yet because I'm hopeful that if I rest and ice it enough and stretch it properly, it will heal. I'm not sure if it's something I can control or not, you know. I have no idea in which column it belongs."

Her small hand enveloped mine and stayed there.

"If I go to the doctor, they'll order a bunch of tests and

force me to rest. The team needs me. Most of the guys are senior. I can't risk messing with their last year. Football season doesn't last long."

I flipped my palm over and knitted my fingers through hers.

"Do you feel like you should seek medical advice?" Melinda asked after a minute.

"Yes and no. I can't let my teammates down. Right now, it's what matters the most."

"Mase?"

I lifted my gaze to hers.

"Promise me something. If you don't see a doctor now, as soon as the season is over, you'll go and get your shoulder checked. Don't put your future in jeopardy for a high school championship or your pride."

I chewed on my inner cheek. "Fine."

Her lips tilted up. "We have a deal." She pointed behind her. "I gotta go if I don't wanna be late for school. See you later." She unlinked our fingers but kept her palm on mine. A little burst of electricity transferred from her hand to mine, and I held my breath.

What would she do if I kissed her? Would she slap me, indulge me, or run away from me?

I wasn't ready to find out. I squeezed her hand, the small touch easing the racing thoughts invading my mind.

Then I remembered Melinda was going to the dance with Landon the following night, and my infatuation died.

I stood and did a few knee-to-chest glute stretches, Melinda following my lead. "We'll go for six miles on Sunday morning. Let's say nine o'clock. Don't get to bed too late on Saturday night." I was being a jerk, but somehow, I couldn't help myself. I knew she was going to the homecoming dance and wouldn't be home before midnight.

Melinda's hand shot to her chest. "Wow, Coach, you're letting me sleep in the morning. How generous of you."

"You're my favorite athlete, so please don't scream for everyone to hear that I gave you a free pass. It wouldn't be good for my hard-ass coach rep."

"Noted." But then reality seemed to dawn on her. "But tomorrow night is—"

"Yeah, but I have plans on Sunday."

"Oh…okay."

Her smile dipped, and I felt bad for being such a jealous asshole and an entitled jerk. Something was clearly wrong with me. "We can postpone and start over on Monday."

She shook her head. "Nah, it's fine. I need this, so I'll make it work."

I closed the distance between us. "I don't want you to overdo it or not rest long enough and exhaust yourself. We can go for a run later on Sunday instead."

"No, morning is fine."

"You sure?"

"Yeah. And don't forget you're already letting me sleep in. I'll be ready at nine. Are you still ditching the dance?"

"Yes. Not going."

"Oh, okay. Have a great game tonight."

"Thanks, Shepard."

CHAPTER 15

I THINK IT'S ABOUT TIME
YOU GET OVER IT

The marching band positioned themselves on the fifty-yard line, forming a tight block behind the drum major, their uniforms, a mix of navy blue and gold, a sharp contrast against the green turf. Attacking a rendition of our school fight song, they began to move, breaking into several lines and spreading across the football field. Their feet marched with synchronized precision as the drumline twirled and tossed their sticks with ease, never missing a beat.

The song ended, and they transitioned into a rhythmic piece, forming patterns as they paraded to the beat of the drums.

The band split into two groups and dispersed on each side of the field as the cheerleaders ran to the fifty-yard line, shaking their golden pompoms over their heads and performing high kicks, infusing the crowd with contagious energy.

I stood on the opposite side of the field with my teammates, waiting for our cue to join the pep rally. I wasn't a fan of the whole spectacle, but I knew how important it was for school spirit.

The cheerleaders formed two parallel lines when the music picked up, the strong intoxicating beat resonating around us. Dressed in their golden-and-navy-blue uniforms, they became the center of attention as three of them stepped forward and executed a series of well-coordinated back handsprings followed by a dozen cartwheels and backflips.

The crowd consisting of students and teaching and faculty staff roared its approval.

"You okay?" Chase asked, next to me, his eyes trained on the cheerleaders' miniskirts that displayed a lot of bare legs.

"Yeah. I have stuff on my mind. I'm trying not to get distracted." It wasn't a complete lie. After my middle-of-the-night discussion with my neighbor, I was still restless about all the things I had no control over—tonight's game and her date tomorrow night included.

I was usually good at compartmentalizing my life so my personal stuff didn't interfere with my sport, but for some reason, this time, it felt impossible. My mind was one big shit show I couldn't keep in line. I blamed my short night for not being able to regain control over my mind.

My brother neared my other side. "Mase. You good, man?"

I shrugged. Every cell in my body was taut. It felt like I was made of glass, and if someone pushed me, I would fracture into a million pieces.

He clamped my shoulder with a muscular hand. "Stop putting pressure on yourself. I know football is your life because it's mine too, but it's also just a sport. All you can do is bring your A-game and hope we dominate the other team. The guys are ready, I'm ready, and so are you. We've been over the plays hundreds of times already, and we've all watched the game tapes more than once. We can kick Cowley High's asses tonight. That's all you should focus on. Have faith in the team."

He let go of me, and I blew out a long breath. His words mirrored some of those Melinda—and my mom—had spoken last night, yet I couldn't seem to relax. I scanned the bleachers for the third time, trying to spot her. So far, no sign of her. Where was she? I knew she had her first training today. I just hoped our morning run hadn't tired her out too much and she had been able to swim. Melinda had been looking forward to going back into the pool since waking up after the surgery, and I didn't want anything to stand in her way.

"Who are you looking for?" Craig asked, following my line of sight.

"No one. I'm counting the number of people wearing jerseys. It keeps my mind busy." Again, it wasn't a total lie. I often did that—count something from a crowd—when my mind went haywire. Ponytails, blonde hair, mustaches, red shirts, hats. Anything to busy my brain for a moment.

"Look." Chase pointed forward. "You don't wanna miss that."

"What?" I brought my gaze forward.

The cheerleaders split into three groups. Interlocking their hands, the base of each group formed a foundation and crouched down. The two outside groups moved back up with their arms bent, loading their mid-bases above their heads. The middle group stretched their arms over their heads, loading Tanya, the flyer, at the top of the pyramid.

Her back was ramrod straight as she clapped her hands to the rhythm of the music. She stood on one leg, holding on to her two mid-bases' hands, their form impeccable. After she hit it, Tanya's base tossed her in the air, and she did a double twist before falling back and landing in the waiting hands of her spotters.

The two mid-bases executed heel stretches, their legs held high above their heads before moving into scorpion poses where they grabbed their curved legs behind them.

People in the bleachers cheered them on at the top of their lungs.

A couple of cheerleaders still on the ground performed cartwheels and handsprings in front of the formation before the pyramid dismounted, the bases lowering their mid-bases. The squad transitioned into partner stunts where one had their feet planted on the ground and lifted the other on their shoulders. After a couple of heel stretches, they propelled them in the air before spotters caught them when they fell back.

Now standing in a line, the squad jumped in excitement, shaking their pompoms and cheering our team.

"That's what I'm talking about," Chase exclaimed next to me. "I'll never get tired of watching girls doing acrobatic shit. Even Tanya is good at this, which is saying a lot."

Sheldon walked up to us, and they fist-bumped. "Me neither. These skirts are a delight for the eyes."

I sighed at their antics. "Guys, stop. Focus on the upcoming game, not on bare thighs. One day, the cheer squad will wear astronaut uniforms, and it will be all because of idiots like you."

"What has gotten into you, Mase?" Peters asked. "Since when are you so stuck-up?"

"Nothing. Keep your eyes and your mind on the game and stop acting like kids." I wasn't in the mood for their stupidities.

"You sure you're okay?" Craig asked again in a low tone.

"Yeah. I'm fine. Let's just get this over with."

"Are you about to have a meltdown? The few times it happened in the past was because the pressure you put on yourself felt like too much, and I was the one who had to get you out of that funk. If you're about to have one, please tell me so I can intervene and calm you before you explode."

I breathed in. "I swear I'll be fine. I'm trying to prevent the stress from getting to me. I'm all right. Don't worry." I smiled, trying to prove I was really fine.

The cheerleaders finished their routine, and Mr. Ross, the principal, walked to the microphone that had been set on the sideline. "Good afternoon, Elk River High."

The crowd clapped and wolf whistled.

Mr. Ross motioned for the students filling the bleachers to calm down with his hands. "People, please behave."

Another round of cheers erupted.

"I know tonight is the night." More cheers. "Let's welcome the Elk River High Bears, our very own football team and last year's State champions."

My teammates and I ran onto the field, pumping our fists and brandishing our helmets over our heads, leaving an electrifying energy in our wake.

"You ready?" Chase asked from beside me.

I shrugged instead of replying. Usually, I succeeded at standing in front of the entire school without freaking out too much, but not today. A ball of nerves bounced around inside me, and I had no idea how to stop it. I clenched and unclenched my fists, waiting for Coach Roberts to call me forward. I wasn't a fan of pep rallies, but as the captain of the football team, it was my duty to be here and lead my teammates and give a feel-good speech to motivate the players and create excitement within the school so people would show up at the games, fill the bleachers, and cheer us on.

"Minutes ago, I learned that a big storm has hit Riverside and wrecked Cowley High's football field. A light pole crashed on the turf and the bleachers. The damage is too extensive to be fixed by the end of the afternoon. Since it's last minute, I offered to host the game here, at Elk River High. Tonight's away game will take place on our very own field."

My teammates jumped into each other's arms, bumped chests, and high-fived. The students filling the bleachers screamed their enthusiasm.

"Yes." I pumped my fist above my head. This was indeed good news. Playing our rivals with the home advantage was incredible. We would have the crowd on our side, our colors filling most of the bleachers, and our team spirit would reach new heights.

"It's like too good to be true," Peters said, his arms draped around Craig's and my shoulders.

"Okay, people," Principal Ross hollered. "I know the news makes you happy, but it doesn't change the fact we have a game to attend tonight. I expect you to be on your best behavior. Cowley High isn't happy about the change of plans, so please don't rub it in their faces. Team, play your best game and make us proud, and students, wear Elk River High colors and encourage them tonight." He motioned to Coach to join him. "I'll pass the microphone to the man of the hour, Coach Roberts."

Both men clapped each other's shoulders, and students applauded.

"Elk River High," Coach's loud voice echoed around us. "Are you guys ready for some football?"

The crowd erupted in a chant. "Bears, Bears, Bears." While some people hollered, "Pierce, Pierce, Pierce."

The cheerleaders dispersed amongst the players, and Tanya locked herself to my side, her small hand circling my biceps in a death grip.

"*Masssse*, have you thought about my proposition?"

I hated when she used that voice. The one she thought was sexy but was everything but. "Your proposition?"

She bobbed her head multiple times. "Yes. Helping me study. I have a test on Monday, and I really need your help."

"Already told you. Not interested. And I won't be tomorrow or next week either. I'm busy."

She dug her fingernails into my flesh, hard enough that I felt it through my jersey. "But Mase..." She batted her eyelashes like it could change my mind. "I wouldn't beg if it wasn't important. My parents are away all weekend, and you know how much I hate being home alone. We could combine study and playtime. I swear it'll be fun. What do you say?"

"My answer is still no." I yanked my arm free and took a step back from her.

As if she recalled we were standing in front of the student body, she plastered a fake smile on her face, shifting position so her side was glued to mine, invading my personal space once more. The scent of her floral perfume tickled my nostrils, and I rubbed my nose with a finger, breathing through my mouth to avoid burning my neurons with the chemical smell emanating from her.

I sensed her tensing beside me, but I refused to engage with her. "About tomorrow night... Have you changed your mind? We could still go together."

"Nope. Not going. Now, leave me alone, Tan."

I sidestepped to put distance between us, and this time, she didn't latch back onto my arm.

Once again, I searched the crowd for the one face I was desperate to see, trying to forget that in an instant, I would step to the microphone and pump up the crowd before Principal Ross dismissed us.

I found her on my second sweep, and I breathed easier. The tension crippling my back melted away. Melinda pushed through the students to reach Paige sitting in the sixth row on the far-left side. From her appearance—a navy-blue school varsity sweatshirt, sweatpants, and a black beanie covering her damp hair—I bet she had just finished training. Even dressed down, she looked magnificent amongst the rest of the students.

Paige and she exchanged a few words, and when Melinda scanned the field, her gaze landed on me. Like she possessed some power over me, I failed to look away. She worried her lower lip, staring at me. My heart fluttered in my chest. Heat flooded my bloodstream, and my throat closed. This time, it wasn't because I was nervous to give a speech. She was the one making me nervous, putting me on high alert. We eyed each other from a distance, and I wished I could translate the words she wasn't speaking out loud right now. I wondered if she could tell I was wishing I could be anywhere else but here at this moment. Her attention never faltered away from me.

My throat bobbed on a swallow, and I swept my dry lips with my tongue.

Even from my position on the field, I could feel the attraction simmering between us.

Melinda nodded once, and I returned the gesture.

As if I had correctly answered a question that had been

nagging her mind, her lips shaped into a smile, and her eyes lit up.

If I walked across the field right now and kissed her, would she push me back, or would she deepen the kiss? I'd been asking myself this question a lot lately.

I shook my head, pushing the thoughts away. Why was I even thinking about kissing Melinda Shepard when I had to be fully immersed in tonight's game and this pep rally?

Trying to get back into the zone, I loosened my shoulders and breathed in, stretching my neck on both sides to infuse my body with a hint of moxie. My head had to be one hundred percent in the game. Bit by bit, the tension in my upper back evaporated.

"You getting your groove back?" My brother watched me with bunched eyebrows, studying my face.

"Yes. We'll annihilate Cowley High tonight. They stand no chance against us. It's gonna be our plays, our field, our game, our victory."

"Yes. That's the Mason Pierce this team needs."

With one last roll of my shoulders, I removed the left-over knots tightening my upper body.

Melinda nodded at me. My confidence returned—tenfold. Craig was right. I could do this.

Tipping my chin up, I firmed my back, looked straight ahead, and waited for my cue.

You okay? Melinda mouthed.

I offered a quick nod this time.

Chase elbowed me in the ribs, and I brought my attention to him. "What?"

He motioned forward with his chin. "Coach called your name. Twice. Go."

"Oh." Of their own volition, my eyes sought Melinda once again.

She pointed to the microphone with a finger where Coach was waiting for me.

With a blink of my eyes, I emerged from my Melinda-induced state and jogged forward. The commotion surrounding us intensified. People chanted my name. The energy in the bleachers and on the field turned electric. My teammates clapped my shoulder, telling me "You've got this" as I passed them. Before I could stop it, I slipped back into my cocky jock persona like it was a second skin, the one my classmates expected, loved, and respected—my very own shield. After all, football was my life, and if they wanted to admire me for my talent on the field, then let them. But for the first time, I also wanted this victory not only for me or my team, but also for Melinda. I wanted her to see me as a champion, as a successful someone. I caught her gaze for a millisecond, and in that instant, I felt more like myself than I'd ever felt in front of a crowd. With fire in my eyes and confidence flowing through my veins, I raised one arm above my head. "Elk River High, are you ready to win tonight?" The sound of clapping and cheers rose to a crescendo around me. "I said, are you ready to win tonight?"

Students jumped to their feet and hollered, whistling and chanting my name like I was some sort of God—their God. "Pierce. Pierce. Pierce."

"That's what I'm talking about. As the starting quarterback, I'll do whatever it takes to make tonight's game one to remember. You have my word. I didn't become your beloved QB and captain for no reason. Am I right? Come on, guys, I'm Mason Pierce. *The Mason Pierce.* Losing isn't part of my vocabulary. Once again, I'll prove to you why I'm the best at my job—why the Bears are freaking war machines on that turf." My lips broke into a satisfied grin, but inside I hated myself for sounding so condescending.

From the corner of my eye, I risked a look at Melinda. She studied me, her lips pinched together, and I wondered if my sudden change of attitude from uncertain to cocksure was the reason. Or if she was trying to decide if my jock persona was genuine or not. Good luck with that, girl, because sometimes I had a hard time deciding. This role I played for the sake of the crowd had become natural to me. So much so that, on some occasions, I forgot to drop the act once away from school.

"Pierce. Pierce. Pierce."

Bella and Tory, two cheerleaders, came to stand on each side of me, shaking their pompoms above their heads. I winked at Bella, and her cheeks turned pink. *All for show*, I reminded myself. A low curse passed my lips. I hated the idea I wasn't strong enough to resist stepping into the asshole persona that wasn't wholly mine, to begin with, in front of all these people.

I returned my attention to the cheering crowd, my grin turning into a blinding smirk. I bet nobody could guess I wasn't at ease in front of the entire school, speaking like I was so full of myself and flirting with the cheerleaders, and yet, here I was, putting on a performance and letting the school spirit rule my actions. Feeling conflicted inside and remembering Melinda's eyes were on me, I dialed down the self-entitled act a bit, trying to end my speech on a humbler note. "Guys, let's play football tonight. Let's show Cowley High who the real winners are and why they should be scared of us. Not because we cheat to win, but because we play to win. Because we're the best. No, scratch that. We're legends. We are courageous and determined, and nothing will stop us. Our team gives their all every game, putting their whole heart into it. I'm telling you the Bears *will* play at State again this year because losing isn't an option. Not when I'm your captain. Not when our team is the one to beat. Go Bears."

The student body went wild. My lips curled up as I enjoyed the energy that zipped through the bleachers. School spirit at its best. I bet Principal Ross was jubilating inside.

As if summoned by the school cheer, he stepped next to me and retrieved the microphone from my grip. "Thank you, Mr. Pierce." He redirected his focus to the ruckus and moved his flat hand up and down in front of him. "Enough, people. Silence. Please. Behave." The sound of his voice barely made it through the brawl.

"Pierce. Pierce. Pierce." Students chanted my name louder, pumping their fists in the air.

"Students." Principal Ross tried to regain some sort of control. "Be quiet now or there will be detention if you don't calm down." The threat worked because everyone sat down, the hectic atmosphere dying down. "You all go back to class now. Don't forget, tomorrow is Homecoming. I expect you to follow the rules and be on your best behavior. Have fun. You're all dismissed."

When I searched for Melinda amongst the sea of retreating figures, she had vanished. A tiny part of me wondered if my speech was the reason.

Craig pulled at my arm, cutting short my train of thought. "Come on, let's get out of here. I'm starving. I need a snack."

I followed my teammates toward the school.

"What was that all about?" my brother asked.

"What?" Would my innocent act work?

"Mase. You froze. It has never happened before. What went down in that head of yours?"

I shrugged. "Nothing. Got lost in my mind for a minute. All good now."

"You sure? This sounds like a bullshit excuse to me."

I clapped his shoulder. "Told you earlier. All is fine."

Weaving through the other students, we made it back to our last class of the day.

———

The score was tied with thirteen seconds left on the clock. The ecstatic crowd, most people on their feet with their hands joined in prayer, was chanting our names. We had the home advantage tonight, a sea of navy blue and gold coloring the bleachers. I called the play, and my teammates dispersed and positioned themselves on the field. The tension was palpable and electric as Cowley High players lined up in front of my guys.

The hair stood on end on my arms, the undeniable sign the crowd's frenzy was getting to me. I took a deep breath in, slowly letting it go. With a rotation of my right shoulder, I loosened my joint, studying the field and picturing how the play would unfold in my mind. Visualization had become a valuable strength of mine. Like I could predict almost to the dot, each movement of my teammates as I put the ball into motion.

Jayden Clarke's eyes searched mine, and he mouthed what I assumed to be threats. As usual, the guy was out for my blood. Our rivalry had started in grade nine when we both attended football camp and I disagreed with his intimidating tactics and called him out in front of everybody. He'd been hating my guts since.

With another full breath in, I blocked all the sounds around me and Clarke's murderous gaze. I hated that guy with a capital *H*. Jayden was a great player, one of the best, but we always butted heads on the field. Maybe our egos were to blame. We both knew we had what it took to make it big one day.

Only the harsh sounds of my breaths and the pounding of my heart were audible in my ears. Now in the zone, a bomb could explode mere feet from me, and I wouldn't react.

I adjusted my grip on the ball, stepped back, and spotted my brother streaking down the sideline, creating separation from his defender. My heart leaped in my chest. Deep down, I prayed Craig would be in sync with me as he usually was. With a quick pump fake to freeze the safety, I scanned the field once again, my tunnel vision latching onto my brother and blocking out everyone else. My palm and the pigskin became one, and with as much precision and timing as I could muster, I launched the perfect spiral that cut through the air toward the end zone.

The clock winded down for the final seconds.

I kept my eyes trained on the ball, holding my breath. Everyone in the bleachers seemed to do the same. Time slowed. This play was the last of the night, and whether or not it reached my brother, its landing would decide the fate of the game.

Craig extended his arms, not slowing down his run, stretching his body out as the football sailed through the air toward him with impeccable accuracy. My heart swelled in my chest. My brother secured the flying pigskin and cradled it to his chest as he crossed the goal line.

Touchdown.

The crowd erupted in a roar of cheers as the clock hit zero, signaling the end of the game.

Helmets flew in the air, and Chase jumped into my arms, his scream loud enough to deafen me. "We did it. We kicked Cowley Dickwad High's asses. Big time. Mase, have you seen their faces? Clarke. Copperman. Ritsy. Jesus, they look like their dog just died. I love seeing these losers eat dirt—our dirt." He returned to his feet, running around the field like a headless chicken, hugging everyone.

If I didn't know better, I'd think we just won State.

Once some of the madness died down, we lined up for the postgame handshakes, exchanging "Good game" praises with CH players.

When I faced Clarke, his hand strangled mine, and his eyes were weapons aimed at me.

"I think it's about time you get over it," I whispered with a wink, referencing the face-off we had a few years ago. "I'm the best. What can I say?"

He grunted something in response that sounded a lot like "You're fucking dead, Pierce. Watch out next time" before moving on.

David Copperman neared me, and he fixated me with a gaze I couldn't decode. Did he hear about my hooking up with Lydia, or was it about tonight's loss?

I straightened my back and upped my chin, projecting as much nonchalance and cockiness as I could. "Don't worry, Cop, your turn will come."

His hand didn't meet my proffered one. Instead, he spit at my feet. Perhaps I deserved his hatred. I cringed inside, schooling my features to let nothing show.

"Don't come near my girl ever again, Pierce, or my guys and I will rearrange your pretty face."

My humor died down, and I nodded. "I won't. You have my word."

He nodded back.

We were good—at least on this front.

Our fans filled the field, with girlfriends, supporters, and family circling us. Hugs, kisses, and congratulations surrounded me, but I felt like a spectator in the whole scene. I perused the space around me and noticed Paige and a group of girls fawning over Craig, Rusty, and Sheldon, but no trace of Melinda. Tanya and the cheer squad hugged me, but I barely registered a word they said. I forced a smile on my lips, pretending I'd heard their praises.

When I cocked my head to the side, I spotted her, walking away, her back to me as she climbed up the steps toward the parking lot. No congratulations, no winning hug, no eye rolls. She ignored me and chose to leave.

Even though it might not have been personal, it still felt as if someone had stabbed my heart and left it to bleed.

CHAPTER 16
ARE YOU BEING STUPID ON PURPOSE?

"I know what you said, and I heard you, but could you maybe reconsider Homecoming tonight?" Craig asked, standing in the doorway of my bedroom, wearing a black suit with a crisp white shirt and holding a violet corsage in a small box.

"Who knew you could clean up nice?"

He shook his head, not engaging with me.

"No. Not going. Sorry, brother. I've already made that clear." I stretched on my bed, pressing my back against the headboard, and grabbed the remote on my nightstand. "I have a very important date with the last superhero movie." I gestured for him to move aside with my hand. "If you'll excuse me, you're in the way. Have a nice night, wrap it up, and don't do anything I wouldn't do."

"Wow, Mase. If these are the tips you give Chase when he goes out, no wonder he's turned into a man whore. Gosh, I'm lucky I'm the older brother between the two of us and that Mom and Dad never gave us a younger sibling. You would be a terrible role model."

"Nah, I'm not buying this. Deep down, you wish I was the oldest so I could teach you how to walk on the other side of the line because we both know that's where the fun is."

"Whatever. So…about Homecoming…?" His phone rang, and he looked like he was expecting it. "Hey. Yes, I asked him." Pause. "Nah. He prefers to watch guys in tights fighting on TV instead." Pause. "I know. You gotta be the one asking him." Pause. "Yeah, I know he'll listen to you better. You're probably right about him. Gimme a sec." Craig handed me his phone.

"Hey, babe. What's going on?" I asked when Paige's voice greeted me on the other end of the line.

"Mase, before you hang up, please listen to me. I need your help… Huh, no. Mel needs your help. It's kinda an emergency."

The mention of my next-door neighbor was enough to trigger the curious side of me. "What about Mel?"

"Landon's dad busted him with weed."

"What?" I pulled myself upright on the bed.

"He's banned from going to the dance and grounded for a month. He's not allowed to use his phone, and his car keys have been confiscated."

"Fuck. How do you know?"

"His sister. She called Madeline who told me because we're in the same Biology class."

"What does it have to do with me?"

"Mel must be all ready by now, waiting for him to show up. Imagine her face when she realizes he's not coming."

"Paige…" If I jumped at the chance to go with her, my brother and she would know about my secret crush. I wasn't ready to be on the hotspot. Not before Melinda and I agreed on what we were to each other—or before we even had the chance to really become friends.

"Craig is coming to my place to pick me up. We were all supposed to meet here, the four of us, and take pictures. I gotta be at school early since I'm part of the home-coming committee."

"And you want me to—?" I wanted her to spill it out so it wouldn't sound like I was the one who'd come up with the idea, but rather that she had coerced me into going.

"Damn, Mase. Are you being stupid for the sake of it? You dress up nice, you store that ego of yours for a few hours, and you go next door, ring my best friend's doorbell, and you ask her to the dance. I can't believe I have to break it down for you."

"Does Mel know about this plan of yours?"

"Not yet. I had to run it by you first. She's not even aware Landon isn't coming. I won't crush her spirits without having a backup plan to make up for his no-show. Jesus. Keep up, please. Do you trust me?"

"You know I do. Why me? Why should I agree to this little scheme of yours?"

"Because. You owe me. I'm always there for you when you need me. And I let you call me *babe* and sip my coffee in the morning. See? I'm a good sport, and you would do me a favor if you agreed."

"I'm kidding, *babe*. You know I can't refuse you anything. And Mel is my friend too. I wouldn't let her be humiliated by Landon. Stupid basketball player."

"So?"

It was like the stars had aligned themselves and heard my prayers. Melinda and I going to Homecoming together. My arm itched. I wanted to pump my fist, but I could feel my brother's eyes on me, so I nodded, acting nonchalant.

"Okay. Fine." I sighed for good measure. "You win. I'll go."

"You will?" I had to pull the phone away from my ear at the sound of Paige's high-pitched shrill to avoid going deaf.

"Yep. Didn't you hear me just now?"

"Yes, but I wanted to make sure you meant it. Okay, here's the plan." For the next five minutes, she told me how we should proceed. "Are you in?"

"She won't be aware I'll be the guy picking her up?"

"Nope. I'll tell her I've found someone, but I won't tell her who. It's gonna be a surprise. Then you'll both meet Craig and me here. I'll call Malory, the president of the homecoming committee, and tell her something has come up and I'll be late. It will all work out."

Excitement bubbled inside me.

Perhaps tonight would prove to Melinda we could be more than friends. I crossed my fingers, hoping Paige's plan would unfold perfectly.

"Oh, just one question before we do this. Mase, are you seeing, sleeping, kissing, or doing whatever with anyone these days?"

"Why?"

"Because the last thing I want is for my best friend to get caught in the crossfire of some of your possessive fuck friends."

A weird sensation tickled the back of my throat. I hated the idea people—mostly Melinda—still saw me as a player and nothing more. I thought keeping it in my pants in the last month had proven to my classmates I'd changed. Perhaps, it was still not a given.

"I am not. I haven't been with anyone since school started. I swear. So, no worries."

"Awesome. See you later then." She hung up before I could say another word.

Craig grabbed his phone and bumped my fist. "Thanks, man. I knew you still possessed a heart underneath all that cockiness. I'll be at Paige's. Meet us there."

I nodded. His joke acted like a knife stabbing me. I knew he didn't mean it in a bad way, but still, it hurt the fragile ego I was trying so badly to hide from everyone else.

———

"Melinda, dear," Mr. Shepard called out from the foyer after he let me in. "Someone's here for you." He redirected his focus on me. "I thought my daughter was going to the dance with some basketball player named Landon?" He crossed his arms over his chest and eyed me with a tipped dark brow. Even though I was two inches taller than him, I felt like a child facing Mr. Shepard right now. Like he could smell from miles away any bullshit I was hiding.

I swallowed. Except for the day we met—which didn't really count—I had never come here to ask Melinda out. In fact, aside from that day, I'd never been interrogated by a girl's father until tonight, and it felt a bit intimidating. Sure, the Shepards were nice people, and I'd known them for years, but I bet they were also aware of some of my extracurricular activities. I hated the idea they could decide that my past actions defined me as a person.

"He…huh…Landon had a last-minute change of plan, and when Paige called to inform me, I decided to step in."

"Does my daughter know? About this little change of plan?"

"No, sir. Paige is supposed to have called her. She

wanted to be the one breaking the news to her about her date."

"Don't sir me, son. We've known each other long enough." He relaxed his stance and so did the muscles of my upper back. "I'm glad she's going with you then. I feel better knowing you're her date."

"Thanks, si—thanks."

"By the way, nice game yesterday. That last pass was perfection."

"Thanks. I'm happy you came." I rocked back and forth on my heels. "It was indeed a great game."

"You really are talented, son. And so is that brother of yours. Don't waste your gift by making stupid decisions."

"I hear you. I won't."

"Good."

I stepped forward when I heard heeled footsteps nearing us.

Mr. Shepard moved aside, revealing Melinda wearing a knee-length dress with a flowing cream skirt and gold sequined top. She had curled her dark hair in some complicated updo, a few loose waves framing her face. The sight of her stole every molecule of air from my lungs. She looked like a princess from my fantasies. I wanted to kiss her, tell her how beautiful she looked, but the words were locked in my throat. My lungs seized up. After a few seconds of shaky breaths, a single word passed my lips. "Wow."

A pink blush crept up her cheeks. "Mase?" The grin she aimed at me made me weak in the knees.

The temperature in the room soared. A prickling sensation spread on my skin, and a flock of butterflies invaded my stomach. We faced each other, our eyes scanning the length of the other, and I felt handsome under Melinda's slow perusal.

"Hey you," I greeted her, my smile no doubt reaching both ears. I raked my fingers through my about-to-be-tousled hair and scratched the back of my neck, not knowing what to do with my hands. Since when did I do nervous? I leaned in, erasing the gap between us, and pressed a soft kiss to her cheek. Her skin felt softer than usual under my lips. A wave of heat swirled in my lower body. My fingertips connected with the back of her hand, and a shiver worked the length of her spine.

She blinked as if I was an illusion. "I can't believe you're here. I thought you said you couldn't care less about the dance?"

I shrugged a shoulder. "Mel, I would have never let you go alone. I can be a gentleman when the situation calls for it. Don't forget I'm Nurse Pierce and it's in my job description to make sure you're okay. I take my profession very seriously when it comes to you."

A low snicker passed her lips. "Huh…thanks. For doing this for me. It means a lot. What would I do without Nurse Pierce, right?"

I mirrored her smile.

"Tell me, though. How did Paige talk you into this? Did she bribe you with cupcakes?"

Paige could get herself out of any situation using her red-velvet delicacies as a secret weapon. "Nah. No need when it's you." I winked and hoped it didn't look cocky, but more like we were in on a secret nobody else knew about.

"I'm very happy you're the one standing here right now."

Her words reverberated against the walls of my heart, sending a buzz throughout my bloodstream. "I'm very happy too." My grin probably looked too big for my face, but I didn't care. I really was happy to be here.

In that instant, I wished Melinda could look past my reputation with girls and see me for who I really was.

"Wow, you two look beautiful together," Mrs. Shepard said as she neared us, breaking the awe we were both basking in. "Move closer to each other. I want pictures of you two."

We both did as she asked, and standing behind Melinda with my arm wrapped around her waist, we smiled for too many photos. Melinda relaxed against me, and it was the best feeling in the entire world. Her touch felt oddly familiar and ignited flames inside me like nothing had ever done before. Done with the photo shoot, Mrs. Shepard handed Melinda her purse with a smile. "Have fun, you two."

Her husband extended a hand and stared at me while I pushed my palm into his. "Thank you for stepping in, son. Take care of our baby girl."

"*Dad.*" Melinda's cheek turned a darker shade of red.

She looked adorable, all flushed because of her dad's comment.

My lips widened into a blinding smile. "I will. It's my pleasure. Night, Mr. and Mrs. Shepard."

I took Melinda's hand in mine as if I'd done it multiple times in the past and ushered her to my car, parked in my driveway next door. "I've got strict instructions from Paige."

Melinda chuckled at the mention of her best friend, and I was pretty sure she could picture her giving me a step-by-step course of action for tonight.

"She and Craig are waiting for us to join them at her house. Ready?"

"Yes." Melinda watched me and blinked twice, still looking shocked by my sudden appearance on her doorstep.

I opened the passenger door for her to slide in. After I climbed behind the steering wheel and the engine roared to life, I switched on the warm air through the vents to chase away the night's chill. With an amused smile, Melinda's eyes flicked back to me, a million questions swirling in them.

"What?"

"It just… It feels surreal. You and me going to Homecoming together."

I grabbed her hand in mine and drew circles with my thumb on the back of hers. "Believe me, it's super real."

Silence stretched between us, and I released her hand.

"You okay?" I asked with a side-glance a few minutes later. "You haven't said a word since we left your house. Are you all right about going with me? I can drop you off if you prefer to go on your own and pick you up later. Nobody has to know."

"No. Please don't. I'm glad we're going together."

"Good."

"Can I tell you something?"

"Yeah."

She worried her lower lip. "If I'm being honest…I didn't really wanna go…with Landon." She scrunched up her nose. "I feel bad admitting it out loud."

"Why did you agree then?" My grip tightened around the steering wheel, my knuckles turning white, as I waited for her to explain.

She stared out the window. "Because… Nobody else had asked me… and…and the one person I hoped would didn't, so…"

I swallowed. If only she knew. "I'm sorry."

"Don't be. It's not your fault."

Yes, it is. I was the one supposed to ask you to Homecoming, and I chickened out.

Before I could explain and question her further, she spun in her seat and pressed a hand to my forearm, my muscles twitching under her touch. "I still can't believe we're doing this. You know how many girls will hate me tonight because I'm the one showing up there with you?"

I shook my head, her words acting like tiny blades shredding my heart. "Mel, I don't care about the other girls. I'm *your* date. No one else's. I wouldn't have changed my mind about going for anyone else."

"Who are you, and what have you done to Mason Pierce?" she asked.

I blinked to hide the hurt I was sure she could read on my face. My smirk returned, protecting me from being vulnerable. "Don't tell anyone, but at midnight, I'll go back to being the no-commitment guy you're used to. And I might transform into a pumpkin." Even though I said it as a joke, my words lacked their usual cockiness, and I wondered if she could tell I was not being myself—not entirely, at least. And once again, I hated myself for the idiocies leaving my mouth when I felt nervous around my neighbor. Why couldn't I be honest instead of hiding my uneasiness under quips?

"Maybe you could wait a little longer. I like this version of you right now."

My discomfort faded, and my happiness returned. "You do?"

"Yeah. Being down-to-earth suits you. Anyway, I always prefer it when you drop the cocksure attitude."

"For real?"

She nodded multiple times.

"Don't tell anyone else. Please. It's not good for my rep."

Melinda traced a cross over her heart with a finger. "I swear. Your secret is safe with me."

We exchanged a grin, and I relaxed in my seat.

"Nice game yesterday."

"Thanks." I swept my lips with my tongue. Warmth filled me at the idea she saw me play one of the best games of my high school career. "You missed the celebrations afterward." I watched her from the corner of my eye.

"Yeah. Huh…I left right after you guys won."

"I looked for you, you know. That's what friends do."

"Oh." She fidgeted with the tennis bracelet around her wrist. "You did?"

"Yeah, I did." The air got charged around us, and my palms got sweaty. "What I'm trying to say is thank you for coming to the game. I'm glad you made it. We appreciate all the support we can get."

We? When I said it like this, it sounded so impersonal. Now she would think her presence meant the same thing as anyone else coming to see us play. Why was there always some defective part of me that took over when I felt uncomfortable?

I begged my brain to save the situation, but instead, I blurted, "I-I thought I would see you at the party afterward."

"The party? I barely ever go to those."

"Well… Paige came, so I assumed that… I don't know… You might show up too, or…"

"I-I didn't feel like going."

I weighed my words before I spoke them. "Is it because of what happened the last time… You know… Nate and his actions?"

Her face blanched, and I felt stupid for mentioning that night.

"Sorry… I didn't mean to…huh…bring that up."

I felt her palm slipping away from my forearm, so I flipped my hand around and intertwined our fingers before she severed the connection without looking away from the road in front of us. I breathed easier now that we were touching, our hands the only thread of connection between us.

We remained silent for a little while, but even our silence wasn't awkward. As if she couldn't take her eyes off me, Melinda turned in her seat to watch me, and I wondered how much longer I could pretend we were only friends when she stared at me with big eyes full of sparks. I felt myself melting under the intensity of her gaze. My Nathan comment seemed to have been forgotten because she smiled at me, the small action beelining straight to my heart and filling it with a fondness I didn't know I possessed before she came into my life. Feeling self-conscious, I let go of her, my hand landing on her thigh and squeezing the flesh underneath it, like it was a normal gesture for us.

Her breath caught in her lungs.

I realized what I had done and brought my hand back around the steering wheel. The heated imprint of her skin lingered on mine, and I missed the contact.

"Hey, Mase. I gotta tell you something…"

"What?"

"Please don't let that ego of yours take over, but I said something the other day, and I'm realizing now it's not entirely true. The thing is… I once said you look better in jeans, but the truth is you look very sharp in a suit."

I hit my chest with a fist. "Wow. Thanks. I didn't expect a compliment, and I'm glad the suit pleases you. I'll add 'looks sharp in a suit' to the list." The corner of my mouth lifted into a mischievous smile. "Just for the record, I've put this much effort into my appearance tonight for you and only you."

"Let me tell you, you absolutely nailed it. The secret-service-inspired look you're sporting is really hot."

"You think I'm hot?"

The temperature in the car felt warmer than it did seconds ago.

She mimicked my smile. "Don't flatter yourself. Most guys wearing suits look hot. That's the way it is, I guess. It's like men in uniforms. I still believe jeans should be your go-to fashion choice, though, but…"

"But dressed to impress, I affect you. Noted."

Paige opened the door wide the moment we stepped on her front porch. "Ohmygod, you two are beautiful," she said, grabbing Melinda's hand and pulling her inside.

A light flush colored Melinda's cheeks, and I wondered whether it was the cool night air, Paige's remark, or our earlier conversation that had put it there.

"Where are we going?" my date asked.

"Bedroom. I forgot my purse."

I joined Craig, who stood by the staircase, both of us wearing matching black suits.

Paige spun to face us and lifted a finger. "Guys, we'll be right back. And thanks, Mase, for doing this."

"Anything for you, babe."

———

Hiding my nervous, wrecked state under a bright smile had become second nature to me. Just like throwing a ball and flirting. This special set of skills wouldn't help me get a full ride to college, but maybe it could help me out tonight. I had no idea the last time so many knots had tied my stomach. So tight that my insides almost hurt.

Trying to look unaffected, I busied myself with the cuffs of my shirt as we waited for the girls to come back downstairs so we could go to Homecoming together, doing my best to avoid my brother's heavy gaze, which I could feel through every layer of clothing on my body.

"You okay?" my brother asked.

I rubbed the column of my throat, pulling at my bowtie, trying to ease the tension coiling there.

I swallowed. Hard. "Yeah. Sure."

"No offense, Mase, but you look like you're gonna pass out. Do you need to sit down?"

I shook my head. "Huh, what?" My brain relayed his words. "No. All fine."

He grimaced. "Tell it to your face."

"Ha. Ha. Very funny. Ever thought about going onstage for your first one-man show?"

"I know you'll be sitting in the first row, front and center, telling everyone we're related." He dropped his head and scratched the hair at the back of his neck. "What's going on between you and Mel? I didn't expect you to agree to accompany her tonight without us having to force your hand or beg. Anything you wanna talk about?"

I stuffed my hands into the pockets of my trousers and rubbed the sole of my shoe back and forth across the tiled floor. "Nah. Why?"

"Oh fuck." His fist flew to his mouth. "I can't believe I never saw it coming. For how long?"

I risked a glance at him. "I have no idea what you're talking about."

"How long?" Craig repeated, his gaze piercing.

"Way too long..." I paused, sucking in a full breath of oxygen. "Five years. Happy?"

He moved into my personal space, his face level with mine, forcing me to meet his gaze. "Five years? Are you kidding me right now?"

I shook my head, shrugging at the same time. Some of the knots around my stomach loosened. It felt good to be honest for once. Until seconds ago, nobody knew about my secret crush.

"Wow. I had doubts a while ago, but considering the number of girls you have"—he lowered his voice—"hooked up with in the last year, I thought you were over her."

"Nope, I wasn't. Just trying to." I avoided his eyes, still heavy on me. "Big difference."

"Did it work?"

My head snapped in his direction, and my lips thinned. I clenched my fists in my pockets. "What do you think?"

"Mase. You dug a hole for yourself. I can't wait to witness how you'll get out of this one."

We both remained silent for a full minute.

"Do you think she has feelings for you too? If she does, that's a whole new level of fucked up. Why would you ruin your chances..." He pinched the bridge of his nose. "Whoa. I'm both impressed and mad at you. Like I wanna slap you behind the head for being stupid and hug you and scream 'Finally.' So? Do you think this infatuation goes both ways?"

"How would I know? The last time I asked her to be my girlfriend, she ran away and never talked to me again."

"You were what? Eleven? Twelve?"

"And so?"

My brother rested his hand on my back, between the shoulder blades. "You two were kids. It means nothing now. You called dibs on her in front of everyone. It was her first day at a new school, and she was so shy. Girls hated her from the get-go because they were jealous of your pseudo-relationship with her and guys hit on her just to screw with you. Imagine how she must have felt? I would have run away and never spoken to you too if you had done that to me." He paused, closing in on me, and lowered his tone. "Do you love her?"

"Like a madman." A chuckle passed his lips, and I elbowed him in the ribs. "It's not even funny. What am I supposed to do? She probably thinks I'm a fuckboy or worse. She'll never trust me with her heart."

"Prove to her you're willing to change. Be who you really are, instead of a jackass. Make her see that she can count on you. And that you're over the bullshit you feed everyone else. If you're honest and show her the real you, I have no doubt she'll fall for you too…if she hasn't already."

"What do you mean?"

"I saw how she—"

The girls' voices reached us from the stairs, and Craig and I stepped away from each other.

"We'll talk about it later," he whispered. "Be on your best behavior tonight and earn some brownie points. That's the only piece of advice I can give you. Blow it up and you may never get a chance."

I bobbed my head, my attention fully on the girls making their way toward us. I held my breath at the sight of Melinda nearing me, a nervous smile playing on her lips. I reached for her hand and blanketed it with mine. There. In that moment, I felt whole and never wanted to let her go.

We said nothing as Paige's mom joined us with a camera and took a dozen shots of us before we left.

Inside, I was a bomb about to explode. There was no way I could spend my night with Melinda Shepard in my arms and not go crazy by the time I drove her home.

CHAPTER 17
I'M NOT A HEARTLESS JERK

"Wow, this is beautiful," my date told her best friend as we walked into the gym and took in the decor. Printed in gold letters on a navy-blue background, the Elk River High logo was surrounded by an arch made of different-sized balloons in the same shades—the colors of our varsity teams. A photo booth with accessories from mustaches on sticks to yellow and bright-pink vintage speech bubbles was set up in a corner. Giant, clear balls filled with golden fairy lights lined the space.

"Babe, you guys did good," I told Paige, who scanned the gym as if to make sure it looked the way it was supposed to. We fist-bumped, and her smile widened.

Beside me, Craig sighed and pulled his girl closer. He was so fun to rile up.

"C'mon," she told him, leading him further inside the gym. "Let's dance. We cannot ruin a good song." She watched us over her shoulder. "You guys coming?"

"Absolutely."

We watched them disappear into the crowd.

With a swirl of my arm, I offered Melinda a hand. Before she could glide her palm into mine, Tanya slid between us, forcing us apart. Anger rippled from her, and she pushed me back with all the strength of her petite size.

"What the hell, Mase. I asked you twice if you were coming to Homecoming and offered we go together, and each time you said you were not setting a foot in the gym tonight. Since when are you a stupid liar?"

She crossed her arms over her burgundy dress, pushing her tits up, not even being subtle about it.

I scratched my forehead. "Look, something came up."

"It's tradition for the homecoming king and queen to attend together. What will people say? You are making me look bad." She closed her eyes and inhaled. When she reopened them, determination flashed in her gaze. She fisted her hands at her sides, and I could tell she was about to deliver one of her poisonous spiels. "Drop this loser, and I'll tell my date we're over. No need to play hero to your brother's sloppy seconds." She clawed my sleeve with her long fingernails. "Come on, follow me. You're late, and they're gonna announce the winners soon."

Standing behind her, Melinda gasped.

Tanya pulled at my arm, but I didn't budge. "C'mon, Mase."

I jerked my arm away, and a growl passed her lips.

"Did it ever cross your mind I didn't agree to go with you because I didn't want to go *with* you?" I quirked one brow, waiting for that piece of information to register in her head.

There. Tanya's eyes rounded, and a curse left her mouth. Hurt filled her eyes. "You don't mean that."

"Yes. I do. In fact, I've been wanting to invite Mel all along."

Before I could anticipate her next movement, Tanya's tiny palm connected with my cheek, the sting radiating across the left side of my face.

"When did you become such a jerk, Mase?" Her high-pitched voice injured my eardrums.

The smirk I'd often used as a shield over the years tugged at my lips. "Never said I wasn't one." With an arm, I reached around her for Melinda's hand, who stood still behind the cheer captain. "Sorry about that," I told Melinda, winding an arm around her waist and erasing the gap between our bodies. "By the way, Tanya, call Mel a loser once more or insult her in any way or any form, and you'll see what I'm really made of. And also, don't ever hit me again. You've been warned." I turned to my date. "Let's go."

I ushered Melinda away, caging her body with mine, evading Tanya's blood-chilling shrill and dagger-throwing gaze. We stopped by the refreshment table.

"Mase, you sure you wanna do this…you know…if you prefer to be with her…huh…it's okay." Her voice quivered in hesitation, and she avoided looking at me.

I hated the resolve painting her features. My brother's words from earlier replayed in my head. *Prove to her you're willing to change. Be who you really are, instead of a jackass. Make her see that she can count on you. And that you're over the bullshit you feed everyone else. If you're honest and show her the real you, I have no doubt she'll fall for you too…if she hasn't already.*

Determined to prove to her I was sincere, I cupped her

face in both hands and tilted her head back, forcing her to meet my eyes. "Mel. If it weren't for you, I wouldn't be here tonight. I only agreed because it was you. I wouldn't have come for anyone else. Already told you. Don't let her jealousy and her insecurities get to you."

Her bottom lip trembled, and I hoped she understood everything I was saying and all that I wasn't. Her turquoise irises stayed glued to mine as if asking a bunch of silent questions. "But—"

"No but, Mel. I don't care about Tanya or anyone else. I swear. And I meant what I told her. Every word."

"Oh."

Like a magnet, my gaze fixed on her plump glossy-pink lips, parted in surprise. The ones I wished I could kiss right now. Too soon. Baby steps. I had to be sure Melinda was seeing me for who I was before I attempted sweeping her off her feet or else I risked scaring her the same way I did when we were middle-schoolers. I had learned my lesson back then, and I was determined not to make the same mistake twice.

"You know what? If we're doing this, we're doing it right."

"W-what do you mean?" Her voice sounded so small I could barely hear it over the music.

"Let's dance." I steered her toward the center of the gym, never releasing her hand. The feel of her skin against mine was powerful enough to inject me with calm, and I hoped everyone would understand Melinda Shepard was mine and not to be messed with. It was a bit possessive of me, but I couldn't care less. For once in my high school life, I would stake a claim, and so be it. The only difference between now and five years ago was that I wouldn't call dibs on her with my words and put her on the spot. This time, I would let my actions speak for themselves.

"Hey, Mase. You came?" someone asked.

"The king is back," someone else shouted.

"Can I have a dance?" a girl whose name I couldn't recall asked, her fingers tracing the length of my arm as we passed her.

"Nope." Leaning closer, I spoke into Melinda's ear. "Ignore them."

Ribbons of balloons marked the perimeter of the makeshift dance floor. A live band, the lead singer being a girl in my Calculus class, played on a stage against the far wall. Melinda and I positioned ourselves front and center.

"Mason Pierce, I didn't know you could dance," she remarked when my arms closed in on each side of her waist.

"Just with you."

"Is this the line you feed every girl?"

I despised the hidden message her words carried. "I never feed lines. I only speak the truth."

"Oh."

"If you haven't caught up with the fact yet, it's true. I don't have time to play games."

Standing closer to each other than we'd ever been before, except the night I'd saved her life, we exchanged smiles and swayed to the rhythm of the music.

A slow country song started playing, and I stepped forward, killing the remaining distance between us. Our chests collided, and the beat of Melinda's heart synced with mine. The side of my face grazed hers, and I relished the shivers traveling down her body.

All my cells reacted to her presence.

At the friction, a whimper rumbled low in her chest, and my body got electrified.

I had no idea what I was doing. Heat washed through me.

Melinda looped her arms around my neck, keeping me close.

Her orange blossom scent enveloped me.

The softness of her skin against mine was all I could feel.

Curtis Burns sang about love and second chances, about forgiveness and happily-ever-after.

Leaning forward, I dropped a chaste kiss on her cheek.

"Mase… what are you—"

Before she could finish her sentence, and fearing she would tell me to stop, I pulled her tighter against me so she had no choice but to bury her face in my chest. "Shhh, let's enjoy now."

My mind, my body, my heart, they all hated me in that instant. I shut the voices in my head telling me to jump headfirst and leave my fears behind.

The *what-ifs* prevented me from acting on what my entire being desired.

Instead, I burned to my memory every second of us. This would have to do for now.

Melinda's hands moved to my chest, and she fisted my shirt as if she was afraid I would vanish.

Pride bubbled inside me. Perhaps I could be the one she needed after all, and my fears were silly.

For the rest of the night, we danced, chatted with our friends, made silly poses in the photo booth, and enjoyed ourselves.

We returned to the dance floor for the last song of the night.

"Mase, I'm having a great time tonight. Thanks for coming with me."

"Thanks for agreeing to go with me." I kissed the top of her head when she nestled herself in my arms like she belonged there.

For the first time after ages of chaos, I felt at peace. I enjoyed the sensation of our bodies touching, of our breaths mixing. My heart pounded in my chest, and I had no idea how to tell the girl in my arms I was so terribly gone for her. If she felt the hard part of me pushing against her stomach, she made no move to distance herself. There were things I could conceal, like my feelings, and some I couldn't, like how my body reacted to her closeness.

———

"Can you tell me why we're doing this again?" Melinda asked from the other side of the door as I tried the shirt on and adjusted it in front of the mirror. Since we had gone to Homecoming together three weeks ago, we'd been spending more time with each other. Alone. I had a play-book full of excuses to knock on her door every chance I got. Math tutoring, figuring out a recipe, her wi-fi password because mine would act up—not really, but she didn't know I had unplugged the router before coming over—a laundry disaster, her opinion about anything even when it didn't really matter. I often went to see a movie by myself so I could catch sight of her on the nights she worked at the theater. That was how lame I had become. And still, I had no regrets because it meant I saw her more frequently.

"Because you can't resist spending a day with me, duh."

I imagined her rolling her eyes, the gesture typical of her when we were together.

I exited the dressing room and fastened the last button. Melinda was sitting in a plush chair, dressed in a pair of jeans and a pink-taupe knitted cardigan, surrounded by mannequins wearing colorful suits.

I adjusted the cuffs in front of the mirror and pointed

to my phone in her grip with my chin. "Have you found the picture I told you about in there? I swear, Rusty really dressed like that to go on a date. It was epic. I can't believe the girl thought he was being cute."

I spun around to look at her, and our eyes locked. A weird expression shadowed her face. She discarded my phone on the seat next to her like it had burned her hands and brought her focus back to me.

"I can understand why she said that. He really went out of his way to impress her. Seriously, it's not every day that your date dresses up like the main character of the most romantic movie ever made, which happened to be *her* favorite movie too. I can see the appeal." Her gaze returned to my discarded phone for a split second, and she winced before staring back at me. "Yes, he looked ridiculous," she continued. "But hey, if he landed a second date, then maybe it was all worth it, no?"

"Maybe. Anyway, back to what matters. We're friends and I need a new shirt for tonight and I don't know which one to get. Therefore, I need a girl's opinion...aka...yours. Spending the day together is just a bonus."

"Ugh, you only befriended me so I would help you dress nice and score a hookup later?"

An uneasy sensation prickled my chest. I hated the fact Melinda still thought I was using her to sleep with another girl. I had invited her to come with me today under the pretense of shopping because I wanted us to spend a few hours together. I'd rung her doorbell earlier, begging for her help. Here we were, at the mall an hour later, as I tried on a bunch of shirts when, in reality, I needed none because my closet was already full of them.

I feared if I told her about my intentions, she'd freak out and refuse to play along. Like all the times I'd invited her to dinner or to watch a movie and she had turned me down, stating it sounded too much like a real date and it would be awkward.

So, this friendship was the only excuse for us to spend actual quality time alone outside of school.

"Come on, Mel, I'm not a heartless jerk. Gimme more credit than that. I wish you were not working tonight so we could go together." I shrugged, acting as nonchalant as possible. "This banquet is important to me, and we had fun at the dance a while back. All the guys will bring dates. And I'd prefer you were mine."

"Mase, don't say things you don't mean. You don't want me at your football thingy. Open the contacts on your phone. I'm sure there's a list of potential dates right there for you to choose from."

I whirled around to face her. "That's where you're wrong. I told you last week I wanted to invite *you*. It's more fun when you're there; otherwise, I have no one else to butt heads with, and things get old super fast. Paige will be there. I'm sure she too would love your company."

She fidgeted with the label of the shirt in her lap, the only one that had passed the test so far. "Sorry. I'm working until ten."

I slouched my shoulders. "I know…"

"I'm sure you can find someone else to accompany you. Mase, you're resourceful." She twisted her lips and looked away as she suggested it. Did the thought that I'd invited another girl weigh heavy in her stomach too?

"Nah. I'll go by myself. It's fine." I turned around to avoid her gaze. "Is red my color?" I asked, tugging at the shirt I was still wearing and doing my best to change the topic.

"Mase, all those fit you. I still think the navy blue looks the best. Bonus point because it matches the Bears' colors."

"Sold." I locked myself in the dressing room and

sighed, dragging my palms over my face. I was so out of my usual game with this girl, and I had no idea why. "Let me change," I said through the door, "then we'll grab a bite. My treat."

Her soft chuckle filled the silence. Despite myself, a smile curled my lips.

"Mase, we had breakfast like an hour ago."

I slipped off the shirt and put my T-shirt and hoodie back on. "What can I say? I'm hungry. I'm a growing boy, Mel. I need more calories."

"I'm just gonna have iced tea."

"Suit yourself, but you only ate a yogurt and some granola earlier. You must be starving by now. I'll order enough stuff so when you can't resist the intoxicating smell of Thai food and change your mind—I'll make sure you do—you'll be forced to eat from my plate."

I joined her, and we walked side by side to the register. I paid for the shirt and pulled at her hand, leading her toward the food court, knitting our fingers. She didn't remove her hand from mine, and the realization sent zings of happiness all through me.

My phone chimed with a text message. I eyed the screen and felt like throwing up. Four unread messages from three different numbers stared back at me, and none of them made me happy.

TANYA

Study time. Help a girl out, I need some real-life biology practice.

picture of her in red lacy underwear, her tits pushed-up

CLAIRE

Wanna spend the weekend at my place?
My parents are out of town, and we could
have some fun. I have booze.

GWEN

Haven't heard from you in a while.
Someone told me you needed a date
tonight. I'm available. We always have fun
together *winking emoji*

My gut told me Melinda had seen the first three messages earlier when I was trying on shirts. That was why she had insisted I invite someone else tonight. I locked my device like it contained some classified information I should avoid, shoved it into my pocket, and scratched the back of my head. Should I say something, or should I pretend I never saw those?

My armpits were sweating while the gears of my brain engaged. I had no idea what the right course of action in this situation was. I hated feeling like this. Like I was stuck in a dead end with no way out. If I said something, would Melinda believe me? If I stayed mute, would I look guilty of something I'd never agreed to? I received a bunch of messages like this every day, and I usually deleted them without a second thought. It had been happening since the day I became the starting quarterback when I started high school. Dirty texts and tit pictures, girls offering themselves for a booty call. None of them surprised me anymore. Once, I had even received a dick pic. No idea if it was a wrong number or a prank. I had dropped my phone on the kitchen counter then as if it was made of hot coal before picking it up and deleting the photo before my parents or my brother could peek at it.

"Are you okay?" Melinda asked as we entered the food court. "You look concerned."

"I-I…huh… After we eat, we should stop by the petting zoo in the town square," I offered. *Nice save, Mase.* "If you're up to it. They're here for the weekend only. I haven't been to one in ages. It could be fun to go together."

"For real?" Without releasing my hand, Melinda turned to face me.

"Yep. What do you say?"

"Yes. A thousand times yes. I love the goats and miniature horses." Her smile lit up her face. "I heard they even have a miniature pig this year. I've always wanted one. They're adorable."

The girl got excited about the smallest things. I had caught that about her in the short time we'd been hanging out together. This morning, I had checked my options after she agreed to run errands with me in case I needed a plan B for us after our shopping spree. When I saw there was a petting zoo in town, I deduced it would be a safe choice after I'd heard her speaking in a baby voice to an alley kitten the other day. And maybe, just maybe, the excitement about going there would make her forget I had girls sexting me minutes ago.

"I thought you would like it."

"Are you kidding? I already adore it. Thank you."

I squeezed her hand still snuggled in mine, hoping she could understand in the simple gesture what my words were unable to express out loud.

CHAPTER 18
SWIMMY. NEW WORD. IT FITS YOU

"Here you go, kids," Mrs. Shepard said, placing a plate with brownie squares on the desk and two glasses of orange juice. "How're the studies going?"

"By the end of this day, I should be the King of Algebra," I said.

Melinda elbowed me in the ribs. "Cocky much?" She raised a brow, and I chuckled.

"Just around you, Mel."

"I'll leave you to it. Keep up the good work, you two." Mrs. Shepard disappeared through the door, the sound of her footsteps echoing down the stairs.

"Your mom loves me," I said.

A loud sigh echoed in my ear. "Mase, you think everyone loves you."

"What? It's part of my charm. Moms love me. It's a fact. What can I say? I'm irresistible."

"You wish."

"C'mon, Mel, be honest here and now. Even you can't resist me. See? You're spending your Saturday tutoring me in math because you want me to succeed. You're not indifferent to my boyish charms. Stop lying to yourself."

"Ohmygod, your ego. Let's finish this because you promised me you'd spend the afternoon timing my laps at the pool."

"I'm almost done." I stretched to grab the plate and devoured two pieces of brownies.

"Geez, Mase. You're disgusting."

I chewed with an open mouth, and Melinda burst out in peals of laughter, hiding her face in her hands.

"See? Irresistible," I said once I washed the crumbs down with a sip of juice. "I thought I was the only one liking orange juice with dessert."

"Nope. Chocolate and orange are the best combination."

"Do you want some?"

"Nah. Not hungry. Thanks, though." She held out her hand. "Let me see what you've done so far while you finish the last few problems." She studied my homework. "Good. I think you understand it now."

The truth was that math had always been a favorite subject of mine. One I aced and needed no help with. Melinda and I had never been in the same math class, so she had no way of knowing that fact about me unless she pried it out of someone, which I knew she would not do.

Earlier, we had gone on an eight-mile run together. Melinda took that getting-back-in-shape challenge seriously. If it had been left to her, all we'd do these days would be running and lifting weights in addition to our regular training hours at school. I didn't want her to overdo it and hurt herself in the process, so I had offered to make a schedule, starting next week.

We worked side by side in comfortable silence for a little longer.

Melinda's bedroom resembled mine a lot. Posters of athletes we liked were pinned on the walls. Hers were Olympic swimmers, while mine were pro-football players, whose footsteps I aspired to follow someday. Her walls were painted in a cream shade. The decor consisted of matching pieces of white furniture in the form of a double bed, nightstand, and dresser. A golden velvet plush chair was positioned in one corner next to a shelf that had books along with trophies and medals she'd collected over the years. A rectangular bright-pink rug was spread between the bed and closet, the same hue as the throw folded on the dresser and the comforter.

I glanced at Melinda, admiring her profile while she scribbled in a notebook.

By now I could decipher every telltale sign of hers. When she was deep in thought, she'd bite the end of her pencil. When she questioned herself, a frown that I longed to erase with my finger creased her forehead. When she got bored, she twisted a strand of her hair around her middle finger.

"I'm only smarter because of the tutor," I said out of the blue.

Her gaze lingered on me for a long moment, her face unreadable. "When you put in the work, Mase, you do amazingly." Her praise beelined straight to my heart and blossomed there. All of me loved it when Melinda Shepard gave me a compliment. Even though I got accustomed to her eye rolls, and they kinda did something to me, I preferred her words of encouragement.

I finished the last two questions and passed the sheet over so she could check them out while I stuffed my books into my backpack, knowing I had nailed both problems. I jumped to my feet, ready to bolt, and pulled my black hoodie over my head, my jersey number gleaming in gold across the front. "Wanna get some food before we hit the pool?" I kicked my legs to remove the numbness that had taken over my lower limbs before squatting to put my sneakers on.

Melinda stood and grabbed the powder-blue cardigan she had discarded on her bed earlier, buttoning it up over her white T-shirt. "Is your stomach bottomless? You just had a snack."

"I'd like to think so." I shouldered her gym bag over mine and carried the empty dishes to the kitchen downstairs before we headed for my car parked next door.

On the way to the athletic building behind the school, we grabbed takeout and ate in the car—well, I inhaled two chicken burritos while Melinda only nibbled on a side of guacamole and chips because she said her muscles would cramp if she trained with a full stomach, which kinda made sense. Thirty minutes later, sitting by the pool, my feet dangling in the water, I timed her on my phone. Every one of her motions was precise and perfectly executed. I could see concentration taking over her features when she was in the zone, reminding me of myself on game day.

Melinda did a few warm-up laps before swimming three one-hundred-meter sets. She stopped in front of me on the last one, her hands clutching the pool edge between my open thighs, breathless. "How did I do?"

A whistle passed my lips. "Careful or Team USA will snatch you and train you for the next Olympics."

"You think? That would be like the ultimate dream."

"Definitive. Let's see how you did." I pretended to study my phone, feeling her sharp gaze locked on my face. "Okay, so… Fifty three point one seconds. Fifty three point seven seconds. Fifty two point six seconds."

She whipped off the goggles from her face and blinked at me. "You sure?"

I flipped the device so she could read the screen.

"Mase…" She blinked fast, drops of water hanging from her long eyelashes. "The last one is my best time ever. I've never swum the one-hundred-meter under fifty two point nine seconds."

Pride flashed in her eyes, and right now, I would have given anything to be able to claim her lips and kiss her senseless. The timing still wasn't right. Too soon. We weren't quite there in our friendship yet. I swallowed, trying to chase the discomfort spreading through my body. My blood felt like lava as it traveled through my veins. My heart pounded like I'd put it through intense exertion when in fact I'd been sitting by the poolside for the last twenty minutes. With my head tilted back, I stared at the high concrete ceiling, sucking air through my mouth to calm the tug-of-war playing inside me.

"You okay?" Her voice helped release the tension coiling me tight.

I cleared my throat. "Sure. I was thinking about some-thing." *You. Me. Kissing. More than kissing. Your body. My body. Those kinds of things really.*

"It must be serious."

"Why? It's no big deal."

"Tell it to your face. You look like you're in pain."

I blew out a long puff of air. "If I were, would you help me out? Cure me? Give me whatever I needed to get better?" I was playing with fire, but I couldn't seem to stop.

She tapped her chin with a finger, her arms now folded on the coping between my spread legs. Each time her elbow stabbed my thigh, I feared my dick would betray my poor self-control.

"It depends. Would you die if I didn't?"

I bobbed my head fast. "Oh yes. I would die a very slow and painful death. You know where you bleed out and no one is patching you up. That would be excruciating, I swear."

She enveloped one of my hands in hers. I was usually the one initiating physical contact between us. I relaxed a bit as her damp skin brushed mine. Everything inside me seemed to agree because it felt as if a big, sturdy knot had been loosened. Melinda flipped my hand over so my palm faced up and followed the lines there with a fingertip—a feather touch that felt like a lightning bolt shooting through my body. "Then I would never let you suffer, Mase. You have my word. If someday you're dying a slow death, I'll be the one patching you up, okay?"

I swallowed. Fuck. How could she say all the right things and appear to have no clue I was really dying here? My words weren't some metaphors. I was really desperate.

"Would you kiss it better?" The gruff sound of my voice surprised me, and I coughed to open my airways.

When she smiled at me, I got lost in the pool of her eyes. I swore she could do some black magic with these enticing abysses of hers. Yeah, it was easy to get lost in them. "Yes, I would."

Now there was a full list of body parts I wished she could kiss better. The thought of it alone was enough to make me lose my mind.

Her tongue traced her lower lip. Was it a reflex, or had she done it on purpose? Was I putting too much thought into her actions? My brain spun in my head, and I felt dizzy. Was the action involuntary or deliberately done to let me know she yearned to kiss me as much as I yearned to kiss her?

Never before had I had such a hard time reading a girl's nonverbal cues. It was usually simple. Lustful smiles, eyelash flutters, a bad case of flushed cheeks, and some eye-fucking.

Deciding to take matters into my own hands, I pushed back a wet strand of her hair that had escaped her cap with a shaky finger and leaned forward. I could already feel her lips on mine, the taste of her skin, the silky texture of her hair sliding through my digits. Anticipation erupted inside me. My body hardened in all the right places. There was no one else but us here. No one to interrupt us or to mess this up.

My lips tingled.

Melinda's eyes rounded. Lust banked low in them. I was sure they mirrored mine.

This was my chance. I was done standing on the sidelines. I wanted her. To hell with everything else.

The rest of the world faded around us. This was it. The moment I'd been waiting for. It had been a long time coming. Five years to be exact.

Before I could claim her mouth and my hands could roam over her body, she looked away and moved aside, lifting herself out of the pool. I didn't have time to understand what had just happened when she walked toward the end of the pool in nothing but her black one-piece swimsuit. My body still vibrated with desire. Melinda Shepard was playing with every one of my restraints, and I didn't even think she was doing it to screw with me. No one had ever kept me up on my toes like her. I was so out of my actual game when it involved her. It was both exciting and excruciating, as if my heart had been left raw and exposed, but she couldn't see it.

She hurried to the row of blocks, and I took in every inch of her dripping with chlorine water and the way her bathing suit molded to her curves. When I looked at her, minus the lust, I recognized the lean and powerful muscles of an athlete. The defined lines of her back peeked through the keyhole opening of her swimsuit. The cut showcased her long and muscular legs that I craved to have wrapped around me.

A new wave of tension stretched the crotch of my swim trunks.

With one hand, I covered the hard part of me, feeling more exposed than I'd ever had before. I had never really *dated* dated anybody. Sure, I'd hooked up with my share of girls, but I'd never actually liked one enough to commit to something more—to crave something real, a relationship.

My heart pounded faster against my ribs.

A relationship. I wondered if it was something I'd be any good at.

Melinda positioned herself at one end of the pool, stepping onto the starting block, and adjusted her goggles. "Ready?"

I gave her my full attention, happy to evade my own crippling thoughts, and nodded. "When you are." I used my most official voice. "Swimmers…huh…swimmer, take your mark."

She bent her knees and leaned forward, then plunged into the pool when I said "Go." I got entranced by her agility as she glided forward, her arms slicing through the water in rhythmic strokes.

She spun around just before reaching the other end of the pool, pushing off the white tiled wall with the strength of her legs. She propelled her body ahead, gaining momentum until her hands connected with the opposite wall. I glanced at my phone, noting the time. She repeated the same course of action three times before joining me. I showed her the numbers, and she grinned as if she'd won the Olympics. "I'm killing it today."

"Yes, you are." I lifted a hand, and her palm connected with mine. "Good job, Shepard."

"Thanks."

"Training with Coach Pierce can do that to you. Excel in everything." I winked, and she burst out laughing. "What?" I asked, pretending to be clueless.

"You. I don't think I've ever laughed as much as when you're being silly."

"Thanks. I'll accept the praises."

"I didn't expect anything else from you. The real question today is, Mase, are you ready for *your* initiation?"

I put my phone aside on a folded towel. Stretching my arms over my head, I cracked my neck and rolled my shoulders back trying to project confidence. "Yep. Give it to me." I had never swum laps other than when I'd hurt my left elbow last year, and it had been part of my physical therapy routine. And that one time as kids when we had raced as a dare.

After I put on a swim cap and adjusted my goggles, Melinda pulled me into the water. "You look very…huh… *swimmy*," she said with a snicker.

"*Swimmy?*"

"Yeah. *Swimmy*. New word. It fits you."

"It sounds bad. I hate it."

"You better get used to it. I usually only see you parade around on a field in tights and a helmet. Let's just say, goggles and a swim cap may not be your best look."

Before she could add another word, I had her in my arms, my palms molded to her hips. Her breathing hitched

—and so did mine. Even soaked in water, heat spread through me, and I was at risk of combusting. Lifting Melinda above my head, I tossed her into the deep end of the pool. The contagious sound of her laughter filled the empty swimming area. And my heart.

She swam toward me, using a hand to splash water at my face. "You cheated."

"Sorry, I couldn't resist. You were there, and it was just too tempting." She shook her head in a half-resigned, half-amused expression, and I broke into a chuckle. "You should see your face."

"What's wrong with my face?"

"Nothing. It's cute."

She raised a brow and scrunched up her nose. "Cute?"

My laughter increased. "Yep. Cute. I stand behind my word. Anyway, it's better than *swimmy*."

She reached me, and we faced each other. My hands returned to her hips, and I kept her at a safe distance.

The last remnants of her smile died on her face.

My humor decreased, and my pulse skyrocketed.

My gaze roamed over every one of her features as if to memorize them.

Melinda's lips parted, and I wondered if she, too, was thinking about kissing me this time.

A fat drop of water slid into her eye, and she blinked, breaking the spell.

Clearly, some invisible force had decided today was not a good day to kiss my neighbor.

My voice sounded rough when I regained its usage. "Okay, what do I do now?"

She leaned back and stared at me with an expression I'd never seen before. "Five…huh…you know…um… laps?" She coughed and cleared her throat. Guess I wasn't the only one bothered right now. "We'll start in the water. Best time wins. I'll give you a five-second head start."

I whacked my chest with my fist. "Nah. If we compete against each other, we're doing it fair and square. No privilege, no head start. I'm not scared of a little competition."

"Fine. Last time we did this, I won."

"Sure you did. I never saw it coming. You never disclosed that one piece of information, you know, the one where you should have told me you were a trained swimmer."

"Oops. In my defense, you had beaten me at basketball all day. I didn't wanna lose again. A girl has her pride."

"If I win this time, what's the prize?" I asked, waggling my eyebrows. We hadn't changed that much over the years. Our competition was still destined to end with some sort of bet.

"Prize?"

"Oh girl, you're adorable. You're as competitive as I am. Don't tell me you're not silently dreaming of beating my ass once again."

She giggled, the sound addictive. "Mase, you know I'll beat your ass. Don't assume otherwise. I'm the pool nerd between the two of us."

"So, what's the prize? For the winner..." I pretended to think. "A kiss?"

Melinda's eyes rounded in surprise. "Huh...Mase... No... Is that what you want?"

I shrugged, trying to look unaffected. "I was joking... but if it's what *you* want, I'm sure we could work it out." *I'm not joking. I've been dreaming of kissing you for years. Please, put a guy out of his misery. Subtlety isn't my strongest suit.*

"It sounds like we're back to being kids. When things were amazing and then became awkward between us within a few days."

"About that——" I said, not knowing how to broach the subject of the game of basketball that had changed everything for me.

"Let's not go there. It was a long time ago."

"I'm sorry. I was clueless back then. I shouldn't have been that upfront and then said those things at school the next Monday. It was wrong to claim you and put you on the hot spot and tell everyone not to talk to you because you were my friend only and that I would kick their asses if they even dared to look at you." I rubbed the back of my neck with my fingers, at a loss for words. "I wish I could go back in time and fix it. I hated it when I saw you crying, sitting all by yourself, because no one would talk to you, and you wouldn't talk to me. I'm glad you stepped up and made it right the next day. Even if it meant you pushed me away while doing so. Anyway, I should have said that I was sorry a long time ago."

"It's okay... We were kids. And for the record, I thought you were adorable back then. I shouldn't have run away that night after I won the race. It was wrong. I wanted to be your friend so bad, but I also didn't want all the attention on me. It was kinda too much, and it freaked me out. I had just moved into town, and everyone knew who I was before I had even stepped foot at school. For a long time, I wished things were different between us. I'm sorry too." She averted her eyes, and I sensed the air tensing around us.

Mentally, I slapped myself for making things uncomfortable between us. Here, I had a chance to make things right, and stupid me had offered a kiss as a prize. I needed to think fast—and fix the moment so we could go back to the camaraderie we'd been experiencing all day.

"What about a horror movie marathon? I'm not talking about one or two movies, I'm talking about an entire night. Three movies of my choice. I'll provide the snacks and the arms to hide when you scream in terror."

Melinda's attention darted back to me, the trip down memory lane seemingly forgotten for now. "You like getting spooked, or you want me to be?"

I smirked. "I hate horror movies. They always run upstairs when the bad guy is after them. Nobody likes jumping out of their skin when he catches them. I know I hate it. Also, the special effects are so bad most of the time."

Her eyes rounded, and she frowned. "Why would you subject yourself to a marathon then?"

"No idea. It seems like a good idea to face my fears and not be alone while doing so." *And because horror movies mean, at some point, we may comfort each other, and I will never turn down the chance to have you in my arms, no matter what brings you there.*

Melinda snickered. "Oh, I had no clue the great Mason Pierce could be spooked easily."

"I am not."

Her grin widened. "Mase, all your secrets are safe with me. Perhaps I should be the one providing the arms in case it gets too much and you have to hide your face, no?"

Yes, please. "Don't get ahead of yourself. I can be brave when I have to be."

"What if I win?"

"If you do, which seems impossible because, come on, as you just said, I'm Mason Pierce"—I winked, my tone teasing—"then you will…" I paused, thinking about it. Deep down, I was aware there was a great chance of her winning since our bet didn't require throwing a ball or running. I had to come up with another excuse where Melinda would have to rely on me. The gears of my brain worked.

Her face lit up. "Huh, I have an idea…"

"Name it."

Melinda stared at me, pinching her lips together. "Not sure you'll agree, though." She wrinkled her nose. "I'm not sure if I should even tell you…"

"Shepard, spill the beans."

She took a big inhale and spoke quickly. "If I win, you-come-to-Winter-Formal-with-me. We had fun at Homecoming, and I wanna avoid a repeat of last time with a guy who'll ditch me like Landon. After all, it's one of my last high school traditions before going to college, and it should count for something."

"Whoa, you want us to go to Winter Formal together?" As much as the idea surprised me, it also excited me. If we went together to Homecoming and Winter Formal, perhaps we could score a hat trick and add prom to the mix at the end of the school year.

Alarm flashed on her face, and she flicked her wrist. "Forget it. It was a bad idea. I'm sure you're already planning on going with someone else."

I lifted my hands in surrender. "No. I accept. Your proposition. The bet is on. If you win, we're going together. If I win, we watch those movies." In my head, I was doing a victory dance, a fist bump, and bouncing around like a kid on Christmas morning. If I won, how could I convince her we should go to the dance together, no matter what? Right now, I wanted to both lose and win. It had never happened to me before. I was a winner. Always had been. But Winter Formal was two months away. Winning would mean spending time together sooner. My brain overworked. How did this dare turn into an impossible choice?

"Wanna shake on it?" Melinda asked, pulling me out of my thoughts.

"Yep." Our palms connected, and tingles jumped from

hers to mine. Shivers lined my spine at the contact. I yanked my hand away before she could tell I was affected or my dick, now hard as a steel pole, embarrassed me. "Ready to be crushed?"

Melinda tapped my arm. "Prepare yourself to lose, Pierce. I know you're not used to it, but this is my pool, my sport, and my winning stroke."

———

Later, we sat at The White Lotus, eating lemongrass chicken and sautéed vegetables with jasmine rice. Melinda had not only annihilated my ass when we had competed earlier, but she had done it by at least eight seconds— which was enormous in swimming time. For the first two laps, I had the advantage, but soon my lack of technique cost me the victory when she passed me like I was swimming backward and she was riding a jet ski.

In all fairness, she deserved the win. I couldn't be prouder to have my girl making me bite the dust. *My girl.* It was a dangerous thought—a recurring one—that I had more and more difficulty chasing away when I thought about Melinda Shepard these days.

After our little competition, we'd spent an hour in the weight room at her request. It was part of my *I'll help you get back in shape* promise. We ended up doing a push-up competition, which I dominated, and a handstand competition, which she won without blinking.

"You know what?" I asked her after I polished off my food like I'd been starving for days.

Melinda had barely touched hers, playing around with her rice, grumbling about a stomachache which brought back Nurse Pierce, who had inquired about her well-being and made sure it was nothing to worry about or the result of too much exercise.

"I still would have accompanied you to Winter Formal even if I had won."

"You would have?"

"Yes."

She watched me, her elbows propped up on the table, a soft expression spread across her face. "It's funny because if you wanna face your fears and do a horror movie marathon, I'm your girl. I'm not easily spooked by rotten zombies, bloodthirsty vampires, or chainsaw-wielding sociopaths." *My girl.* Again, those two words. Heat swirled through me. Could she tell I'd combust soon or kiss the shit out of her if she didn't stop staring at me like this? Like I was hers.

I discarded my napkin, crossing my arms. "You think you won't get scared?"

She forked a tiny piece of chicken into her mouth. "I know I won't. I may not look the part, but I pack some courage underneath my skin."

"We should do some sort of trial. See if you can eat your popcorn and not scream when you can't take it anymore because blood has splattered everywhere the moment the bad guy catches his victims."

Melinda studied me for a second. "You think I will run and hide?"

I shrugged. "No idea. There's just one way to find out."

"Oh geez, you serious?"

"Mel, I never do anything half-assed."

"But *I* won the bet. I need something in exchange if we do this."

"Oh, I love a girl who holds up her own and knows how to bargain." I paused, reflecting on it for a minute. "If you watch the movie with me, I'll do any dare you throw at me. I'm a team player, and I lost, so it would only be fair that you get to decide my fate."

Melinda's face flushed, and she shook her head, a hand cupping her mouth, laughing. "Are you always so dramatic?"

"Can't help it. It's part of my charm. But I lost, so I'm all yours." *And not just for a few hours. For as long as you'll have me. Can you put me out of my misery now and kiss me?*

"We can brainstorm something together."

"Nope. A bet is a bet. I'll survive anything you put me through." I stood and offered my hand for her to grab. "Let's go. We have a movie to watch."

She slipped her palm into mine, and nothing had ever felt so right. "Then surprise me, Mase."

On Monday morning, Melinda rode with me to school. It took a bit of convincing over the weekend, but she had finally agreed. It turned out she hadn't lied when she said she could watch horror movies without blinking. She had proven I was the bigger coward of the two of us.

We ambled down the hallways together after she grabbed books from her locker.

"I'll walk you to your homeroom," I said.

"Mase, I can do this."

"I know. It makes me happy to do it."

"Oh, okay."

I draped an arm over her shoulders to make sure she did not run away when we crossed paths with a pissed-off Tanya, who murdered me with her brown irises framed by thick eyeliner and fake eyelashes.

"Wanna go to the weight room during lunch?" Melinda asked once we halted in front of her classroom. "I was thinking we could get ahead of that schedule of yours."

Hope swirled inside me. It was the first time Melinda offered to spend time with me on her own. I was usually the one scheming up excuses just to be with her.

"Sure, but we went for a run earlier, and you have swimming practice after school. Isn't it too much in one day?"

"Nah. I can take it."

I stared at her with one raised brow.

"I swear."

"Okay then. Coach wants to talk to me after the bell about Friday's game, but it shouldn't take more than five minutes. We can walk there together. Won't you be hungry? I know I will, but I have a free period after lunch, so I'll eat then."

"I've been snacking all morning. I'll do the same this afternoon. It's easier to go for smaller meals throughout the day than a big lunch when I have practice. It's part of the latest diet plan I've worked out with Coach Vivien. We're trying this new thing to see if it helps with my performances." She turned to walk away. "See you later, Mase. And thanks for doing this."

My name rolling on her tongue had never sounded better. She flashed me one last smile over her shoulder. Every part of me prayed the happiness shining on her face had everything to do with me.

My eyes were trained on her backside as she disappeared through the mass of students entering her homeroom. It was hard to explain, but ever since the surgery, there was something different about her. She looked frailer. More fragile. Perhaps it was all in my mind. The protective part of me, who had been scared she wouldn't make it that night, had been stuck in worry mode since.

I was being silly. She was fine. She had told me so herself. Her coach would intervene if it weren't the case, right?

With one last glance in the direction of her classroom, I walked away, silencing my thoughts.

I hit the row of lockers with the heel of my hand, the sound filling the empty hallway.

Something didn't sit well with me. I just wished I could tell what it was.

I shook my head to chase the feeling away.

Why was my life so confusing these days?

CHAPTER 19

DO YOU TRUST ME?

When we halted in front of my house, Melinda and I bent forward, our hands pressing on our folded knees, breathing hard. We had gone for a ten-mile run and raced the last mile. The sun was shining high for a late October morning, and I felt like tearing the fleece off my body. Even the breeze wasn't enough to cool me down right now.

Melinda guzzled the rest of the water from the bottle she had left on the front lawn earlier and pinched the fabric sticking to her abdomen away from her as if to air her upper body. "I think I gotta stretch now. Geez, I had to run twice as fast as I normally do not to lose track of you. How fast are you?"

"My long legs can be considered a superpower, Shepard."

She panted. "I-I...I won't argue with that statement."

"Glad we agree." I peeled off my shirt and used it to wipe the sweat from the back of my neck. When my gaze returned to Melinda, she stood there, a few feet from me, ogling my sweaty, bare chest. "See something you like?" The heat of her stare was enough to burn holes through my flesh.

She dropped her gaze to her feet. "Huh... It's not... I-I should go. I'll see you later." She looked flushed, and I relished the blush coloring her cheeks.

"Mel." I stepped closer and held her upper arms before she could flee the scene. "Look at me."

She stared down, pretending to adjust the hem of her shirt, not meeting my eyes.

"Mel. Look. At. Me." She lifted her eyes to mine in the slowest possible motion. She swallowed, and I followed the movement of her slender throat. I pulled her closer, my other hand landing on her hip. She felt thinner than usual beneath my palm. Our breaths mingled. Her chest pushed against mine, and I could feel the wild rhythm of her heart. Her lips parted, stealing every bit of my attention. Even if I tried, I couldn't look away. "There's something I've been thinking about doing for a very long time." I inhaled and gathered all my courage. "Do you trust me?"

I moved my hand to her chin, smoothing her lower lip with the pad of my thumb. She shivered against me. My heart jumped around in my chest. It seemed we were both reacting to each other's proximity.

"I do. I trust you, Mase."

I framed her face with a hand, leaning in.

"Oh, Mason, you're back. Hi, Melinda." Mom couldn't have chosen a worse time to interrupt us. "Can you come inside? Your father and Craig left, and I need the oversized pot from the shelf in the garage. I would really appreciate your help because I'm not tall enough to get it without a stepladder, and since my son is almost a giant compared to me, he can grab it without a hitch."

I sighed, not releasing Melinda. "Can it wait?"

"Not really. It will only take you a minute. You'll be back out here in no time."

"Mom."

"Mason."

"Fine." I let go of Melinda. "I'll pick you up at noon. We'll grab food and study for that test. Don't make other plans, okay?"

She nodded.

I tucked a strand of her hair behind her ear and kissed her forehead. "Good."

———

"What's up, people?" Chase said as he spun the empty chair around and sat with his arms folded over the backrest. "You don't mind, right?" He didn't let us speak a word before he picked fries from the basket in the middle of the table, the one I was adamant Melinda and I should share when we'd ordered.

"Why don't you go elsewhere to see if you're needed?" I asked, mouthing *Sorry* at Melinda as my best friend bit into my burger next.

"Nah. All good here. Mel, mind if I stick around and order some food? I'm kinda starving."

Before she could utter a word, he had stuffed our textbooks in her bag and placed it on the empty chair next to his.

Melinda snickered and pointed to the chair he already occupied. "Suit yourself."

"Don't indulge him," I told her. "We were studying here. Can't you read between the lines?" I then asked Chase.

"Enough schoolwork. You both will get those full rides to college next year. Don't stress over it. You're like royalties in your own sport." His humor faded. "Also…I kinda don't want to be alone." Chase and I exchanged words without speaking any. "You know how my old man is when he comes back from a work trip…"

Chase's dad was a motherfucker with a capital *M*. Every time Mr. Hillman returned from one of his business trips, he drank to oblivion and screamed profanities at my best friend before passing out on the couch in a drunken stupor. Once, his father had even thrown a beer bottle at Chase's head and laughed it off as if it was a joke. Since his dad was home only one weekend every month, Chase usually did his best to disappear during that time.

"You can stay, man. Don't worry. We won't kick you out." I chewed on a handful of fries. "I'll tell Mom you're staying over this weekend."

Chase nodded, glancing down. "Thanks, man. I appreciate it."

The server came to take his order, and when he left, my friend turned his chair around, resting his elbows on the wooden surface of the table, his chin braced on his fists, watching us.

Space Burger was the hangout spot for students after school. It was located in a small shopping plaza that also housed a coffee shop and a pizza place. During the summer months, there was a small outdoor stage where local bands performed every weekend. During school year, students from Elk River High often came here to study, fraternize, or grab food. Contrary to its name, it didn't have a space-themed decor. The tables were dark wood, the chairs an array of pastel colors, and the walls were whitewashed wood, with blackboards filled with motivational quotes and menus written in white chalk. Pool and foosball tables were set in the far corner by the hallway leading to the restrooms. They served a mean black bean patty and avocado burger, and their cheese fries were legendary in all of Michigan.

Melinda pushed her plate away like she was done. I intertwined our fingers under the table and rested our joined hands on her thigh. I risked a side-glance at her. She smiled at my best friend, who was biting into his food like there was no tomorrow and moaning in delight. She hadn't even eaten half of her Greek salad, the one thing I had convinced her to order after she stated she wasn't hungry because she had eaten before I picked her up. We'd been here for two hours, and I hoped she would change her mind by the time we were done. With all the training hours she put in a week, I rarely saw her eat more than a few bites each time we were together. I knew girls like Tanya and her friends counted all their calorie intake and checked their figure every ten minutes, but Melinda had never been that kind of girl. I'd seen her indulge in burgers and pizza plenty of times in the past. Maybe the anxiety was weighing on her these days. All the student-athletes around the country, hoping to be recruited by their dream college, were waiting for offers. I knew how stressful the process could be. I was one of the lucky ones who had already received a bunch of them. I just had to commit to one. I knew where I wanted to go, but my parents were adamant I took my time and thought it through.

Chase went on about a pro football player at the top of his game who had just announced his retirement after another knee injury, and I scooped a black olive from Melinda's plate and chewed on it, listening to him.

Melinda let go of my hand. "I'll be right back." She stood and walked toward the restrooms.

"You guys are spending your weekends together now?" my best friend asked, sipping his strawberry milkshake with a slurping sound. "Anything you're not telling me?"

"I'm helping her train so she can go back to her pre-surgery fitness level. She said she's behind her teammates, so we've been running and lifting weights during our free time. With the occasional yoga practice. Stuff like that. No big deal. We both had a free day today, so we decided to study together."

He glanced over his shoulder as if to verify Melinda wasn't back yet. "Don't train her too much or soon she'll break."

"She's on a new regimen her coach has put her on. Said it should help with her performances. I'm no swimmer and no nutritionist. I trust her coach to watch out for her."

"You're probably right. Remember when Coach ordered DeKosky to work with that lady last year? He shed eighty pounds and went from fat to fit within a few months."

I pushed a piece of fry into my mouth. "Mel's coach has her eating all through the day instead of regular meals. I've heard about that. Not sure I could survive on snacking, though."

"Fuck that. Me neither. I like food too much, and I'm always starving." He lifted his shirt to give me a glimpse of his toned abs. "These babies never complain."

I tossed a balled-up napkin at him. "Stop showing off, man. I'm not interested in your six-pack."

"You're more interested in a set of swimmer thighs and rubber ducks nowadays."

"Rubber ducks, really?"

Chase waggled his brows. "Oh, it's not what you guys are doing when you're together? Taking baths and playing with yellow rubbers?"

"Shut up, man. For once, shut it."

Melinda returned minutes later, resuming her seat next to me.

"Mel, I have a very important question for you," Chase said in a serious tone.

"Careful, man." I didn't want him to spin his yellow-rubber thing on my girl.

"Can I finish your plate? I'm a growing boy, and I'm always famished."

Her laughter vibrated across the room. "Super original. Mase is always feeding me the same line."

A mischievous smirk brightened my best friend's face. "I thought he was too busy feeding you other things?"

"Chase," I warned through gritted teeth at the same time Melinda said, "All yours."

"Man, don't be a pig." I watched him and shook my head.

"I'm sure Mel here loves it when you're being a pig. I'm just helping you out in case you lack some moves these days. The rumor is that you can't score anymore." He flashed me a smile and attacked Melinda's leftovers like he hadn't just inhaled a burger minutes ago.

"Chase," I warned.

"Just keeping you up with what people are saying about you, man. True best friends watch out for each other."

I shot him a pointed look and scooted on my seat until my arm brushed against Melinda's. "You good?"

She turned to look at me. "Yeah."

"You've barely eaten anything. You sure you don't want me to order you something else?"

"I had breakfast after our run this morning and a protein shake when I woke up. Already told you." With a finger, she combed away a curl of my hair that was covering my left eye.

Goose bumps blossomed over my back. I shut my eyelids and took a deep inhale, trying not to lose my self-control. We stayed like that, suspended in time for a minute. Chase kept talking, but we both had blocked him out.

"Mase, wanna stay here or go home and have a rematch?" Melinda asked before dropping her hand.

I popped my eyes open. "A rematch?" I cleared my throat. Why did my voice sound rough?

"I haven't dribbled a basketball in years. It could be fun to…I don't know…play again, you and me. Make up for lost time… What do you think?"

We stared at each other. Was I imagining things, or was Melinda trying to ditch my friend so we'd be alone, she and I?

"We're out of here," I told Chase, jumping to my feet and slinging both our bags over my shoulder. "I'll see you later, man. Don't go home. Your old man doesn't deserve your giving him that much power over you. Some of the guys are playing laser tag at three. You can have my spot. Be at my place at six for dinner and bring your stuff so you can spend the night."

"Thanks, Mase."

"Call me later. We can have a bonfire tonight. I'll let you know."

I grabbed Melinda's hand in mine. "Come on, let me prove to you I've still got it."

She nudged up against me, her warmth seeping through. "Mase. I would expect nothing less from you."

CHAPTER 20
I'M WAITING FOR A SIGN

"**M**ason Pierce, what are you waiting for? Why haven't you asked my best friend out by now?" Paige asked as I entered the kitchen a week later. She was busy baking something while my brother was doing his homework, sitting at the table.

"Hello to you too, babe," I told my brother's girlfriend, sneaking up behind her and dipping my finger into the chocolaty batter she was stirring with a whip.

She slapped my hand away. "You know the rules, Mase. No touching and no tasting before the final product is ready and served."

I made a show of licking and sucking on my digit.

Paige spun around and pushed me back with both

hands. "Gross." She folded her arms across her chest. "Answer the question. Now."

I mimicked her stance. "No. First, it doesn't concern you, and second, you're gonna babble everything I say to her. No thank you." I knew she wouldn't, but I liked to mess with her. Just like my brother, Paige was fun to rile up.

"I won't say a thing, I swear."

"Not even under girls' code or sleepover-hair-braiding confession or shit like that?"

She fake-zipped her lips with her thumb and forefinger.

I snorted. "What about nail-polish-and-facemask-night promises? Or naked-pillow-fight and truth-or-dare nights?"

"First, you're a pig. And second, those do not even exist."

"Are you *really* really sure?"

"Yes. Don't change the topic."

"It's just… I'm not okay knowing all my fantasies aren't real," I argued.

From his seat at the table, my brother chimed in. "FYI, I wish all of these existed too. All those stupid teen movies have been lying to us."

Paige shook her head with so much velocity it could have detached from her neck. "Not you too. Don't side with Mase on this one."

He lifted his hands in surrender. "All right, I'll stay out of it."

He and Paige exchanged smiles and stupid love-filled gazes, and I sighed. "You two, get a room. I'm serious, this is a kitchen, not a motel. Take your PDA somewhere else."

"Relax, we're not even touching." Craig met my eyes with a funny expression.

"In your case, I think it's even worse. I can feel your sappy love spiraling all around me. I don't need to get caught in your web of love tentacles."

Paige failed at hiding the curl of her lips. "Mase, stay away from poetry and focus on football instead. Better yet, you could become an author of Valentine's Day cards if one day you need to reorient your career."

"Everyone needs to stop meddling in my life and pushing me to reorient my future. Geez, are you all in on this?" I swept my gaze back and forth between my brother and his girlfriend.

Craig shook his head. "I swear I have no idea what it's all about."

"Me neither," Paige added.

"Something Mom said the other night. It doesn't matter anyway. The point of this conversation is to let you know you can bang in a bed upstairs instead of eye-fucking each other when I'm around. I'm younger than you guys. You should protect my innocence."

Paige snorted.

Craig made a gagging sound and returned to his schoolwork. "I'm done with this conversation."

Page watched him for a few seconds and then brought her attention back to me. "I'm your friend too, Mase. I can be impartial. You need to tell me what's going on between you and Mel."

"No. As I said, I don't."

"She's my best friend. I don't want you to mislead her."

"I am not. And I would never do. See? We're on the same team, you and I."

"Stop stalling. Be honest with me. The three of you, Craig included, always confide in me, and I keep it all to myself. Your secrets are safe with me."

I sighed. "Maybe." I failed at holding back the smile threatening to form on my lips. "Okay, fine." I pulled her under my arm. "You know I trust you… It's just…"

"Just what?"

"First, let me ask you a question." I raked my fingers through my hair. "Do you feel like there's something off with Mel lately?"

"Like what?"

"We are spending more time together these days, and I don't know… It's like a hunch. Hard to explain."

"I know she's stressed about college and stuff. Her surgery killed her spirits, and now she's obsessed with her training. She said she felt bloated for the longest time and that her body wouldn't cooperate when she swam. I think she's back to normal now. She finished first three times at her last meet. She's not behind at all. Sometimes, Mel needs to process things in her head, but it doesn't usually last long."

"Okay then. Anyway, I'm not asking her out because I'm not sure we're there yet. I don't want to screw it up with her. Some days, I'm convinced I'm not good enough to be with a girl like her."

"Mase, why do you think you would screw it up? And since when do you doubt yourself? It's out of character for you."

I shrugged. "I have my moments. Anyway, in the past few days, every time the mood was right and we almost kissed, we were interrupted. I believe in the universe and timing shit. Maybe our time isn't *now* now, so I'm holding back. I'm waiting for a sign."

"Oh…huh…okay."

"Why? Did she tell you something?"

"Nah. Just that you guys are friends and she likes spending time with you and she doesn't want to rush it either."

"Do you think she likes…huh…that she *likes* likes me?"

"I do. Give her some time, though. Like you said, maybe wait for a sign. She hasn't been with anyone before. It can be intimidating to date a guy like you, Mase."

"Why?" I offered her my cockiest smile. "Because I'm good-looking and I have special skills on the field?" Why was the cocksure side of my persona always making an appearance when I was crippled with doubts?

Paige tapped my chest. "Keep believing that. When you're ready to drop the smug act, let me know. We'll assess your dating history and start there."

Like I wanted Paige to throw my past hookups in my face. Hard pass. "Sure." I turned toward my brother. "What's for dinner?"

"No idea. Paige's parents invited us over. You'll have to be a grownup and make your own food. Mom and Dad are having drinks with friends and won't be home for a while."

Melinda and Chase were both working tonight, and I didn't feel like entertaining Sheldon or having any of the guys on the team over.

My phone pinged with a text just when I entered my bedroom after I left the lovebirds to their business downstairs.

JACKSON

Party. Johnny Wilson's. Eight pm. Bring your ass.

I had nothing better to do, so I texted him back.

ME

Count me in. Later

Johnny Wilson was a senior mostly known for his ragers and his stoned ways. The guy was high twenty-four-seven. The rumor mill even said he woke up in the middle of the night to smoke a blunt so the buzz would never fade.

It was a little over eight thirty when I turned into his street. There were so many cars that I had to park two blocks down his house. I had no idea how Johnny could throw these parties without any of his neighbors complaining. It was like his place was a frat house. His father was some sort of CEO for a medicinal pot company, and his mother was never around, traveling the globe for a foundation dedicated to African elephants or something like that. The house was a revolving door of people staying over and moving out soon after.

"*Masssssse*," Johnny said when I climbed the three steps leading to his front porch. We exchanged a handshake and a bro hug. "What's going on, superstar?"

Anyone else calling me that would usually receive one of my retorts, but for some reason, I didn't care when it came from him. Johnny Wilson was harmless and the kind of person nobody could ever get angry at.

"You know, the usual."

"In that case, enjoy. Come see me if you need a"—he made a smoking-a-joint gesture with his hand—"and I'll hook you up."

"You know I don't smoke that crap, man. No offense."

"None taken. By the way, I wouldn't have given it to you even if you had asked. No reason to spoil such talent."

"Thanks." I clapped his shoulder and made my way inside. The place was cramped. I couldn't take two steps forward without brushing elbows with other people.

"Pierce Junior, over here," Rusty screamed, waving an arm over his head. I spotted the sucker's face in the crowd and made my way to him.

A hand sporting red-manicured nails wrapped around my left biceps. "Mase, you made it."

Another girl walked up to me, kissing my jaw. "I thought you'd be a no-show tonight."

More girls joined us, and in that moment, I felt like my own clothes were too tight to house my body. I wanted to be far away from these people. I stepped back, bumping into a guy who complained I should watch where I was going, and lifted my hands before me. "Not in the mood, okay," I said to all five pairs of expectant eyes. I scratched the back of my neck, trying to grow some kind of bubble around me. As if they could read the situation, two of my teammates neared us and flanked me on each side, fending off two more girls walking toward me. "Thanks," I muttered. We reached Rusty and Sheldon, busy playing poker, and I grabbed a drink, slouching in the empty chair near the table. "Fuck. I forgot how Johnny's parties got. It's like every teenager in a fifty-mile radius has decided to show up tonight."

"There's a hockey game on TV, and the bets are high. Don't go into the basement unless you're ready to throw in two grand."

I choked on my drink. "Two grand? Where are those fuckers getting that kind of money to bet on a hockey game?"

Rusty shook his head. "You don't wanna know, man. I swear. Last month, a guy from Cowley High left this place ten grand richer."

"I'll bet on my football career instead. Seems like a surer way to get that kind of pocket change."

"Wanna play?" a guy I recognized from my biology class asked.

I usually partook in low-stakes poker games with my friends.

"Nah, thanks. Not feeling much of a gambler tonight. I'm good sitting this one out and watching."

Sarah, a girl who had been in all my classes last year, joined us. There was no seat left, so I offered her my lap.

She wasn't a clinger and never showed any interest in me, so I was safe. Her brother had played offensive for the team before graduating two years ago. He'd gotten recruited by Crestwood University, and Sarah started showing me footage of his last game on her phone.

"Okay, this is sick. These guys are war machines. I can't wait to play there next year."

"Are you going to CWU? Have you signed with them?"

I hadn't told anyone about the college offers I had received so far. This was only between Coach, my parents, and me. For now.

"Look who the cat has brought in," Sheldon said with a wolf whistle, saving me from answering. "Is it just me, or does she look hotter every day? Think she'd date a guy like me?"

"If I were you and if you value your balls, I wouldn't get too close. Pierce Junior will turn them into a stew if you touch what's his."

"Who?" I shifted in my seat, pretty sure they were referencing Tanya or even Lydia, only to catch sight of Melinda walking toward us, with my brother and Paige close behind arguing about something. My eyes zeroed in on my girl. Her brown hair was tied in a high ponytail, and she was wearing a simple black, V-neck cropped top and a pair of jeans that molded to her curves, nothing provocative or super short, and yet, she was the sexiest girl in here.

Our eyes locked, and her lips curled. And so did mine.

Her smile faded when she came face to face with me, her gaze traveling between Sarah, still perched on my thighs, and me. I released my grip around Sarah's waist and leaned back as if I'd done something bad.

Hurt flashed on Melinda's face. Her lips shaped into an *O* before she halted, blinked, and turned around, ready to bolt from here.

"What's wrong?" Paige asked her when she came to stand next to her friend. She scanned the space, and anger blazed in her eyes when they landed on me. "Mase, really?"

My heart sank as Melinda scurried away, Paige after her.

"Fuck." I pushed Sarah off me and rose from the chair in one swift motion. "Hey man," I told my brother when I passed him. "Save my seat. I'll be right back."

I reached Paige and stopped her with a hand on her shoulder. "Don't. Please. Let me do it."

She pivoted to face me. "What the fuck, Mase. We talked about it. Are you sabotaging your chances on purpose? Or is Sarah Beaufort your sign?"

"No." I shook my head, glancing at my feet and rubbing my hands on my jean-clad thighs. "She's not."

"Come on, you had your arms wrapped around her, and she was sitting on you. From where I stood, you both looked cozy together."

I grabbed the roots of my hair and pulled. "It's not like that. We were watching some football on her phone. Nothing else. Anyway, why am I even explaining myself to you? I gotta go. I'll fix this."

She rested her fists on her hips. "You better, Mason Pierce. Don't you dare break her heart."

I wasn't used to Paige being angry with me. She usually was pretty chilled even when I messed up. "I will." I weaved through the bodies filling the makeshift dance floor in the living room and landed in the kitchen. I perused my surroundings. No sign of Melinda. My heart leaped up in my throat. I had fucked it all up. Dammit. I turned around and headed for the den on the other side of the house.

I noticed her by the door, wiping her eyes. She looked over her shoulder like she could feel my presence.

I was about to follow in her footsteps when a very drunk Tanya appeared in front of me as I entered the living room, one hand cradling my face and the other fisting my T-shirt. "*Massse,* baby. I *misssed* you. I didn't *knooow* you would be here tonight. Why haven't you *callled?*"

From a distance, Melinda blinked and left the room, and once again, I lost her in the crowd.

I clamped Tanya's wrists and lowered her hands. "Not now, Tan. And not here."

Her bloodshot eyes rounded. "So later then? I've *misssed* you, Mase. I've *misssed* us. There's a free bedroom on the second floor we can use. Wanna *meeet* me there?"

"No. I already made myself clear. Many times. You gotta move on."

She pouted. "But I don't wanna *movvve* on. I want *youuu.* We're *goood* together."

"No." My tone was firmer this time. Her hands returned to my face, and I lowered them once again. "Tan, I gotta go. Find someone else."

Tears shone in her eyes, and she tugged at my shirt with one hand.

I closed my eyes for a second and breathed out. "Geez, why are you doing this? We're not together, and we won't ever be. I can't deal with you right now." I pushed forward, and at that point, she had to let go of me. I searched the space for Melinda, but she was nowhere to be seen. "Dammit," I screamed louder than I intended.

I crossed the room in a few strides, on a mission to find my girl. I spotted her as she cut in line and locked herself in the bathroom. "Sorry," I said as I elbowed my way through the partygoers. I knocked on the bathroom door. "Mel? It's me. Open the door."

No response.

I tried the knob, but it didn't budge.

"Mel? Can we talk? That thing with Sarah… It's not what it looked like. I swear. I-I wouldn't… I wouldn't do this to you. Can I come in? I would—" Someone bumped into me from behind, and my chest hit the door. "C'mon, man," I spoke through gritted teeth. "Get lost somewhere else." I tried the knob again. "Mel, let me in. Please. I don't know why I'm begging you… I did nothing wrong. Let's talk."

I held my breath at the sound of the door being unlocked.

My heart split in two when Melinda appeared on the other side, wiping mascara streaks down her cheeks with a piece of toilet paper. She raised a hand before I could say anything. "Not now, Mason. I don't feel like talking to you."

I raked my fingers through my hair. "Don't shut me out."

"Don't push my buttons. I'm not in the mood."

"Can we go somewhere else and talk?"

"Nope. Not going anywhere with you. Not now. I need some space." She cast a glance at her feet. "I thought we… I believed that… It doesn't matter what I… Never mind." She looked me in the eye and delivered two words that shattered my heart: "I'm leaving."

"I'll drive you home."

"No. You stay. Enjoy the party."

"I don't care about the party."

"Too bad. I don't wanna be around you right now, Mase."

"Well, I wanna be around you, so that cancels it out."

She folded her arms over her chest. "Not funny. Anyway, get out of my way."

She pushed past me, but I stopped her with an extended arm.

"Mase, let me go. I'm done here. Move."

I raised my hands in surrender. "Fine. We'll do as you say. This time."

"Don't…don't look so dejected. I was wrong thinking things would be different…"

As if summoned by the God of bad timing, Bella, one of the cheerleaders I had flirted with multiple times in the past, edged closer to us. "*Massse.*" My name sounded like a purr on her tongue. She traced the length of my biceps with a finger. "Wanna have some private fun away from here? I wanna see for myself if any of the rumors are true." She batted her eyelashes and flipped her long blonde hair over her shoulder. "What do you say?"

"Geez, not you too. I'm in the middle of something here, Bella. I won't go anywhere with you. If you seek company, find someone else because it won't be me."

"But, *Massse…* Why would you pass the opportunity to be with me? I broke things off with Matt. There's no one standing in our way anymore."

"I'm not inter—"

Melinda motioned to leave. "Night, Mason."

"Mel, wait."

"No, I'm done here. Don't follow me." Her voice shook. "Stay. Away." I had never seen her so pissed off before, and I had no idea if I should do as she said or do the opposite. Girls were hard to read sometimes, and I had no experience in this kind of situation.

Before I could make up my mind, Bella's hand wrapped around my arm. "Let her go. I can make you forget all about—"

"No." I scurried away, breathing hard through my mouth, trying my best to calm down. This wasn't the place to make a scene. "Tonight is a disaster," I muttered to no one but myself. I searched for Melinda for the next ten minutes, but she had already left because Sheldon told me he saw her climbing into Sandra Nolan's—one of our neighbors from down the street—car.

Get out of my way. Mase, let me go. I'm done here. Move.

Melinda's words played on a loop in my head, driving me crazy. A part of me yearned to go after her and demand to be heard. The other part of me thought I should give her some time to blow off some steam and realize our fight was silly because it was just a misunderstanding before facing her again.

My shoulders sagged in defeat. I couldn't decide which part of me I should listen to.

"Shots?" a guy on my left asked, balancing half a dozen shot glasses filled with cherry-colored liquor on a tray.

His offer felt to be a sign that I should allow Melinda some time to think before I went after her. "Why not?" I had already screwed up everything so far tonight, so it couldn't get worse. Anyway, I needed to kill the anxiety surging inside me with something or else I'd go crazy. Without hesitation, I grabbed two shots and gulped them down. "Thanks." And before I changed my mind, I took three more and downed them as fast. I wasn't used to drinking during football season, and the alcohol made its way to my brain in no time.

Getting wasted wasn't the solution to my problems, but right now it sounded like a great alternative to patch the hole in my heart. I had done nothing wrong, but Paige was right. From an outsider's point of view, sitting with Sarah nestled against me, our heads touching and my arm around her, must have looked bad. No wonder Melinda was upset with me.

I reached the kitchen and poured myself a hefty amount of whiskey from one of the bottles on the countertop and knocked it back in two swallows. I was more of a beer guy, but liquor seemed like a faster road to Waste Town right now.

"What are you doing?" Craig asked, removing the empty cup from my grip and discarding it on the kitchen island that was already trashed with beer cans, empty bottles, and crushed cups. "You never drink until the season is over. Don't start now."

"I-I *fuuucked* up." I blinked, my brain not in sync with my mouth and my thoughts. "Mel... I screwed it all up. She hates my *guttts* now. She left... She-she doesn't want any...anything to do with me tonight."

"Mase, don't."

I stabbed his chest with a finger. "I didn't *fuuuck* Sarah Beaufort. I didn't even *kisss* her. And I didn't want to. It was just...just football." I buried my face in my hands, tears prickling the back of my eyes. "We were...we were just watching ga-games. Her brother...he...he plays for Crestwood U. Mel thinks... She probably thinks I've been with her. And then Tan. She *stoppped* me when I was chasing after Mel. And then *Bellla*. She said th-things. It's...*dammmit*...it's complicated. Now, Mel will hate *meeee* forever. Pouf. Gone are my chances with her. She left. I-I... I don't remember *whaaat* I was saying just now. And I'm... I'm plastered. Shit. Why am I...?"

"Why are you what?"

A somber chuckle passed my lips. "*Nooo* idea, brother. I'm going... I'm going home *nowww*. Before I do something else *thaaat* I'll regret."

He shook his head, and I hated the expression he cast on me. Like I was a stupid asshole, someone he pitied. I couldn't tell. I hated pity.

I closed my eyes and massaged my temples with my fingers. "Out of here."

"I'll give you a ride. Let me tell Paige. I'll be back in a few. Don't go anywhere. Wait for me outside."

I did a military salute. "*Yesssir.*"

He opened his palm. "Keys."

I sighed and fished the set out of my pocket and handed it to him.

"Good. I'll join you in a bit."

After what felt like hours, my brother met me outside as I sat on the front porch steps and tossed me the letterman jacket that I had probably left by the poker table. My reflexes were off because I failed at catching it. "Come on. Paige and I will drive your car home later."

For the twelve minutes the ride lasted, we both remained silent. My heart sank down to my heels, and my hopes were long gone.

The car stopped in front of our house, and I climbed out. Before I slammed the door behind me, Craig's voice boomed in the dark, and I turned to face him. "Explain yourself, Mase. Tell her the truth. Mel is a smart girl. She'll listen."

"I tried. She *stilll* left."

"Give her some time. Whatever it is, I'm sure it can be mended."

I rubbed a fist over my prickling eyes. "You think?"

He nodded. "I do. Go to bed and sober up. Tomorrow, you go over there"—he pointed to the house next door with his chin—"and you fix the mess."

I stood in the driveway, watching his car pull away, the taillights retreating in the darkness enveloping me, when an idea hit me.

Yes, I could fix the Melinda situation. I had to or else I'd be miserable for the rest of time.

Rushing to my backyard to avoid triggering the motion-sensor light by the Shepards' driveway, I walked to the wooden fence separating both our properties. Maybe I could attempt to jump over it in my drunken state without breaking my spine—or maybe not. Anyway, Melinda Shepard was worth the risk.

I rolled my shoulders back and squinted, trying to gauge the height of the fence, because for the life of me, right now, I couldn't remember. I took a few steps back to gain momentum and ran forward, unconvinced I could jump over it.

Airborne, I flapped my arms and legs, realizing I should have just climbed the damn thing instead of trying to leap over it. I hit a wooden post with my left foot and tumbled forward, face-first.

Oh no. Please don't let me hit my right shoulder again.

CHAPTER 21

HELP A GUY OUT. PLEASE

Instead of landing on my two feet like I'd pictured myself doing—and like I should have done, thanks to my athletic abilities—I faceplanted on the lawn once I jumped over the wooden fence. Classy. Pushing my body up, I struggled to my feet, glad to see I was still in one piece. On shaky legs, I dusted myself off and rotated my right shoulder to check for any damage. I exhaled in relief and neared the side of Shepards' house on my tiptoes, praying I was as silent as I believed myself to be. The clouds parted, and under the light of the thin sliver of moon, I craned my neck back to guess the height of Melinda's bedroom window. It appeared much higher right now, thanks to my brain being unable to process much information clearly.

Holding on to the gutter, I climbed onto the roof of the small woodshed, shrugged off my jacket, and tossed it to the ground. I was burning hot, the cold air doing nothing to cool me down. My jacket was in the way, and I needed a full range of motion if I expected to make it to the second-floor window.

Slipping the tips of my shoes in the trellis lining the side of the house, I climbed the wall. Even with a half-functioning brain, I could tell this was a bad idea, but I was Mason Pierce, and I never did anything half-assed. I wasn't about to start now. My T-shirt got stuck on something, and I pulled the fabric to free it. Even the sound of tearing cotton didn't distract me from my mission. Melinda deserved an explanation, and I would give it to her. At the cost of my life…or at least, my shirt.

I continued my ascend. The trellis cracked under my weight, and I held my breath, imagining myself free falling, as it shattered underneath me, and breaking my neck when I landed on the ground. I peered down and blinked. Was I that high, or was my mind playing tricks on me? I could take a hit on the field and run thirty yards with guys three times my size after me, but this, opening my heart to a girl was a first for me. And climbing a wall that I wasn't sure I could trust to get to her room in the middle of the night was another first.

I secured my forearms on the windowsill, the tip of my left shoe wedged on the ledge a few feet away, and knocked on the glass panel. From where I was balanced, I couldn't see a thing on the other side. The curtains had been drawn, and no light shone through the opening.

Was Melinda even back home? Did Sandra drive her here after they left the party earlier, or did she drive her somewhere else?

I rested my forehead against the cool glass, not sure

how to climb down if she wasn't in her bedroom. Clouds blocked the moonbeams, and now I was here, under-dressed, in the dark, with no clue what to do. I tried to fish my phone out of my back pocket to call my brother. He would have a blast helping me off here. Hopefully, he could save my ass without Mr. Shepard noticing. If he did, I would forever be forbidden to near his daughter again. My night was going from awful to horrendous way too quickly for my liking. My device wasn't there. I cringed. I had placed it in my jacket pocket earlier.

I knocked on the window once more.

The glow of a night-light appeared through the gap in the curtains. I squinted, trying to spy through the slit, but couldn't see anything. "*Pleassse*, don't let it be Mr. Shepard. *Pleassse*, whoever is listening to *meee*, don't let it be Mr. Shepard on the other side."

I held my breath, a weird acidic taste coating my throat.

Time stilled as I stayed suspended on the side of the house. My muscles burned, and the grip of my shoes on the ledge below wasn't so strong anymore. My legs shook. Soon I would crash and shatter into fragments of bones.

Gathering every last piece of my ego, I tapped on the glass again.

I almost bawled my eyes out when Melinda's figure appeared on the other side of the glass. It took her a second to notice me. I offered her my best apologetic half-smile. Her hair was damp and loose on her shoulders, and she was wearing a tight pale-pink top that did nothing to conceal the outline of her nipples that grew harder the longer she stared at me. Because I had no fuck left to give tonight, I trailed my eyes down her toned legs, only covered by a tiny pair of black night shorts, and gulped.

Melinda opened the window and folded her arms over

her chest, pushing her tits up, the swell peeking from the neckline doing weird things to my body. At least, my dick wasn't as intoxicated as I was.

Melinda did nothing to help me out of my neck-breaking precarious position, watching me with a frown. "Mase? Care to explain what you're doing here at one in the morning?"

I coughed to ease the tightness around my vocal cords. "I'm *heeere* to make amends… and to *explaaain* myself."

She snorted. "Make amends. Yeah, right. You owe me nothing. I thought we… Never mind."

"You thought *whhhat?*" I was hanging on to every word coming out of her mouth while hanging on for dear life, my grip loosening with every ticking second.

"Doesn't matter now. Forget it. You shouldn't be here. It's late, and I'm pretty sure"—she looked down—"you're five seconds away from falling down a two-story window and breaking your neck."

"I'm *druuunk.*"

"Yes, you are."

"It was *stupppid.* Help…help a *guyyy* out. *Pleassse.*"

She stepped back. "And why would I do that?"

"I *screwwwed* up. Huh, I-I didn't. Sarah and I were just watching some football games on her *phonnne.* Her *brottther.* He…he plays for CWU. I was curious *abouuut* their team."

"Why would you be curious about Crestwood University? Didn't you commit to Alabama last year?"

"*Nooo.* Don't believe everything you hear." My foot slid from the top of the ledge. "*Helpppp* me inside and I'll tell *youuu* everything you wanna know. Don't let me *diiie.*" I winced when I risked a glance down, now that the moon was peeking from between the clouds and I could see better in the dark.

Melinda opened the window wider and tugged at my

arms until I was half in, bent at the waist, my feet dangling outside and my head and torso kissing her bedroom floor. "This is ridiculous. You could have fallen and killed yourself."

"*Thannnks*," I slurred once I stood on my feet. I felt lightheaded, thanks to the booze still swirling in my veins, but I didn't feel as drunk with Melinda standing before me, her breaths hastening as my eyes zeroed in on her chest once more.

"Stop ogling me." She pointed to the door. "You should go."

I pushed my hands into my pockets and nodded. "Yeah." All the words I had rehearsed in my head since I started climbing her house vanished. I had no idea what I should tell her now. I took two steps to the right, ready to forfeit my mission when her small hand reached for my wrist, and she stopped me.

"What is this?" Melinda lifted my T-shirt, exposing the side of my stomach. Her fingers were cold as they traced my flesh. A shiver skated the length of my back. She leaned forward before bringing her eyes back to mine. "Mase, you've hurt yourself."

I shrugged. "It's probably nothing. Just a *scratttch*."

"You're bleeding. It's not nothing. Let me look at it, okay?" Her fingertips lingered on my taut skin, sending a ton of mixed signals to my body.

"Don't *worrry*. Tomorrow it…it won't show."

"You need to clean it."

"I'm *finnne*."

She let go of my shirt. "Stop saying it. You're not invincible." Her eyes drifted toward the window I'd just climbed through. "Not that you got the memo tonight, but… Anyway, let me do this for you." She stepped closer, eating the small distance between our bodies.

Heat spread through me.

"Please."

I leaned forward, my lips so close to her ear I could lick the shell if I poked my tongue out. "Okay."

She trembled against me.

"I *neeed* to tell you something. I'm not *suuure* I'm drunk on *boooze* anymore."

The Earth stopped its rotation. Everything stilled between us.

The orange-blossom fragrance of her shampoo was all I could smell. The pulse of my heart throbbed in my ears.

I drew the line of her nose with mine. Melinda gasped, and I pulled her closer, my hands locked around her waist. This was not how I imagined our first kiss to be. Me, drunk and messed up. She, barely dressed, in her bedroom, with her parents sleeping down the hall.

Her lips parted on a moan when I kissed the corner of her mouth.

The lower part of my body grew rigid.

My lips lingered on her jaw, the column of her neck, the exposed skin over her breastbone.

Her fingernails dug into my ribcage as if she needed to grip me to anchor herself to this moment.

I was about to steal a kiss when I recalled I was drunk and it would be wrong to take advantage of her when I wasn't fully myself.

"Mase."

"Mel."

We breathed each other in.

My hands found her face and I dropped a kiss on her forehead. "I won't *kisss* you like this. Gosh, I *waaant* to, believe me. There's no one else. I swear. Everything *youuu* witnessed tonight wasn't what it…what it appeared to be. It's just a *biggg* misunderstanding."

"It hurt." She paused, taking a deep inhale. "To see you with them."

I pressed my forehead to hers. "I know. I never meant to hurt *youuu*. Never. You gotta trust *meee*."

"I'm trying to. You never gave me a reason not to, but—"

"But what?"

"You have a rep with girls. I'm not like any of them."

"I'll never *askkk* you to be."

"They're prettier and have more experience than I do."

"*Bullshittt*. Never compare yourself to anyone else, Mel, because the truth is… They-they all wish they were *youuu*."

"Yeah. Only because we spend time together."

"Are you kidding me right *nowww*? They wanna be *youuu* because *youuu're* perfect. Smart, beautiful, talented. It has nothing to do with *meee*."

"You wish."

"Mel…"

"It's okay. I'm me, and it's enough…or I hope it is."

"Mel."

She silenced me with a finger against my lips before leading me to the bathroom down the hall. Once she closed the door behind us, she pushed me to sit on the edge of the bathtub. "Don't say a word. If my parents catch you here, it'll be the end of you. I don't think Dad owns a shotgun, but he would kick you out, no matter that you're *you*… and he likes you. Never say I've never warned you."

I nodded.

Lifting my T-shirt over my head, Melinda kneeled between my legs with a first-aid kit and attended to the cut on my abdomen. "You don't need stitches." She pressed a disinfectant pad to the wound. "Sorry," she murmured when I flinched, then blew on it, easing the burn, before covering it with some ointment and a bandage. "Good to go."

She picked up my shirt from the floor and handed it to me when we both moved to stand.

Her gaze scanned my chest before they returned to my eyes. "I'll help you out of here…unless…"

I used my thumb to push a strand of hair away from her beautiful face. Without her guard up, and fresh-faced, she looked like an angel. My angel.

"Unless you prefer to stay here."

"*Sleeep* here?" I wasn't sure I was computing her words correctly. My heartbeat kicked up a notch. Was I dreaming this conversation?

"Yeah." A soft blush colored her cheeks. "After all, you might need a nurse to watch over you in case this awful wound gets infected and you have a fever or something."

"Shepard, you wanna *playyy* nurse to *meee?*"

"Maybe." A mischievous smile formed on her lips.

"How can I *stoppp* you from doing the right thing? This would be *verrry* careless of *meee*."

She laced our fingers and led me to her bedroom. Locking the door behind us, she got into bed and flipped the covers over to make room for me.

I kicked off my shoes and my jeans, standing in red boxer briefs in front of her. "Is it *o…kay?*" I didn't want her to think I was expecting stuff from her. "If I sleep *withhh* clothes on, I'm gonna *diiie* of heatstroke."

She beckoned me with a finger. "It's fine."

"Huh…can I *havvve* the left side?"

"Why?"

"I-I don't *likkke* to lie *onnn* my right shoulder."

"Are you injured?"

"*Nahhh*. It's just a…a preference." *Lie.*

We slid under the covers, neither of us brave enough to break the thick silence enveloping us.

On my side, I splayed my palm across Melinda's stomach as she lay on her back next to me, her eyes trained on mine.

Without breaking eye contact and feeling brave, I slid my hand under the hem of her top. She shivered as I rubbed slow circles over her bare skin with my fingertips.

The sight of her, trusting me, sent a warm feeling through my being. How many nights did I dream of doing just that? Too many to keep count.

Her pillow carried the sweet scent of her shampoo, and I wished I could sleep here every night.

"I—" Why were my thoughts so hard to express when they mattered the most? "I…I wouldn't *wannna* be anywhere else. You are *heeere*, and I want to be *heeere* too, you know, because that's where you live and I climbed the wall to see *youuu* because…" That was lame. I could do better. But how could I open my heart and lay it on the line for her to see? All the things I'd never said and kept to myself, all that I felt for her? If only my thoughts weren't so *boozy* right now. I should have never gotten drunk tonight. But if I hadn't, would I have been brave enough to come here in the middle of the night? Would I have chickened out at the last minute? My brain was a rambling mess.

Melinda's breath hitched as I caressed her breast over her top, her nipples hardening under the pads of my fingers.

My own breath came in and out in harsh pants. "You *likkke* it?"

She nodded.

"Want me to *continuuue*?"

"Please."

I nuzzled her cheek with my nose, burning her sweet

scent to my memory, and lowered my hand down her front. I felt the heady beating of her heart under my touch.

With a finger, I grazed the hem of her night shorts. Melinda's hand enveloped mine, pushing it lower.

"*Youuu* sure?"

"Yes. Don't stop, okay?"

I traced the seam between her legs, and her hips buckled off the mattress.

"Mase." My name became a plea on her lips.

My dick enjoyed every minute as I rubbed her over her clothes, eliciting whimpers and heavy pants from her.

She rocked her hips, meeting the movements of my hand. This was the slowest torture I'd ever endured. Melinda Shepard was coming apart under my touch, and I was about to jizz in my pants because she looked so hot while trusting me to make her feel good.

A muffled cry escaped her mouth, and she arced her back before coming undone. We both froze. Melinda watched me with hooded eyelids.

"*Fuckkk,* you're *beautifulll.*"

"Don't say things like that if you don't mean them."

I leaned up on an elbow and lifted her chin toward me. "I mean it. Every *singggle* word. You are *sooo beautifulll.*"

"You can't—"

"What do *youuu* mean I can't?" I tried to make sense of her words, but my stupid brain couldn't seem to come up with anything logical. "I can't *whaaat?*"

"Shhh. Don't say anything."

She hesitated for a beat before dipping her hand under the waistband of my boxer briefs. I sucked a gulp of oxygen in when her cold hand met my warm flesh. Was it the alcohol still swimming in my blood or Melinda's touch making me dizzy right now?

She curled her fist around my length.

I breathed through clenched teeth. "*Jesusss.* Mel, what are *youuu* doing?"

"Isn't it obvious?"

"*Yesss… Nooo…* You-you don't have to."

"I want to. Please let me. Unless you don't."

I took her face in my hands so we could watch each other and she could read the truth in my eyes. "Let me *makkke* it clear. I'll never not want *youuu* to touch me." I pushed myself up to kiss her, but she cocked her head to the side, and my lips grazed her cheek instead.

Melinda pumped my hard-as-hell erection slowly and I swore I saw stars and I hadn't even come yet. "I'm not… I've never… I'm not experienced in this."

I wrapped my hand around hers, increasing the pace of her movements. "*Youuu* are pretty *goood* at this. I swear." I closed my eyes, so many sensations washing through my body that I had a hard time telling what was real and what was a side effect of the whiskey and shots I had drunk earlier.

Feeling cheap for touching her the first time when I wasn't even fully conscious, I stopped her before I could jerk off.

"What?"

"Not tonight, *okaaay.*" Why was I doing this? I was about to burst at the seams. "I'm still *drunnnk,* and I don't want our first time to be when *I'mmm* not quite sober. I'm not *thattt* guy. The one…the one taking advantage." My arguments sounded better in my head.

"Oh." She withdrew her hand and scooted away from me, and I had never felt so angry with myself.

Tonight, there was no excuses. I was an idiot.

"Can-can…huh…can I *stilll* stay here?" The last thing I wanted was to leave. My heart wouldn't survive being rejected by this girl again.

"Sure. I'm not kicking you out…unless you choose to go."

I tensed at her clipped tone.

A wall had risen between us, and I was the one who had complicated everything by touching her first. I sealed my eyelids, trying to stop my brain from racing so I could save the night.

Knitting our fingers, I tried to mend the emotional distance between us. I opened my eyes, fishing courage from deep inside me. "Are *weee* okay?"

"You tell me."

"We *arrre*. I'm trying to be a *goood* guy here, and for some reason, you're pissed at *meee* for it. If I had acted like an asshole, you wouldn't have liked *meee* either. This is confusing to my…to my wasted brain."

"I'm not mad… Not really. I've never let anyone…do things…touch me like that before. And then I touched you, and you pushed me away… I don't know how to react. It's—"

"I wanna *kisss* you so bad right now." Her pink lips were like a drug I had to taste to stay alive.

She flipped to her side to face me and shook her head. "Mase, you can't kiss me."

"Why?"

"If you do, it means more than this is. It would be real, and I'm not ready for it to be real between us. I need a little more time, okay?"

"Huh…okay. I'm *nottt* sure what's going on right now. I'm…huh…I'm confused." My brain was clearly affected because none of her words made sense.

"I'll tell you. One day. Just not tonight."

"No pressure."

"There's a lot you don't know about me."

"There's a lot *youuu* don't know about me either, but I

want us to be able to open up and share…huh, to share those things."

She inhaled but said nothing.

"Just so you know. I'll wait for *youuu* for the rest of time because you're worth it."

"Whoa, that's a pretty big statement. I would never ask you to, though." She squeezed my hand. "I'm sorry if I overreacted earlier."

"Nah. It's all on *meee*. It won't happen again."

"Mase, can you hold me? I really don't want you to leave."

"Okay." My heart did a victory dance in my chest. We shifted positions until Melinda's back was molded to my front. My eyelids weighed heavy, and with the only girl I'd ever loved nestled in my arms, I drifted into a deep sleep.

The last words I thought I heard her whisper were "Soon I'm hoping to be good enough for you." My *boozy* brain was now making things up. Maybe the entire night was a dream after all.

———

The next morning, I woke up early, the sun barely shining through the curtains we didn't close last night. It wasn't a dream. Melinda was spread over me, her brown hair fanned around her shoulders, and her small hand splayed across my chest.

Last night replayed in my head. Some parts were clear, while others were a bit blurry. One thing was sure, though, Melinda Shepard had ceded all power to me for a moment. That I recalled perfectly.

Easing myself from under her, I stood up by the bed and put my torn T-shirt and my jeans back on, noticing the bandage across my abdomen. This wasn't a dream either. I really had hurt myself last night. Nearing Melinda's sleepy figure, I brushed her hair back with my fingers, admiring her for an instant. "I'll come to knock on your door at nine for our morning run. Thanks for taking care of me last night and letting me sleep here."

She stirred as I tucked the covers over her but didn't wake up.

"I'm so gone for you. You'll see, I'll be worthy of you," I whispered before I kissed her temple and made my way outside.

In the morning light with a fully functioning brain, jumping from the second-story window didn't seem as perilous as it had been hours ago. Hanging from the windowsill, I balanced my legs and landed on the ledge below, holding on to the trellis before jumping on the woodshed and then onto the lawn. After I picked up my jacket, I made my way back home, desperate for a shower, a toothbrush, and some food.

CHAPTER 22
SHUT UP, DRAMA QUEEN

"Seriously, Mase, what's going on between you and Mel?" Chase asked after we finished practice and walked toward the athletic building to change a week later.

I heard that question at least once a day lately. As if Melinda's and my friendship was that interesting to the rest of the school.

"Why?"

"Because." He bumped my padded shoulder with his. "I'm your best friend, and you don't tell me shit these days. When I saw you guys at Space Burger, you both looked… huh…cozy. Then I heard about the party and your getting drunk. And we all noticed, how you two have been pretty much joined at the hip in the last week."

"Cozy?"

"Yeah. Is that all you heard from what I said?"

I shrugged. "Pretty much."

"You spend all your free time with her, and also, you've skipped most parties since you two have started hanging out, which isn't like you. You haven't closed the deal yet, so either she stole your balls or you're obsessed with her or you're turning into an old and boring man."

"Who's turning into an old and boring man?" Sheldon asked as he jogged past us.

"Mase," Chase replied. "He's been hanging out with Shepard for months and won't close the deal or talk about it."

"My sex life and my relationship are no one's business."

"Sex life? Relationship? What did I miss?" Jackson asked as he joined us. "Are you guys talking about Pierce Junior and Shepard K. I. S. S. I. N. G. in a tree or something?"

"Jesus, Pierce Junior. Are you all right?" Rusty piped up from behind. "Have you lost your legendary swagger? Did you break your dick?"

Someone slapped me between the shoulder blades, and soon my brother's face peeked from my left side. "I heard you lost your swagger, bro?" he asked in the same teasing voice he used each time Melinda was involved. "Need my help to find it?" And now he was using my own expression against me.

I nudged him with my elbow. "Nobody has lost their swagger, guys. For the record, my dick is fully functioning. I'm taking my time, not rushing into it because she's worth it, not that it's any of you stupid fools' business anyway."

Sheldon hit his chest with a fist in mocking hurt. "It's not? I thought we were a team. And you are our captain.

Our quarterback. Our leader. Our future Prom King. Don't play coy. You are *The* Mason Pierce. You fear no one and nothing. You would walk through a bed of nails and scorching coal to take us to victory. Come on, man. Share with us the matters of your heart. We can help you."

Laughter echoed around me. "Wow. If football doesn't work out for you, try drama, Sheld. You are a born actor."

He stopped by the locker room door and curtsied. "Thank you very much, Mase. For recognizing I'm such a talented gentleman."

I pushed him aside with a hand. "Shut up, drama queen."

The guys followed me inside, and we each reached for our lockers, discarding our practice jerseys before removing our shoulder pads.

"FYI, guys. Nothing that's going on between Mel and me is up for discussion. Nothing. And it will never be. Don't act weird around her, don't ask her stuff, don't mess with her. Have I made myself clear?"

One arm raised. Then another. And a third one.

"What?" Seriously, my teammates were acting like five-year-olds.

"Have you kissed her yet?"

"Are you planning to break your no-dating rules for her?"

"Can I ask her out once you move on? She has one of the best asses in Elk River High."

I killed the fucker with my eyes.

"Is what you two have serious, or it is like a bet or something?"

"Would you be pissed if I kissed her first?"

"Is she blackmailing you to spend time with her?"

"Will we be invited to the wedding, or are you ditching us?"

"Have you ever thought of naming your firstborn after me?"

"Do you think she's saving herself for marriage?"

I lifted both arms in front of me and splayed my palms. "Again. Enough. None. Of. Your. Business. Didn't you guys hear anything I said before?"

"Why her?"

"Is it serious?"

"Are you two dating in secret and no one knows because that would be *soooo* cool."

"Oh, wait. Is she pregnant and that's why you're sticking by her side? So your baby isn't fatherless?"

I blocked out their voices. Every question was more ridiculous than the previous one.

Chase turned to Craig. "Any spoilers for us? I swear over my dead body whatever you tell us about Pierce Junior and Shepard will stay in this room."

Someone snorted.

Craig's smirk reached both ears. "You guys are the worst kind of tattletales. None of you know what the term *keeping what you hear here between these walls* means. You'll walk out of this room and repeat everything to whoever is stupid enough to listen to you."

I gestured to my brother. "Point made. Thanks, man."

He nodded and stretched his arm forward so we could bump our fists. I could read on his face what he didn't say out loud. *I have your back. Even though I will give you shit when we're home alone.*

"Just one piece of info," Chase begged, his hands linked together under his chin in prayer. "Give your best friend something."

I tossed a lone sock at him. "You wish."

"You, Pierce Junior, are no fun," Sheldon chimed in.

"True," Peters, a linebacker, agreed.

"Okay, I'm done with the twenty questions. Nothing to say, nothing to add. Find gossip elsewhere and get a life."

I walked to the showers, unable to erase the grin plastered on my face. If only my teammates knew about my infatuation for the girl next door, I would never hear the end of it.

Dressed in a pair of Heather gray sweatpants and a coral-pink hoodie and ready to go, I hauled my bag over my shoulder and tucked my letterman jacket under my arm, about to take off and pick up Melinda from swim practice when my phone chimed with an incoming notification.

MELINDA

Mase, I'm sorry, but Coach Vivien asked me to swim fifty additional laps before I go home. She said something about increasing my endurance. I'll be late. Leave without me. I'll call my dad so he can pick me up later.

ME

Nah. Forget it. I'm in no rush. I'll meet you at the pool. Take your time.

MELINDA

You sure? It will take me a little while.

ME

Yep. No stress. See you soon.

"What's with the smile?" Sheldon asked when he returned from the showers with a white towel wrapped around his waist. "Is it Shepard who makes you grin like a fool?"

"Nope. My mom. She just informed me she made lasagna for dinner. It's my favorite. And before you ask, no, you're not invited." I winked and hurried away before any of the guys could follow me.

I sat in the bleachers section of the pool and grabbed my physics textbook, wanting to finish the last pages of the homework due the next day. Every few minutes, I scanned the pool area, watching the one girl my eyes were trained to find in a crowd, slice through the water, her strokes timed and precise. She stepped out of the turquoise body of water and rushed to drape a towel around her waist before waving in my direction. I was aware Melinda was on a new training program, but I was an athlete too, and I didn't understand what her coach and nutritionist were trying to accomplish. She looked skinnier than she used to be, and her muscles appeared, not stronger or leaner, but smaller and weaker.

Since it wasn't my sport nor my place to say anything, I decided to mind my own business when it concerned the swimming part of her training. Going on runs five times a week with her and spending time together at the gym to work on her figure was the part of the deal I'd agreed on.

"I'll shower and change fast and be right back," Melinda called from the poolside.

I gave her a thumbs-up, and she disappeared into the locker room.

I finished my homework and read two chapters of the mandatory novel for my English lit class before she joined me with a timid smile and her duffel bag slung over her shoulder. I grinned when I noticed she was wearing the hoodie I'd given her the night I walked her home at the beginning of the semester over a pair of deep-blue yoga pants.

"I was right the other night. This looks much better on you."

She mirrored my smile, tying her damp hair in a messy bun at the top of her head before slipping a knitted hat on.

I shoved all my stuff into my own bag and stole hers from her grip.

"You don't have to."

I tugged at her hand. Even her digits felt bonier than usual. "It makes me happy. Let me." I steered her outside to my car, and she didn't remove her palm from mine, which pleased me a lot.

I watched her after we both sat in my car. Something was off. "You look tired."

"I didn't sleep well last night."

"You were missing my amazing arms, Shepard." I flexed my biceps to make a point even though she couldn't see the muscles under my jacket sleeve.

She snickered. "Maybe." Her humor died down. "I have been dealing with a pounding headache most of the day." She massaged her temples with her fingertips. "Practice has just stolen every last bit of energy I had left."

Since the night I'd spent in her bed over a week ago, we hadn't broached the subject of our dating again. What we did that night felt like a dirty secret we shared, and I had no idea if she had any intention of pursuing what we had started. I said I would follow her pace, so I didn't feel confident about rushing her to talk about it when clearly, she was acting like it had never happened.

"Headaches are the worst. Last year, when I had that concussion, it took weeks before they totally disappeared. It was horrible."

"I haven't had one in a long time. I used to have migraines when I was younger. I just hope it's not everything catching up with me. The last thing I need is to give my parents a reason to worry about me and for Coach to declare me unfit to swim."

"Why would they do that if it's just a headache?"

She sighed, avoiding my eyes. "No reason. My mother is just always on my case since the surgery."

"It sucks." The engine roared to life, and I pulled out of the parking lot. "Hungry?"

She winced. "Not really. Headaches always kill my appetite."

"Do you have any plans tonight?"

She shook her head. "Unless a warm bath and PJs count as a plan."

"If you decide it is, then yes, it definitely counts."

She offered me a tiny lopsided smile. "Why? Anything on your mind?"

"What about a movie and takeout? My treat. I would have invited you to eat out somewhere, but I'm not sure noise and fluorescent lights would help that headache of yours."

"We could go to my place. My parents are out with friends, so it'll be just the two of us."

I wanted it to be an invite to continue what had gone down between us the other night, but I doubted it was. "Pizza sounds good? We could add cheesecake bites for dessert. I usually eat cleaner than that during football season, but I think we both deserve some comfort food tonight. Training was a bitch earlier. Too many burpees and suicides. Peters threw up, and Jackson almost fainted."

Melinda extended her arm in my direction and took my hand in hers. "It's perfect. Thanks for being my friend, Mase."

Yep, I was right. I was still stuck in the stupid friend zone. Whatever. Spending time with her was all I longed for, so for now, it would have to be enough.

Sitting beside Melinda on her bed, we ate while talking about a million different things. Melinda had changed into pink fluffy pajama pants with gray kittens printed on them while keeping my hoodie on after she'd blow-dried her hair. Even dressed down with her hair braided over her shoulder and no makeup on, she looked magnificent.

Her turquoise eyes searched mine. "Do you wanna visit the pumpkin patch next weekend? It could be fun. I saw an ad announcing ax-throwing and log-chopping competitions and a giant corn maze."

"We could hit the fair afterward. Unless you already have plans?"

"Paige and I talked about going together on Sunday because I have a meet on Saturday. Maybe we could go… the four of us…and you know…hang out. Just a thought."

"It's a date then."

"A date?"

I cleared my throat. "It's a plan."

She untied her hair and positioned herself against my arm, a yawn parting her lips.

I cupped the back of her head, staring at her. "Want me to go so you can rest?"

"Not yet." She yawned again. "I'm comfy."

"Fine by me."

I was just about to dig into the cheesecake bites when Melinda slumped against my side, the weight of her head heavy on my upper arm, and I realized she had fallen asleep. I put the container down and pulled the comforter over her figure. For the longest time, I watched her sleep before moving to my feet and tucking her in. She had shadows under her eyes, and her silhouette appeared slighter than usual dressed in baggy clothes. I wished I could pull her into my arms and sleep here, but we hadn't discussed it, and I couldn't invite myself over. I lifted the pizza box to discard it when I noticed she had put her own slices back inside, barely having taken a few bites. On top of her physical changes, her headache and loss of appetite, it looked concerning. Was she sick again? Could someone get a complication from an appendectomy weeks later? Paige had said Melinda was stressed about college applications. Could that be enough to affect her health? Could it be more than that?

A part of me dreaded to leave her side. What if she really was sick again and I was too far away to help her out this time? I debated my options in my head. I couldn't panic every time she didn't feel well, and anyway, the Shepards would be home soon.

I touched her forehead. No fever. I pressed two fingers to the pulse point on her wrist. Her heartbeat was steady. Maybe she was just overdoing it and was tired. We should ease up on the training schedule until she got some strength back. Yeah, I would talk to her about it tomorrow.

I grabbed a pencil and a piece of paper from her desk, wrote a note, and slipped it under her phone, which was charging on the nightstand.

Holding the leftovers in my hand, I made my way to the door only to go back to her side and kiss her cheek. This would have to be enough to get my fill of Melinda Shepard for the day.

"Night," I whispered as I closed her bedroom door behind me.

CHAPTER 23

IT'S CALLED LUMBERJILL

"I can't believe you finished second in ax throwing," Paige said, jumping into Melinda's arms. "I had no idea you could swing an ax and hit a target like you've been training for it all your life."

"Me neither," she said, laughing when they stepped apart and she took her jacket from my hands. Melinda had won a teddy bear wearing a tiny plaid shirt as a prize for winning the last ax-throwing round and received an offer to join the local women's team.

"Who knew? Perhaps you should join the circuit and become a lumber…lady," Craig said, high-fiving her.

"I think it's called *lumberjill*," Paige argued. "Not sure, though. Sounds weird. Who cares?"

I draped an arm over Melinda's shoulders, pulling her

against me. "You're a rock star, Shepard. That was pretty impressive."

"Think you can do better?" She watched me with expectant eyes.

I raked my fingers through my hair. "I'm not sure I wanna try. You kinda upped the stakes."

She smiled as I sang her praises.

"All the pressure is on me now."

Craig chuckled. "Stop being a chickenshit, Mase, and prove to us you can do it too." He turned to Melinda. "I'm so thankful you're putting a dent in his ego. Good riddance."

I elbowed my brother's side. "Shut up."

Craig grinned bigger. "You wish. Come on, superstar, show us what you've got."

I entered the competition and listened to the instructions and safety guidelines before taking a stance in front of a wooden target.

"You have ten takes," the man in charge of the stand told me. "The first five are practice runs and don't count. There are six people competing against one another. The person with the best overall score wins a prize. Are you ready?"

I rolled my shoulders back and nodded, blocking all sounds around me and putting my game face on. My competitive side had taken over, and I was about to make the other contestants look like kids.

My first take was a miss. The ax struck the target but didn't stick. I adjusted my stance, played around with the tool in my hands, modified my grip, and threw it as if I'd done it multiple times in the past. It hit the highest-value mark. A slow smile spread across my lips. Yes, I could win this.

I risked a look at my supporters. Melinda stood still,

her hands clamped together, as she watched me. Craig had his arms around his girlfriend, their eyes locked on me.

The man in charge neared me once I was done. "Okay, wow. I must admit this is the best score I've seen in all the years I've done this."

My name went at the top of the best-score board, and I returned to my friends with a stuffed beaver, a plaid shirt, and a miniature golden plastic ax.

"You guys are so cute," Paige said, her gaze traveling between Melinda and me. "Ax-throwing champs. You two should start a team and compete. Screw football and swimming, you'll be the perfect little lumberjack duo. You could live in the woods and perfect your skills every day. Why go to college when you can enter the ax-throwing circuit and have ax-throwing babies dressed in plaid shirts one day, right?"

"Beginner's luck. On my part. Not sure plaid shirts match my complexion." I turned to face my brother. "Are you giving it a try?"

"Nope. Wouldn't wanna beat your ass and make you feel like second best. See? I'm doing it to preserve the peace between us. And that giant ego of yours."

I hit my chest with the side of my fist. "So generous of you, man."

We reached the corn maze.

"First one to reach the center wins," Paige called out.

"If you're lost, call for me, I'll come find you," Craig told her.

"It's cheating," I said while Paige cooed, "Oh, you're so sweet. I love you."

They kissed like they were alone in this world for a long minute.

Melinda and I exchanged an amused gaze.

You'll be okay, I mouthed.

Watch me win, she mouthed back.

I loved it when she was confident about her own skills and didn't shy away from it.

I clapped my hands. "Stop the PDA, guys. We've seen enough of your tonsils for the rest of our lives. Let's go. I'm ready to wait for you at the center."

Craig and Paige broke apart, and we all rushed toward the maze through different entry points.

The blazing autumn sun shone high in the sky, and little beads of sweat pearled on my forehead under its warmth. From my hiding spot, I watched Melinda take the same route for the third time.

"This maze is a joke," she complained with a huff. The skinny jeans she was wearing made her legs appear mile-long, showcasing her lean thigh muscles. Combined with her snug cream knitted sweater and matching hat, she was a sight for sore eyes. And one my body had a hard time resisting.

Giggles and whispers resonated from somewhere on her right, and she moved forward, distancing herself from the noise—probably not wanting to risk seeing something her eyes could never unsee—and tearing my eyes away from her.

In a few strides, I stepped behind her and covered her eyes with my hands. "Shepard, are you lost?"

A shiver traversed her body when I spoke close to her ear. My front pressed against her back, the firmness of my muscles molding to hers and the fabric of our jeans not thick enough to conceal how my dick reacted to her proximity. She relaxed against me, like she was expecting me to stand there. "No. I'm just killing time so you can finish first in case you throw a second-place tantrum when you lose."

"Liar. You're almost there. I've been waiting for you to

join me in the center for almost ten minutes. And I don't do second place. Never."

She turned in my arms, her soft breasts pressing against my hard chest. Our gazes collided. "Ten minutes?" Her soft voice sent a zing through me. Like supercharged tiny particles of electricity moving throughout my body and lodging in my crotch.

"Ten minutes," I repeated. "Paige and Craig are on the south side, doing who knows what."

"Ugh."

"Don't remind me. I ran the other way when I bumped into them. Now, I've been waiting for you to join me because I'm all alone over there. Winning isn't as much fun when you're not competing against me."

"First, don't put images in my head about your brother and my best friend. It's a load of information I don't need. And second, it's not that I'm losing on purpose. This maze leads nowhere. And by the way, what are you doing here if you've already found the center?"

"Cheering you on."

"Why?"

"Because, like I said, it's lonely in the middle without you. And life is much more enjoyable when you're around."

She pushed my chest in a teasing manner, her hand lingering on my hoodie-covered torso for a few seconds. "Drama queen."

I shrugged. "Please deliver me from my loneliness, Mel." She melted a little more against me. My hands found her waist, and I contoured the length of her jaw with my lips. She shuddered but didn't push me away.

Her voice sounded rougher when she spoke again. "Yeah, I'll meet you there."

"What are you waiting for then?"

Her breath caught in her lungs. I loved that she reacted to my presence as much as I reacted to hers.

She closed her eyes, and I fought with myself not to kiss her. Recalling her words from the other night, I disappeared before she opened them back, hiding in the same spot as before.

When she did, she blinked, her gaze roaming around, but not spotting me. "Mase? Where are you?"

My heart thundered in my chest, and I cupped it with a hand to calm its storm. I was so screwed. I had been seconds away from sweeping her off her feet and kissing her senseless.

Before I retreated to the middle of the maze again, I heard her low whisper. "Get a grip on yourself, Mel. It's just a corn maze. You can beat it."

Standing on a big rock, I spied on my girl as she turned left and right instead of left again. "I'm right here, waiting for you."

She glanced around, but I squatted so she wouldn't notice me. "Gosh, you're impossible, cocky man. Where are you?" Her soft laughter dissolved as a group of teenagers walked past her.

"Focus, Mel. You can do this. Listen to my voice. Feel my energy."

Shutting her eyes, she relaxed her shoulders and inhaled deeply, all gracious, just like she did on meet days when she stepped on the block.

I closed my eyes too, listening to the same things she did. Birds chirping. The breeze rustling the corn crops. Giggling. A man speaking in a loud voice. A baby crying.

Melinda stepped forward, and minutes later came face to face with me, sitting on a hay bale, smirking with a *I'm proud of you, but I still finished first* expression. "You made it, Shepard."

"I made it," she echoed. "Seriously, how long have you been here?"

I shrugged. "Fifteen minutes, give or take."

"Are Paige and Craig still somewhere doing who knows what?"

"I guess. I went to look for them again but couldn't find them this time around."

She moved between my open legs, her hands resting on the top of my thighs. "Huh. What should we do? Wait for them?"

I cradled her cheek with a hand and smoothed her bottom lip with my thumb. The world fell away, and we lost ourselves in each other for an endless minute. "Nah. I'll text them. Hungry?"

Her attention drifted to my mouth. My breath stuck in my lungs, and my cells vibrated in anticipation of what she might or might not do when we were standing this close to each other. For the umpteenth time today, I wondered if she was thinking about kissing me too.

I grabbed her hand and drew the lines of her palm with a finger. Melinda said nothing, erasing the gap between us and pressing her forehead to the crook of my neck. She exhaled loudly, and I curled a hand around the back of her head, brushing her hair. I could tell she was scared of something, but unless she opened up to me, we were stuck in this push-and-pull relationship endlessly.

"When you're ready to tell me, I'll be here, okay? No matter what it is. I won't go away. I'm not scared that easily."

She planted a kiss on my cheek, and I pretty much dissolved inside. Melinda Shepard held so much power over me, and I didn't think she knew just how much. "Thanks."

"Let's go and eat something. I'm starving."

As if I'd shocked her, she jumped back and grinned. "Geez, Mase, you're always hungry."

I winked. "Only for mouth-watering stuff, though." I licked my lips, and she backhanded my chest. I grinned bigger. "Don't make me wait. Come, feed me."

Her face turned a deep shade of red at my words.

My one-track mind formed dirty images of her lips on me and all the things I yearned to do to her body with my mouth, and heat blossomed through me in addictive waves.

I stood and kicked my legs, killing the tension between my thighs.

I was way over my head in love with the girl next door, and I had no idea how to tell her without scaring her away.

If by Winter Formal, Melinda and I hadn't made it our relationship official, I would spill my guts to her that night.

Yes, that would be my deadline for everything. I would gather all the courage I needed by then and show her we were perfect together. I had one month left to sweep her off her feet. This was doable. I had to prove to her I had changed and that I was looking for a lasting relationship—with her. I had to solidify our friendship before putting my heart on the line, though.

If I played my cards right, Melinda would have no choice but to trust me with her heart and jump in with both feet, without a net to break the fall.

Tension drained away from my back. I had a plan. Something tangible to hang on to.

CHAPTER 24
WE MUST FILE IT AS A MISTAKE

"Anyone in for the Ferris wheel?" Craig asked after discarding our food wrappers into the nearest trash can.

Melinda finished nibbling on her plain Caesar salad—no dressing, no croutons—and pushed her plate away. "I'm done." She'd only agreed to order a salad after I argued she had to eat something and she counter-argued saying she wasn't allowed fat or carbs on weekends, except on meet days.

"You sure?" my brother asked, eyeing the half-eaten salad like he was still starving.

She nodded. "Yeah. I don't wanna get sick on the rides. Just thinking about it and I already feel nauseous."

"Mel is not really a fan of heights," Paige chimed in,

sipping her soda. "We'll sit the Ferris wheel out. You guys go ahead."

"The whole thing about the Ferris wheel is to go with you," my brother told Paige. "I love my brother, but I don't wanna ride with him in a pod for ten minutes. I have nothing against his sorry ass, but it is a big fat no. The only person who's climbing in that thing with me is you."

"Oh," Paige said, a blush spreading across her cheeks.

"You guys all go. I'll grab cotton candy or something while you have your fun," Melinda said, pointing to the concession stand behind her with a thumb.

The whiff of the sugar treat had been tickling my nostrils the entire time we'd been here, but I had eaten enough junk food today without adding the sugary treat to the mix.

"Or…" I neared her and grabbed her hand in mine. "We could ride together. You and I. I promise I'll keep you safe. The view from the top is to die for. And now that the sun is setting, it will be even more beautiful. It's a sight you don't wanna miss."

She shook her head. "I'm doing just fine on solid ground. Take a picture or something. I'll look at it later."

"Not good enough for me. I wanna do this together."

"Mase."

"Mel."

"You protected me when we did that horror movie marathon. It's my turn to protect you when something scares you. I'll let you bury your face in my chest if you freak out."

"Oh, so sweet," Paige said, cupping her heart with one palm.

Melinda glared at her with a *Not helping* expression and twisted the ring around her thumb.

"Please. Pretty please. It won't be as much fun if I have

to ride alone. I hate third wheeling with these guys." I motioned to my brother and Paige with my chin.

"Okay. Fine. You win. Geez, you're so dramatic. I'll ride the Ferris wheel with you, Mase. Under one condition."

"Name it."

She plastered an expression that said *I mean business* on her face. "I get a treat afterward."

I waggled my eyebrows, unable to conceal the amusement I knew was brightening my features. "A treat? Any treat? Am I the one choosing what I feed you?"

She scrunched up her nose and seemed to catch up with her own words. "Oh no. Mase, I didn't mean food… or something else. When you say it like that, it sounded…it sounded…"

"Dirty?"

She nudged my side. "Stop. Ohmygod, I can't believe you said it…like that." She sighed, fanning herself. "What I meant was, if I survive this ride, you ride the haunted house with me. I know firsthand how much you like being spooked. Something like that."

I watched her with a wicked grin. "I knew what you meant. I just think red suits you, and shy is a good look on you." I shrugged and snickered as her cheeks flamed hotter.

She closed her eyes and breathed out before bringing her attention back to me. "Anyway, do we have a deal?"

My lips stretched into a victorious grin too big for my face. "Yes. And Mel? You won't regret this, I swear."

The girls jumped into a conversation about some movie actor as we waited in line.

I pulled my brother aside. "Everything okay between you and Paige?"

"Yeah, why?"

"Nothing. Just some tension I've noticed between you two lately. I promised I wouldn't eavesdrop, but I heard you arguing in the maze earlier. And the other night too. I told Mel I caught you guys doing the nasty so she wouldn't walk in on you, but it's happening more and more often these days. Your bedroom is not as soundproof as you would like to believe."

He hung his head low and gave it a shake. "It's nothing. She thinks… She thinks I'm hiding stuff from her."

"Are you?"

He shrugged. "It's complicated. I wouldn't say I'm hiding stuff, but more like withholding some details until I'm certain we gotta discuss it. Does it make sense?"

"Huh…not really. Does it have anything to do with your secret meetings in Dad's office most nights?"

"Yes and no. It's not something either one of you has to worry about, okay? It's my shit, and I'm dealing with it the best I can."

"Fine. She loves you, man. Don't screw it up because you think withholding information from her is the right thing to do, okay? If I were her, I'd want to know too."

Pain flickered across his face, and he peered into the distance. "If it doesn't work out as planned, I'll lose her anyway. I'm not ready for the day it happens, but I won't lead her on either. I'm in no rush to find out how it will play out."

"Anything I can do to help?"

"Promise me you'll be there for her if things go south. Promise me you'll be the friend she needs if it all implodes and she's collateral damage."

"I promise. Man, are you dying or something? You are scaring me."

"Nah. I would tell you if I were. As I said, it's nothing

for you to worry about. It's my big brother's job to protect you too."

"What did you do?"

"Me?" He pointed to his chest and let out a sarcastic laugh. "Nothing. I wish I could blame this on myself. It would be much easier to wrap my head around everything it implies."

"I'm here if you wanna confide in someone who's not Paige."

"Thanks, Mase."

Paige waved at him, and he returned to her side, pulling her in for a hug. He stared at me over her shoulder, and I nodded, sealing the promise I'd just made.

"I love you," he whispered, kissing the crown of her head.

Beside me, Melinda tilted her head back and squinted, probably trying to guess how high the top car hung in the air.

"Don't do this," I murmured in her ear. "And don't look down when we're up there. Just straight ahead. And you'll be all right."

"And you know that…because?"

I stepped around her until we faced each other. "Because I'm Mason Pierce, duh. What else?"

She exploded in a fit of laughter and relaxed. "For once, that cockiness of yours is welcome."

I winked and pumped my fist mentally at the idea I had succeeded at easing her fears with one of my comebacks.

Paige closed in on us. "You sure you wanna do this?"

Melinda blew out a breath and bobbed her head twice. "Yes. I can overcome my fear."

Paige squeezed her forearm and turned to talk to my

brother when he wrapped his arms around her waist from behind.

"Mel, what's going on with you and your fear of heights?" I asked in a low voice once it was just the two of us.

"When I was a kid, I jumped from the highest platform at the pool and did a belly flop. It hurt so bad. I jumped with my eyes closed, not making sure I hit the water properly. I burst into tears once I returned to solid ground, and I've been hating heights since."

I could relate. We had something more in common.

I held out my hand, and after hesitating for a couple of seconds, she slid her palm into mine, my thumb lingering on the pulse point of her wrist. "No chance of your getting hurt this time around."

The car stopped at the lowest level, and it was our time to climb inside. Craig and Paige had taken the previous one and waved at us as the wheel moved them up.

"It'll be okay," I told Melinda in a calm voice that I hoped would soothe the wild beating of her heart.

We settled ourselves next to each other, and I kept my arm over her shoulders in a protective stance. "You good?"

She nodded, stiff as a rod, her teeth worrying her bottom lip.

"Relax."

"I'm trying."

The wheel started its upward motion, and she shut her eyes, cursing under her breath. I pulled her closer until she was almost sitting on me. I massaged her upper back with my other hand, dissolving the knots lodged there.

The ride stopped every few seconds until all the cars were filled. On its first rotation, Melinda buried her face in my chest when we reached the top instead of admiring the view. I cradled the back of her head with my hand, holding on to her.

We were about to reach the top a second time when I leaned back and kept her at a distance, my hands locked on her shoulders. "No more hiding. When we're at the highest point, you take a moment to look around. You'll see miles ahead and realize how beautiful our town is. I love the Ferris wheel because it's the only spot high enough to let us see well past Elk River. Like our world doesn't end here and there's an entire planet out there for us to explore. It puts things into perspective. And opens us up to new possibilities."

"Wow. It sounds inspirational."

I shrugged. "There's so much more we haven't seen or experienced yet. I have all these dreams, but I'm sure there are a thousand more for me to grab in this lifetime."

"I never thought of it like that."

I pointed to our far left. "See that? The park next to the white building between the lines of trees?" She nodded. "It's where I went to football camp when I was a kid. It's where I fell in love with the sport. Craig and I, we were on the same team because we were born the same year, discovered we had talent. And that this talent multiplies when we play together." Next, I gestured to the green expanse of lawn in front of us. "That's our school and our football field."

"Whoa, it looks so different from up here. So much bigger even though it's smaller. If that makes any sense."

"Yeah. It does. And right there?" She followed the direction of my pointer finger. "That's our street. We can't see our houses because they are behind those trees, but they are there. When I was little, I recall seeing my roof before the trees got so big they acted like a screen."

I kept showing her places, and Melinda got engrossed in the pieces of information I was providing.

"I didn't think the river was so sinuous," she said.

"Me neither. I was surprised the first time too."

"How many miles ahead do you think we can—"

The jerky motion of the ride coming to an abrupt stop propelled us forward. Melinda screamed, and I extended one arm across her chest to prevent her from crashing into the opposite seat.

We heard a commotion below us, and I repeated the same words I had spoken earlier. "Don't look down, just straight ahead. And you'll be all right."

"What—? What's going on?"

"Emergency break. Huh…I think."

"You…think?"

"Seems like it." I framed her face with my hands. "Breathe in. Breathe out. You're okay, Mel. I'm here, remember? I'm keeping you safe. That was the deal. You. Are. Safe. I'm right beside you. Everything will be okay. I'll feed you that treat once we return to solid ground." My lips stretched at the corner, and a small chuckle passed hers.

"You won't let it go, like ever, right?"

"I haven't decided yet." I intertwined our fingers. "We're okay. Look at that view. We're lucky because we now have more time to admire it."

She surveyed our surroundings. The sky was picture-perfect, a work of art made of pink, orange, and purple brush strokes. "Wow. It's even more mesmerizing from up here. Thanks. For offering me a front seat to this."

With our fingers laced together, we watched the colorful display for a little longer before the reality of our situation came back. "Can-can we like *fall?*"

"Nah. Nothing to worry about. Keep your eyes on me, or that sky, and don't stare down."

Melinda sucked in a long breath.

I pressed a kiss to her forehead—the one thing I kept doing whenever we spent time together. We were suspended in time, the world around us spinning faster as we both remained frozen until I sat back and cleared my throat but said nothing.

"Thanks, Mase. For being here with me. Not like you have a choice since you didn't activate the emergency brake, but still… Oh gosh, I'm rambling."

My attention drifted back and forth between her eyes and her mouth. My body temperature soared, and I had no idea what to say or do. Other than football, Melinda Shepard was the only thing in my life that could hold my focus, and yet I was out of my depth with her, with no playbook to follow.

"Mase?"

I coughed, trying to break the spell. "Yeah?"

"What are you thinking?"

"Of doing something I should have done a long time ago."

I leaned forward, and my heart stopped.

Her breath hitched.

My entire being felt like it was being lit from the inside as I erased every inch separating our bodies one by one.

My lips were a hair's breadth away from hers.

My palms got sweaty.

The thrum of my heart accelerated, stronger and faster than ever before.

I moved closer. I could feel Melinda's minty breath tickling my upper lip.

If she didn't want me to kiss her this time, she had

point five seconds to react. Either she let me mold my lips to hers or she leaned back and put an end to it.

My brain became a mushy ball.

I pushed her hair behind her ear with my fingers.

Melinda's eyes darkened, their turquoise shade now a penetrating dark-cyan abyss.

It felt as if we were seeing each other for the first time again. "Hey."

She swallowed. "Hi." Her tongue swept her lips, and I followed the slow movement with my eyes.

I looped one hand around her waist, pulling her closer. "Mase…?"

"Mel… I know a few tricks that can make you forget we're hanging in the air and that we're stuck here for a while. Also, I've been thinking about kissing you for a very long time. Permission granted?"

"Mase, I can't…"

"Mel, I wanna kiss you."

"I wanna kiss you too."

"So can I? Kiss you, I mean."

"Not sure it's a good idea."

I blinked. "Why?"

"You've kissed a lot of girls, and I don't wanna be just another girl you do this with. The last time I kissed someone, he thought I was willing to offer more than I was ready to. I don't want the player you are with everyone else. If I'm kissing you, it has to mean something to you too."

"So, it's a *me* problem? I'm aware my rap sheet isn't all clean…"

"Nah." She shook her head multiple times. "It's about me this time."

"Mel, I wanna say… I'm not a player around you, okay? Never have been. I would never mislead you. In case you have doubts, I wanna put it out here. I love this friendship thing we've got going on. It's important to me. But it doesn't mean I don't want to explore this crazy chemistry we share and see where it takes us. It's nothing I've ever experienced before, and lately, I'm kinda unable to think about anything but you."

"Our friendship or whatever we have going on is precious to me too. For now, though…that's all I can be… your friend." The lust in her eyes said the opposite. Like she was dying to kiss me too, to lose herself in what we could be. The expression on her face looked painful. Was she going against everything her heart was urging her to do?

"The other night… I didn't imagine it. I was drunk, but not enough that I would have mistaken your coming apart in my arms for a dream."

A light blush colored her cheeks. "We must file it as a mistake. A moment of weakness. We cannot fool around because I'm not that girl, Mase. I cannot give you something without the assurance it's real for you too."

"I would never take something you're not willing to give, Mel. You know me better than that."

"I'm aware. It's just… You've been telling everyone since you turned fifteen you would never date. So, what does it make me then?"

"The one."

"Don't stay stuff like that."

I dragged a hand over my face. How could I make her see it was real for me too? "I'm not interested in playing the field anymore. I want you. I've always wanted you. I've acted stupid for far too long. All along, you were the only one I dreamed of being with. I know it doesn't erase my stupidity, but it's the truth, and it's about time I come clean about my feelings."

"I don't want you to have feelings for me. Not yet. If you do, it's gonna mess it all up. I can't… It's too hard if you do. The pressure. I'm not sure I'm strong enough to deal with it. Not right now."

"What do you mean?"

She blew out a breath, looking away. "Nothing you have to worry about."

I gripped her chin and turned her head so she was facing me. "Talk to me. Nothing you just said makes sense."

"It makes sense to me."

"Let me in. Please. I wanna help you. No matter what you need."

"I gotta do this on my own."

"But—"

"No but. Gimme a few weeks so everything works out."

I studied her, trying to decipher the hidden meaning of her words. "Are you like sick or something?"

The tiniest upturn of her lips told me she wasn't.

"Do I stand a chance? With you?" I had to ask. Better knowing I didn't now than hoping for something that could never exist.

"You do." She moved forward, resting her lips along the column of my throat and breathing me in. We stayed like that for a beat.

"What do we do now? It's torture spending all this time with you and not being able to act on my feelings."

She lodged herself in my arms, and I held her close to my heart. "I don't know."

"Winter Formal?"

Melinda leaned back to watch me. "What about it?"

"Our deadline. I'm gonna prove to you I've changed, and I'll help you figure out whatever you gotta figure out by then. We'll reassess what we are that night."

"Are you sure?"

"Yep. I'm not missing out on a chance to be with you if you wanna be with me as well. You're too important to me."

"Okay."

A heavy silence descended upon us, and time and gravity didn't seem to matter anymore.

A squeaky sound above us caught our attention, breaking us out of the invisible bubble that had risen around us in the last few minutes. Paige and Craig's pod was rocking back and forth, but from where we sat, we couldn't see what was going on inside, only caught bits of laughter.

"You think they're fooling around?" Melinda asked as we both stared at the car.

"Yep."

We watched the motions for a full minute, and a part of me wished I could be my brother. The one head over heels in love, making college plans with the one person I cared about the most in this world. The one who possessed every fragment of my heart.

An announcement blared from below us, breaking the moment. "Attention, attention. Due to technical difficulties, the Ferris wheel will stop all activities until further notice. To all passengers stuck on the ride right now, please remain seated at all times and keep your arms and legs inside the cars. Don't try to exit the ride on your own. Stay calm as we are working actively to resolve the issue. Emergency units and repair crews are on their way and will proceed to the passenger evacuation in a timely manner. Thank you for your cooperation, and we'll keep you updated on the situation."

"Ohmygod. We're gonna die. I can't be stuck here. *I'm*

going to die. This isn't happening. No. *No, no, no.* This is a nightmare. I can't breathe."

I swiveled on the seat to talk to Melinda. "Relax. No one is going to die. And if, and I say if, we were to die, I promised you earlier that I would keep you safe. Your life won't be in danger, no matter what."

She watched me, but I wasn't sure my words were registering.

"Just breathe."

She snapped out of her panic state and followed the rhythm I set, inhaling and exhaling in sync with me.

"Yes, like that. Again. See? You're doing good. You are safe, Mel. I'm with you. At least we have the best view. *I have* the best view." My sole focus remained on her, my hands enveloping hers and preventing them from shaking. "It's gonna be all right."

My phone chimed, and I slid it out of my pocket. I typed something, then added something else before flipping the device so she could read the exchange.

PAIGE

Mase, how's Mel? Please tell her not to freak out, okay? I wasn't kidding earlier. She hates heights.

ME

I know. She's okay. Don't worry.

You guys all right?

PAIGE

Yes. Take care of her. You promised.

I put the device back into my pocket and motioned to Melinda. "Come here." I lifted her and positioned her over me until she straddled me.

She splayed her small hands across my chest, and my heart cartwheeled in its cage.

"Mase, you're good at this. Making me forget. And caring for me."

I pushed down the bulge in my pants with a palm, trying to conceal the effect she had on me.

"Oh." She pinched her lips together as she followed my movements. "What now?"

I wrapped my arms around her body, and she relaxed against me. "You enjoy the ride."

A bit later, gone was the sunshine and the breeze felt colder against my skin, and chills traversed her body.

"Cold?" I asked.

"A little."

I removed my hoodie, now dressed only in a red T-shirt and a pair of jeans.

"What are you doing?"

"I'm running hot. Here." I slipped the hoodie over her head.

"No, you should keep it."

"Nah."

"Thanks. Soon you won't have any sweatshirts left if you lend them all to me."

"They look better on you. Don't worry, I have plenty."

We returned to our previous position, with her head in the crook of my neck and my arms around her. "You good?" I asked.

"Yeah. And you were not kidding. You really always run hot."

I kissed her temple. "I told you. It wasn't a ruse the other night." We stayed like that for infinite minutes. "Remember when you used to hate me?" I asked after a while.

She shook her head, her face still resting against my chest. "Hate is a strong word. I never really hated you."

"Come on. Don't lie to me."

"Never. I would never lie to you, Mase."

"Then tell me the truth."

She sighed. "I wanted to hate you. It was easier than to like you."

"So, you're telling me all the banter, the eye rolls, the pushing me away was because you liked me?"

"When you say it like that, it sounds bad…but kinda. The day I moved next door to you, I watched you play ball and wanted to be your friend. You had that poise, that agility and confidence I admired. I recognized a part of me in you, but you appeared to be braver than I was. Then you wanted us to date, and it scared me. I wasn't interested in boys, and I had never thought about dating anyone before you mentioned it. I had no idea what I should do or say. This was all new to me. Days later, you claimed me in front of everyone at school, and it made me so sad because I thought we had something special going on. You were my first friend in town, and people hated me because of it. I couldn't understand what I had done wrong to deserve their hatred. After that, I tried to hate you, but it faded away with time. So, it was never just hate…mostly hurt or something like that. You forgive me?"

"Yes. I'm still sorry. I never had a girlfriend before, and I never thought about dating someone before you appeared in my driveway. There was just something about you I found enticing, and I didn't like the idea of sharing you with my friends. It was clumsy. What I'm trying to say is that we both did stuff we're not proud of. I've just realized something, right about now, though. I wouldn't change the past if it meant you're stuck here tonight with no one else but me."

Once the ride went back into motion, four hours after it stopped midair, a part of me was ready to go back to the ground, but the bigger part of me wished we could have stayed in our little suspended bubble for longer. Because even though Melinda and I still hadn't defined what we were exactly to each other, I was aware that tonight had changed us. And since being together wasn't an option right now, I had no idea how to return to how things were before without making things weird again.

CHAPTER 25

IS MY OUTFIT THE REASON YOU'RE DROOLING ALL OVER YOURSELF?

Melinda stood at the end of the driveway, her jaw slack and her eyes traveling all over me, leaving a burn in their wake. I wiped my hands on a rag, watching her with an amused smirk playing on my lips. The intensity of her stare sent bolts of desire through my being, and I inhaled, doing my best to look unaffected.

"Shepard, is my outfit the reason you're drooling all over yourself?" I asked, pointing to the stained white T-shirt and old pair of jeans I was wearing.

She forced herself back into the present. "Ha. Ha. Very. Funny."

"So? Drooling again?" I pointed to the corner of her

mouth, and she ran the back of her hand across her lower face.

I pinched my lips together, doing my best to keep my chuckle leashed in.

"Oh, Mase. Stop. I'm not drooling."

"From where I stand, that's not what it looks like." I waggled my eyebrows in a teasing manner.

She poked her tongue out, and I finally let out the laugh I'd been holding in.

She wiped her mouth with a hand again, trying to look subtle but failing. I winked, and she shook her head, grinning. "Anyway, I came over because my dad said you have taken my car hostage."

I walked out of the garage, not bothering to put on a sweatshirt or a jacket. When Melinda stood in front of me, looking this hot in a pair of jeans and *my* hoodie, I couldn't care less about the November breeze. "I may have stolen your car earlier, that's a fact. But in my defense, I'm changing the brakes. I noticed they were due last week when you gave me a ride after practice. I didn't like the idea of your driving around town with worn brake pads."

"You…? Huh… You're fixing my car?"

I gestured to her vehicle lifted on jacks behind me and shrugged one shoulder. "Yep."

"I had an appointment for it next Friday after school."

"The thing is, I had free time today, and you would have missed the game next Friday if you'd gone to the mechanic. Anyway, working on cars is my secret superpower. Don't tell anyone or my schedule will blow up."

Since I was fourteen, I had been working at D&D Automobile in town during the summer. There was just something about cars and mechanics in general that fascinated me.

"That's… Wow, that's nice of you. And generous. I

should buy you a gold-painted wrench, but first, I gotta pay you back. How much do I owe you?"

I grinned big. "Nothing." I flicked my wrist because it really was no big deal. "I went shopping for parts with your dad because he insisted on paying, and my time is free—for you."

"You went shopping with my dad?"

"Yeah. We worked together on his car earlier. We fixed his rear wiper while we were at it and installed his winter tires. He helped me with my physics homework during lunch, so we're even."

I had gone to the Shepards' house this morning and asked for Melinda's keys when I knew she would be gone all day. Paige had picked her up yesterday, and they had a sleepover at her place. Melinda was scheduled at work all afternoon, and Craig had told me Paige would give her a ride, so the timing was perfect.

Before me, Melinda blinked a million times. "You went shopping with my dad and he helped you with your schoolwork?"

"Yep. As I said, all good. Your car will be ready tomorrow by the end of the day because I started it just thirty minutes ago, and I wanna do the oil change and replace the filters while I'm at it. And switch your tires for a winter set."

She stood there with her mouth hanging open.

"Don't worry, I'll give you a ride to the meet tomorrow. Just let me know what time we gotta leave and I'll be there."

"O-okay." She blinked again. "You're coming to the meet?"

"Yeah. I thought you would enjoy more supporters."

"Thanks?" She shook her head as if she just realized her reply sounded more like a question. "That's nice of you. To do this for me." Staring at me, she twisted her hands before her, looking nervous.

"Everything all right?"

"Wanna come over for dinner? Dad said he made too much food tonight. I think it was his way to let me know I could invite you."

My smile must have reached my ears. "Sure. I'll shower and change and meet you at your place afterward?"

She nodded, not saying a word. Her eyes sparkled, and I got hypnotized by her beauty.

The time we'd spent together hanging in the air on the Ferris wheel had sealed something in our friendship. I still wasn't sure what it was exactly, but I could feel how she looked at me differently these days. Something I had a hard time to define with words.

She cast a glance down, and when her eyes met mine again, something had changed in them. A confused expression shadowed her face. This time, it didn't look like lust, though, but more like she was far from here.

"Mel? You okay?" I stepped in front of her, coiling my hand around her wrist, pulling her closer, and inspecting her features.

She pulled herself back into the moment. "Yes. Sure. Sorry. I was… Lots on my mind."

I molded my palm to her cheek. She pressed her face into my touch, closing her eyes. "Hey, are you sure you want me to come over for dinner?"

She opened her eyes. "Yes. Please." She coughed to clear her throat. "Come knocking when you're ready." Her eyes lost focus, and she swayed on her feet. I clamped her elbow in case she fainted or something.

"Hey. Are you sure you're fine?" I tilted her head until I could look at her, and for a fraction of a second, confusion filled her gaze. From up close, she looked a bit pale.

Dark circles rimmed her eyes, and her cheeks appeared hollow.

"Huh…yes. A bit dizzy. I had a long day and barely slept last night. Paige and I talked till three in the morning." She breathed out. "I'm better now."

"Okay. You would tell me if something was wrong, right?"

"Yes. Don't worry about me. I'm under a lot of stress, and with the new training, the diet, school, and my work, I'm drained these days. I can't wait for the winter break."

We stared at each other for an infinite minute.

"You would tell me if it was something else?"

She nodded, and I let go of her.

"Thanks. For inviting me."

"Thanks. For fixing my car."

We exchanged smiles. A brick of the wall I'd erected around my heart a long time ago turned to dust.

Melinda Shepard's smile was definitely the most beautiful thing ever. It brightened even the grayest of days. Now I had the certainty my heart would never be whole without her holding it.

———

Later that night, we returned to my place and were in my bedroom, watching a movie, sitting on my bed. Melinda lay half spread on top of me, my fingers entangled in her hair. This had to be the most confusing relationship I'd ever had with a girl—and the only real relationship I'd ever had with a girl if I were being honest. We were acting as if we were dating, but there had been no attempt to take things further since we'd had the conversation that night at the fair.

"I should let you go so you can catch a full night's

sleep. You have a meet tomorrow and need the rest. Do you want me to prep you a snack before you leave? You only ate the veggies on your plate at dinner and a small piece of chicken. You must be starving."

"No. It's my night-before-meet diet. Lean protein and vegetables. I'll have a breakfast with carbs in the morning."

"Mel. I promised myself I wouldn't say anything, but this seems a bit harsh." I lifted myself up on one elbow to look at her. "I've worked with trainers and nutritionists for years, and they've never put me on such a restrictive diet. It's not like you're training for the Olympics. Are you sure you're in good hands and these people know what they're doing?"

"Mase, don't worry, okay? It's all under control. It's only temporary."

I lowered my hands to her hips. "You look exhausted all the time and those headaches… I'm not trying to piss on your training program here, I'm just…"

Her lips lingered on my jaw in a soft kiss. "Thanks, but I'll tell you if it's not the case." She rested her face in the crook of my neck.

"Even though I believe you should ask them to review your training and diet programs, I'll mind my own business, but I still think you should be in bed." I checked the time on my phone. "It's almost midnight."

"Mm-hmm, I'm going now." A yawn passed her lips. "It's hard because you make such a great pillow."

"Not sure your dad will invite me over again if you fall asleep here."

"Probably not." She sounded like she was already halfway to dreamland. "I'm just so comfy."

"Come on, Shepard. Even though I wish nothing more than to have you here all night, I'll walk you out." I shifted from under her weight and moved to my feet, holding out a hand for her to grab.

She sighed. "Fine."

Standing up, the full length of her body pressed against mine, and once again, I couldn't control how it reacted to the contact.

Melinda watched me with wide eyes. "Mase?"

I cleared my throat and shrugged because it was basic biology, and I had no idea how to respond to this.

Flames licked the inside of my body. My cells vibrated. I cupped the back of her head with a hand and leaned in to kiss her cheek. "Let's get you home."

We stood on Melinda's front porch, and I was about to leave when she grasped my hand. "Mase? I feel it too, you know. Just gimme a little more time."

"No pressure. I'm not going anywhere. Night, Mel."

"Good night, Mason."

———

I watched Melinda as she annihilated Emery Mellencamp, her rival from McKinley High, at the 100m backstroke event the next afternoon. She whipped her goggles off to look at the scoreboard, her victory grin splitting her face in two.

She skimmed the bleachers with a quick look, spotting where her parents and I sat, and I offered her a thumbs-up when our stares collided.

You did it, I mouthed. *You beat her ass.*

Melinda chuckled behind her closed fist, her eyes illuminating the entire pool area, pride evident on her features.

"She's really talented," Mrs. Shepard said in an

admiring tone. "She's been wanting to win against this girl all semester."

"Yeah." I nodded. "I'm sure the victory is really sweet right now."

Mr. Shepard nodded. "She works hard. It makes me happy when she sees the results of her efforts."

I was glad to know that the football team was not the only one having an obsession with beating their rivals. Today's meet was taking place at McKinley High, so a victory against their best swimmer was no doubt even more satisfying.

Back home, we ditched the Shepards' dinner invitation and decided to hang out at the park at the end of our street.

My phone rang when we stepped on the turf. The name *Peters*, a guy on the team, flashed on the screen.

"Hey, Cap. Throwing a rager tonight. Interested?"

"Tonight?"

"Yep. Nine. We have the whole basement to ourselves. My sister Jenny will be there too with some of her friends. Sheldon and Jax are already in."

"Gimme a sec." I blocked the speaker with my hand to address Melinda. "Peters is throwing a party. Wanna go?"

"Huh… Would you be mad if I said I'd prefer a laid-back night? You can go, though. I'm sure all your friends will be there."

"I'll pass. I'm not in the mood to be social tonight. I prefer hanging out with you."

We exchanged timid smiles.

"Hey, Pete. Not coming. I already have plans. Raincheck, okay?"

"Sure, Cap."

Melinda and I climbed on each side of the teeter-totter, and every time I pushed up with my legs, she only went halfway down because she wasn't heavy enough to balance my weight.

"Name something that grosses you out?" she asked, suspended in the air.

"Easy. People who chew with their mouths open. You?"

"I can't decide between oysters and snails. Equally disgusting."

I grimaced. "I agree. Clams and caviar. Just thinking about them and I want to barf."

"Favorite season?"

I didn't have to think about it. "Summer. It feels like everything is possible when the weather is perfect."

"True. Something from your childhood you miss?"

"Huh…That's harder. I'd say feeling like you can achieve anything. Like no dream is impossible and summer lasts forever."

"Oh, I like that. I was about to say, the ice cream truck. You know that creepy clown-like song that gave you the chills and brought excitement at the same time? There was one where I used to live in New Jersey that came every Tuesday night and Saturday morning. It was the highlight of my summers when I was little."

"Craig was convinced ice cream truck drivers were serial killers targeting children because he watched some scary movie once. We never neared one after that."

"No. Ohmygod, this is terrible. You missed out on all the fun."

"For the longest time, I thought it was Dad who made him watch that movie so we would stop annoying him about letting us buy ice cream."

She laughed. "That would have been a genius plan. Diabolic, but smart."

"Only he saw it at one of his friends' place, so my theory was proven false."

"Who knows? It must have been their parents who put that movie on."

I joined in on the laughter. "Yes. That makes perfect sense." I lowered the teeter-totter so she could climb off and motioned to the swings. "Come on, I'll push you. Maybe you can touch the sky with your toes."

"Oh, I used to love doing that. With my friend Jolie, we tried countless times to go all the way around."

"Craig broke his arm when he jumped from as high as he could get and landed badly. He was nine, I think."

"Ouch."

"He had the best-looking cast in all of Elk River. Let's just say it was full of penis drawings and genital and sex words we thought were funny. Mom was so desperate that she painted over it at some point. Only, black marker bleeds through paint after a while—we learned it that day. There was no way out of it for the six weeks it lasted."

"Boys are terrible. Nobody draws vaginas on girls' casts."

"I have nothing to say in my defense. We are indeed terrible."

We both burst into contagious laughter once again.

I sat on the swing to her left and pulled at the chain to close the distance between us, using my legs to swing us back and forth. The sun was low on the horizon, the sky a fading mixture of pink and orange paint splatter. The wind picked up, and soon scattered snowflakes danced around us. They melted as soon as they touched the ground.

We both stared at the sky, the white specks of snow glistening against the darkness, thanks to the park's lighting.

"It's beautiful," Melinda said with awe. "I love snow."

"Me too." A snowflake landed on the tip of her nose, and I captured it with a finger. "Make a wish."

"Isn't it something you're supposed to do with eyelashes?"

"Yeah, but let's pretend it is. C'mon, Shepard. Play along."

She closed her eyes and breathed out before opening them again. I presented her my digit, and she blew on the melted ice crystal.

We remained silent as we swung back and forth for a little while. The snow stopped, and it felt as if we had been the only witnesses to the very first flurry of the season.

Melinda chewed on her thumbnail as I set the pace. "Can I tell you something I've never told anyone, not even Paige?"

"Sure." My heart hammered in my chest at the thought she was choosing me to confide in.

"When I was ten, I was the only girl in my class wearing a bra. I was an early bloomer as they call it. One day, I removed my sweater during lunch hour, and my T-shirt got stuck to it, and I flashed everyone. Mean girls started calling me *perky boobs*. I would feel sick before school in the morning because I was so stressed out. It lasted for about two months. Some other kid did something stupid, and it diverted their attention from me. After the winter break, most girls were wearing bras and suddenly, I wasn't so awkward in their eyes."

"It went down before you moved here?"

"Yeah. It was the most humiliating experience of my life. I thought I would die of shame for the time it lasted. For some reason, I never told my parents. I kept it a secret. Now I wished I had involved them so I wouldn't have felt all alone and afraid to go to school."

"Kids are stupid. Is that why it hurt you so much when I put you on the spot on the first day of seventh grade?"

"Kinda. It reminded me of that episode of my life, and

I really didn't want to be in the spotlight anymore. I usually prefer when I'm behind the cameras than the main protagonist. Except when I'm swimming. Then I like to win, be in control, and succeed. It's like another part of me takes over when I'm in the water."

"I'm sure I look like I crave being the star of the show, but I swear, I do not. I understand what you mean."

"Why are you always so…so exuberant at school? It seems like you love the fuss."

"It's a role I play. People love that guy, but he's not me. Not entirely."

"Why do you do it then? Why pretend to be someone you're not?"

I shrugged, glancing down to avoid her heavy gaze on me. The one full of questions. "It's easier, I guess. I show people what they expect, and they enjoy it. It's a façade. Many things in life aren't what they seem…"

The night fell upon us, and we kept asking each other questions, slipping back into the easy chemistry we'd shared before Melinda opened up about her past insecurities.

"Favorite ice cream flavor?" I asked.

"Pistachio. You?"

"Brownies."

"Which one of your friends is the craziest?"

I rubbed my jaw with a hand. "This is a tough one. I feel like they're all crazy in their own way. Rusty forgets to think before he acts sometimes. Sheldon is afraid of nothing which is not always good news. Chase is just a jack-in-a-box, and you never know what to expect from him, but the guy is loyal to a fault. He's like a puppy. If he adopts you, then it's for life."

"I love the comparison. He really is a ball of contagious energy."

"Yep. Other than Craig, he's the one guy I would put all my trust in. I just wish his life was simpler."

"What do you mean?"

"It's not my story to tell." I jumped to my feet and held out a hand. "Come on, let's walk."

"Movie? You can come to my place."

"Okay, but I choose what we watch. Nothing gore."

She snickered and used a baritone voice. "Don't be a pussy, Mase."

"Ha. Ha. Don't impersonate Chase."

Melinda linked her arms with mine. "I would never dare to."

———

"Melinda, honey, is Mason still here?" Mrs. Shepard asked around midnight. "We're going to bed. If he is, it's time for him to go home."

"I'm not ready for you to leave," Melinda whispered after pausing the thriller movie we were watching.

I kissed her forehead. "It's okay. We'll see each other soon." I winked and moved to my feet.

"Mase, wait. I'll walk you out."

"Night, Mr. and Mrs. Shepard," I said when I passed them in the living room.

"Good night, Mason," they both replied.

"Wanna go for a run tomorrow?" I asked Melinda, the moment her parents disappeared upstairs, and it was just the two of us in the dimly lit entryway.

"Yeah. Eight?"

"Sure." I pressed a kiss to her cheek. "See you."

For the next ten minutes, I stood in their driveway, watching as lights were turned on upstairs and turned off soon after. Once I was sure it was safe to proceed, I went home, showered, and changed into a pair of charcoal sweatpants, a white wife-beater, and a black hoodie, and returned outside.

Climbing the wall leading to Melinda's bedroom like I had done the night I was drunk, I tapped on her window with a knuckle. It took seconds for her to open the curtains.

"Mase? What are you doing?"

"You said you were not ready for me to leave…and… well, I wasn't ready to leave either. Can I come in?"

She bobbed her head fast. "Yes, but it can't become a habit."

"Why not? I like sleeping here." I hoisted myself over the windowsill and landed inside. "It's not my fault. Your bed is comfier than mine."

"Yeah, right. Your mattress is a big fluffy cloud, and it's like twice the size of mine. Try again."

"Okay. Fine. I lied. It's not the bed that attracts me but the company."

She shook her head. "I have nothing to say to this. Wanna finish that movie?"

"Yes." We resumed our previous position on the bed, sitting with my back against the headboard and Melinda lying on her side, her head resting on my lap while I twisted strands of her hair around my fingers. It felt oddly couple-like even though we were just friends—or friends who cuddled.

"At the beginning of the summer, I acted without thinking first, and that's how I hurt my good shoulder," I said when the credits rolled on the screen. "I've been pretending it's no big deal, but sometimes, it doesn't feel like it's fully healed, like something is wrong with it."

She flipped to her other side to face me. "Have you changed your mind about seeing a doctor?"

"Nah. Back when I hurt my elbow, it affected my

season. I only have a few games left, playing for the Bears. I can't risk being benched when this season matters so much and we're on a winning streak."

"You've been playing really well."

"I think it's the adrenaline. I'm so in the zone during the games that I think even if I lost a limb, I wouldn't notice."

"Did you tell someone else?"

"Nope. Only Craig and a few of my teammates who were present are aware. They all promised never to say a thing about it unless I was the one coming forward. They don't wanna risk their season too."

"How did you manage to cover it up?"

I snorted. "A lot of icing and not walking around bare chest for a while. It was purple all around. I've been resting it as much as I can... I don't think anything is broken, though. It's just a feeling... It doesn't hurt. It-it's just stiffer than it used to be."

"Mase, you should really get someone to look at it."

"Maybe."

"You said you would. The last thing you need is for that injury to have long-term consequences and affect you in college or when you go pro."

I traced the contours of her face with a fingertip. "It's hard to ask for help when you feel vulnerable."

She looked past me. "I'm well aware..." Her gaze returned to my face, and she squeezed my hand. "Please think about it."

CHAPTER 26

I NEED ICING. NO, NOT ICING, BUT ICE. A LOT OF ICE

My lips broke into the largest grin known to humankind when I opened my bedroom door and bumped into Melinda a week later. A too attractive sight early on a Saturday morning. "Mel? What are you—" The cupcake she'd been holding lay smashed between our bodies, blue frosting spreading all over my bare skin. My eyes darted between my chest and her face, the amusement playing on my lips impossible to hide.

"Huh… Happy birthday?" She winced. "Sorry?"

"Are you my gift?"

She blinked. "Your what?"

"My gift? Since it's my birthday and you're standing here first thing in the morning."

"*Ohhh.*" A red hue skated up her cheeks. "No. I'm

here because I thought it would be fun to surprise you and spend the day together. Unless you have other plans."

I cradled the back of her neck and kissed her forehead. "Nothing sounds better than spending my birthday with you."

I let go of her, and she appeared shaky on her feet. She zoomed in on the blue mess right above my heart. "I'm sorry for this. It was meant to be eaten."

With a finger, I scooped some of the frosting and brought it to my mouth. "It still serves its purpose, and it tastes amazing."

"You think? Paige coached me over the phone while I whipped it."

I used the same finger to scoop more frosting and brought my digit to her mouth. "Open up and taste it." My words sounded dirty even to my own ears. The flush on her face darkened, and my body pulsed at how magnificent she looked when she was bothered.

She did as I asked of her, swirling the tip of her tongue and sucking my finger clean to capture every bit of the buttercream.

"Fuck, Mel." I breathed hard, my voice huskier than I intended it to be, turned on. Dressed in only a pair of neon-colored boxer briefs, I couldn't hide anything as we stood a foot apart.

The air around us became charged. I watched her with hooded eyelids, not sure how to shy away from the lust taking over every inch of me.

She batted her lashes and said, "I should clean up the mess I made."

I blinked, trying to compute her words, but before I could ask what she meant, Melinda leaned forward and licked the icing off my chest, taking her sweet time. My heart rate picked up, and I was sure she could feel every thump against her lips.

I sucked in a harsh breath and grabbed her hips, my fingers pressing into her flesh and bones. I grew rigid as she laved my bare chest with her tongue until there was no trace of icing left.

"Mel…"

She stepped back, averting her eyes.

"Look at me." I cocked her face toward mine with a finger. "Whoa. You can wish me happy birthday every day for the rest of my life if that's how you do it."

We watched each other for the longest beat.

Her throat rippled.

"I'll shower now. A very cold shower, okay? I need icing. No, not icing, but ice. A lot of ice. An icy shower."

She followed the motion of my hand as I cupped my erection to keep it from drilling a hole through my boxer briefs.

Her face turned fire-engine red.

I lifted the bottom edge of her buttermilk-yellow ruffled top a few inches and smoothed my thumb over the pink scars the surgery had left on the lower-right side of her abdomen. Melinda held her breath, goose bumps rising on her skin under my gentle touch. "Does it hurt?"

She shook her head.

"Good." I released her top, and she trembled when I removed my hand. "Can you wait for me? You can stay here. I won't be long."

"Okay."

I picked the cupcake from her grip and engulfed it in three bites after she shook her head when I offered her some. "Best birthday ever. Thanks, Shepard."

I kissed her cheek and disappeared into the bathroom next door before I did something like kissing her to oblivion or eating her up like I'd dreamed of doing every night. I was playing with fire. The dance was in four weeks. It was our deadline. I had to keep it to myself until then. I could do this. Under the hot stream of the shower, the realization dawned on me. Melinda Shepard had licked my bare chest. By the time Winter Formal rolled around, I would be an aching mess if I didn't regain some self-control.

I turned the temperature of the shower to the lowest setting, but the cold water did nothing to decrease the desire tightening my body.

I rested my forehead against the tiled wall, breathing in and out to slow the wild rhythm of my heart. For a second, I thought about rubbing one, but knowing Melinda was on the other side of the wall, in my bedroom, waiting for me, killed the idea. That thing she did earlier—licking my frosting-covered chest—was hot as hell, and I'd frozen, mesmerized by everything she was. I loved this new side of her, bolder and more assured around me. She was slowly breaking out of her shell, and I wanted to be the one she did it for—the one she did it with.

The tension in me lessened, and I toweled myself dry before dressing in a pair of jeans and a dark long-sleeved T-shirt with my jersey number printed on the front in gold ink.

An ache built inside me when I opened my bedroom door and found her there, in my personal space, and I had to fight with myself not to lay her on my bed. She wasn't ready. I could tell she was still unsure about us. About me. Not about our friendship, but how much she could trust me. Since the beginning of the school year, I'd stepped up my game, and I wondered what else I could do to make her have total faith in me.

Melinda was busy going through the books on the shelf

mounted on the wall opposite my bed, her back to me. Like a stalker, I admired her for a minute, relishing the way her stretch dark-indigo jeans made her legs look infinitely long, before I cleared my throat to announce my presence.

"I hadn't pictured you as a fiction reader," she said, her hand tracing the spines of the paperbacks before she spun around to face me. "I don't know why I've never noticed these before."

I shrugged. "Everyone needs to escape real life once in a while."

A faint smile touched her lips. "Good answer. Are you ready for a full day of fun?"

"It depends. What do you have in mind?"

"A lot of things. Come on, Birthday Boy, let's get out of here."

Melinda treated me to a mountain of waffles with berries and whipped cream at Breakfast at Midnight, a twenty-four-hour little eatery on the outskirts of town. She ordered a side of fresh fruit for herself after telling me she'd had a protein shake earlier and was perfectly happy to watch me eat my weight in carbs, as long as she didn't have to join in. We spent the rest of our morning at the indoor roller-skating rink, something she had never done before. Not willing to risk Melinda falling and hurting herself—that was the bullshit excuse I fed her—I held her hand the entire time. It gave me an excuse to touch her without seeming too obvious about it.

For lunch, we sat in my car and devoured a picnic she had prepared earlier while we chatted about everything, and then spent the afternoon at the arcade where she beat me at air hockey. Twice. I got my revenge when we played roll and score right after, and I won all three rounds.

Things were simple and easy between us. I didn't

remember the last time I'd had this much fun and laughed for so many hours.

Until I bumped into Tanya when we were ordering tea at Beans, the coffee shop on Main Street. Melinda was waiting at the counter for our order to be ready while I was on a mission to pick a table by the wall-length window. The place was small and popular amongst teenagers who often came here for a coffee break or to study. It had cream walls, a dark exposed ceiling, blush-pink tables, and black chairs.

"Here you are," Tanya exclaimed as if she'd been looking for me. She jumped into my arms like she had the right to, as if we were best friends who hadn't seen each other in a while. "Happy birthday, Mase." She smacked my cheek with her heavily painted lips, no doubt leaving an imprint behind.

I rubbed my cheek with a finger and stepped back, stuffing my hands into my pockets to create some sort of physical barrier between us.

"Thanks," I spoke the single word with as much indifference as I could muster, my eyes traveling between the clingy cheerleader and Melinda, who had no idea we had company, deep in conversation with the barista, her back to us. How Tanya remembered my birthday was a mystery, one I had no intention of solving. Like ever.

"Are we celebrating or what?" She took a step forward and dragged her fingernails down my chest. "I have a gift for you." Her lips swelled into a pout. "But I don't have it with me right now. You'll have to come to my place so I can give it to you." She smiled in a way she probably thought was sexy. "I'm not sure it's meant to be given in front of an audience anyway."

"I'm not interested, Tan. I thought I'd made myself clear multiple times already."

She flicked her wrist like I was being silly. "Nonsense. Everybody loves to be spoiled on their special day. When you meet me at my house later, I will—" She stopped her rant the moment Melinda neared us, two cups in her hands. "Aren't you clingy?" She sighed. "You can keep walking, swim girl. Can't you see you're interrupting us? It's Mason's birthday, and we're making plans for him to pick up his gift later." She winked like we were both in on whatever she meant.

I took one cup from Melinda's grip and draped my free arm over her shoulders. "Actually, Tan, I'm not available to come to your house today or ever. I'm here with Mel. If you would excuse us. See you around…or not." I laced our fingers and led Melinda away. We sat across from each other at a table in the far back. "I'm sorry. About that." I pointed toward the door behind me with my thumb, where I suspected Tanya was still standing, fury probably straining her features as she spied on us.

Melinda shook her head, but the smile that had been a permanent fixture on her face all day had dipped. "Mase, if you've got places to be, don't let me keep you."

I squeezed her hand over the table. "No. I'm here with you. No one else."

Her eyes followed something over my shoulder, no doubt Tanya being her despicable self, and I could tell the easy bubble we'd been basking in since the morning had burst.

"I have to go home for dinner," Melinda said after we finished our drinks and walked toward my car parked at a short distance from Beans.

"O-okay. I'll drive you. About earlier…Tanya…she was messing with you. I have no intention of going to her place if that's what you're worried about."

"Mason. You and I aren't a couple. You're free to be

friends with whoever you want. I'm not the police of you." She forced the widest grin onto her lips. "And by the way, you still have a red lipstick smudge on your left cheek."

I wiped my face with my sleeve and turned my head to the side. "Better?"

"All gone. Just so we're clear on this, you don't have to justify your actions to me. We're friends, and it doesn't come with a free pass to know everything that's going on in each other's lives."

Her words acted as if she had slapped me. A wall rose around her, and I despised the distance she was forcing between us.

I unlocked my car and we hauled ourselves inside, sitting there as I made no move to start the engine. Tension filled the cab, suffocating me.

"And just so we're clear," I said after a beat, using her own words against her, "it didn't feel like we were just friends when you licked my chest this morning." My words were clipped, and I hated myself the moment they left my mouth. "You know we're way past the friend zone by now. That chemistry, those sparks, I've never felt them with anyone else."

She remained silent, her stare staying trained on the passenger window, her back to me.

"I don't know what you want from me anymore."

Finally, she refocused her attention on me. "Trust. I've seen you sleeping around for over a year, Mase. Everyone has. And I see how girls are around you. You're like a magnet. I know we're more than friends by now, and yes, I admit there's something sizzling when we're together and I'm a sucker for it, but I'm scared. I'm scared that if I give you my heart, you'll stomp on it because I'm not like the girls you usually hang out with."

"Is it about Tanya or something else? You gotta talk to

me when things bother you. I thought we were fine. I thought we had decided we'd be together once you figure out whatever stuff you gotta deal with."

"That's the thing. I won't act like a jealous girlfriend when we're not even officially together."

"Not yet."

"You owe me nothing, Mase. As long as we're not *together* together, it would be hypocritical of me to ask things from you."

"Winter Formal is in a month. We agreed we would date by then. I'm trying to go at your pace here. Talk to me or else I can't guess what's going on in that pretty head of yours."

"Would you wanna know?"

"Yes. All of it. The good, the bad, the ugly. I can't do better if I don't know what's wrong."

"Is it Tanya? Maybe. Or the girl at the pizza place you flirted with yesterday without even realizing it. And the girls at school who follow you like you own the secret to the next makeup trend. Or the clerk at the library who can't stop ogling you whenever you step foot in. Oh, and I forgot the three girls who have slipped you their number since we left your place this morning without being discreet about it, even though I was standing right beside you. It's not fun, Mase."

"Are you hearing yourself right now?"

"There will always be someone else who's flirting with you or begging you to follow them home. I'm not stupid, Mase. You are you, and I am me."

"What's wrong with you being you? And what does it mean, *I am me?*"

"Nothing." She shot both arms over her head before dropping them back to her lap. "I don't wanna compete with the others. I'm not pretty enough to compete with them. My shoulders are too broad and my eyelashes, not long enough, and unlike you, I'm pretty much inexperienced."

"Is that how you think I see you? Because let me tell you it's a load of bullshit. I don't care about the other girls, Mel. I only care about you. They could parade naked while you are wearing a snowsuit, and I would still think you're the most beautiful one in the room. I'm aware I have a rep, and I can understand why it would put you off, but I'm not that guy anymore. It has never been me. It was all an act. Something stupid I did to… It doesn't matter. What matters is that I want you, but I have no clue how to make you trust me once and for all. How to move forward with you without my past tainting our future."

She said nothing, hugging herself with her arms.

"Is it about the night of the party? The one I spent at your place? The night I was drunk?"

No response.

"I thought we were past that. I said I was sorry and explained myself. I proved myself to you. Over and over. Why can't you still not trust me with your heart? For your information, I trust you with mine. Fully. I've been trusting you since you moved next door and we were just kids."

She gasped at my revelation.

"See? I'm fully invested in an *us*. I'm just waiting for you to join me."

"I need more time. That first night…when you slept at my place…you touched me like no one ever has. When we're together, I forfeit all my defenses. I'm used to being in control. I hate when my heart takes over and my head cedes all its power. And today, it's your birthday and we've spent an amazing day together and now we are fighting and I don't wanna fight with you. I hate fighting with you." Tears rolled down her cheeks. "I'm a mess. I can't think clearly these days. Everything feels like a battle. It's like all I am doing is climbing an invisible mountain, and I still can't reach the top."

I pulled her into my arms over the console between our seats. At first, she resisted, but eventually, she let go, and I lifted her up until she straddled me. I kept my arms fastened around her and slowly, she relaxed in my embrace. "Shhh. It's okay. For the record, I don't wanna fight with you either. I'll give you more time to get used to the idea we are it. And I'll keep proving to you I'm not that guy who used to sleep around. He's the past version of me. The chickenshit version of me. I can do better. No, I *will* do better. By you. For you."

"Mase. You don't have to change for me. You would hate me if you did."

"I'm doing it for me. I wanna be a guy who's worthy of you. All day. Every day. The one you'll trust, no matter what, and whom you will always come back to. The one I am beneath all the bullshit I've been hiding under for too fucking long. I hate playing a role to please people, but over time, it has become second nature to me. It's a hard habit to break, but I want to because I'm not happy. Only you and the game feel real to me. And I want both. No, scratch that. I need both."

Her cries intensified. "Why do you always say the right thing when I feel vulnerable? Some days, I wish I could go back to hating you…or pretending I did… When I pushed you away, I was in control, and things were not so scary… and confusing"

"I've always liked being in control too. We have that in common. It's the first time I've let someone else in, and I'm still not used to it. It's the first time I let my emotions do the talking too." I shrugged. "Maybe we can learn how to do it together."

She looped her arms around my neck. "I'd like that, but… I'm not the person you think I am."

I tried to lean back, but Melinda tightened her grip around me, making it impossible for me to see her face. "What does that mean?"

"Nothing. Forget I said anything." She paused. "Did you really mean it when you said I was pretty?"

"Mel, I would never lie to you."

She relaxed against me, and I held her close, enjoying the bond that had emerged between us. For the longest time, we hugged each other, not saying anything. It felt as if our bodies and our souls could mend the distance that had materialized between us in the last ten minutes.

Leaning back, she brushed my cheeks with her fingers and offered me a hint of a smile. "Mase, for what it's worth, you are pretty too…for a boy."

A loud chuckle tumbled out of my mouth. A load of memories from our younger selves replayed in my mind. Years later, Melinda Shepard still enticed me as much as she confused me. Maybe we'd be all right after all.

CHAPTER 27

YOU AND ME, WE NEED THIS

"Why are we heading toward the cabin?" Melinda asked from the passenger seat. "I thought we were going home."

"I know, but Jax texted me and said he messed up. It sounded urgent. You know what it means. I'm not going to abandon him when he needs me. It shouldn't take long."

"Fine."

I was almost relieved that, after we'd left Beans, my teammate had sent me a 911 text. Our fight over my past fuckboy persona had left me feeling raw, and I wasn't ready to let go of her just yet. I needed more time by her side, wanting us to go back to the way we'd been lately. This awkwardness between us made me uncomfortable in my own skin. I couldn't find the words to convince her we could be something real, if given a real chance.

I drummed my fingers against the steering wheel. "Sheldon called last night and said he was throwing a party tomorrow to celebrate my birthday. You're invited too. He told his parents he was having a pre-Thanksgiving barbecue with some friends, and they bought it, so we'll be meeting at his place around nine if you can make it."

"I work tomorrow night until eleven, but I'll try to make an appearance afterward. I took more hours at the movie theater since school is off this week for Thanksgiving. I'll check if Paige is going, and maybe we can share a ride."

I nodded. Melinda's back was ramrod straight, and her smile hadn't fully returned. She still seemed a bit shaken about our earlier confrontation, but at least now we were talking to each other instead of screaming.

I stretched my arm and enveloped her hand with mine. "Are we okay?" I needed the confirmation we were fine. That whatever our fight was about, we would get over it.

"Yes."

I didn't release her hand as I took the exit leading to the cabin belonging to Jackson's uncle. "I wonder what he did. I swear, the guy only thinks with his dick."

Melinda snickered. "Like someone I know…or how he used to be."

I sighed. "Touché." If her sense of humor had returned, we were halfway back to our normal selves.

I drove on the dirt road along the lake, killed the engine, and turned toward her. "Come inside with me? In case it takes longer than I planned, or he's handcuffed to a bedpost and I need a witness to confirm it really did happen. One day, he'll meet his match, and it'll actually happen."

"You think some girl left him in there and ran away with the key?"

"Who knows? It's a possibility. With him, nothing surprises me anymore. And I'm best friends with Chase, so can you imagine?"

"Chase is terrible."

"I won't argue with that statement. I swear, these guys always think after they act. I can't figure out how they can be so good on the field and so idiotic off it."

"My parents used to say the same thing about my brother when he still lived with us. Like he never thought about the consequences before he acted. I hope he's done doing stupid shit nowadays."

"Any news? It feels like he's never been around much."

"Nah. He's in Nashville, playing gigs in bars, hoping to get a record deal. He's not really the chatty type, never has been, so I'm not sure what else is going on in his life."

"That sucks."

"As long as he's happy, I supposed it's good enough. Sometimes, I wish he was more of a big brother, you know. I could use a sibling relationship like you and Craig…or his outlook on stuff…someone who sides with me when my parents are treating me like a kid or gives me advice. Having a guy's point of view would be useful sometimes. Anyway, those kinds of things."

"I hit the jackpot when I landed Craig as a big brother. I know I'm lucky. He's the best."

She mirrored my smile. "He really is. You guys have the kind of bond everyone would wish for."

Melinda unbuckled her seatbelt and followed me on the path leading to the cabin. I slowed my steps and locked my fingers around hers when she neared me. We climbed the few stairs leading to the front porch and stopped. I cracked my neck on both sides and rolled my shoulders back. "Okay. Wish me luck. And stay behind me if you're not ready for whatever we witness in there."

"You think it's gonna be that bad?"

I bobbed my head. "It usually is. The last two times he called me stating it was an emergency, well, let's just say it was…" I scratched my head, not sure how to describe my friend's antics. "I wanted to bleach my eyes afterward."

"What did he do?" She whispered as if we were in on a secret. "Now I wanna know. You can't tease me like that and not say anything."

"All right. I'll save you the details, but one of those times, Jax thought he would have a threesome. Turned out he was dating two girls at the same time and one of them offered him a fun time with her twin sister. The twins were not identical, and he was indeed dating both of them and had no clue. They got their revenge by tying his wrists and ankles together behind his back like he was a piece of meat, pulling his pants down, and strapping a gag ball into his mouth. It was epic. Traumatizing, but spectacular all at once."

Her hand flew to cover her growing smirk. "*Ohhhh.*"

"Yep. Not a sight I wish to ever see again. They wrote *Pig* on his chest with red lipstick. It took him over an hour to be able to make a phone call."

"I bet. That is horrible. I'm glad you didn't bleach your eyes, but I understand why you wanted to." A low chuckle parted her lips. "Let's be brave. How bad can it be this time around?"

"You're right. Let's get it over with." I knocked on the front door before making my way inside. "Jax? Man, are you there? If you're naked, please warn me or grunt or stomp your foot so I'm not walking in on a scene that will traumatize me for life. I'm still not over your latest fuck-up. And I have company, so please don't scar us for life."

"Why is it so dark in here?" Melinda murmured from behind me, her grip around my fingers tightening.

"No idea. It's already sketchy. No matter what it is, I hope he's dressed." Running my palm over the wall, I flipped the light switch on, and a loud "Happy Birthday" resonated through the room when my friends and teammates popped out from behind furniture and cheered me on.

I cocked my head to look at Melinda, who stared at me with glint in her eye. "Happy birthday, Mase." Gone was the heaviness that had settled over her features in the last hour. Her smile was back and blinding and looked genuine.

I clamped the back of my neck with a hand and turned toward her. "You knew?"

"Yeah. I'm glad the surprise worked. I was in charge of keeping you busy all day. I didn't have to go home either. It was a ruse so you wouldn't suspect a thing when Jax texted you."

I lifted her in my arms and twirled her around. "Thanks. I had the most amazing day with you today."

We fixated on each other for an infinite minute before I lowered her to her feet as my friends came to clap my back.

"I'm not naked this time," Jackson said as we fist-bumped.

"Thank God. I wasn't ready for a repeat experience of last time."

"Happy birthday, Captain."

"Mase, my man." Sheldon walked up to us, handing me a shot glass. "Just to be clear, there's no party tomorrow."

I laughed with my head tilted back. "I kinda guessed it."

We clinked our glasses and downed them in one gulp. When I searched for her, Melinda had disappeared into the crowd. A piece of my heart cracked, and I prayed we really would be fine after all.

"Birthday, man," Craig said as he pulled me closer and ruffled my hair. "Glad you could make it. We're finally the same age again. How was your day?"

"Great..."

He pulled me aside. "What happened?"

I hung my head as the name "Tanya" left my mouth.

"And?"

I returned my gaze to his. "She said things...and it looked very bad...for me. No matter how many times I tell her to leave me alone, she doesn't get the memo. It's harassment, I swear. Double standards, man. Big time. I would be arrested if I did the same thing to her. Anyway, Mel freaked out. Said trusting me wasn't always easy. We got into a fight."

"Well, I hate saying this, but you kinda brought it on yourself when you fraternized with the she-devil."

"You're supposed to be on my side."

"Geez, Mase. I am. But if you play with fire, don't be surprised when you get burned. No matter what, don't play Tanya's games. She's not worth the trouble. Keep proving to Melinda you really are a different guy than the one you used to be months ago. That's all she's asking for. The proof can't be a temporary fix, but a permanent one."

I quirked one eyebrow. "Insider information?"

"Not much. Paige is tight-lipped about everything. The only piece of information I got, and man, you owe me big time, is that Mel wants to trust you, but she's being extra cautious before jumping in with both feet. Her main priority right now is that scholarship to Crestwood U. Paige says she's more obsessed about it than she has ever been before. It's all she talks about when they're together."

"She does? She barely broaches the subject with me. For the record, I talked to her about her training program and her diet the other day because, no matter what everyone says, it doesn't sound healthy to me. She's always tired and is complaining of headaches."

"And?"

"Nothing. I said I would mind my own business since she's convinced it's all under control."

"Fuck, but we can't blame her. We'd both do just about anything to play pro," Craig said. "She had that surgery, and perhaps it has affected her mindset. Her coach wouldn't let her put her health at risk. They have shrinks and specialists at school for athletes. If it's serious, I'm sure Mel will ask for help. She's smart."

"Yeah, I guess you're right. It still feels off somehow."

"I'll talk to Paige, see if she has noticed something else."

"Thanks."

More drinks were handed to me, and soon I felt tipsy but happy—and relaxed.

After half a dozen slices of pizza and more beer, I joined some of my friends outside, all of them bundled up in jackets and hats and standing around the bonfire. From the crisp late-November breeze and humidity in the air, we could tell December was just a little over a week away.

My eyes were trained to find Melinda because I spotted her the moment I exited the cabin through the back door.

She was deep in conversation with two girls, looking cozy in her white fluffy jacket. I inched closer to them and wrapped my arms around her from behind. A shiver danced up her back when she relaxed against me, and it shot me with renewed joy. Her body couldn't lie. We would be okay.

"Dance with me?"

"Mase…"

"Don't." I spun her around and placed a finger over her lips. "You and me, we need this…we need to connect. Today was amazing, and I'm not ready for it to end." I stared into her eyes. "For the record, I hate fighting with you too."

She nodded, her cheek brushing mine, then tipped her head back to look at me. I released her and tugged at her sleeve to usher her further away from our friends to a dark secluded corner.

Melinda swirled and looped her arms around me, connecting us once again. "Are you drunk?"

I nuzzled her neck, my lips stretching wide. "Just a teeny tiny bit. Are you drunk?"

"Nah. I only had sparkling water."

"Is it true we're all sleeping here? Chase told me they'd put the stuff Craig brought over in one of the rooms upstairs." I kissed her cheek, my lips lingering on her soft skin while I breathed her in.

"Yes. That's the plan."

"Did you bring your stuff?"

"Paige and your brother did. I'm not sure if I'm staying yet."

I leaned back to watch her. "Shepard, will you stay in my bedroom with me tonight?"

We were nestled deeply in each other's arms, swaying to the music playing inside that was barely audible from here.

"Mase."

"Mel."

"I'm not sure it's a good idea."

"Why not?"

"Because." She glanced down. "You know…"

"Is it about this morning or our earlier conversation?"

She swallowed, and even in my tipsiness, I heard every ripple of her throat. "Both."

I leaned back and placed my hands gently on her cheeks. "Tanya and every girl before you were mistakes. A lack of judgment on my part. I have a history, but I don't want to go there ever again. I'm sorry I hurt you. I never meant to. No one else means anything to me. But you? You mean everything."

She said nothing, and I let go of her face. She buried herself deeper in my arms, her head resting against my throbbing heart.

"If we make it to State in two weeks, will you come to see me play?"

"Isn't it like a three-hour drive from here?"

I nodded. "I checked. You don't have a meet that weekend. I'm longing to see you in the bleachers, cheering me on."

"Maybe I can come. I'll check my work schedule. Paige said she was going. If it works out, we could ride together instead of riding the buses the school provides."

"Good. I-I…huh…I wanna ask you a favor."

Melinda raised her eyes to mine, waiting.

"Will you wear my jersey?"

Her lips parted. "You want me to wear your jersey? Isn't it like something only girlfriends do?"

"Yeah, so? Will you? It's kind of important to me if you do. I swear I'll play better if I see you wearing it."

Her heart banged in her chest, every thump reverberating through me.

"Mase, what are we?"

"Bound by fate."

"You really believe it?"

"More with every minute we spend with each other."

"I like that." She repositioned herself against me, and I tightened my arms tighter around her body as we danced the night away.

Lying on our backs on top of the mattress in one of the bedrooms, fully dressed, we linked our fingers together, barely exchanging a word, our energies doing all the talking. Melinda had said nothing after my earlier confession, but she'd stuck by my side all night and agreed to share a bed with me. "As long as we keep our clothes on and our hands to ourselves," she had said. It was meant as a joke, but I could tell that was what she wished too.

"Hey, Mel?"

"Yeah."

"Thank you for today…or, huh, yesterday now, I think. Anyway, it was the best birthday I've ever had. Because we spent it together." She remained silent next to me, and I wondered if she had fallen asleep. "Can I hold you, or does that count as touching you?"

She rolled to her side and pushed her ass against me. I pulled her into my arms, drawing her close to my chest, relishing her warmth and the softness of her body. I had turned seventeen with a smile anchored to my face. One I hoped would never be flushed away.

"Happy birthday, Mase. I had a great time too. Please, don't let go of me."

"Never."

CHAPTER 28

JUST DOING MY JOB

With my fingers laced behind my head, I paced the hotel room, unable to stay still for more than a few seconds.

"Please, stop." Chase moved to stand before me and put his hands on my chest, stopping me in place. "You're making me dizzy. What's going on with you, man? We were supposed to meet the team ten minutes ago for our pre-game dinner, and you're still walking across the room like this place is about to explode if you don't cut the right wire and you can't decide which one it is."

"I-I…" My throat was parched as if I had swallowed sawdust. I coughed, trying to ease my vocal cords. "Go. I'll meet you there in a minute."

He shook his head. "Nope. No way am I going without you. If our captain isn't there, the guys will know something isn't right, and the coaching staff will ask questions. I'm a shitty liar. I don't wanna be on the hot seat because I am sure to stutter, and it will be grade six all over again, where I tried to cover for you when you skipped school because you'd found a stray dog. I don't need a repeat performance. Lying makes me sweat."

"I'm not asking you to lie. Just tell them I've decided to go to bed early."

"Are you?"

"Am I what?"

"Going to bed early?"

I offered him a noncommittal shrug. "I'll try."

Chase studied me, a frown forming across his forehead. "Want me to bring you food?"

"Sure."

"You swear you're okay?"

I swallowed. How could I tell him it felt like the walls of our shared hotel room were closing in on me? "I just need a few minutes of rest and a hot shower, and I'll be fine."

My answer seemed to satisfy him because his grin returned. "Good. I'll bring you a plate when I'm back. Can you believe we're playing at State, man? Tomorrow's game will be epic. I can feel it." He slapped my shoulder, relief flashing in his eyes. "See you later. I'll keep a seat for you at the restaurant…just in case."

"Thanks."

The door clicked behind him, and finally alone, I relaxed a tiny bit.

Sitting on the edge of the mattress, I bent forward, my elbows propped up on my knees and my face buried in my hands, and my eyes closed, counting my breaths. It'd been a while since I felt so much pressure on me hours before a game. This wasn't any game, but the last one my teammates and I would ever play together and our last chance to set a record as a team. Never before in their history had the Elk River High Bears won two consecutive State championship titles.

I evened my breathing and pictured the field we would play on tomorrow. When we arrived in town earlier, Coach had asked the bus driver to make a small detour so we could see where the game would take place this year. We walked on the turf, admiring the vast green space that was so much bigger than our own field. My heart rate decelerated. The knots tightening my back loosened as I saw my guys lining on the field, the referees, the supporters filling the bleachers in my mind.

We would kick butt tomorrow. We were more than ready. For once, no players were injured or sick.

A soft thud on the door snapped me out of my visualization process. At first, I thought I had imagined it, but when a second and a third knock broke the silence surrounding me, I moved to the door, expecting Coach to be standing on the other side. My eyes grew big when I took in Melinda standing on the carpeted floor, a paper bag in her hands, the aroma of jasmine rice and chicken encircling us and hitting my nostrils.

"Hey. I've brought you food. Thought you might be hungry."

I stared at her, not sure if I was hallucinating or not.

"Mase? Is something wrong? Why are you looking at me like that?"

I blinked and recovered from my state of shock. "What are you doing here? I feel like I am imagining things right now. Weren't you supposed to arrive tomorrow?"

Her lips tilted into a soft smile. "Paige and I decided to drive early. We booked a room. We thought you guys would love to have supporters a day in advance, and we didn't feel like arriving at the same time as the school buses and families."

"Whoa. I'm hearing you, but it still feels like a dream."

"It's not." She lifted the bag of food to just under my nose. "It is real, Mase. I grabbed this for you at the restaurant downstairs. Chicken breast, steamed broccoli and carrots, wild rice, a baked potato, and a green salad. Chase said it was your favorite meal the night before a big game."

"Yeah." I recovered from my daze and moved aside to let her in. "You brought food. I hope you're staying." I raised one eyebrow, waiting for her to answer while I kicked the door shut.

"Maybe."

"You are." I took the bag from her hands and placed it on the dresser. "Wanna share?"

"No. Paige and I grabbed takeout on our way here. We left later than we had planned for, so we decided to stop to eat. Do you have water, though? I'm thirsty."

I uncapped two bottles from the sixteen-pack I'd brought with me and offered Melinda one.

We sat cross-legged on the bed, and I attacked my food, hungrier now than I was minutes ago.

"Chase told me you felt off…"

I swallowed a mouthful of chicken. "He said that?" I hated the idea my best friend was telling everyone I was on the verge of a panic attack earlier.

"Don't worry. He told me in confidence when he took me aside after I asked why you weren't eating with the team."

I pushed my plate away, a new set of knots tying my stomach. Closing my eyes, I counted my breaths.

"Mase?" Melinda's fingers grazed my hand, and I relaxed. "Wanna tell me what is happening? Is it your shoulder that is bothering you? You haven't said a word about it since you confided in me about hurting it last summer?"

"Nah. My shoulder is fine. I think… Remember when I told you that sometimes I freak out and let other people's expectations get to me?"

She nodded.

"Tonight is one of those times. I keep replaying everyone's words of encouragement in my head—Coach, the guys, my parents, Principal Ross. Even though they all meant well, they also told me to bring my A-game. Principal Ross and Coach want us to make history by winning State a second time in a row. The thing is… I know we can, and we have what it takes, but my brain is having trouble right now shutting down the voices in my head. It will be okay. I just need a little more time to get in the zone. And some peace and quiet."

"Do you want me to leave?"

"No. Please. Stay." I returned to my food. "This is freaking good. Where are you sleeping?"

"Second floor. Room two-twenty-two."

"Twenty-two…my favorite number…"

"And your jersey."

"Mel, you know what it means, right? You're my lucky charm." I pulled her hand and rested it on my knee, drawing circles on the back with my thumb.

"I am not."

"You are. Did you…did you bring the jersey I left at your place? Your dad told me he would give it to you."

"Yes. It's in my bag."

I exhaled my relief. "Tomorrow will be a great game."

"You think?"

"I'm sure."

———

Retreating a step, I extended my arm back, adjusted my grip on the pigskin, pivoted, and then voiced a prayer as I threw a Hail Mary. With my eyes half-closed, I followed the ball and hoped my brother was in sync with me to catch it. It was a long shot, but with seconds to go and over thirty yards to cover for the win, it was all or nothing.

Seconds felt like hours.

My heart jumped in my chest.

If Craig caught it, we would set a new record for the longest pass in high school football history.

I perused the field. Playing here felt like a dream, and I tried to burn as much of this moment to memory as I could. We'd almost lost in the semi-finals, but we pushed through, even though two of the guys were hurt. Today was the pinnacle of my high school football career. The one day that would cement the efforts of the last four years of my life.

Silence fell upon the stadium.

All eyes were on the ball slicing through the air in a perfect spiral.

My heart lodged in my throat. I had given the game my all today, and the fate of our victory resided in this one pass.

Time slowed.

I watched the space all around me. The coaches were waiting with bated breath, following the trajectory of the ball spinning above our heads.

The entire crowd stood, most of the people wearing our colors with their hands folded in prayer.

Sweat pearled on my forehead, a drop rolling into my eye.

I found my girl with my number displayed on her chest, and our gazes collided. She nodded at me, and it filled me with a new surge of confidence.

I turned my head to watch Craig, running with his arms stretched above his head, never losing speed, his gaze trained on the ball while he avoided the guys after him with twists of his body and jumps.

Time resumed its speed.

My brother was the fastest guy I knew. He was a force to be reckoned with on the field. One hell of a badass football player.

All his movements screamed confidence and precision.

The ball rotated in a perfect curve, its brown shade a contrast to the early December ice-blue sky, landing between his hands, milli-seconds before he crossed the end zone.

Touchdown.

The crowd erupted in a deafening cheer. Helmets were thrown in the air.

Two players emptied the sports drink cooler over Coach Roberts's head.

A wave of navy-blue surrounded us, our supporters screaming and clapping.

Running as fast as I could, I reached Craig as he was being shoved around in celebration by our teammates.

Unable to hold back the grin forming on my face, I lifted him into my arms and twirled him around. "Man, I knew you were the greatest, but I'm still impressed you caught that pass." He was, without a doubt, the best wide receiver in Michigan and had just proved it once again. Big time. Yeah, raw talent ran in our bloodstream.

"When you throw a perfect ball, Mase, I can't help but

catch it. Just doing my job." My brother, always the humblest guy on the team.

"Man, it's more than that. You're a goddamn king on the field, man. I'm proud of you." I lowered him to his feet as Paige ran toward us and jumped into his arms, locking her legs around his middle, kissing him like he had just won the Big Game. They exchanged sappy love words, and I blocked them out. Nah, I didn't need their lovesickness after we won the game against Castle High. Up until the last second, our victory wasn't a given. We were losing by two points. Chase and I bumped chests, and Sheldon gave me a noogie. Laughing, I dropped my helmet on the grass and wiped my sweaty forehead with my sleeve.

"We fucking did it, guys. We *did* it."

Nothing in this instant could steal my happiness away. I was surfing the greatest high.

My parents walked up to me, my mom hugging me. "My babies did great today." She stepped back and wiped her eyes with a tissue.

"Mom, are you crying?"

"No. It's the cold air. It makes my eyes watery."

I smiled. "Okay. Not crying. Noted."

"It's just… My babies are growing too fast. This was your last high school game. I'm not ready for Craig and you to be freshmen in college next year and live elsewhere."

I stepped forward and hugged her a little longer than I normally did. "It will be okay. We're not leaving just yet."

She bobbed her head. "You're right."

Dad ruffled my hair. "You did great, son. That last play was fantastic. I think I caught it on video, so you'll be able to watch it later. You make me so proud. I love you."

"I love you too, Dad."

"Come on, let's leave the boy alone and find Craig."

"Careful, he's sucking tongue over there. If I were you, I'd stay far away." I made a gagging sound. "Super gross."

Dad clapped my shoulder with a chuckle. "Like you're an angel, Mason. We know much more than you give us credit for. You should follow in your brother's footsteps. Paige is good for him."

"Nah. Hard pass." *I'm trying. Doesn't mean it's easy, though.* "I am enjoying my celibate life way too much." If only he knew. *I feel all alone these days. I wish I had what Craig and Paige have.* "Thanks for coming, old man. I'll see you at home later."

He shook his head and left, his lips curving at the corners.

As soon as they were gone, I spotted Melinda standing on the sidelines, her arms around her, smiling when I hurried in her direction. She was wearing my jersey over a white sweater, a pair of jeans, and brown ankle boots, and I couldn't look away. Her brown hair was loose over her shoulders, and she was wearing a navy-blue beanie with the school logo embossed in golden thread on the front. She was every shade of beautiful as she grinned at me.

"Did you see that?" I asked when I neared her. "We did it."

"Mase, I've always known you were the best."

I lifted her in my arms, her body molding to the length of mine. She radiated joy today. How could she ever doubt her beauty?

"Aren't you the one always trying not to indulge my ego?"

She jerked her head back in a contagious laugh. "You can have today. Tomorrow you're not allowed to feed that gigantic ego of yours anymore."

"I'll take all I can get."

She slid down my front, and we stared into each other's

souls. Her lips parted on an exhale. I leaned forward, unable to resist tasting her for another minute when I got ripped away from her. Melinda landed on her feet, her cheeks flushed and her eyes bright. Amusement brightened her features.

"Mase, you king of the field." Three of my teammates lifted me on their shoulders. "No kissing, just celebrating."

I glanced at Melinda, and her smile widened. "I'm sorry," I yelled, hoping she could hear me over the roaring of the still-enthusiastic crowd.

"Go." She gestured to where the rest of my team was. "I'll catch up with you later."

My teammates steered me away.

"Are you gonna be at the party tonight?"

She shrugged. "Maybe. It depends."

"On what?"

She winked instead of answering.

I kissed my fingers and blew her a kiss. "You better be. You're wearing my jersey. It has to count for something, right?"

She burst into a fit of laugher before I lost sight of her as more people stood between us.

Something clicked into place inside me.

I was exactly where I should be. Once Melinda and I made it official by Winter Formal, every piece of my life would make perfect sense.

"Where's Mel?" I asked Paige as she poured herself a glass of soda in the overcrowded kitchen. The loud music pounded in my skull. Today's State victory still felt surreal. After our game, we had ridden the team bus back to school. Before Paige and Melinda left, a bit before we did, we'd all agreed to meet at the party tonight.

We were celebrating at Rusty's. His dad had ordered enough food to feed an army and promised not to make a big deal if we drank booze as long as we were not driving afterward. Paige had even offered to be our designated driver tonight.

"Home."

"Home? I thought she'd be here. Was I supposed to pick her up?" In the midst of everything, did I forget about our deal?

"No. She was supposed to ride here with me. She wasn't feeling well when we drove back after the game. She said her stomach bothered her, and she felt nauseous."

"Dammit. I should go to her. See if she's okay."

She laid a hand on my chest. "She made me promise to tell you not to leave the party. She said you deserve to have fun tonight and enjoy every second and that she would talk to you in the morning. I think it's that time of the month."

"Oh."

"Mase. I don't wanna be a party pooper, but I think something else is going on with her."

I took a sip of my drink. "What do you mean?"

She hesitated for a second, twisting a strand of her hair around a finger. "Forget it, okay? I'm sure I'm being paranoid."

She moved to leave, but I stopped her. "Babe, what are you not telling me?"

"Don't worry. I'll let you know if it's serious. It's better if you don't get mixed up in this, or she'll get mad at you."

"Paige. Talk. Now."

"Mase, I'll deal with it and let you know if you need to get involved. It's going to be okay. I'll catch up with you later." She weaved through the mass of people toward the living room where I knew most of my team-mates were.

An unknown sensation weighed heavily on my heart. Had I missed something? What had Paige noticed that I hadn't?

Before I had time to think it through, two sets of arms lifted me up, and the crowd parted as the guys carried me further into the house. "Mason Pierce, the best captain this team has ever had."

Deafening cheers and wolf whistles resonated all around me. A bottle of beer was handed to me, and a cardboard crown decorated with fake blue and gold gemstones was placed on my head.

Chase stood on a chair and motioned to everyone to shut up with a hand. From the width of his smirk, I could tell he was wasted.

"Are you giving a speech?" I asked, not drunk enough not to remember tonight.

"*Tryinnng* to." He slurred his words a little bit. "Mase. You are my *bestest* best friend. I-I'm not sure I wouldn't be in juvie right now if you hadn't been in my life and convinced me to give…to give football a try when I used to be a little *shhhit* back in middle school. I'm glad you stuck by my side all these years. Even when things got…huh… tough and I couldn't go home, you never made me feel like a burden. *Youuu're* not only my best friend, *sorrry*, Craig, but also my brother and a guy everyone should look up to. You-you're royalty on the field and one hell of a QB." He lifted a finger. "Seriously, I'm not sure that right arm of yours is human. Anyway, I'm *proooud* we won State today." He raised his hand over his head, showing our champi-onship ring. "Whatever I do next, I…I can say that for once in my life—or twice if we count last year's victory too —I've been a…I've been a freaking champion. My dad wouldn't agree with this…huh…statement, but right now, he can go to hell. Anyway, I *am* a champion and I feel like one and I have *youuu* to thank for it. And Pierce Senior, because he-he caught that pass and *youuu* guys made history today. It was *wilddd,* and I still…I still can't believe we won. *I lovvve* you fucking much."

My throat closed, a bunch of emotions stuck there. It was weird having my best friend make a speech about me. Sheldon and my brother lifted their drinks in my direction and nodded. I did the same.

"Thanks," I told my best friend. "I love you too, man."

The guys lowered me to the floor, and I adjusted my shirt.

"Now that the season is *ovvver,* people, let's get this party started." Chase stumbled when he tried to jump from the chair, and two girls broke his fall, nestling themselves under his arms. He grinned like he had won the lottery before leading them away.

I shook my head. I didn't need this—a girl under each arm ready to be at my beck and call. I had something more special to protect now. A relationship—or an almost-relationship, if you cared about semantics. A special someone to care for. One who would love me back too.

When Paige dropped Craig and me home around two, I contemplated climbing the house next door to Melinda's room. I wanted to sleep beside her, holding her, and to wake up with her in my arms. Then I recalled the last time I'd climbed the wall to her bedroom while drunk, which had almost killed me, and I chose to wait until I was sober to give it a try. If she was sick, she was probably already asleep by now anyway. Waking her up for my own selfish needs wasn't my best idea.

After I studied the Shepards' house for a bit longer, I followed Craig inside after Paige drove away.

"I-I'm in *lovvve* with her." I kicked my shoes off once the door clicked behind us. "And it hurts when I can't… when I can't see her for more than a few hours."

"It's about time you admitted it out loud. Now you know how it feels." My brother said nothing else as we both climbed the stairs to our bedrooms.

I hated it when he was wiser than me.

CHAPTER 29

ONLY IN PORN MOVIES

"Wanna go shopping for Winter Formal before your shift at the movie theater on Saturday?" I asked Melinda on Monday morning as she joined me in my driveway so we could ride to school together. She would be training after school, and I wanted to hit the gym so our schedules matched, and riding together had become our thing whenever we could make it work. "I thought it would look cool if my tie matched your dress. Just an idea."

Winter Formal was in two weeks.

"You want us to match? Are you sure you're not sick?" she asked, hoisting herself onto the passenger seat after she discarded her book bag on the backseat. Leaning forward, she touched her hand to my forehead. "Nope. No fever."

I laughed, something I seemed to do a lot around her. "Not sick, I swear. And here I almost wished I were so you could transform into Nurse Shepard. The time you bandaged the cut on my abdomen is branded on my memories forever. And the nurse uniforms are hot. Just sayin'."

"Only in porn movies, Mase. Real-life uniforms are not sexy, I swear."

"And just like that, you killed one of my fantasies." I rolled my eyes in the most exaggerated manner possible. "Thank you very much, Shepard."

She patted my hand. "You'll survive, Mase. For your information, if you had been sick, I would have cared for you."

My face lit up. "For real?"

She sighed. "No questions asked. Until you transformed into a big baby and I had to quit."

"I love your faith in me. I'm tougher than you give me credit for." We both laughed. "Back to business." I put on my most serious expression. "The theme this year is Midnight Frost. It could be fun to dress the part. Think about it and let me know what you decide."

"I'm free Saturday morning. If we do this, indigo or arctic blue would work best. If I can find a dress in those hues."

"That sounds like something doable. Not that I know a lot about dresses, but I'm sure blue is a pretty common color."

"Yeah, but there's a whole rainbow of shades. We gotta find the right one." Melinda toyed with the radio button for a moment. "Hey, Mase. Do you have plans for the winter break? Craig and Paige talked about going to the mountains to snowboard. They're renting a cabin for two nights, and they have a spare bedroom. Christmas present from her parents. Could be fun to join them if you're up to it. They offered. I've never snowboarded before, but I heard it's not that hard. I would like to give it a try. And three days away from everything would be amazing after the semester we just had. As long as I can fit my work schedule around it and my parents agree."

"Craig said something about it the other day, but we were interrupted, and we never broached the subject again. Could be fun, though. You sure it's okay with them if we tag along?"

"Yes. Paige called me last night. They're going the weekend before Christmas. She said they would love for us to join them. We would only have to pay for our tickets and our food. We could split the money for gas. She even offered we ride together, the four of us…" She twisted her hands in her lap. "Or the two of us can ride alone. Whatever we decide."

"You'll love the slopes. Let me run it by my brother first and get back to you." I stopped at a red light and watched my girl when an idea hit me. "Wanna skip morning classes?"

"Skip? Like skip school?" From the look on her face, it was like I had suggested we commit murder and bury the body together.

"Yeah. Like you said, we had one hell of a semester, and I need a break. Time to cool off. Football season has been exhausting with the extra training I put myself through. I kinda feel like going to the lake and walking… and talking." Last Saturday, we won the state championship, which meant practices were over—and my high school football career too. The guys and I were still hitting the gym at least three times a week to stay in shape for the spring off-season training. Dedication was the key to our well-oiled machine. And even if technically my high school football days were over, I was still the captain and called the shots—at least until the end of the school year.

Melinda sighed and flipped her hair over her shoulder. My fingertips itched to brush the silky strands. "Even though it sounds tempting, I can't. I have a quiz and if I miss it and my parents hear about it…let's just say it's a complication I'd prefer to avoid."

I scratched my temple. "Oh, okay. Maybe another time."

I really wanted to talk to Melinda alone. It was time we had *the* conversation. We'd been tiptoeing around each other for months now. Our deadline was approaching, and after sleeping in the same bed on my birthday, I was done pretending we weren't together when we did everything, except kissing and the physical stuff, like other couples did. I couldn't have her so close to me all the time without being with her—like really being with her—anymore. It had become torture. I was combusting inside each day, not knowing how to get rid of the tension tightening my body. All I wished for was to hold her hand and kiss her whenever I felt like it. Watch movies tangled up together under a blanket and go on dates. I didn't want to have to come up with excuses to see her anymore. The other day, I'd caught myself doodling her name next to mine in my notebook when the math teacher went on and on about limits, and I couldn't care less about the lesson.

"Are you okay?" Her voice brought me back to the present.

"Yeah. Sure. All good."

Craig met us in the parking lot. "How is it going, lovebirds?"

I made a cutthroat gesture and glared at him.

He winked as if he could read my thoughts. I would

have vaporized him with my eyes if they had been laser beams.

"Need something?" I asked, not in the mood to kill him this early in the morning.

"Nope. Waiting for Paige. I thought I should come and say hi since it would be impolite not to say hello when you cross paths with your favorite brother and his gir—and his friend in the school parking lot."

Fucker, I mouthed at him.

He clapped my back as I pushed him aside to walk past him. "I'll see you later, man." The sound of his chuckle still made me want to murder him with my own hands. I didn't need my brother to mess up my plans. No thank you.

We entered the building, and I fist-bumped a couple of guys before making it to the seniors' wing to walk Melinda to her locker.

"Can you give me a minute?" she asked as we passed the restroom.

"Yeah, sure. I'll wait here."

With my back against the wall, I scrolled through my phone, studying every picture we snapped of us in the last few months.

My heart would burst if I didn't come clean to Melinda soon. If we started dating before Winter Formal, we could go as a couple. Officially. The real deal. And spend our winter break together with nothing standing between us. Not being some third or fourth wheel on Craig and Paige's mountain vacation.

Chase joined me, offering me a donut from the box in his hands. I hesitated at first, but indulged, picking a vanilla one with chocolate frosting and violet sprinkles. After all, football season was over, and I deserved a treat—and some sugar courage. "What's up?" he asked.

"Waiting for Mel."

"Are you two—? Is this real? You guys have been hanging out together like a couple for months, and I don't understand why you haven't tapped it yet."

I pivoted and glared at him. "Respect, man. Don't talk about her like that. Whatever we are or aren't isn't your business or anyone else's."

"Relax, Mase. I was just kidding. I have eyes, you know. I've been seeing how you two have become inseparable. I'm just surprised because it's not like you to spend time with a girl without banging her on the side and dumping her ass afterward. What happened between you two at State?"

"Drop it. She's not like the others. Anyway, why am I even explaining anything to you?" I waved him off. "Shoo. Now. She'll be back, and I don't want you in my space."

Chase burst out into a fit of laughter, grabbing another donut from the box and pushing it whole inside his mouth. "If I didn't know any better, I would think Mason Pierce was in love." He spoke with a mouthful, waggling his eyebrows as he did.

I poked his shoulder. "Shut up. Again, none of your business."

He sidestepped and shook his head, a smirk curling his lips. "You're so screwed. You're my idol, Mase. Jesus, you are the best. How have you been surviving the longest case of blue balls known to mankind?"

He walked away, the sound of his laughter reverberating through the hallway as he traipsed toward the rows of lockers.

"Everything okay?" Melinda asked from behind me.

I turned to face her and grabbed her hands in mine. "Yeah, just Chase being his idiot self. Are *you* feeling all right? You're staring off into space."

She flicked her wrist. "I was dizzy. Moved too quickly. It's better now."

I nodded. Something wasn't right. The nagging feeling I had experienced in the past returned.

"Don't worry, okay?"

I removed Melinda's bag from her shoulder and slung it over mine.

We walked side by side, and the instant I spun to reach for her hand, her eyes lost all focus, and seconds later, her knees buckled. I caught her limp body right before she hit the floor. I kneeled down with her in my arms. "Mel. Open your eyes. Talk to me. Mel? Wake up."

One by one, her eyelids peeled open before closing again.

"Mel. No. Someone get the nurse. Mel, open your eyes." I pulled her against me, cradling her inert body, urging her to wake up. My eyes burned with unshed tears. "Mel. It's not funny. Don't do this. Open your eyes. Now."

A palm molded to my cheek. "Mase?"

"Mel. What happened?"

A ghost of a smile touched her lips. "I'm fine." She pushed herself up onto her elbows. "Help me up."

"Huh… Not sure it's a smart idea. Your face is ghost-white right now. You've just scared the shit out of me."

"I wanna sit." Her eyes traveled all around us. "Everybody is staring."

"Let them stare."

Still in my arms, she motioned to sit, but seconds later, her eyes rolled back, and her body sagged against mine. Her eyes lost focus, and her blush-pink shirt contrasted with her pale complexion. Her quivering lips looked blueish as they parted, but no word escaped her mouth. I took her hand in mine, and it felt colder and smaller than usual.

"You're not fine. Don't feed me bullshit."

With one hand, and never releasing her, I pinched the back of my sweatshirt at the nape, pulled it over my head, and draped it across her legs in case she was cold. I held her limp body in my arms, using my upper body as a shield to hide her from all the commotion around us and inquisitive stares as much as possible.

She shivered and I pulled her closer to me, wishing my body temperature could warm her up.

"Mase? Don't leave me, okay?"

"Never. I'm not going anywhere. You are safe. Hang on."

Minutes later, the school nurse appeared and took charge, checking Melinda's vitals before helping her stand and urging her to her office.

I trailed after them, carrying Melinda's bag. "Is she gonna be okay?"

"Yes, Mr. Pierce. Miss Shepard needs a little time to recover. Water and some calm."

"I'm already feeling better." Melinda's fingertips grazed the back of my hand. "I'll be right behind you. Don't worry, okay?"

The late bell rang.

"I'll check on you after first period." I handed her bag to the nurse, then dropped a kiss on her forehead before walking away.

"Mase?"

I looked at her over my shoulder, my heart breaking for the girl I loved. Her eyes were shiny and unfocused, tears hanging from her lashes. "Thanks. For saving me again."

"I would save you a thousand times. That's what personal nurses are for, no?"

We exchanged a hint of a smile before I left and hurried to my homeroom. That feeling weighing heavy on my heart wouldn't go away. My insides had turned into one giant knot. Something wasn't right. I had no idea what it was, but I knew it in the marrow of my bones.

A part of me was afraid to find out I was right.

———

"Okay, Mase, this has to stop. You can't follow me around all the time like a sick puppy. I'm not gonna faint again. I was dehydrated yesterday. It was a one-time thing."

"Explain to me why I'm not convinced then? You're wearing a white blouse and right now it looks the same color as your skin, which says a lot. Luckily for you, you're wearing maroon pants because otherwise, I would have mistaken you for a ghost."

She let out a low chuckle. "You worry too much. I swear I'm no ghost. Anyway, I'll catch you at lunch." We stopped in front of Melinda's second-period social studies class. "This is me."

"Wait for me when the bell rings. I'll be right here when your class ends."

She pushed me back with a hand before catching her book bag that had slid down her arm. "Get lost, Mase." Even though she tried, she couldn't hide the smile in her voice.

The clock ticked by too slowly, every second stretching into hours.

"Mr. Pierce. Please come see me." Mr. Rockwell called my name after he dismissed the class. I would be late. I had told Melinda I would walk her to her next class.

I stood by his desk, rocking on my heels, not sure what he wanted as we waited for the students to rush out of the room, flooding the hallway, the mayhem of their footsteps and chatter echoing around us.

"You wanted to see me?" I strangled the strap of my bag as if it could make him speak faster.

"I was tasked to ask you to walk Miss Shepard to the athletic building. Don't ask me why, but that was the order I got from Coach Vivien. She's waiting for her in her office. I told her I would send you right after class."

I pointed to my chest. "She asked you to tell me to bring Mel over there? What's going on? This sounds sketchy as hell."

Mr. Rockwell lifted his hands in surrender. He was a retired cross-country coach, and all the students had a soft spot for him. "Hey, Mr. Pierce, don't shoot the messenger." He shoved the stack of papers he had to grade into his bag and waved me off with a flick of his wrist. "Go now. You're dismissed."

"Fine. See you tomorrow, Mr. Rockwell." I hurried down the hallway, catching Melinda as she was strolling toward her locker.

"Mase. Have you seen Paige? She wasn't in class, and I know for a fact she was looking forward to today's assignment."

"I crossed paths with her earlier." I tugged at her hand, and she got in step with me. "We gotta go to the athletic building. It seems like Coach Vivien wants to talk to you or something."

She clasped her hand, a large grin lighting up her face. "Do you think she has received college offers on my behalf or something? I'm still waiting for Crestwood U to make an offer so I can commit to them." I hadn't told her yet that I had already committed to them too because I knew Melinda wouldn't go anywhere else. "My times are amazing this year. Mase, I think this could be it. Yes, I feel it in my bones."

My lips pulled into a smile, mirroring hers.

She stopped and frowned. "Huh, but why did they ask you to tell me?"

I shrugged and then swept a hand down myself as we resumed our walk. "I'm irresistible. Maybe your coach needs to take a peek at my exceptional handsomeness to get through her day."

Melinda elbowed me in the ribs. "Careful with the ego, Mase. If it inflates and grows too much, you won't be able to play ball anymore because it'll be in the way."

"Never. I'm Mason Pierce, remember."

"Gosh, you sound just like Chase."

"What can I say? We spend too much time together, and it must have rubbed off on me."

She shook her head, her smile widening. "You don't need Chase to be cocky, Mr. Football."

"That's why you can't resist me. Want to grab your jacket from your locker?"

"No, it's fine. It's just a two-minute walk. Anyway, you're wearing your letterman jacket inside like it's a sweater. So, if I'm cold, I'll steal it."

"No need to steal it. I'll give it to you. All you gotta do is ask. For what it's worth, I like the idea that if you receive an offer, I'll be the first person you tell it to."

Her fingers squeezed mine, bringing me peace and calming the crazy thundering of my heart.

"I kinda like it too."

We both halted when the door of Coach Vivien's office opened and Paige exited, glancing at her feet instead of us. "What are you doing here?" Melinda asked with a tightness in her voice that wasn't present before. Oh God, this meeting wasn't about college. Melinda realized it too because the blood drained from her face, and it appeared like she had seen a ghost—for real this time.

I pressed a palm to the small of her back, trying to

inject her with some courage. The thundering of my heart turned erratic. This meeting was a setup. It screamed bad news.

"Paige?" Melinda's gaze bored into her best friend, whose guilty expression was impossible to miss.

Tears brightened Paige's eyes, and her cheeks were flushed. "I'm sorry, Mel. I…I really am."

"You are sorry?"

"What is she talking about?" I asked, not sure I was understanding the scene unfolding before my eyes.

"What did you do?" Melinda asked her friend, her tone accusatory.

"What needed to be done. You know I love you, right? And I will always love you. All I want is for you to get better."

Melinda clenched her fists, her entire body tensing. "What…? How?"

"Paige? Mel?" I looked back and forth between them both. "Can someone tell me what's going on right now?"

Before either of them could say something, Coach Vivien exited her office and motioned for Melinda to enter. "Melinda. Please, come on in and take a seat."

Instead of going in, Melinda stood there, as if she was rooted to the tiled floor, sorrow flooding her face.

"Melinda," Coach repeated, more insistent this time.

"Go. I'll be right here when you're done," I murmured in her ear.

She nodded, casting a glance down, and let go of my hand. She plodded forward in silence, her head hanging low as if she was on death row.

Melinda jerked her arm away when Paige tried to grip it. "Mel? Please don't be mad."

"Don't. Don't talk to me" were the only words she told Paige before the office door shut after her.

I turned to my brother's girlfriend. "What's this?" I asked, pointing to the closed door with my chin. "What did you do? What did Mel do?"

Paige stepped away until her back hit the wall behind her and dropped down to the floor, folding her knees and burying her face in her crossed arms. "I did something terrible. I broke my best friend's trust." Sobs rocked her. "She'll hate me for this, Mase. I may have destroyed our friendship."

CHAPTER 30

YOU FUCKING LIED TO MY FACE

I sat in front of Paige, untangling her arms, taking in her bloodshot eyes and reddened cheeks. "Hey, talk to me. We're usually pretty good at communicating, you and I, and what you are saying is gibberish right now."

"Mase, you don't get it? I snitched on my best friend. I hurt her because I love her. She's been lying…to-to me. To you. To everyone. For months. Her parents had doubts, her…her coach had doubts, and I just confirmed them all." She hid her face in her hands as a new batch of sobs escaped her.

"She lied to me?" A big knot tied my insides. "What does that even mean? And why would she lie to you? You two are like inseparable. Care to explain?" I knew something was off. I'd known for a while, but I never could determine what it was. Had I been too blind to see the truth? "Is it about what you told me the other night? The day we won State?"

"I didn't—"

The door of the office opened with a bang, and Melinda bolted out, cutting short Paige's reply, her eyes puffy and her lips trembling. She used the sleeve of her blouse to wipe her face. I moved to my feet to block her escape. "Mel, what's wrong? What happened in there?"

She jumped into my embrace, wrapping her arms around me, her face buried in my chest. Her entire body shook with heart-wrenching sobs. "Mase, take me away from here. Far away." She tipped her head back to look at me, defeat painted across her features. "Please."

I swept her hair away with a delicate touch. "Why? What is this all about? Talk to me."

"You're not taking her anywhere, Mason." Mr. Shepard's icy voice came from beside us.

I stepped back, not releasing Melinda. This whole situation was getting more confusing with every passing second. "Mr. Shepard? What are you... Can someone explain to me why everyone is here and what is happening?"

"Melinda will do that. Once she calms down. For now, we gotta drive her to the clinic. They're waiting for her."

"No." Her rebuttal sounded more like a shriek. She broke free from the safety of my embrace and rushed outside, looking like an injured animal afraid to get caught.

"Mel, wait." I jogged after her. "I'm super confused right now. Why are your parents here? What did they say to you? And why does Paige look like you kicked her puppy?"

We faced each other, Melinda hugging herself, shivering. I removed my jacket and draped it over her shoulders.

"You wanna know what happened? They all teamed up against me." Her sadness had switched to anger. "They think I have an eating disorder. Again. I'm banned from training or competing unless I see a doctor and receive medical help."

My blood froze in my veins, and it had nothing to do with the cold seeping through my clothes. "Do you? Have an eating disorder?"

"No. It's not like that. They're being paranoid. I was only controlling my calorie intake…to be in my best ever shape."

"What did you mean when you said *again*?" I swept the length of her body with my eyes, taking every single detail in.

"I used to starve myself. Freshman year. Because… because some girls on the swim team were making fun of me because I-I had boobs and hips and they hadn't blossomed yet. I'm cured, though. I-I'm over this… I've been for years."

I remained silent for a whole minute, digesting that piece of information. I knew my words would break her, but I had to be honest. I loved her too much to lie to her. "Mel…I think you should listen to your parents."

"No." Her scream pierced my heart. "Not you too. Are you teaming up with them? You're supposed to be on my side here."

"I am on your side. Always. But I'm also on the side of what's right." I gestured to the length of her. Even my jacket looked bigger on her than it used to. "If I replay the last couple of months in my head, I gotta be honest. Mel, you *are* starving yourself. All the times we had lunch or dinner together, you barely ate anything. You toyed around with your food, never actually eating it, and you only ordered the smallest appetizers on the menu. You always came up with excuses for why you weren't hungry. The new training program, the diet your coach had spun on you, it was all a lie, wasn't it?"

"It's not like that."

"You've been lying to me. You fucking lied to my face. The entire time. I thought we were friends, that I could trust you. I was honest with you. I confided in you…told you things I've never told anybody else. But you never opened up to me…not really. Even when I offered to listen and not judge and said I'd be there for you… You kept me in the dark and avoided discussing such a vital piece of information with me. Not just that, but you gambled with your health." I clenched my jaw and breathed out, trying to keep my tone even. "I'm so angry right now. You got mad at me, saying you had a hard time trusting me, when all along, it was you I should have been doubting. And here I was, thinking you felt safe enough around me to open up about your struggles and that deep down, you were honest with me."

"We are… I-I am. None of this has anything to do with trust."

"I agree to disagree. If all we'll ever be is friends, then as your friend, I'm telling you that you need help. That what you're doing to your body is not only unhealthy, but also dangerous. I care too much about you to turn a blind eye to your behavior. If I had known what was going on, I would have reported you myself or helped you through it. I feel stupid for not seeing it sooner. All the signs were there. I'm so ashamed of myself right now. I trusted you. I ate up every lie…every excuse…because I thought you were honest with me. Gosh, I'm so stupid." My voice cracked. "I feel like I've been played."

"Is this really what you think?" She pressed her fists to her hips, her eyes boring into mine.

"Yes." I breathed in through my mouth, doing my best to keep my anger in check.

"You didn't need to know shit because it was all under control. You're not allowed to be upset with me right now. It's not your problem. *I am not* your problem."

"You don't want me to be upset? Wow, are you kidding me right now? What else am I supposed to do? Think what you're doing is cool and watch you kill yourself slowly and forfeit all your dreams? The ones you've been working so hard for? No thanks. All this talk about control... You duped me... All along, I-I thought you were passing some athletic wisdom to me and that we were bonding. What a joke." I dragged a hand over my face, not sure what to say. This was not how I saw my morning going. I was no shrink and wasn't sure what the right things to say were in that moment. "Mel...be honest with me. Here and now. Was there really a new training regimen, or was it some bullshit you made up? I need you to tell the truth to my face."

She remained silent for a full minute. "Mase, you can't call me out on things I did or said."

"Sure, I can. The fasting, the extra hours at the gym, the fifty additional laps at the pool, the nausea and stomachaches, the migraines—were any of them true, or were they all ruses?"

She cocked her head to the side, looking away.

"That's what I was thinking. You played me like a fool. Can you imagine how fucked up this is? In case you haven't caught up yet...I'm infatuated with you, Mel. I would have rearranged the stars for you if you'd asked me to. And now...now, I feel cheated." My entire body shook from the new surge of anger building inside me. "I would still drop everything and give it to you if you ask me, even though I know what I know now. I just feel like it's a one-way kinda relationship. I'm not sure I know you...the real you. Do I? Was any of it, the times we spent together, genuine, or was it only real in my mind?"

"I care about you, Mase. I do."

"If you do, let me in. Let me help you."

"No."

I sighed. "Why not? I'm here. That's all I'm asking."

"Because I don't want you to."

"I don't believe you." *I love you.* "You need someone in your corner, someone to rely on when things get tough. I'm that guy for you."

"You can't be. I won't let you."

"But—"

"No but. We're done. If you can't respect my way of doing things and you believe I'm not in control, then this thing between us leads nowhere."

"Nowhere? What are you talking about?"

"Mase, I'm setting you free. You don't have to feel obligated to be by my side." She glanced down for a long second before staring back at me. "I…I don't want you in my business anymore. This is over."

"I would actually think you were serious, had you sounded like you meant it. This situation…it's just a bump in our road…in *your* road. You've said it yourself. You have been doing great for a long time. I don't see you not being able to heal again. Don't say stuff, thinking you can chase me away, because it won't work. Anyway, we're good for each other and—"

"Nah, we're not. Look where our relationship has gotten me."

"Are you putting the blame on me?"

She dropped her shoulders, some of the fight leaving her. "I can deal with my own shit. Stay out of it. Leave me alone, Mase. We can't be friends anymore."

"Why? Because I said your parents were right and you

should get help? Because I wanna help you and be there for you?"

"No. Because I don't have a freaking problem and you think I do. Can't you guys see I'm okay? I'm tired of people thinking they know better than me about what's best for me. I'm the boss of my life and my body… Not my parents, not Coach, not you. If you can't accept it, then this relationship is over. Effective now."

"Mel…" I spoke slowly, praying my words would make her rethink her pushing-me-away act. "I get it, but this time around, I'm not sure you understand how bad it has gotten. And also, stop acting as if you're the only one who gets to decide what's good for us. I'm not the boss of you, true, but you're not the boss of us either."

"There is no us—that's the thing—and there's never been one. Stop pretending we're more than what we are to each other…"

"You're impossible right now. Do you hear yourself?"

Was she hurting me on purpose? Was this her attempt to chase me away? Because it was pretty lame.

"I stand behind what I said. You're not better than any of them, and if you think I have a problem, then you're not on my team."

"Whoa, that's how you wanna play it? We don't agree on something and you flush me from your life like I've never mattered? Mel, this is how cowards act. I never pictured you to be one."

"I'm no coward."

"Then prove it."

"I don't have to prove anything to you. I'm banned from training and swimming because people decided so without my consent. How would you feel if football was taken away from you because of your shoulder, huh? Tell me."

"My shoulder has nothing to do with your health."

"But it has everything to do with lying, no? Don't pretend like you're not doing the same thing I did to protect your future and the sport you love and to get recruited by your dream college next year."

"It's not… I'm not…"

"Yes, you are. See? We're not so different after all. The only difference is that I didn't judge you for not telling your coach, your parents, or your teammates about your injury. And I didn't force you to see a doctor right away, because I trusted you would do what's best for you."

"I didn't put my life at risk by playing with a stiff shoulder. You did. You gambled with your health…with your life. Can't you see it? Our situations aren't the same."

"Believe what you want, I'm done with this conversation."

"I'm not. You once said you hate fighting with me."

"Well, maybe I lied. After all, haven't I been lying to you for weeks?"

Her words were cruel. A mixture of fury and pain weighed heavily on my heart. Melinda didn't mean any of it, right? She was hurt. I had to repeat it in my head so I wouldn't end up with a broken heart. "You don't mean it." I took a big inhale to avoid losing my calm. "I was there too, you know. All along. What we have is much more than just a friendship. It's everything…it's—" I swallowed the lump forming in my throat, my emotions running high inside me. "I never asked anything from you other than for you to give me a chance. I'm not the one starving myself, so don't try to make it all about me to avoid dealing with the real problem."

"I can't. I just can't do it. You don't know how it is. It's —" Instead of finishing her thought, Melinda turned and ran in the opposite direction.

Each time I neared her, she fled further away. Until I stood before her, and she had nowhere to escape anymore.

"Mel, stop running."

"I don't need you to save me, Mase. I can save my own self. Go play hero to someone else."

"I don't wanna be anyone else's hero. All I want is to be *your* everything. I can help you through this. You won't be alone."

"Not interested."

I flinched as if she had slapped me. "You-you don't mean that."

"Wanna bet?"

"How can you heal if you're lying to yourself? Your swimming career isn't over. All the people who love you just need you to get better first so you can go back to it. How will you be able to swim and beat Emery Mellencamp if you're"—my throat closed—"if you're dead?"

A single tear rolled down her cheek, and she wiped it away hastily. "I-I'm…I'm fully capable of taking care of myself."

"You've been repeating that, but are you sure? Because, right now, I'm not convinced. You're not alone. Just say the word and I'll—"

Paige arrived, putting a stop to our face-off.

Melinda pointed an accusing finger at her. "Not you. We're not friends anymore. You stabbed me in the back. You planned this intervention with my parents. I can't trust you from now on. You're a hypocrite."

"Mel…"

"No. Don't Mel me." She motioned her finger between Paige and me. "I'm done with all of you. You two can rot in hell, for all I care."

"I had to do something. I saw it, you know. At State. When we grabbed food and you hid it in a napkin while pretending to eat. I saw it when you measured the circumference of your biceps with your fingers and when you jogged up and down the emergency stairs for over thirty minutes after you failed to join me for breakfast and told me you had lost track of time because you had bumped into Stacey. She wasn't even at State because her car broke down on the way there. I'm your friend, and as your friend, I consider it my job to care. I tried to talk to you about it. Multiple times. The night you spent at my place and your own night clothes were too big on you or when I brought you cupcakes and you dropped the plate and threw them away so you wouldn't have to eat any of them. I'm not stupid. I was there in freshman year when you starved yourself for months before it got out of control. I was the one you confided to after therapy or when you almost relapsed in sophomore year after Jason Smith said your shoulders were too big for a girl. I was the one wiping your tears that night because you thought you weren't pretty enough for boys to notice you."

Melinda's lips trembled. "It-it's not like that this time around. It's temporary… I'm…I'm not sick. I have it all… I have it all under control. You guys are making a mountain out of a molehill."

My heart bled for the girl I loved, who was in denial over the seriousness of the situation. I stepped forward and pulled her into my arms, tears building in my eyes. She kept her back taut, never relaxing against me. "Let me be there for you. Please. Let *us* be there for you."

"No. It's too late. You picked your side. Cut me loose."

I swallowed the rock down my throat. "I don't want to."

"It's not your call." Melinda pushed away from my embrace when

Mrs. Shepard neared us. Before I could grab her hand,

my girl strode toward the parking lot. I was about to go after her when her mother stopped me.

"Let her go. She needs some space. Please don't take everything she said personally." Her attention traveled between a heartbroken Paige and me. "I know you both care about my daughter. We all do. She's having a relapse. We thought this episode of her life was behind her, but it's not. She needs medical help. Give her some time to calm down, okay? I'm sure she'll be willing to talk to you both once she's calmer and realizes we're doing this for her own good. Because we love her. She'll need all the love she can get once her anger diminishes."

"Is she...will she be okay?" My voice sounded foreign to my own ears.

"Yes. Eventually. With medical treatment and therapy and support. And time. She did it once, so there's no reason why she can't do it again. If she wants to get better. It has to come from her, though."

"Will she continue to swim?" If someone could understand what her sport meant to her, it was me.

"Since there are no other swim meets before the winter break, we'll reassess how it goes once school resumes in January. For now, it's too soon to tell. Coach Vivien promised it wouldn't affect her college offers. She'll deal with them herself in the meantime to remove as much pressure from Melinda as possible."

I nodded. "Good. Do you think I can come over to see her tonight?"

"No idea. We have a doctor's appointment in an hour. Come knocking after dinner and we'll see how she's doing."

I looked over my shoulder to watch Melinda as she hauled herself onto the backseat of her parents' car. Mrs. Shepard squeezed a dejected Paige's hand. "She's not really mad at you, honey. She'll understand it once the truth doesn't hurt so much anymore."

I draped an arm around Paige's heaving shoulders and pulled her to me, wishing Melinda was the girl I was comforting right now. "Shhh. It's okay."

"I know I...I did the right thing when I shared what was going on. It's just... I hate the idea Mel hates... that she hates me." Her sobs shook her body.

"She doesn't hate you," Mrs. Shepard said. "Her ego is hurt and doing all the talking at the moment. Even though it's hard, don't take any of her accusations personally." Mrs. Shepards patted my shoulder. "I know you love my daughter, Mason. Someone would need to be blind not to catch up with that fact. She'll need you in her corner. Don't lose faith in her." She turned around and walked to her car.

I turned to Paige. "Babe, why didn't you tell me?"

"I knew she'd be mad at me, and I didn't want her to be mad at you too. I thought with you by her side, she would accept help. I'm sorry, Mase."

"If you had told me first, we could have avoided this."

She shook her head. "If I had confided in you, you would have tried to deal with it by yourself. It's not your job. Mel needs doctors. Even though we love her, we can only hold her hand through this."

With Paige still sobbing in my arms, I watched the Shepards leave, with my bleeding heart in fragments and my spirits sinking.

In my head, only one question remained. *How can I help Melinda through this without messing it all up for both of us?* Because no matter what Melinda claimed minutes ago, we weren't done.

CHAPTER 31

DIFFERENT IS A GOOD THING

I stood on the Shepards' front porch, pulling at the roots of my hair, not sure if I should knock or go back home. Melinda's and my battle of words earlier had left a bruise the size of Texas in my chest. She was the last person I wanted to fight with and the last person I wanted to push away. And I'd succeeded at doing both earlier. Not my finest moment. Since she exposed her truth to me this morning, I'd been pacing like a lion in a cage every chance I got, in between comforting a dejected Paige and trying to go on with my day. Craig had no clue how to up our spirits and finally stopped trying after lunch.

I gathered my courage and knocked on the wooden door. Mr. Shepard greeted me. "Hi, Mason."

"How is she doing?" Did I sound as distressed as I felt?

"I mean, good evening, Mr. Shepard. Can I see her?" I blew out a breath.

He opened the door wider and motioned me inside. "We met with the doctor earlier. Melinda is in her room. I'm not sure if she'll agree to see you. She's mad at all of us right now."

I traced the pattern of the tiles on the floor with the tip of my shoe. "Can...can I try? I gotta talk to her. I hate how we left things earlier."

"Sure." He led me to his daughter's bedroom. We both stopped in front of the closed door and exchanged a gaze before he rapped his knuckles on the panel. "Honey, Mason is here to see you. Can he come in?"

No answer.

He cracked the door open and peeked inside. "Mel?"

I heard her mumble something but couldn't make out what she said from where I stood.

"Mason is here. Can he talk to you?"

Melinda answered something.

Mr. Shepard spun to face me. "Go ahead, son." He patted my shoulder like his wife had done earlier.

"Hey you." I tiptoed inside the dimly lit room, unsure how Melinda would react to my presence.

She was sitting on her bed, with her back to me, and I couldn't read her facial expression. Dressed in a pair of pajama pants and a sweatshirt, she appeared minuscule in her clothes. How did I not realize what was going on before it went too far?

I swallowed my uneasiness and cleared my throat. "I'll sit right here." I pointed to the chair set in the corner even though she didn't look at me or acknowledge my presence. This had to be one of the most uncomfortable situations I had ever put myself in, yet I couldn't walk away unless I had the certitude we were all right.

The silence stretched between us, so heavy against my chest that it suffocated me.

Unable to bear the distance between us, I stood and circled the bed, sitting next to her.

I extended an arm to hold Melinda's hand, but she scooted away from me.

"Mel… I… Please…" Emotions prickled the back of my eyes. My throat stung as if I'd eaten shards of glass. "We… I'm not going away. I'm right here. With you."

She ran the back of her hand under her nose, still avoiding a look in my direction.

I kneeled in front of her and cradled her face with both hands. She closed her eyes, silent tears streaming down her cheeks. I could clearly see everything I'd been too blind to notice before, everything I'd convinced myself wasn't there. The hollow cheeks, the shadows under her eyes, the slimmer fingers, the thinner waist, the smaller chest. The girl I loved had been suffering in silence, and I had done nothing to alleviate her anguish. How clueless I had been.

"You…huh…you tried to tell me. That day. When you confided about being bullied in middle school… You tried to tell me you were suffering without naming it. I should have picked up the hints. There were so many, and I was blind to them all."

My own tears drenched my cheeks.

I pressed my forehead to Melinda's lap, wrapping my arms around her, holding on to her like she might vanish. "I'm sorry, baby. I didn't know… I-I'm so sorry." I choked on my sobs. "I…I need you. Please stop… Stop hurting yourself."

A tentative hand brushed my hair back, and I shivered under the feather touch.

My sobs doubled in intensity. I felt so powerless. So out of my game. I knew nothing about eating disorders except the few things I had learned while searching the internet this afternoon.

We stayed like that for what appeared to be hours.

"You need me?"

Those were the first words she'd spoken to me since we parted ways this morning.

I raised my head, searching her eyes. "I do. With every fiber of my being. With every bit of my heart and my soul."

"Mase, you can't need me."

I jerked back. "W-why? Gimme one good reason why."

"Because. I don't want you to."

We watched each other for a beat.

"You don't want me to?" I blinked, pretty sure I was dreaming the entire scene. "What if… What if I wanna be with you?"

She shook her head. "Nah. I won't let you. I'm defective…broken. You can date any girl you desire. I'll always have this voice in my head telling me I'm not good enough or beautiful enough or smart enough to be with you. When I look at Tanya or any of the girls on the cheerleading squad, all I see are long legs, tiny waists, shiny blonde hair. Everything I'm not."

"That's a load of crap. I don't want the other girls, Mel. I-I want you. All of you. Even the not-so-healthy version of you. The rest, I don't care."

"Too bad. I can't do this with you. It's asking too much from me. I was doing better before we started hanging out. Dating you seems a lot like a one-way road to getting my heart broken. I…I can't risk it. I gotta be focused on what matters, and right now, it's not…it's not you."

Was she serious, or was she willingly chasing me away once again?

"Don't say it like I'm the reason you feel like you're not

good enough. I've always been there. I cared for you when you were sick, and I held you in my arms at night. I never made you feel this way. I've told you how beautiful you are. You're the only one I see. I've never given you a reason to feel insecure about your physical appearance."

"No. You didn't. I did. It doesn't change the fact I feel like I'm not good enough to be seen at your side. Sometimes... Not always… It's just… It's hard to explain. All the girls I find pretty look the opposite of me. They have less curves, smaller shoulders, slimmer waists."

"This doesn't make sense."

"I'm not blaming you. I just don't wanna go back to being that insecure girl."

"I can help you through this. I know I can if you let me in…if you gimme a chance."

"Yeah, probably, but I gotta do this on my own, like a big girl. It's my battle, my body, and my screwed-up perceptions. For once, I must put myself first. Find…find my groove back, make swimming my priority. That and huh…my mental health. Even parading in a swimsuit these days is like asking a lot from me. I never wanted you to see me naked before I looked like the girl I had pictured in my head. I only had five more pounds to shed. Five. Since our deadline was Winter Formal, I wanted to be ready and beautiful by then so whatever happened between us that night, I wouldn't feel ashamed of my body."

"No. Don't say that. I would have never put pressure on you. I-I don't care about those five pounds. I've always thought you were pretty. Did I say something to make you believe otherwise?" I replayed some of our conversations in my head, trying to find out where it went wrong. If I'd said something she could have interpreted badly. Nothing. I couldn't think of anything.

"Don't blame yourself, Mase. It-it's all on me."

"What does it mean…for us?"

"There can't be an us. And I'm not sure there can ever be one. We're too different."

"Different is a good thing. Different is great. We can help each other out. I'm not perfect. I struggle too. With how people see me… You've witnessed it. Thanks to you, I'm just starting to be myself again. You get me. You never ask me to be perfect or to put on a brave face when I feel down. See? We can help each other out. We're good together."

"Mase, you can't be my crutch. I gotta do this on my own. I'm sorry if I'm hurting you. If we are together, you'll be collateral damage. Eventually… I'm going away for the winter break. My cousin Jeremy lives in Traverse City. My parents found a clinic there... I'll be staying at his house while I receive treatments. Please don't call me or show up. It would just make things messier than what they already are."

"So, it's like that? You-you're ditching me, and there's nothing I can do or say about it?"

"Sorry… It's better this way. We'll talk when I return in, huh…January… Or maybe we won't."

"Mel… don't push me away. Not like this."

"I have to. You should go home now."

Her cold tone surprised me, and I froze, unable to speak.

"I was serious at school this morning, Mase. I don't need you to save me. Stop playing superhero."

A part of my heart died. Why was she being cruel? Was it a new attempt to keep me at a distance?

I let go of her and stood. "You don't mean that. I know you, and you don't mean a word you just said."

Melinda moved to her feet, avoided looking at me, and walked to the door, opening it wide and showing me out.

"We're done. I also meant it when I told Paige I was done with her. I never wanna talk to her ever again. She ratted me out."

"She's your best friend. Flush me from your life, but don't flush her."

"She *was* my best friend. I'm not sure I can forgive a traitor."

"You don't mean that." *You don't mean this; you don't mean that.* Were those the only replies left in me? "Nothing you're saying sounds like you right now."

"Well, maybe you don't know me as much as you thought you did."

Before I could argue further, she closed the door on me. For the longest time, I stood there, my palm flat against the door, wishing she would change her mind, say she was sorry, and we would make out and that she would agree to accept my help through her struggles.

It never happened.

For the very first time, I found love and lost it just as fast.

Back home, I hurried to my room, avoiding my parents' questions, before Paige and Craig cornered me upstairs.

"I can't do this," I said, breathless as if I had run drills for hours. "She wants nothing to do with me anymore."

"Oh, Mase." Paige pulled me into her arms, her tears mirroring mine. "It's all my fault. I should have said something sooner. Mel was good at changing the subject and finding excuses to explain her behavior. I had to go to Mr. and Mrs. S. They had to know. But I messed up everything for all of us when I did. I'm so sorry."

I hugged her tighter. "You did the right thing. Never believe you didn't. I just wish you had told me first. I don't know what I could have done differently, but I would have tried."

"Now she hates us all. I lost my best friend."

I swallowed around the lump, now a permanent fixture in my throat. "I'm sure she'll forgive you. Once she's healed."

"What about you?"

"She just doesn't love me back."

Paige stepped away from me, drying her cheeks. "She loves you, Mase. That's the thing. She's been loving you for quite a long time. She was just too proud to admit it."

"Maybe…maybe that's not enough."

I locked myself in my bedroom, and for the first time in my entire life, I cried myself to sleep. For what I had and what I lost. And for the girl next door who owned my heart but refused to hang on to it or trust me to help her fight her demons by her side.

CHAPTER 32

I'VE ALWAYS LOVED YOU

Jitters invaded me as I stood in front of the bathroom mirror. "You can do this, man," I told my reflection. "Today is the day. You've bid your time and are ready to see Melinda Shepard again. Am I right?" I nodded at my reflection.

It'd been six weeks since I last talked to her, and the truth was that I missed her like crazy. My feelings for her hadn't faded during the time we were apart. In fact, her absence had only solidified what I already knew. I was in love with her. The hole in my heart her absence had created had only deepened over the last few weeks. All I longed for was to be her sidekick again. To rejoice with her when she had a good day and celebrate her victories, no matter how small or inconsequential they might seem. To be her support system when she had a bad day and needed some cheering up and to be her shoulders when it became too much and she had to cry it out. I prayed a month and a half had been enough time for her anger and hurt to have waned and her common sense about us to have returned.

Every week since she'd been gone, her parents had updated me about her well-being. I'd spent so much time at her house over the last few weeks that I'd had breakfast there twice. I'd even helped her dad hang a giant wreath from the cedar gable bracket the week before Christmas. They'd invited me to dinner once, too, but it had felt strange being there while their daughter was away, getting treated for an eating disorder. They missed her—*how could they not? I did too*—and had driven to see her for Christmas, but she had refused to talk to them. They'd warned me it was part of the process. That it was normal for her to reject the people who cared about her most at first. They said that, in time, she would get better and the anger would fade.

"I love you," I told the mirror, pretending it was her. "I've always loved you. I'm done standing on the sidelines. If you love me too and you think what we have is real and worth fighting for, then let's figure this out together. I wanna be by your side while you fight this. I believe we can work out our shits better if we do it together as a team. If you're not ready for more, there's no rush. We can go back to being friends. I'm okay with that too. Take all the time you need to heal and feel better, but please don't push me away again. I'm right here… I'll be right here when you need me. If a part of you believes we can be much more and you're ready to take a leap of faith, I'm asking you: Melinda Shepard, will you go out with me?"

My heart thundered in my chest, and my hands felt clammy. I exhaled. I could do this.

Before they left to pick her up in Traverse City three days ago at her aunt and uncle's, her parents had reassured me that Melinda was doing much better. She still had a long way to go in her recovery, but they were confident she would get through it. She'd even been given the green light to start training with the swim team again, as long as she kept up with therapy and her weekly meetings with a nutritionist and continued having her sessions and meals monitored.

My heart beat wild in my chest. Seeing Melinda again after all this time apart felt like a big deal, and I didn't wanna look desperate, yet a part of me yearned to see her with my own eyes to assess whether she really was recovering. Sometimes, I wondered if she missed me too. If she missed what we had...or what we were... I'd never contacted her like she'd asked, and I knew for a fact she'd never reached out to Paige either. When she'd come over for dinner two days ago, Paige had confided that she was just as anxious as I was to have her best friend back in her life and to see where they stood.

At night, when I was alone, missing her, I wrote her letters. I found it helped untangle my messy feelings and thoughts—and it made me feel closer to her in a way. There were a dozen of them stored in a shoebox under my bed. I still hadn't decided if I would give them to her one day.

I gave my reflection a thumbs-up, fixed my tousled hair, and dressed in a pair of jeans and a vintage-looking white T-shirt I'd bought during one of our shopping sprees, one she'd approved of. We had spent an hour at the arcade that afternoon. I hoped she remembered the day as much as I did, and that the sight of the shirt would trigger her memories of what we used to be. Back then, I thought she was being cute when she'd suggested we skip dinner so we could catch a movie and cuddle in the dark. Even though Mom told me multiple times Melinda's disorder wasn't on me and I wasn't responsible for her struggles, I still loathed myself for not realizing sooner that she was suffering in silence.

"Ready?" Craig asked as I passed him on the staircase on my way downstairs.

"As much as I'll ever be."

"Did she try to contact you after she made it home last night?"

"No. I swear it took all my inner power to stay away. I almost knocked on her door at nine because I was becoming restless. I didn't want to look like a creep, so I didn't spy next door like I craved to. Maybe it would have been smarter to ring their doorbell and not wait until we were at school to talk to her… What do you think?"

"I think you're worrying too much. Her parents told you she was doing better. If I were her, I'd be anxious to come back to school after everything. She wouldn't be back if it was bad, no? Paige had been pacing her own bedroom all day yesterday, hoping for a call that never came. I'm sure it'll all be okay."

"Yeah. You're probably right. It still feels like a big deal, though."

"I know. I'll root for you, Mase. I'll root for you two. I know she's the one struggling right now, but I swear she's good for you too. You've dropped the act since things started becoming serious between you guys. I feel like I'm getting my brother back—the real him."

"Don't get all sappy on me, man."

"I'm not. I've just missed the guy, that's all."

I nodded. "Thanks." We fist-bumped, and I reached the landing with a jump.

"Mason," Mom warned. "There are stairs, use them. No need to start an earthquake this early in the morning."

"Sorry, Mom," I said, planting a kiss on her cheek while I grabbed the protein shake I'd made earlier from the table.

"You're in a good mood this morning. I'm glad the gloomy attitude you wore during the entire break is gone. I've missed my happy son." *It seemed like my whole family had missed me while I'd been here the entire time. Go figure.*

"It is, Mom. And don't call me your *happy son*. It's lame." I winced. "And disturbing."

"Your brother is the serious one, Mason. You're usually the laid-back one. *Chillax*. It's nothing to be ashamed of. It's one of your most endearing qualities."

"Whatever. And don't say *chillax* either. You're too old to talk like that."

She blinked. "To talk like what? Am I not cool enough for the likes of you?"

"You're cool enough usually, but no weird teen slang, please."

"Teen slang? I just made up the word. I'll say *Easychill* instead."

"Nope. No more made-up expressions."

"Fine. Anyway, like I was saying, I'm glad happiness is back in your life. It broke my heart to see you blaming yourself for Melinda's disorder. You can help her much more if you're in a good mood than if you're miserable. The girl will need all the positivity she can get, now that she's back."

"I'm choosing to let go of the guilt and the pain and to look at the future with a positive outlook. I think I can help her out. Let's just hope she gives me a chance to be there for her. See? I'm trying to be Mr. Optimism."

"I love this new mindset." She turned, studying me with a frown. "How are you really doing? The truth. There are shadows under your eyes. I can tell this whole situation is weighing heavily on you, and I worry about you."

I averted my eyes, but she cleared her throat, and I brought my focus back to her. "I'm fine… I think… Melinda returned last night, and it took all I had not to go over there... I stayed awake hoping she would reach out. She never did. After that, I didn't sleep well. There are millions of scenarios playing in my head every day. I have no clue if she still wants nothing to do with me. It's hard not knowing where we stand. I've missed her like crazy, and… I-I hope she misses me too…and that she's healing. I hate the idea she did this to herself and thought I would like her more if she looked different. I want her to be healthy, you know?"

"Mase, we've already discussed it. It's not on you. And it's not up to you either. Eating disorders are serious, and it's more than just a warped-up perception of physical appearance. It's a mental health struggle, and it impacts self-confidence too. Melinda put herself under a lot of stress last fall, and with her health history, it just became too much, and she cracked. Don't blame yourself for not seeing it. And don't blame her either. Instead, be there for her if she lets you in. Be her moral support, her confidant… I know I would have wanted someone in my corner if it had been me in her shoes at that age. Someone I could have been honest with and who I knew had my back, no matter what."

"Okay."

"Have you talked to her at all while she was away?"

"No." I sighed. "She asked me not to contact her, and I

kept my promise. We haven't talked since the night I went over to her house, and she said we were over. Her mom told me she was hopeful about her progress the other day so…" I scratched my temple. "Mom, do you think we can go back to what we once were? Or do you think our relationship will be forever broken?"

"Is that what you want? To be with her in a romantic way?"

"Yes. Why do you even ask? It's not even a question."

"Oh, Mase." My mom caressed my cheek. "You're a special one, my son. Don't rush her, okay? She's been through a lot. I could tell every time I saw you two together that she cared about you a lot, too. Give her some time and some room to breathe. For now, be her friend and see where it takes you. She'll need all the support she can get. I'm sure deep down she knows you only want what's best for her too."

"Yeah. I wanna care for her."

"I know. It comes with great responsibilities, though, and I don't want you to put too much pressure on yourself. You are no doctor, and you're not supposed to be one either. Your job is to be there for her if she lets you in, but not to try to heal her. Don't take over someone else's job because you think you have to."

Her words simmered between us for a minute.

"Since the day she moved next door, I've always thought there was something special between the two of you. I'm glad you found your way to each other after all this time. This chemistry, it won't fade because of a bump in your road. If you two are meant to be, you'll find your way back to each other again one day if now isn't your time."

"You think so?"

"I truly believe that." Her words beelined straight to

my heart and confirmed what I already knew. Melinda and I shared a connection. Our getting together had been a long time coming.

"Thanks, Mom. I gotta go. I don't wanna be late."

"I love to see you so enthusiastic to return to school after a month-long break." Her laughter wrapped around me like a warm ribbon as I made my way outside, relishing the crisp winter air as it hit my lungs. Two inches of freshly fallen snow covered the ground like millions of tiny diamonds gleaming under the sun's rays, giving the street a fairytale appearance.

The weather wouldn't make a dent in my day. The sun was shining high, and my heart was bursting with hope—and love. Nothing could go wrong today. I had a plan and I would follow it and everything would unfold perfectly.

For long minutes, I watched the house next door, waiting for a movement—or a sign. Anything that would make it easier for me to engage with my neighbor before we arrived at school.

Craig joined me on the front porch. "Are you chickening out?"

"No. She's worth it. I was waiting to see if she came out so I could have offered her a ride to school." I sighed. "Are we riding together?"

"Nah. I'm going to pick up Paige. I don't like the idea of her driving when the roads haven't been plowed yet."

"You know she's a big girl, right?"

"Yep. I have to do this since I may not be able to be there for her next y—"

"Wait, what? Why wouldn't you be able to do this next year?"

"Nothing. Forget I said anything."

I blocked his way down the steps. "It's not nothing. Talk to me. What did you mean by that?"

"It's complicated. Nothing you gotta worry about."

"Does Paige know?"

A mixture of sadness and resignation swam in his eyes. "Don't say anything. It's messier than you think. Don't bring her into this." I saw the plea in his gaze. "Please, Mase."

"Don't lead her on. If you do, it's your ass I'll kick and her side I'll choose when it all goes to hell. Don't screw this up."

He nodded, pushed past me, and seconds later, his engine roared to life. After he cleared the snow off his car with a brush, he pulled out of the driveway, not sparing me another glance.

"Fuck," I said, not sure what to do with the information I'd gotten from my brother.

Parked in the school lot twenty minutes later, I repeated everything I wanted to say to the girl who owned a big chunk of my heart. Six weeks without seeing her had felt like forever. I was ready to have her back in my life. Full time. Mom's words from this morning replayed in my head. They'd been invading my thoughts every second since I left the house. *Since the day she moved next door, I've always thought there was something special between the two of you.*

A sports car stopped in front of the main entrance. Black with orange stripes. Tinted windows. Chrome wheels. I had never seen it around before. Was it a new student? Or some kid showing off the new ride he got for Christmas? Students gathered around the idling vehicle, probably trying to guess who was hiding inside.

Standing still, I kept my gaze trained on the scene, my feet heavy as if they had been encased in concrete.

My pulse accelerated. Goose bumps rose on my arms. My insides twisted.

Something was off.

I had no idea why, but my gut told me I wouldn't be happy about the whole thing. That I should brace myself for whoever climbed out.

A guy exited the driver's side, and when he spun around, I recognized him as Jayden Clarke, linebacker for the Cowley High Cobras, our biggest rival, and the one guy I couldn't stand. It'd been a while since we last crossed paths. Annoyance bubbled deep inside me. My instinct hadn't been wrong. Cowley High's and our school's football teams had a long history of feud over the last fifty years. The rivalry was no joke. Cobras and Bears didn't mix well together. We each stayed in our respective towns and avoided running into each other as much as we could. Jayden Clarke was a cocky son of a bitch. Not that I wasn't one myself, but he took the word cockiness to an all-new level. He had no reason to be on our school grounds. If he knew what was good for him, he would flee our parking lot before all my teammates arrived and shit hit the fan.

Unless he had transferred schools. Had he? None of my teammates—me included—would welcome him with open arms if he walked the hallways of Elk River High. It would be a catastrophic scenario. I watched him like a hawk, waiting for his next move.

The passenger door opened, and someone climbed out. A girl with long brown hair. Time stopped. A piece of my chest splintered, and it hurt like hell. I almost fainted right there. *Mel? What the fuck.*

Clarke rounded the idling vehicle to meet her, handing her the book bag he had fetched from the backseat. Melinda smiled at him, and he leaned in, capturing her lips in a kiss after grazing her cheek with his knuckles, the gesture sweet and gentle. Like he really did care. He wrapped one arm around her shoulders and pulled her to him, murmuring something in her ear before kissing her one more time.

I blinked a million times. What. The. Actual. Fuck. What did I miss?

Craig and Paige, who I hadn't seen arriving, stood next to me. They turned to follow my line of sight.

"What's going on?" my brother asked. "Why is Jayden Clarke here? Is he looking to have his ass kicked?" He must have taken the entire scene in because he stiffened beside me. "Is that Mel? Oh shit—"

I breathed around the growing rock clogging my airways. "Yep."

My brother nudged my side. "Since when?"

"Fuck if I know."

Paige remained silent between us, watching the debacle unfold in front of us.

"No. This isn't happening," I said. "It's. Not. Happening. This must be a mistake or a prank." I stepped forward, ready to intervene and put an end to this circus. I could feel the sweat lining my temples even with the cold winter breeze hitting my face. My body grew hotter by the second. Soon I'd combust if I didn't do anything.

"Mel, wait up."

Paige backhanded my chest, forcing me to a stop. "Mase, no. Don't do anything stupid. Please don't make a scene."

I motioned to the train wreck happening in front of us. "Paige, what's going on? Tell me it's all a big mistake and that I'm not seeing what is right before me." Rage flooded my bloodstream now. My fists clenched so hard I feared my nails would draw blood.

"Mase. I swear I didn't know. He's a friend of her cousin. They have a band together or something. They spent their break together. The three of them. I saw pictures online last night. She told me nothing. We haven't talked since that morning when…you know. I tried to contact her a few times, but I think she blocked my number."

"What? What are they? Don't hide anything from me."

She glanced at her feet. "They are dating… I think. Three days ago, Jayden posted a picture of them kissing on that photo thing online with the tag *My girl is hot.* I'm so sorry, Mase. I thought it was a sick joke or something. A way to get back at you somehow. I never believed they were actually an item and that it was serious."

"Sorry? Sorry? Sorry doesn't mean shit right now. It doesn't fix anything. I listened to everyone who said I should follow her lead and give her some time while she was healing. That she was prioritizing herself and getting better. I did all of it. I didn't reach out. I gave her space. I didn't drive to Traverse City when I missed her like crazy. Or call her when I was awake in the middle of the night, wondering if she was scared or if people were treating her right. I haven't seen her in six weeks. It-it's a long fucking time. Her parents told me she was doing better and was ready to come home and that I could see her today so we could fix our relationship because she was more stable emotionally and mentally. And now that she's back, she's with him? No. *No, no, no.* She can't be. It's a mistake. She was supposed to come back *to me.* To be *my* girlfriend. Not Clarke's. Jayden *I'm-gonna-kick-his-ass* Clarke." I tugged at my hair, pacing the parking lot. "No. I don't agree with that. Are you sure? Is it a prank you're playing on me? Are you all in on this?"

Craig pulled me aside. "Mase, calm down and let it go. For now."

"No," I screamed despite myself. "This was not how it was supposed to be…how it was supposed to go down."

My body vibrated with all the anger and sadness spreading through me.

My brother hugged me. "I know. Stick with me, okay? I have your back. Always."

I leaned back and adjusted my jacket, trying to look unaffected. Even though I wanted to, I couldn't put my cocky jock suit on this time. My head and my heart weren't in the game. My attention drifted to the main entrance where Melinda had disappeared.

Nausea filled my mouth. My eyes burned with unshed tears.

I was a bomb about to explode.

How many nights had I spent lying awake, imagining our reunion? I would open my arms, and she would run into them, telling me how much she'd missed me. Then she would kiss me, saying she should have done it a long time ago. The scene I'd just witnessed looked nothing like that. For a moment, I wondered if this morning had been nothing more than a nightmare I would wake up from.

My heart raced faster in my chest. I felt dizzy. My mouth tasted like chalk paint.

Craig elbowed my side. "Come on."

Following Paige and my brother inside, I met with Chase who was waiting by my locker. "Hey, Cap. How was your break?" Chase had spent the last two weeks in Bora Bora with his mom and older brother, far away from his deadbeat father.

"Later," I mumbled, not meeting his eyes.

"Whoa, did your cat die?"

"I don't have a cat. Gimme a break."

Tanya walked by, waving her fingers. "Morning, baby," she purred.

"Who are you calling baby?" my friend asked. "Me? No thanks, I would rather die than get too close to you. I'm afraid your poison is lethal. That bitch attitude of yours might be contagious, and I haven't received the vaxx."

She pushed my friend aside with a hand. "Go. Get lost somewhere else, Chase. I'm not talking to you. I'm here for my king."

"Jesus," I groaned.

"Your king?" Chase's attention traveled between us. "Something I missed?"

Tanya sighed. "Haven't I told you to get lost already? Come on, *Masey* Baby."

"*Masey Baby*?" Chase's loud chuckle vibrated around us. "That's precious."

"Don't," I said, pointing at him.

He inserted himself between Tanya and me, blocking my view of her. "Tan, hear me out. No way will I let my man here alone with a viper like you. Your behavior is bordering on harassment."

Tanya circled him and draped herself all over me. I wanted to push her away, I really did, but I was hurting and couldn't care less what anyone thought right now.

Chase nudged me. "Are you okay with her being here, or do you want me to kick her ass to Neptune? Your call, Captain."

My conscience made a comeback before I did something I would regret. "Kick her ass, Chase. Far away from here. She's bad news. And she doesn't understand the word *no*."

Seconds later, Tanya was pried away from me. "Mase. You can't do this. What about us? Our reign over ERH? We said it would be you and me. We agreed. Don't you remember your promise to me?"

"You're a psycho, Tan. I never promised you anything. You are accusing me of things I never said or agreed to. Don't come near me ever again, or you might hate the person I turn into. Keep walking and forget I exist."

"What? You can't be serious. We had a deal."

"Nah. No deal. You never meant anything to me, and you're done screwing up my life."

Hurt flashed in her gaze. "You don't mean it."

I stepped forward, towering over her by almost a foot, forcing her to tip her head back. "Wanna bet? I'm in a very bad mood right now. I suggest you go annoy someone else."

Fury poured out from her. She transformed right under my eyes from kitten to evil. "You're a mean person, Mason Pierce. I'll tell everyone you gave me crabs. We'll see who's gonna let you bang them now."

"Do that and I'll tell everyone you're a lame fuck," Chase added. "Worst I ever had."

She rested her fists on her hips. "You wouldn't dare."

"Watch me," my friend said. "You're lucky I was too drunk that night to realize I was making the biggest mistake of them all."

I had no idea what had gone down between them, but right now, I didn't care. I enjoyed seeing Tanya being handed her own medicine for once.

She gritted her teeth, stomping her foot. "You'll both regret this."

"Whatever," I said as she scurried away, adjusting her tiny cheerleading skirt as she did.

Chase's palm met mine, and I sighed in relief. "Thanks. For having my back."

"I have no idea what happened to you or between you two," he said. "I can't wait to be updated on all the latest gossip."

"Well, I won't be the one feeding them to you. I haven't seen her since the last day of school before the winter break. She's making up stories about us in her mind." I filled my book bag and hoisted it over my shoulder. "I'll see you around."

Before he could utter another word, I stormed away, wishing the day was already over.

For the rest of the week, I lay low, spending all my free time in the weight room of the athletic building or jogging around the indoor track, sweating my anger and pain away. I watched Melinda from afar, making sure she was okay, even though she pretended I didn't exist. She not only looked different nowadays, but also acted different too. Every time our paths crossed, she switched directions, not acknowledging my existence. She did the same thing with Paige. Even after all this time, she still refused to talk to her best friend. Craig had told me Paige had tried to mend their friendship and explain herself multiple times, but Melinda had reiterated she was done with backstabbing people, whom she couldn't trust, pretending to play nice.

It hurt because I concluded she had included me in that statement.

Yesterday, she was having lunch by herself in the library when I walked in. I had noticed she only ate when she wasn't surrounded by other people. At least she'd had food on her tray when she walked out of the dining hall, and her plate was empty afterward, which reassured me that she really was doing better. Our eyes locked for a long moment, and I saw the flames bank low in hers. All was not lost. I still had a chance. Before I could say anything to break the uncomfortable silence between us, she picked up her things and left without a word.

My heart had cracked into thousands of pieces.

I had to talk to her. Whatever it took, I had to make things right between us.

CHAPTER 33

THE BIG FUCKING THING THAT STARTS WITH A CAPITAL L

"**H**ey, Mel. Wait up." I jogged after her when she exited her science class a few days later.

She hurried forward, holding a textbook to her chest, not even sparing me a glance.

My fingers closed around her elbow from behind, but she yanked her arm away, putting more distance between us. "Talk to me. I deserve to know what's going on."

My words—or my tone—must have done the job because she stopped, took a deep breath in, and spun on her heel to face me.

She looked radiant. Gone were the shadows under her eyes and the ghostly complexion, even though we were in the middle of January and lacking sunlight these days. She was wearing a golden corduroy romper over a white shirt with black knee-high socks, her hair braided over her shoulder, a light coat of lip gloss coloring her lips.

I swallowed. "You look…wow…you look beautiful."

Not acknowledging me, she glanced down.

"Aren't you gonna say anything? I deserve an explanation. You've been avoiding me like the plague since school has resumed."

She snorted. "I don't owe you anything, Mason."

Mason? What happened to Mase?

I lifted her chin up with a finger, capturing her eyes, the turquoise pools that I wanted to sink in for the rest of time, mesmerizing me. We remained like this for what felt like hours, neither of us saying anything. As if our souls could say it all. And then I saw it again. The tiny glint. The small hint that we were not done. That there was still something powerful simmering between us. Melinda must have felt it too because she stepped back as if my skin had burned hers and looked away.

"I-I missed you."

She said nothing, her gaze snapping back to me. Emotions crossed her eyes, lingering there for a small second before vanishing.

I made another attempt and grabbed her hand in mine, lacing our fingers. They fit just like I remembered. This time, she didn't remove her hand or try to escape my proximity. "We haven't seen or talked to each other in over six weeks." I swallowed around my own emotions blocking my airways. "I was worried about you. I tried to give you space like you asked, but I can't do it anymore. I need to know where we stand and if we can salvage what we had."

"Mason, we had nothing." Her voice was barely above a whisper.

I stepped forward. "Wrong answer. Please say it like you mean it this time."

"I won't play games with you." Her gaze drifted everywhere but to my eyes as she spoke.

"I'm done playing games too. I truly believe we belong together. I'm just waiting for you to catch up with the fact."

The iciness of her laughter sliced through my heart. "Sorry, but it won't happen. You better find someone else to be with."

"Stop feeding me bullshit. What we had was real. Why won't you recognize it?"

"I'm dating someone else. I'm with Jayden now."

"Yeah, right. Clarke." I clamped the back of my neck with a hand, the feeling of my fingers around my spine grounding me. "Like you had to run away and fall for my number one enemy."

"Jayden is not the bad guy here, Mason. He's nice to me and doesn't expect anything from me. He treats me well and makes me smile. There are no groupies after him everywhere we go. We have fun together and he was there when my world crumbled around me and I was all alone because everyone had turned their backs on me. It's simple with him. He listens to me and... I don't have to explain him to you."

Her words acted like a punch in the gut, and I jumped back. "You're kidding, right? I have never turned my back on you. Not once. I know you've been through something hard and recovery is a long road ahead and it won't always be easy, but dating Clarke is not what you need right now."

"Like you know better what I need. Yeah, right."

"As a matter of fact, I think I do. Whether you wanna admit it or not, I know you. The real you, not the one you are pretending to be right now."

She snorted. "You know me so well that you didn't notice when I was struggling."

I flinched like she had just kicked me in the stomach.

"Why are you so mean? You know it's nothing like that. Jayden Clarke is bad news. You don't need more complications in your life. You need someone who really cares about you."

"Like you?"

"Yeah. Like me. I've always been there for you. You can't deny it. You and I, we're great together. We're much more alike than you think. We have history, and we can make it work. I'll give you your space and wait until you're ready to be with me. In the meantime, we can resume our friendship."

"Here's the thing, Mason. I don't wanna be with you. Not anymore. Not even as a friend. I'm with Jayden. You gotta respect that."

Sadness and fury mixed inside me. I fisted my hands at my sides, not sure how to protect myself from the punches she kept throwing at me. "Is this a new thing of yours? Part of your therapy?"

"What?"

"Hurting the ones who care about you?"

Her teeth left indents in her lower lip. "That's not what I'm doing."

"Isn't it? Because from where I'm standing, that is exactly what is happening. Why won't you give me a chance? Why won't you give *us* a chance? What is so wrong about me that you won't even consider dating me?"

"Because there is no *us* and there never will be one. I thought I made myself clear already."

My eyes prickled with the tears building in their corners. I wouldn't lose my cool here. I wouldn't break down in the hallway en route to my next class. Melinda Shepard might be able to break my heart, but she wouldn't break me.

"Keep lying to yourself, but it's not a good look on you. I thought we'd already agreed on that."

Red crept up her cheeks. "Drop the sarcasm. Can't you see I'm setting you free here?"

I threw my arms up in frustration before I realized what I was doing. Anger underlined my tone. "You think I wanna be set free? What kind of world do you think you're living in? You know what, keep pretending all is fine. I'm no shrink, but I'm pretty sure the first step in healing is to stop lying and blaming others. I guess you skipped that lesson. Congrats, you wanted to lose me. Well, you did just that. Are you happy now? Does it make you feel better? Help you sleep at night?" I pointed an accusing finger at her, the opposite of how I had seen this conversation going. I wanted to shield her, help her, protect her, not make an enemy out of the only girl I ever had feelings for. "Next year, I'll be everywhere you'll be. I signed with Crestwood U. It's been official for a long time, but I was waiting for the perfect moment to tell you. I was supposed to come clean on that snowboarding vacation we never went on. I had ordered a bunch of CWU merch and swag as your Christmas gift after your dad told me they offered you a full ride too. Stupid matching stuff for both of us because I could picture us dating, going to college together, and doing all the shit kids our age do when they're in love. Anyway, forget I said anything. It's not important now. It doesn't mean a goddamn thing anymore. I left the bag at your house this morning. Throw it away, burn it, give it to charity for all I care."

A lone tear carved the length of her cheek. "You did that...for me?" Her lips quivered.

"Yep. Like a fool in love. Because what I've been feeling for you, Mel, all these years isn't friendship, it's much more powerful than that. It's love. The big fucking thing that starts with a capital *L*. I'm sorry I snapped at you. It won't happen again. And I'm sorry I made you late for your next class. It wasn't my intention either. Just remember that for the next four years, I'll still be around. I'm not going anywhere. I just hope Clarke treats you decently because he'll be in Maryland in a few months. Don't come crying on my shoulder when things don't work out between you two when you realize he's an asshole and not worthy of you. Remember what I told you once. I don't do second place. Never. Goodbye, Mel." My own words became a stabbing pain that left me bleeding everywhere.

"Mason…" The single word sounded like a plea. "It's not that simple… I-I can't be with you. I hope you forgive me one day. It's too hard…being with you. When you look at me like I'm your whole world, it puts too much pressure on me… I feel like I'm not enough, and…and I can't…I just can't."

Sobs passed her lips, and I fought with everything I had not to pull her into my arms.

"Mase…" Her voice trembled. "I'm sorry."

I whirled around, gathered the last threads of self-preservation I had left, and strode away, my heart so heavy in my chest that I feared it could burst at any moment. "I'm sorry too," I said to no one but myself.

CHAPTER 34

I ALWAYS PLAYED FOR KEEPS

I skipped lunch and didn't recall any of my afternoon classes. Sitting on the floor by my locker, my back and head pressed to the wall, my eyes closed, I waited for the ruckus of the students leaving school to fade before making a move. My conversation with Melinda had replayed in my mind countless times all day, and I still couldn't wrap my head around the fact she'd dismissed me so easily. Time stilled, and I blocked out the noisy chatter and loud footsteps until everything became quiet around me. Enjoying the silence, I stretched my legs before me and breathed out, trying to get rid of the heaviness gluing me to this floor.

Someone sat beside me, and I didn't have to open my

eyes to know it was my brother. "How are you holding up?"

I snorted. "What do you think? She's dating the one guy I can't stand and making it sound like he's Prince Charming."

"That's messed-up. Do you think it's serious?"

I shrugged. "She made it sound like it was."

"Damn. You talked to her?"

"Yep. This morning."

"How did it go?"

I remained silent.

"That bad?"

I cracked my eyes open and stared at him. "Yep."

We said nothing for the longest time.

"What's going on with you? Want to tell me what it's all about for real? We can feel dejected together. I heard you arguing with Paige last night again. Your secret late-night meetings with Dad aren't so secret. I just don't understand why you two are shady as hell about whatever is going down behind those walls. What you said the other morning… It's still nagging at me."

A shadow passed through my brother's eyes, and he dragged a hand over his face. "I screwed up, man. Well… not me. Dad did. But I couldn't hold my end of the bargain, and now it's too late. His actions will impact me— and Paige—and I'm not sure what to do about it. If I come clean, my girlfriend will hate me, and I can't deal with her hatred. I love her, man. She's the one for me, and I can't imagine having to let her go."

I blinked, not sure what he meant. "Why would you have to let her go?"

"Because… As I told you that morning, it's complicated. I'm still trying to find a way out of this one, but I'm not sure I'll have enough time to right the wrong."

"Wanna tell me what it's all about instead of speaking in riddles?"

He shook his head, toying with the leather cuff around his left wrist that Paige had gifted him for Christmas. "No. She might never forgive me for this. I gotta see if I can fix it before I accept it's my reality. If I tell you all about it, it will make it real in my mind, and I'm not sure I can survive the truth. Not now. I'll be honest about it, I swear. Just not now, okay?"

"Fine. But you tell me if it gets too much, okay?"

"Deal."

"And please don't break her heart. I know firsthand how shitty it is. She's already lost Mel, so she can't lose you too. Whatever it is, fix it."

He nodded. "Do you think Mel will ever forgive her?"

"No idea. She's pretty hurt. It was like she was pushing me away earlier not because she wanted to, but because she thought it was the right thing to do. Maybe therapy will help. She's not on speaking terms with her parents either. I think until she decides she wants to heal and it comes from her instead of from the people around her, there's nothing we can do. If she doesn't recognize there's a problem in the first place, why would she want to deal with it?"

He moved to his feet and held out his hand to help me up. "That's sick. Sucks to be you right now."

"Yep. It sucks balls."

"Are you going to survive?"

"Yep." It felt like this was one of the only few words remaining in my vocabulary today. "What other choice do I have?"

"None. Sorry, man. I wish I had some words of wisdom right now. Wanna grab some food before going home?"

"Yep… Huh, sure."

"Follow me then. My treat."

———

I made my way inside, trying to avoid my parents and having to explain why I probably looked dejected. I felt crestfallen inside, so I had no doubt I looked the part too.

"Oh, it's you," Mom said, walking to me with an empty mug in hand. "I thought it would be your dad. He's working so many hours these days that it's like he's never home anymore."

I gave her a half-shrug. "At least Craig sees him."

"They're going through something. Nothing that concerns you for now."

"Nothing ever concerns me these days. Everyone keeps me in the dark. Now that we won State and I've committed to college, nobody cares what I'm doing anymore. I have served my purpose, and now I'm not useful to anyone. I'm just fucking tired of people pushing me away."

"Mase, language."

I snorted. "Sorry. I'm not fucking tired. I'm just tired."

Mom stared at me with a quirked eyebrow. "And you think sarcasm will work on me?"

I kept quiet, glancing at the hardwood floor, avoiding her eyes. If I knew something for sure, it was that my mother could smell bullshit from miles away.

"Want to tell me what's on your mind?"

I shrugged, my eyes still glued to the floor. "Not really."

"Where's your brother?"

"Paige's."

"Come, sit with me. Let's chat."

"Mom…"

"Don't Mom me, Mason. I know the look, and I would

be a very awful mother if I let you go to your bedroom before making sure you're all right."

"I'm fine."

"If only you were a great liar. Where's Mr. Optimism? I only saw him for a few minutes days ago. Care to tell me where he's hiding?"

"He doesn't exist. Dead. Buried with his heart."

We took seats next to each other at the kitchen island. Mom put a cookie on a napkin on the counter and poured tea into a mug and pushed them in front of me. She was using my chocolate-chips-cookie weakness against me, and she was well aware. She'd been using the same cheer-me-up method on me since I was just a little kid. It was like she had a sixth sense and always knew when I needed a home-baked treat to make the sting of something a little less bitter.

"Is it Melinda?" she asked after a full minute.

I broke a piece of cookie but didn't bring it to my mouth. "How can you tell?"

"Only love—and football—can put you in a sour mood when things don't go your way."

"I talked to her today… It-it didn't go well."

She said nothing as if she knew I had more to confide in her. I told her all about our encounter. The way Melinda had rejected me, the sadness in her eyes, the connection we shared that she was fighting and trying so hard not to acknowledge. Mom didn't say a word, listening to me as I poured my heart out.

"Do you recall what I told you on the day you returned to school after the break?"

"Which part?"

"The part about the chemistry you both share that won't fade because of a bump in your road. Also, if you two are meant to be, maybe your time isn't now, but you will find your way back to each other again one day."

I braced my elbows up on the countertop and buried my face in my hands, doing my best to conceal my emotions from my mother. "The thing is… I-I told her that I…that I loved her. And…and she didn't…she didn't care."

"Oh, Mason." She moved to her feet, and so did I when she wrapped her arms around me. "It's okay to be sad."

At that moment, I realized how small my mother felt in my arms. I had always pictured her as strong and tall, but right now, even though I towered over her by many inches, her petite frame was the glue keeping me in one piece instead of a million shards.

"I saw her… Melinda, I mean. She came by earlier."

I leaned back and wiped under my eyes with the back of my hand. "She did?"

"Your car wasn't in the driveway, so I believe she thought it was safe to come over. Anyway, she gave me this for you." She pointed to a white rectangle and a small box on the breakfast nook table.

"I don't want them. You can give them back to her."

"No. It's yours. You can keep them, look what's inside, throw them away, but if I were you, I'd wanna see what Melinda has to say. Sometimes, putting our thoughts into words on paper feels easier than speaking them aloud. She looked sad when she dropped by." She went to grab the envelope and the box and handed them to me. "I'm no mind reader, but this may answer some of your questions." She turned to walk away. "I'll leave you to it. If you need me, I'll be in the living room."

I swallowed around the mountain of rocks stuck in my throat. "Thanks."

Showered and changed into a pair of sweatpants and a white T-shirt, I stared at the envelope I'd discarded in the middle of my bed as if it were an explosive device about to blow up.

"What are you doing?" Craig asked as he entered my room a while later and stood next to me, his eyes landing on the white rectangle. "What's that? You look like it's about to bite you."

I sighed and rolled my shoulders back. It did nothing to ease the tension inside me. "Mel. She dropped this earlier."

"Have you opened it yet?"

"Nope. I'm still trying to decide whether I want to or not."

"Maybe it's important."

"Maybe."

He placed a hand between my shoulder blades. "Let me know if you want me to read it first in case it destroys that heart of yours."

He left, and after debating the pros and cons in my head for another minute, I finally concluded I would never be able to go to sleep without looking inside.

I sat on the edge of the bed, and with shaky fingers, I opened the tab and unfolded the piece of paper.

Dear Mason

This is not how I imagined our relationship going. All day, our conversation has been replaying in my head, and the last thing I've ever wanted was to hurt you.

Walking away from you that day when my parents staged the intervention is the hardest thing I've ever done, but I was so ashamed. I didn't want you to see me differently, and I didn't want to pull you down the rabbit hole with me.

I'm doing better, yes, but for the first time, I really wanna heal for me, not because everyone else is asking me to. It's hard. I understand now why I relapsed, and it's not easy to accept. Remember when you told me that dealing with the pressure others put on you is hard and you feel like you're suffocating? Well, I put that same pressure on myself and paid the price with my mental health.

I know you care about me, and I care about you too (a lot), but I need to stay away from you, Mase. Not because I want to, but for my own good. You once told me you never made me feel like I wasn't enough, and you were right. Again, I did all of that to myself. In my warped mind, I put these expectations on me. Please don't blame yourself. In all the months we spent together, you've been nothing but amazing and respectful and patient. You gave me your all, and I kept you at arm's length because I thought I had to become the perfect girl for you. I didn't believe you when you said I was beautiful in your eyes because I couldn't see myself as beautiful and thought you were lying. I'm sorry I pushed you away, but believe me, you're much better-off without me and my problems in your everyday life. If you stick around, you'll become collateral damage, and you're too amazing to be sucked into my vortex of self-doubt.

Being far from you is the only way I can truly heal.

Otherwise, we'll go back to where we left things off, and I won't prioritize my health. After we went swimming that afternoon, you told me you'd accept any dare I threw at you because I'd won the race. Today, I'm daring you to cut me loose. For good.

Please respect my decision.

And in case you still believe Jayden is bad news, just hear me out. When I was broken, he was there for me. We connected. He's been through some hard stuff himself, and he's been nothing but nice to me. He never judged me or made me feel like I was damaged. He's not the bad guy here. He is who I need at the moment. I'm not dating him to hurt you, Mase, and I didn't plan to fall for him. It just kinda happened one day. I was sad and he was there, and it just clicked. Deep down, I wish seeing me happy will make you realize we're not it, you and me—no matter what we tell ourselves—and help you move on. For the time it lasted, I really enjoyed being your friend, and I'm thankful for everything you did for me. You saved my life twice (or three times if you count the fainting episode), and I'll never forget it. You're still my hero and will always be, no matter what I let you believe when I was upset.

Mase, listen to me. You deserve the moon and the entire galaxy, and I wish I could be the one giving it to you, but since I can't, please find someone who will. Someone who is free to love you like you deserve to be. Someone who will make you smile and treat you well.

Please tell Paige I'm not ready to forgive her. I don't hate her anymore, and I now understand she was trying to do the right thing, but her betrayal still stings, and I don't know if I'll ever be able to trust her again.

Perhaps we'll all reconnect sometime in the future, or maybe we won't, but I'm okay with it. I have to be. I'm aware we'll both be at CWU next year, but I believe the campus is big enough that we won't have to be around each other. I won't get in the way. That's my promise to you.

I wish things had been different, but they are not. I hope one day you'll forgive me and understand I'm doing all this because I love you, just not the way you want me to.

Thank you for always having my back and caring for me when I needed a friend. I'll cherish the time we spent together forever.

I wish you the best in life.

Goodbye,
Melinda x

With my tears blinding me, I read the letter again, just to make sure I'd read it right the first time. A sense of panic spread through me at the idea Melinda and I were done for good. Being dismissed by the one person you wished would hold on to you hurt a lot. My heart fractured into more fragments inside my chest, and I pressed a hand against my ribs to keep all the pieces inside.

Curious about the contents of the box, I got up and grabbed it from my dresser before sitting back down on my bed.

I removed the tab and fished out the small object it contained. A piece of paper fell from it, and I skimmed the message.

Mason (or should I call you Nurse Pierce?)

I had it custom-made after my surgery as a thank you.

And also, because I promised you a trophy.

Here I am, following up on my words.

I hope you like it. I added a cape because all superheroes need one.

Melinda x

It was a bronze trophy of a football player with a jersey that read number twenty-two and *Pierce* on the back. Melinda had sewn a red cape embellished with gemstones and had attached it to its neck. A load of memories from our time together hit me like a tidal wave, and a new surge of emotions washed through me. She did care. About us. About me. About all of it.

Three soft knocks resonated on my bedroom door.

I ran my forearm over my eyes, trying to stop my tears. "Yeah?"

"You okay?" my brother asked from the other side. "Just wanted to check in on you before going to bed."

I cleared my throat to remove the tension tightening my vocal cords. "Yeah."

"Okay." He seemed to hesitate for a moment. "If you wanna talk about it, you know where to find me."

I swallowed and blinked to erase the sadness from my face even though he couldn't see me. "Thanks. Night."

His footsteps echoed on the hardwood floor as he walked away, and I relaxed a little. Turning the bedside lamp off, I lay on my back, my arms under my head, staring at the ceiling in the dark, my mind racing a thousand miles a minute.

In between excerpts of Melinda's letter, my night out with my brother replayed in my head, keeping me awake. Sometimes, I believed he was born first because he was wiser and could teach me a thing or two. Since I had no intention of being miserable and ruining the rest of my last year of high school, I had to come up with a plan. Something to keep me going and not lose hope. Melinda cared. She did. We were not over.

I turned the night light on and sat on my bed with a notepad in hand.

I was a damn good football player, but also a born leader. If I used my skills on the field in my personal life, perhaps, in the end, everything would work out. I had nothing to risk, nothing to lose. When an opponent tackled you on the field, you took the hit, stood back up, dusted yourself off, and came up with a new playbook. I decided to use the same strategy in my personal life.

If Jayden Clarke was who Melinda needed right now, then so be it. Perhaps the guy could help her see what we had all failed to make her see—that she needed help. Who knew, right? I wouldn't fight him over her. That would just alienate her further if I did. Maybe he was just a dick on the field, but not so much off it and really cared about her wellbeing.

As Mom had said, if now wasn't our time, it didn't mean later wouldn't be. We would be spending four years together at Crestwood University. A new chapter for both of us. Once Melinda was healed, I would sweep her off her feet like my brother had suggested earlier and show her we were still *it*. She just needed time to realize that I wasn't about to forfeit the match because she had pushed me away for my supposedly own good.

Perhaps if she missed me enough and realized she didn't share the same chemistry with other guys as she did with me, she would come to her senses and realize I was the one. Eventually.

I had no intention of following her advice and moving on. Not unless I had the certainty we were over—for good and forever. Who knew what the next few months had in store, right?

For now, my only option was to set her free like she'd asked.

I wrote it all down on the blank page. Even though it tore my heart to shreds to think she was with somebody else, I locked down the uneasiness seeping through every part of me. This new plan sounded like the smartest thing I could come up with. I would stay out of her way and see how it all played out. What other choice did I have, anyway?

Step one: set her free + wait

Once in college, I would revise my strategy because

Mason Pierce 2.0 would show Melinda Shepard what she was missing. Yeah, that sounded like a solid plan. I could do that. Prove to her I was the real deal. That she could trust me and lean on me when dealing with her shit became too much for her to handle alone. I rubbed my palms together, newfound energy coursing through me. It felt like I was about to enter the field to play an important game.

> *Step two: See how things evolve between us when in CWU*
> *(Note: check if still dating Clarke first)*

The sadness infiltrating my heart faded a little as my plan took form.

> *Step three: to be revised once step two is underway*
>
> *Step four: get the girl*

I watched the trophy I had set on my nightstand for a long moment. *She cared.* It was all that mattered.

After I put down my notepad, I turned off the lamp and lay back on my bed.

Shifting to my side, I chased sleep. I needed my brain to go on a break or else I would turn my strategy over in my head all night, and I really needed to evade reality for a few hours.

My mind wandered, and I pictured myself on the football field at Crestwood U, aiming the perfect kickoff. Soon it wasn't the ball I saw, but Melinda standing in front of me, her smile blinding. Maybe I could aim that perfect kickoff both on and off the field. It would prove to her I wasn't bluffing all along and that I was the only choice. Yes, I would steal her heart. Forever.

I just hoped everything went according to plan.

My eyelids weighed heavier. My heartbeat decreased its rhythm.

I was Mason Pierce, and losing wasn't part of my vocabulary.

No, I always played for keeps.

Sleep claimed me, and hope replaced my tears.

CHAPTER 35

LIKE I'M THAT GIRL

Elk River High - Freshman year

It was the first training session of the year. The sixteen of us stood in a semicircle, dressed in navy-blue swimsuits, while the coaching staff stood front and center in matching white polo shirts with the school logo sewn on the pocket. I hated this moment. When we were all standing next to one another half-naked, while coaches went over the schedule, their roles, and any other information they considered useful. Eyes roamed over swimsuit-clad figures, assessing the competition. Being naked wouldn't have been any more revealing for me.

Once we were in the water, this wouldn't matter anymore, but as long as we were standing there like statues, it made me feel self-conscious. I knew only six of my team-mates because we'd swum together in middle school. Everyone else was new to me.

A guy across from me gave my body a full once-over and winked in my direction. I felt my cheeks warming up. Then he did the same to a girl on my left. Pervert.

Another boy nudged the one next to him, and they stared at me until I was sure my face was flushed.

Trying to be subtle, I surveyed my teammates. All the girls had less curves than I did. I was the only one with boobs and a full ass. I felt even more naked than I already was when I realized why the guys were checking me out. I was the outsider.

Once the coaches finished their spiel about sport ethics and what they expected from us this year, we were asked to stand in line by the end of the pool so they could see our form. Two laps. First, breaststroke. Second, backstroke. I could do this. I was good and fast.

Someone behind me started giggling. "She should be good at breaststroke since she looks like her parents gifted her breast implants for her birthday. And that ass should be considered a flotation device. She is wearing her own buoy. I would die of shame if my butt looked like I had slipped a watermelon in my bathing suit."

"Maybe she's older and got redshirted too many times. She has no right to compete in grade nine. Do you really believe her boobs are fake?"

I kept my head down, blinking fast to avoid crying. If these girls saw my tears, they would never leave me alone. Chris, my half-brother, had taught me that. Growing up, he had always told me to never show my weaknesses in front of bullies. I repeated his words in my head to block out the sound of the mean girls' voices.

"No idea, but I didn't think they allowed fat people on the swim team."

"Shut up, Reagan," a voice I recognized as Matteo's spoke up. "Leave Mel alone. You'll see. She's much better than you'll ever be. She has always been the fastest on the team."

When it was my turn to show my form, I did just that. I dived forward and put everything I had into those strokes.

After I returned home at the end of the afternoon, I spent too much time browsing through magazines and analyzing my figure in front of the mirror instead of showering. Sure, I had curves, more than most girls my age, but Mom had said that eventually they would have them too. I had grown up faster than the girls in my class. Perhaps if I lost some weight and dressed differently, people would not notice them as much. Perhaps they would go away until I was a bit older and ready for them to show.

That night and the days that followed, I learned all about calories and how I could cut them so my body would shrink, and I wouldn't appear much different than my teammates.

That was when I started obsessing over what I looked like.

It was the first time since the *perky boobs* incident when I was ten years old that I felt bad in my own skin. Where I felt like being invisible would benefit me.

As long as I could control what I ate, how I trained, how I looked, and still be the best one on the swim team, I believed nobody's words would ever hurt me again.

———

Elk River High - Senior year

Pre-Homecoming Dance

I kicked the wall with all my strength, slicing the clear water with precise arm strokes while executing a perfect flutter kick. I reached the opposite side of the pool in no time, doing a flip turn and going for another lap. My heart pounded in my chest, my breaths hastening, each movement of my body fluid and resolute.

Every inch of me hurt with the exertion, but I had nine-hundred more meters to cover. Now wasn't the time to slack off. I had missed too many swimming hours in the last few weeks due to my appendectomy, and I had to make up for it.

Counting in my head to keep pace, I pushed through the water, kicking my feet and rotating my arms with perfect precision. My lungs burned as exhaustion settled inside me. Eight hundred-fifty meters to go. I kicked the wall and kept the count. Six hundred meters to go. Two hundred. I could do it. I was almost done. Seventy-five meters. Yes, I would make it.

Reaching the end of the pool, I removed the silicone swimming cap, freeing my hair, and resurfaced after diving my head in to push the wet strands back. I panted, my heart racing inside my chest. I placed a hand over the left side of my abdomen, trying to catch my breath. My arms had turned into spaghetti. I couldn't recall the last time I had swum this big a distance in one go. Usually, midday swims on Fridays were more about form than beating a personal record, not this time, though. I had all these numbers swirling inside my head—the ones obsessing me —and I had to do something about it. Even though I had pushed myself almost up to my breaking point, the exercise helped get rid of the tightness in my chest that had been lingering there for the last few days.

Lowering my hand back into the water, I ran my fingers over my scars. Just to make sure they were still okay. I felt no discomfort, and relief washed over me. I would be back at the top of my game in no time. With my crossed arms propped up on the white tiled coping, I relaxed, waiting for my breaths to even and my pulse to decelerate. Swimming had always been my favorite way of dealing with my conflicted emotions or the stress in my life. It helped me think more clearly. And get rid of the angst suffocating me. Tomorrow was Homecoming, and I felt giddy at the idea of dressing pretty and having an evening of dance and fun planned with my friends. My only concern was fitting into the cream dress I had bought last summer with my grandma. Since my surgery, my body hadn't just felt different—it looked different too. I just hoped the dress would still fit me. Somehow, I'd always felt like an outcast whenever I tried to dress cute. My body was more muscular than the other girls my age. Since the surgery, my stomach looked swollen all the time, my arms saggy, and my thighs touched. Nothing to be proud of. I was desperate to go back to my pre-appendectomy figure.

"Good job, Melinda," Coach Vivien said as I lifted myself out of the pool and toweled my body dry, pushing away all my conflicting thoughts about Homecoming to a safe corner of my brain. "Your form was impeccable today. We'll work on your speed next Tuesday. I'm glad you're back. Don't push yourself too hard, okay? Your body went through a trauma, follow its lead. I would prefer if you stuck to shorter distances next time. No need to overdo it. You're not training for the long distance anyway. The meet is in two weeks. You have enough time to be ready and perform like we both know you can. I have hopes you'll make the podium again in freestyle and backstroke. If you hurt yourself because you are pushing too much, it will only slow down your progress."

"Do you think I can make it to number one even though I haven't swum in a while?"

"Absolutely. You gained speed since last year, and I'm confident in your abilities. Even with the setback of the surgery, you're still my top swimmer. You possess every quality of a winner." If only she knew how much I needed to hear that word. *Winner.* "There's no reason you can't grab the gold."

"What about the medley relay?"

I wanted to be the best, the legend. If only to shut the voices in my head. The control and the perfection I was aiming for, it wasn't to prove something to myself, but to prove something to everyone else. It was warped, I was aware, but I had no idea how to stop. I watched Tanya and her squad, pretty and thin in their cheerleading outfits. I checked Lydia, Beth, Gabriella, and all the other girls Mason was usually seen with. They all shared something: willowy figure, shiny blonde hair, perfect smiles, long eyelashes. I had none of those things. My hair was brown and not shiny because of the time spent in the chlorine pool water, my feet were a size too big, and my shoulders were wide due to all the training and swimming. I sighed. Since when had I started comparing myself to other girls again? I knew how destructive it could be, and yet, in my head, I was competing with those girls for Mason's attention, and I didn't fit the profile he always went for.

"I'm optimistic we can score high if the doctor clears Sonja for the meet. That pneumonia has kept her on the sidelines for far too long already. You two make a great duo." Her attention switched to Dillon and Raoul, two of my swim mates, closing in on us. "Hey, guys. Get set. I'll be with you shortly." She clapped my shoulder. "Melinda, I'll talk to you next week. Get some rest this weekend. You deserve it. Have fun tomorrow night. Don't party too much, though." She winked.

"Like I'm that girl."

Twenty minutes later, I showered and changed into a pair of Heather gray sweatpants and an oversized navy-blue sweatshirt with the white swimming team logo stamped on the front. My choice of clothing wasn't optimal. Sweats always covered my figure and made me look like I'd gained twenty pounds, but right now, I didn't feel like sliding my damp legs into a pair of jeans. I averted my eyes when I crossed the locker room and passed the row of mirrors mounted above the sinks.

With my bag slung over my shoulder, I hurried across the yard toward the football field. A black knitted beanie covered my still damp hair that I was too much in a hurry to dry. Mom wouldn't be happy if she knew I'd ventured into the crisp fall air with wet locks, but right now, I had no time to blow-dry them because Paige was waiting for me. I had promised I'd make it on time.

Dizziness made my head spin, and I had to decrease my pace. The cup of tea I'd drunk this morning and the handful of grapes I'd eaten were long digested. I had skipped lunch earlier and had gone for training instead. No need to ingest more calories when I already doubted I'd fit into my dress. I fetched my bottle of water and took a big gulp, praying it would silence my grumbling stomach. This would do for now. It had to.

Sitting amongst my classmates on the bleachers, I watched the cheerleaders doing their routine, noting every detail of their anatomy. I wanted to look like them. Long legs, slim waist, glowing skin. No wonder all the guys' attention were solely on them.

Part of me wished I could blend in so no one could see how different I looked from everyone else.

Another part of me wished I could be just like them and attract the same attention they did. Because those girls were beautiful, and I longed to be too.

———

After Winter Break

I spotted Mason hurrying after me and increased the pace, doing my best to evade him without looking like I was trying too hard. Maybe he would stop chasing me if he thought I hadn't seen him. The truth was that I missed him. A lot. Our friendship and our almost-dating relationship had been the highlight of last semester. Having Mason by my side and keeping me busy had helped me not to cede too much control to my thoughts. I was afraid I would have really starved myself much more than I had if he hadn't been around. Not that I would ever admit it to him.

"Hey, Mel. Wait up."

I closed my eyes when I heard his voice. The one that had been with me since the day my parents drove me away from school before the break. I had missed Winter Formal and almost two weeks of school, plus they had also stolen my dignity that day. They had exposed my secrets in front of the boy I loved. Never again would he see me for who I was. Forever, I'd be the broken girl. The one obsessed with her weight and her appearance. And I'd seen how Mason had been staring at me since school had resumed. He was sad for me. And I hated the feeling.

I had done my best to avoid him so far, but it was just a matter of time before he asked for the explanations I wasn't sure I possessed.

"Talk to me. I deserve to know what's going on."

I had to push him away for good or else he would pursue me. Mason Pierce was tenacious and never gave up. It was my job to put a stop to it. And fast.

I halted my escape and turned to him, trying to be brave while facing him.

His gaze swept over me for a long moment. Up close, he looked even more handsome than I recalled. "You look…wow…you look beautiful." I glanced down, not wanting to acknowledge him, as he continued, "Aren't you gonna say anything? I deserve an explanation. You've been avoiding me like the plague since school has resumed."

I snorted. "I don't owe you anything, Mason." *I wanna talk to you, but I don't know how, and pushing you away is the only way I'm not overwhelmed by your proximity. I've missed you. I'm sorry I'm broken. All I wanted was to be perfect for you, and I screwed it up big time.*

He gripped my chin and lifted my head so he could stare at me.

I lost myself in his eyes. I had forgotten how it felt to be on the receiving end of Mason Pierce's attention. The contact of his skin on mine felt familiar, and it calmed the throbbing of my heart. Then I remembered I had decided to cut him loose, and I jumped back, looking away.

"I-I missed you."

Those were the words I had waited years to hear. Despite myself, my gaze snapped back to him. I felt exposed under his stare. I pressed my tongue to the roof of my mouth, determined not to show any weakness.

Mason laced our fingers, and I was unable to jerk my hand away this time.

"We haven't seen or talked to each other in over six weeks. I was worried about you. I tried to give you your space like you asked, but I can't do it anymore. I need to know where we stand and if we can salvage what we had."

"Mason, we had nothing." *We had everything.* Why couldn't I say it like I meant it?

He neared me, almost erasing the space between our bodies. "Wrong answer. Please say it like you mean it this time."

That stupid expression. Could he read my inner thoughts? I couldn't look him in the eye, just in case.

"I won't play games with you." There, I said it.

"I'm done playing games too. I truly believe we belong together. I'm just waiting for you to catch up with the fact."

"Sorry, but it won't happen. You better find someone else to be with." I had to force iciness into my laughter to keep myself from shattering.

"Stop feeding me bullshit. What we had was real. Why won't you recognize it?"

"I'm dating someone else. I'm with Jayden now." Why did speaking this fact out loud feel wrong? I liked Jayden, and we got along great, but he wasn't Mason. It was supposed to be a good thing. Why did it feel nothing like that right now? Why did I still miss Mason?

"Yeah, right. Clarke. Like you had to run away and fall for my number one enemy."

"Jayden is not the bad guy here, Mason. He's nice to me and doesn't expect anything from me. He treats me well and makes me smile. There are no groupies after him everywhere we go. We have fun together and he was there when my world crumbled around me and I was all alone because everyone had turned their backs on me. It's simple with him. He listens to me and… I don't have to explain him to you." *I'm aware you must see me as a traitor right now, but it was never my intention to hurt or disappoint you any more than I've already done. I'm so sorry.*

"You're kidding, right? I have never turned my back on you. Not once. I know you've been through something hard and recovery is a long road ahead and it won't always be easy, but dating Clarke is not what you need right now."

"Like you know better what I need. Yeah, right." *I do need you. I was just too ashamed to admit it, and now it's too late. I've moved on. You should move on too. Why does the idea of being away from you and of your dating someone else hurt so much?*

"As a matter of fact, I think I do. Whether you wanna admit it or not, I know you. The real you, not the one you are pretending to be right now."

I snorted, trying to hide how I truly felt inside. "You know me so well that you didn't notice when I was struggling." I barely recognized myself as the words passed my lips.

Mason flinched like I had punched him. "Why are you so mean?" *I'm asking myself the same question right now.* "You know it's nothing like that. Jayden Clarke is bad news. You don't need more complications in your life. You need someone who really cares about you."

"Like you?"

"Yeah. Like me. I've always been there for you. You can't deny it. You and I, we're great together. We're much more alike than you think. We have history, and we can make it work. I'll give you your space and wait until you're ready to be with me. In the meantime, we can resume our friendship."

"Here's the thing, Mason. I don't wanna be with you. Not anymore. Not even as a friend." *Lies. Lies. Lies.* "I'm with Jayden." Maybe if I said it often enough, it wouldn't sound so weird anymore. Jayden was a safe choice. My heart wasn't at risk with him. "You gotta respect that."

"Is this a new thing of yours? Part of your therapy?"

"What?"

"Hurting the ones who care about you?"

His words stung. I deserved his hatred. Hatred was good. It was safer—for me. "That's not what I'm doing." *Yes, it is.*

"Isn't it? Because from where I'm standing, that is exactly what is happening. Why won't you give me a chance? Why won't you give *us* a chance? What is so wrong about me that you won't even consider dating me?"

"Because there is no *us* and there will never be one. I thought I made myself clear already." *Why is my heart breaking as I'm speaking the words I don't mean out loud?*

"Keep lying to yourself, but it's not a good look on you. I thought we'd already agreed on that."

"Drop the sarcasm. Can't you see I'm setting you free here?" *Why couldn't he see I was doing him a favor?*

"You think I wanna be set free? What kind of world do you think you're living in? You know what, keep pretending all is fine. I'm no shrink, but I'm pretty sure the first step in healing is to stop lying and blaming others. I guess you skipped that lesson. Congrats, you wanted to lose me. Well, you did just that. Are you happy now? Does it make you feel better? Help you sleep at night? Next year, I'll be everywhere you'll be. I signed with Crestwood U. It's been official for a long time, but I was waiting for the perfect moment to tell you. I was supposed to come clean on that snowboarding vacation we never went on."

No. *No, no, no.* He couldn't do that. He knew what Crestwood University meant to me. Why couldn't he let me have that?

"I had ordered a bunch of CWU merch and swag as your Christmas gift after your dad told me they offered you a full-ride too. Stupid matching stuff for both of us because I could picture us dating, going to college together, and doing all the shit kids our age do when they're in love.

Anyway, forget I said anything. It's not important now. It doesn't mean a goddamn thing anymore. I left the bag at your house this morning. Throw it away, burn it, give it to charity for all I care."

Oh. *Wow, he did that? Could he be any more amazing? Was I making a mistake by dating Jayden?* Mason was all in, and for years, I'd dreamed about the day he would show interest in me. And now that he had, I was the one not ready to be together, the one pushing him away. Once again, I was lying to his face.

Tears leaked from my eyes. "You did that…for me?" We needed to wrap up this conversation because I wouldn't be able to keep a straight face much longer.

"Yep. Like a fool in love. Because what I've been feeling for you, Mel, all these years isn't friendship, it's much more powerful than that. It's love. The big fucking thing that starts with a capital *L*. I'm sorry I snapped at you. It won't happen again. And I'm sorry I made you late for your next class. It wasn't my intention either. Just remember that for the next four years, I'll still be around. I'm not going anywhere. I just hope Clarke treats you decently because he'll be in Maryland in a few months. Don't come crying on my shoulder when things don't work out between you two when you realize he's an asshole and not worthy of you. Remember what I told you once. I don't do second place. Never. Goodbye, Mel."

He loved me. Mason Pierce just admitted he loved me. "Mason…" *I love you too.* "It's not that simple. I-I can't be with you. I hope you forgive me one day. It's too hard… being with you. When you look at me like I'm your whole world, it puts too much pressure on me… I feel like I'm not enough, and…and I can't…I just can't." *More lies.* "Mase… I'm sorry."

He spun around and left me there without another word.

Why did it hurt so much?

Was doing the right thing supposed to shatter me, or was I wrong in losing the most important person in my life because I believed I was doing him a favor?

I stood there, my tears now freely rolling down my cheeks.

I had never felt so fractured before. Like every piece of me was splintering and I had no idea how to stop it from happening.

Perhaps therapy wasn't such a bad idea after all. I wasn't strong enough to deal with the pain of losing Mason for real. As long as we didn't face off, I could pretend we were nothing, but now that he'd opened up to me, there was no more hiding how I felt.

I fished my phone out and called my mom. "Can you pick me up from school?"

"Honey, what's wrong?"

My sobs drowned my words. "I…I'm not doing so good. I think I made a mistake, and I-I'm ready to see that therapist now."

"I'll call in an emergency meeting. I'll be there in fifteen minutes. And Mel? I'm proud of you."

I wanted to be proud of myself too. When I was in Traverse City, I'd accepted the medical help they gave me because I had no choice, but now it was my choice, not anyone else's. Maybe losing Mason was the wake-up call I desperately needed.

Deep down, I prayed I hadn't lost him in vain.

———

Thank you for reading the first part of

Mason and Melinda's story.
Now that high school is over and they're both attending Crestwood University, can they patch up their relationship and move on from the past, or are their scars still too raw to be healed?

Find out in ***Game Plan***
book two in the ***Touchdown series***
emmanuellesnow.com/products/game-plan

Curious about Mason's letters to Melinda?
Keep reading for some bonus content.

ELK RIVER HIGH

BONUS

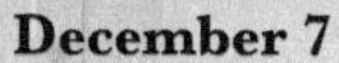

December 7

Hey, Shepard

Tonight is Winter Formal. I got dressed up and everything and decided not to go at the last minute. Chase, Craig, Jax, and a bunch of guys on the team decided to throw their own party instead.

I couldn't convince myself to go to the party that we were supposed to attend together.

Jax got his uncle's cabin for us, and we had a big sleepover there. I really like my friends. They've gone out of their way lately to up my spirits. Nobody knows what went down that morning between us, but I'm pretty sure they believe you dumped my ass or something. Don't worry, I won't tell a soul about what you're going through. Your secret is safe with me.

I heard our song earlier while I was getting ready, and I know we never discussed having a song together, but the lyrics made me think of you and me because it was *Curtis Burns's* song that we danced to at Homecoming.

> You are the stars in my eyes
> Every time I look at you, I can't help
> but think
> About what life has in store for us
> About how I miss you when you're not
> around

Anyway, I listened to it on repeat. Right now, I'm wondering what you're doing and where you are. Paige told me your cousin is cool, and I hope he takes good care of you since I can't.

Please get better.
I love you,

Mason xx

———

December 10

Hey, Shepard
It's Nurse Pierce checking up on you. You've been gone for more than a week now. It's crazy how time slows when you want it to go faster, no?

Anyway, I nailed the last math exam. I thought you should know since you helped me study all semester.

Chase and I thought we should try winter camping during the holidays, but we can't decide if it's better to sleep in a tent or build some sort of igloo. No idea if it will happen. If Sheldon or Rusty hear about it, they'll want to join us, and things will get complicated super fast. You know how they are.

Last night, I almost climbed the wall to your bedroom, only to remember you were not home these days. I wish you were back already. I have so much stuff to tell you. Elk River High has been a revolving door of gossip lately. And you will never guess who Jax hooked up with. I'll tell you when I see you because I kinda wanna see your face when I say the name out loud.

I have a personal question to ask...and I'm not sure I want the answer to this.

Are you still mad at me? I hate thinking that you are.
If we're being honest, I'm still a bit upset with you too, so it's okay if you feel the same toward me. I hate that you lied to me. I really do.

If you feel alone, please reach out. Even if it's just to say "Hi" and nothing else. I know you won't receive this letter, but maybe if I write my wishes down, you can hear them at night.

Please get better.
I love you,

Mason xx

December 16

Hey, Shepard

Craig and Paige just left for their mountain vacation. They asked me to come with them, but I declined. It didn't feel right joining them while you can't. I'm sure we'll have plenty more occasions to go snowboarding together, the four of us, in the future. And let's be honest, being a third wheel isn't fun, and I don't feel like listening to them proclaim their love for each other for three days with no way out. No thanks.

Last night, I baked three dozen chocolate chip cookies with my mom. She wanted to talk to me, and she always uses cookies as a bargaining chip. Anyway, we talked about a lot of things, but mostly you. She explained stuff to me. Every second of every day, I'm wondering how you're doing. It's hard for me not to come to find you and make sure you are doing okay.

I miss you. A lot. Nothing is the same without you around. Even Winter Break isn't as much fun, now that you're gone. I was hoping this holiday would be the first of many we would celebrate together as a real couple. I didn't even get a chance to ask you to be my girlfriend before your parents drove you away. Now I regret not asking you sooner.

For the record, I'm not mad at you anymore. I was hurt at first because I thought you were pushing me away... It's hard for me to understand why you thought you were not pretty enough and why you chose to starve yourself, but I have accepted it's your journey and something you have to overcome. I just wish you had told me, so I could have been there for you and helped you through it. Maybe, as Mom says, you gotta figure it out on your own. I hope that's why you never opened up to me about your struggles.

I gave your parents a batch of cookies. They are sad, so I tried to bring them a bit of sugar comfort. They told me you guys would spend Christmas together, and your mom had a glint of hope in her eye when she announced the news yesterday. Please don't hate them anymore. They love you. So much. All they talk about is you whenever we cross paths.

I need to tell you something. I've committed to Crestwood University. I did a while back but was waiting for you to get their offer before coming clean about it. Your dad told me you've committed too. I knew you had what it took to be noticed by them. I'm so freaking proud of you right now. Anyway, since we'll both be there next year, I bought you something...or many things if I'm being fully honest.

I'm not gonna send them over with your parents because I want to be the one giving them to you when you're back. Sure, maybe we'll look stupid in our matching sweatshirts and track pants and shirts, but I don't care. We'll be one of those couples, I guess, and I'm perfectly fine with it. I hope you are too.

A bunch of the guys on the team have invited me to go ice skating with them later. I wish it was something we could do together.

I think this is the longest letter I've written to a girl, my mom included. No, scratch that, this is the longest letter I've written in my entire life.

I wish you were here, but I understand why you're not.
Please get better.
I love you,

Mason xx

ACKNOWLEDGEMENT

Wow, this book was such an adventure from the first to the last draft. What started as a short story ended up in a book so big I had to split it into many parts. Let's just say Mason and Melinda had more to say and to live through than I first thought.

I wrote the first draft over a year ago while I was working on the **Wrecked** series because I wanted to write Mason and Melinda's backstory after falling in love with them in **Cast Away**. Through the months, I lost a big chunk of my manuscript after an update on my computer took the book back to an older version.

It took me months to pick it up again after that. In the meantime, I went through my own health scare (just like Melinda, I underwent emergency surgery for a condition that could have been fatal if not addressed when it had been) and it felt like I had somehow predicted my own fate through Mason and Melinda's story. I believe everything happens for a reason, so let's just hope my health scare was necessary to finish writing this book.

To my husband. Thank you. For being there every step of the way and listening to me talk about my characters and my storylines over and over again. Thank you for taking care of me when I was at my lowest point. Thank you for holding my hand when I thought I would die and for taking over every aspect of our family's life when I was too weak to even stand on my feet. Thank you for loving me and being the best dad to our kids. I wouldn't have ever survived this ordeal if you hadn't been by my side.

To my kids. I'm so sorry I scared you. It was never my intention. Just know I would never leave you on purpose. I know my afternoon at the ER ended up being a full week followed by a long recovery, but your love and faith in me have made me stronger. Thank you for cooking my favorite food, baking my favorite desserts, making sure I took my meds on time, and entertaining me when I couldn't do it myself. You guys rock, and more than ever, I'm so happy we went on that year-long trip when we did because we never know how fragile life can be. Enjoy every single moment because life is precious.

To Dr. Shinde. The fictional Dr. Shinde saved Melinda's life, but the real Dr. Shinde saved mine. Thank you for not worrying me when I was scared and in so much pain by not telling me how serious my condition was (Yeah, I learned it afterward once the pain meds wore off and I could ask questions). We talked books while I lay on a stretcher, and you said that one day I should write a character based on you. The surgeon in the story has a small role, but it's the one that's very important. Without him, there would be no story because there would be no heroine. Without you, there would be no author to write this story and no mom to my kids. Thank you, Dr. Shinde, for saving my life that day when most doctors didn't believe the excruciating pain I was in was real. Not all heroes wear capes.

To Shalini. I know this book was a mess at some point, but I found my way, and I'm happy you pushed me to make it the best version it could be. This book took a long time to see the light of day, but I love everything about Mason and Melinda's story, and I'm so proud of this final version. The Medora Beach universe is one that is very emotional and sweet and full of hope and love, and I can't wait for what comes next. Thank you for the pep talks when I feel like I can't do it, and for your professional knowledge that always helps me make my stories as realistic as they can be (and helps me in my personal life too). I'm very thankful.

To A, my alpha reader and favorite book nerd. Thank you for cheering me up after I lost a big part of this book and recalling some of the key scenes that had disappeared so I could write new versions of them. Thanks for always brainstorming with me when I'm stuck and re-reading the same pages over and over again when I have doubts or I'm not sure about a character or a scene. You've been beside me since the very first book I wrote years ago, and I always love your enthusiasm.

To Mason and Melinda. I know your lives aren't always easy, and heartbreak is just around the corner, but sometimes you have to take a step back to fully appreciate what's in front of you. You two deserve your happily-ever-after even though it may take more time to reach it. Don't lose hope. What you share is precious. Falling in love with your best friend is scary, but it's also the greatest feeling when you go all in, because they'll always have your back. No matter what.

To my readers, thanks for being so patient with this book. I know I said I wanted to release it sooner, but life happened and wreaked havoc on all my plans. I'm glad the release was delayed because I feel like it's even better now.

To all the bloggers, Bookstagrammers, Booktubers, Booktokers, and influencers loving and sharing about my books, you are the absolute dream team.

Mason and Melinda's story isn't over yet, as they will both soon attend Crestwood University together. I can't wait for you to find out what I have in store for them.

Kickoff is a wrap.

Cheers!

Emmanuelle

ABOUT THE AUTHOR

Soulfully Beautiful Love Stories

USA Today Bestselling Author Emmanuelle Snow is an author of contemporary YA and women's fiction love stories, who gives life to strong characters who'll fight with all they have to reach their life goals and find their own happiness. She loves her characters to be relatable and realistic.

She writes soulmates emotional romance that should be read with a box of tissues. Or two.

You'll want to be best friends with her heroines and have her heroes rock your bed and take hostage your heart.

Emmanuelle is in love with love. Especially complicated, deep, and passionate feelings that make a relationship extraordinary and complex all at the same time.

In her spare time, when she's not writing or reading, she likes to go on road trips—with her four kids and her own soulmate—watch movies, paint, or do some DIY, always with a cup of green tea in her hand and listening to country music.

She splits her time between beautiful Canada and the small US towns she adores.

Find all of Emmanuelle's books here:
emmanuellesnow.com

———

Want to connect with Emmanuelle online?
YOU CAN FIND HER HERE:

Website
Author's bookstore and merch store

Snow's VIP newsletter
emmanuellesnow.com

Readers' VIP group Snow's Soulmates
facebook.com/groups/snowvip

amazon.com/author/emmanuellesnow

goodreads.com/emmanuellesnow

bookbub.com/authors/emmanuelle-snow

facebook.com/esnowauthor

instagram.com/snowemmanuelle

x.com/snowemmanuelle

pinterest.com/snowemmanuelle

tiktok.com/@snowemmanuelle

ALSO BY THE AUTHOR

CARTER HILLS BAND UNIVERSE

(suggested reading order)

Carter Hills Band series

False Promises

Heart Song Duet

Blindsided

Forevermore

Whiskey Melody series

Sweet Agony

Second Tear Duet

Cruel Destiny

Beautiful Salvation

Breathless Duet

Wild Encounter

Brittle Scars

Upon A Star Series

Last Hope

Midnight Sparks

Love Song For Two Series

Summer. Secrets. Music country...
and the boy I should stay away from.

WRECKED
Cast Away
MEDORA BEACH
a love story BOOK ONE

SUMMER FEVER
SURFING DAY

USA TODAY BESTSELLING AUTHOR
EMMANUELLE SNOW

Chapter 1

Thirteen year old

January 19

Dear Ava,

I can't believe I've missed your birthday again this year. I'm so sorry about the change of plan. I was looking forward to spending the entire weekend with you. I swear, since we moved down south, we barely ever make it to Michigan anymore. There's always something coming up. Not that I miss the chilly winters, though. I prefer the warmth of the weather here.

Before winter break, I went to school wearing only a hoodie and sneakers. I could've never done that in Elk River in December. Can you imagine it? I'm sure you're covered in ten layers right now because you're always cold.

How was your winter break? Did you like spending your vacation in Aspen? I wish we could have come with you guys, but Dad's business has just started picking up, and I understand it was better and more logical for my parents to stay here. Not for me, though. I really wanted a white Christmas. Hopefully, next year we'll be able to go together.

My friend Riri and I decorated a palm tree with blue lights because I thought it would look good. I'm sure you would have approved.

You probably have received your gift by now. Well, I'm sure Mom sent you something pretty to wear, but I wanted you to have something I made. I used purple, white, and navy-blue threads because I know they're your favorite colors. I made a matching one for myself too, so it means we're connected even though we live far apart.

Riri helped me with the wrapping. We talk about you all the time. Sometimes it feels like you're here with us. I can't wait for you to visit and you two to meet. I'm sure you will get along just fine.

Mom and I recently redecorated my room, and now I have a bigger bed. Do you remember the old one in the cottage our parents rented that summer? So cramped it was when both of us tried to fit in it. I just had a flashback of the time you fell off the bed in the middle of the night, and we decided to lie in our sleeping bags on the floor instead. No, I still say I didn't push you. And no matter what you believe, I don't kick in my sleep. But now when you come over, there is enough space, and we can share my bed.

Do you have plans for next summer? Maybe

I could come visit you for a week or two. It would be fun to spend some time together like we used to. I'll talk to my parents. See if they agree. I'll be fifteen so it makes more sense if I'm the one who makes the bus ride on my own. I wouldn't want you to travel alone.

I miss you.
Happy thirteenth birthday, Ava!
I wish you all the best.

Love,

Cici xxx

P.S. Call me after you read this letter.

P.P.S. Riri says hello.

P.P.P.S. Don't forget to write back.

———

March 6

Ava!!!!
You won't believe it. I auditioned for the cheerleading squad for next year, and I got in. Riri helped me practice until I knew the choreography by heart. This was so

stressful. I thought my heart would jump out of my chest. But I did it. I made the team.

How are you doing? Did your parents agree to let you spend your spring break with Iris at her cottage? I heard Mom talking to your mama about it the other day.

Last Friday, during lunch break, I was reading your letter, and some friends at school were asking why we write letters to each other instead of emails. And when I said it was more exciting to receive a real envelope through the mail than a chime on a computer, they looked at me like I was crazy. I wish you had been here that day because you would have thought it was funny. Their faces... OMG. I almost told them we use pigeons to deliver the mail (you know, like in that movie), and I'm pretty sure they would have believed me. Anyway, thanks for the pumpkin cookie recipe you sent in your last letter. I can't wait to try it with Mom.

Dad promised we'd talk about my coming to visit you next summer. He's not really enthusiastic about this cross-country journey at my age. But he's being a good sport and said we'd discuss it. Cross your fingers. Hope he says yes. Cross your toes too, Ava. Just in case.

Or maybe...just maybe...the three of us will come to Michigan, and it will all be like it used to be. Sleepovers and camping nights in your backyard. And painting our nails and doing our faces. Dressing up. Having scary movie marathons.

Oops. Look at the time. I gotta go. I'm not done with my math homework. And I really need to finish that novel for my English lit class tomorrow. I hate tests.

See you soon (hopefully).
Fingers and toes crossed until then!

Love,

Cici xxx

P.S. There's a new boy in my English class, and his name is Camden. He has blue eyes, and he invited me to the movies on Friday night. I said yes. I'll keep you updated.

P.P.S. Oh, I forgot. My friend Riri and I

finished in second place at the school science fair last week. Life is awesome these days.

————

April 3

Dear Ava

Okay, there's so much I need to tell you. Remember when I told you Camden, the new boy in class, invited me to the movies? Well, the following week, we played mini golf together, and he kissed me. And now I have a boyfriend. I'm sure you would approve. He's nice and sweet and always wants to hold my hand and carry my backpack. I'm super happy, and I wish you were here to hang out with us. And meet him.

Well, I want you to meet all my friends. You should move down here. You would like it since it's summer almost all year-round.

I received the silly pictures you sent me and the one of us when we were little kids. I can't believe we were that small.

I was thinking that when we're both in

college, or some time after, we should be roommates. Imagine how much fun it would be to spend all this time together and have our own place... I know it's a few years from now, but it's never too early to start planning. And maybe we can also go to see the Eiffel Tower together after graduation. Have a girls' trip. Let's talk about it when I visit you this summer and we make a list of all our dreams.

I miss you.
Can you believe I have a boyfriend? I don't. LOL.
Mom is here and says hi. She's making your favorite dish for dinner.
Tell Iris I said Happy Birthday.

Love,
Cici

P.S. I wish you were here.

P.P.S. Dad said he'd call your father next weekend to figure something out for our summer vacation. Fingers and toes crossed. For real this time!

Chapter 2

Sixteen years old

The blade fell from my grip, landing next to the discarded letters on the floor as I watched the line of blood dotting my fair skin and trickling across the surface of my forearm. I held my breath, waiting for the sting of pain. The one I couldn't seem to run away from. Something that would remind me I was alive. In the last three years, I had become an addict. To physical pain.

Every time the memory of who I'd lost took over my thoughts, it twisted my insides. Made me vulnerable. I couldn't think straight, disconnected from my emotions, but dying to feel something. Anything.

Blood dripped onto the floor, and I followed the path, hypnotized by the pattern.

Still, I felt nothing. Blank.

My head spun, and I blinked.

My gaze drifted to my arm, mentally begging for the aftershock to kick in. For the physical pain to erase the mental one.

After what seemed like forever, the twinge on my forearm, just below the crease of my elbow, finally hit me. Oxygen returned to my lungs as I took a deep inhale, escaping the prison of numbness that had suffocated me seconds ago.

My eyes flitted to the mirror above my dresser. I looked haunted. Shadows undermined my eyes. And a sadness—though I wished it would vanish—lingered in my irises.

The first time I used a blade was the summer after my thirteenth birthday. At the time, I had no idea how to cope with my grief. Until a girl from my gym class shared how she relieved the paralyzing emotions that sometimes crippled her after her mother's death.

She put into words the feelings that were drowning me inside. The ones I refused to talk about because they hurt too much. Her words resonated with me. For once, they made sense to the confused and heartbroken girl I was back then.

In a way, grief broke me. It made me weak. And ashamed of myself when I let my emotions rule me. The ones I tried to conceal deep inside for as long as I could remember. Until I couldn't bury them anymore. That was the moment I started cutting myself. Because in a twisted manner, it helped relieve the suffering from the crater lodged deep inside me. And to soothe my troubled mind.

That spring, my favorite person in the world had been taken from me.

In the most hurtful way.

She didn't get a chance to fight back. That chance was stolen from her.

She didn't have the opportunity to say her goodbyes. No one had heard her last words.

She had been forced to put all those dreams of hers to rest. Forever. We would never visit Paris together. Nor would we ever be roommates once in college. She never came to visit me that summer, and I never met all her friends.

Three years later, all those memories still haunted my nightmares. Sometimes. Most times.

I lost not only her that day, but also a part of myself. And the people I considered to be second parents. They all disappeared from my life. And I had no idea if I'd see them again someday. I knew it was for my own good that they stayed away. I was suffering. So lost in my own pain that just the idea of seeing them was enough to send me back spiraling. But the realization didn't hurt any less.

Eyes brimming with tears, my heart fractured in my chest. I hated everything about being me right now. I was failing myself. Again. In so many ways. My teeth dug into my lower lip as I swallowed the sobs about to wreck me.

Harming myself wasn't a habit of mine. I had only done it seven times in the past. When the pain became unbearable and too hard to hide, when I felt like I was falling down the rabbit hole, it helped me remember I was still here. Alive. And that all those chances she would never have were still waiting for me.

"I miss you," I said to a picture of us that we'd taken on my eleventh birthday. Wearing matching blue polka-dot dresses, both of us grinning at the camera. The last one we celebrated together.

Dizziness filled me, and for an instant, I thought I would faint.

The cut should have already started clotting by now. Instead, a thick film of blood covered my skin, oozing down my forearm.

My hand clamped onto my desk, my body growing weaker by the second.

Ohmygod, what have I done?

How deep did I cut this time?

It was usually only a surface scratch, but right now it felt to be much deeper than that. My fingers shook as I wiped the mess off my skin, trying to stop the bleeding.

My bedroom whirled around me.

Trying to stay calm, I fixed my gaze on the photo. Could she see me hurting from wherever she was? If she were here, she would be so disappointed in me. She loved life. Always cheerful and dancing around for the smallest of things. Everything gave her joy. Thinking happy thoughts. And befriending everyone.

My eyes darted to the injury I'd inflicted upon my body. Chills worked through me. I didn't wanna die. Just the thought scared the shit out of me. I wanted to live.

I watched my forearm. "Please, blood, stop. I'm sorry." Tears burned the back of my eyes. My heart did some awkward jump inside my chest. Tremors shook me.

How did I end up here? Again?

The cut stung, and pain radiated from the wound.

Sadness wrapped around me, suffocating every piece of my being.

I needed to do better. Be better.

I hated feeling like I had no grip on my own life.

I was done being sad. And miserable. I was done wreaking pain upon myself, thinking it would help. I had to take back control of my life. For me. For her. She wouldn't want to see me like this. Broken and suspended in time. Everything hurt so bad. Inside and out. Blood trickled down my arm. I was getting light-headed. Grief seemed like a weight, crushing me. I needed to fight. For both of us. She wasn't given the chance to reach for her dreams. Why was I forfeiting mine? It sounded selfish to waste a life when hers had been stolen. She would tell me to fight back. Yeah, she certainly wouldn't want me to drown and give up.

Using the heel of my hand to put pressure on the wound, I let my sobs out. I squeezed my arm in a vice. The bleeding wouldn't stop.

Shame filled me. I had let the letters get to me. I hated the idea I hadn't been strong enough to deal with the emotions today with a clear mind.

Tears drenched my face, and I used my shoulders to clear my foggy vision.

I needed my mom.

With slow and unsteady steps, I staggered toward the kitchen where my parents were making breakfast. I had draped a black T-shirt over my arm to conceal the result of my actions. A chill crawled up my back. Cold sweat pearled on my forehead. Suddenly, I felt so tired.

The smell of bacon hit my nose first. Followed by the crisp aroma of freshly brewed coffee.

Dad stood with the frying pan in his hand, listening to my little brother Collin's retelling of his last soccer game, while Mom was busy pouring caffeine into mugs. I could hear them, but it was hard to understand what they were saying. Like I was standing in some sort of bubble, far away from them. The numbness I felt inside was now spreading to my physical body.

I tried to move forward but was paralyzed, my feet heavy.

My body overheated. As if lava was traveling in my bloodstream. Seconds later, my teeth chattered when the heat was replaced by cold shivers.

Bracing myself and doing my best not to collapse, I neared them. Black dots danced in my vision. Breathing became harder. My pulse pounded in my head.

"Morning, Miss Sunshine," Dad called out when his eyes landed on me, the carefree grin drawn on his lips slowly dissolving. Worry swam in his eyes.

I stood there with drenched cheeks, holding my arm tight and wishing for the bleeding to stop. The pain to leave. And the fog filling me to recede.

I wished the wound would heal.

The pan dropped from his hand. Mom seemed to be alerted by the ruckus because she turned around at once. A gasp passed her lips, and her eyes rounded when she looked at me. In seconds, they were both standing by my side.

"What happened?" my father asked, his strong arms enveloping me and helping me stay upright as a new surge of dizziness made my head spin. "Are you hurt?"

Time slowed down.

Once again, I heard their voices, but they sounded distant.

I saw their faces, mere inches from mine, but they looked to be miles away from here.

Dad lifted me in his arms. I buried my face in his chest, my safe place, while he carried me to the living room and sat me on the sofa, my hand still clamped tight over the T-shirt covering the wound on my forearm.

"Ava, talk to us," my mother urged, kneeling before me. She combed my hair back with her fingers as her eyes roamed over my face. "What happened?" Her attention drifted to my T-shirt-covered arm, and she asked a silent question as she stared at me.

I shook my head, never releasing the pressure on the slit across my flesh. My gaze was stuck to the corner of the chevron-patterned rug underneath the coffee table. I refused to admit what I had done. But I also knew I had to tell her how bad it was. Another wave of exhaustion hit me. The stickiness of the blood made it through the cotton fabric.

Dad sat next to me, carefully removing the piece of clothing around my arm. His eyes widened, overflowing with worry as he took in the wound.

"I'm sorry," I whispered, unable to look at any of them.

"She needs stitches," I heard him tell my mother.

More shame grew roots inside me, and I mumbled, "For...for a moment...I...I missed her and wanted to be with her." I swallowed the constriction in my throat. "I found the last letters… And life seemed unfair. I don't want to hurt every time I think about what happened. I can't do this anymore."

He fastened his arms around me, holding me closer. His lips descended to rest on the top of my head. "It's okay. We'll get you more help, okay? We'll figure it out. I'm sorry, baby. We're here."

In a heartbeat, Dad was bandaging my forearm, Mom providing him with gauze and tapes from the first aid kit. The entire time, I rested my head on my father's chest, fighting the sleepiness invading me.

"Ava, put pressure on it," he said while he secured the bandage with the last piece of medical-grade tape.

With my eyes closed, I could hear my mother's whisper. "Okay, I'll drive Collin to the Jensens'. I'll meet you at the clinic." She kissed my forehead. "I love you, honey."

I was lifted from the couch, and seconds later, I felt myself lying on the backseat of the car.

My lids stayed close the entire ride. I refused to see the pain on my father's face as I felt the weight of his gaze through the rearview mirror. None of it was his fault. Or my mom's.

Growing up, I just happened to be an expert at masking my pain. And my feelings. Instead of talking about it, I would plug music into my ears and escape to another world where I was safe. And nothing could hurt me.

My parents were my anchors, and I knew if I opened up to them, they would help me through this ripping pain affecting me. This void I sometimes felt inside. They did save me once. Could they save me a second time?

Soon, exhaustion won the battle, and my mind took me far away from here. The last thing I heard was my father's panicked voice saying, "Ava, wake up. Stay with me. Come on, Miss Sunshine, open your eyes," while he lifted me from the backseat, and everything went black.

Don't miss Ava's story,
Read Cast Away now

emmanuellesnow.com/products/cast-away

Author's bookstore at emmanuellesnow.com

22
PIERC
22